PRAISE FOR
THE LEFT-HANDED BOOKSEL

INDEPENDENT BOOKSELLER E
YALSA BEST FICTION FOR YOUNG ADULTS

"The world building is exquisite—the broad, immersive world and the specific rules for types of booksellers maintain a sense of discovery, and Susan and Merlin, the heroic protagonists, have vibrant, entertaining personalities (and a realistic romantic story line). Readers will beg for more adventures in this London." —*KIRKUS REVIEWS*

"An immersive fantasy. Nix builds meta mentions [and] marries fey elements and spectacular bookshops with booksellers who wield mystical artifacts, cold steel, and magic. Unflappable Susan and wonderfully costumed, magically gender-fluid Merlin make for a fantasy that genre fans, teen or adult, won't want to miss." —*PUBLISHERS WEEKLY*

"Nix throws readers headlong into the splendid new world alongside the bewildered but determined heroine. It's an incredibly diverse, detailed universe, and Nix puts in enough twists to make it his own. A remarkable romp through a fantastical new world." —*ALA BOOKLIST*

"A thrill-packed fantasy adventure. Strong world building is clearly informed by a deep knowledge of local mythologies, and the allusions, literary shoutouts, and pseudo-historical references become a game for the clued-in reader. Overall, this is a fresh, engaging fantasy." —*BCCB*

"As in his high-fantasy novels, Nix puts a strong, capable, and resourceful young woman front and center within a diverse cast [with] tropes from British spy stories. A thrilling, suspenseful romp with lots of humor and romantic tension; we haven't seen the last of Susan and Merlin." —*THE HORN BOOK*

"Fans of Garth Nix's other works, such as the Old Kingdom series or *Angel Mage*, should enjoy this exhilarating volume. Action, light romance, and otherworldly machinations keep the tension flowing as Nix reveals a warm-hearted and clever fantasy. Readers will almost certainly leave this magical London searching for hints of the Old World peeking through our own." —*SHELF AWARENESS*

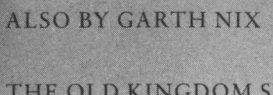

THE
LEFT-HANDED
BOOKSELLERS
OF
LONDON

GARTH NIX

 KATHERINE TEGEN BOOKS
An Imprint of HarperCollins Publishers

To Anna, Thomas, and Edward; my parents,
Henry and Katharine Nix; my brothers Simon and Jonathan
and their families; and to all my family and friends.

THIS STORY TAKES PLACE IN A VERSION OF ENGLAND IN THE YEAR 1983, BUT IT IS NOT ENTIRELY AS THOSE WHO WERE ALIVE THEN WILL REMEMBER, OR THOSE WITH A HISTORICAL BENT CAN CHECK UP ON. BUT WHICH IS REAL?

PROLOGUE

IT WAS 5:42 A.M. ON MAY DAY, 1983, IN THE WEST OF ENGLAND, AND A sliver of the sun had edged above the ridge. But it was still cool and almost dark in the shallow valley, where the brook ran clear and straight until it made a sweeping left-hand curve before the weir a mile farther downstream.

A bridge of three planks crossed the brook near a farmhouse, carrying the footpath to the farther side, diverting walkers away. Not that this path was ever well-traveled. Walkers somehow failed to see the start of this particular path, under the ancient oak next to the crossroad at the hamlet near the weir.

A young woman came out of the farmhouse, yawning, her eyes half-shut, her mind still mostly lost in a dream that had seemed so real.

Susan Arkshaw, who had turned eighteen years old as of two

minutes ago, was striking rather than immediately attractive, with her vibrant black eyebrows in stark contrast to her closely razored head, the stubble dyed white-blond. She wore a 1968 Jimi Hendrix Summer Tour T-shirt given to her mother fifteen years ago by a roadie. The T-shirt was big enough to serve as a nightdress, because she was not tall, though very wiry and muscular. People often thought she was a professional dancer or gymnast, though she was neither.

Her mother, who was tall and slight without the muscle, said Susan took after her father, which was possibly true. Susan had never met him, and this was one of the few details her mother had ever shared.

Susan walked to the brook, and knelt to dip her hand in the cool, clear water. She'd had the recurring dream again, familiar since her childhood. She frowned, trying to recall it in more detail. It always started the same way, here at the brook. She could almost see it. . . .

A disturbance in the water suggested a fish rising at first, until it became a great roiling and splashing, too big for any fish. Slowly, as if drawn up by an invisible rope, a creature rose from the heart of the swift current in the middle of the brook. Its legs and arms and body were made from weed and water, willow sticks and reeds. Its head was a basket shaped of twisted alder roots, with orbs of swirling water as limpid eyes, and its mouth was made of two good-sized crayfish, claws holding tails, crustacean bodies forming an upper and lower lip.

Bubbling and streaming clear, cold water, the creature sloshed a dozen yards across the grass and then stone paving to the house and, raising one long limb, lashed green willow ends upon window glass, once, twice, three times.

The crayfish mouth moved, and a tongue of pondweed emerged to shape words, wet and sibilant.

"I watch and ward."

The river creature turned, and walking back, lost height and girth and substance, until in the last few paces it became little more than a bundle of stuff such as the brook might throw ashore in flood, the only sign of its presence a trail of mud upon the flagstone path that lined the front of the house.

Susan rubbed her temples and looked behind her. There was a trail of mud on the flagstones. From house to brook. But her mother had probably gotten up even earlier and been pottering about, shuffling in her gum boots. . . .

A raven cawed from the rooftop. Susan waved to it. There were ravens in her dream as well, but bigger ones. Much larger than any that actually existed, and they talked as well, though she couldn't remember what they said. She always remembered the beginning of the dream best; it got confused after the brook creature.

Besides the ravens, there was also something about the hill above the farmhouse. A creature emerged from the earth there . . . a kind of lizard thing of stone, possibly even a dragon.

Susan smiled, thinking about what all this meant. Her

subconscious hard at work fantasizing, fueled by too many fantasy novels and a childhood diet of Susan Cooper, Tolkien, and C. S. Lewis. The brook creature and the huge ravens and the earth lizard should all make up a nightmare, but the dream wasn't frightening. Quite the reverse, in fact. She always felt strangely comforted after she had the dream.

She yawned hugely and went back to bed. As she crawled under her duvet and sleep claimed her again, she suddenly remembered what one of the huge ravens had said in the dream.

"Gifts your father gave us, we creatures of water, air, and earth, to watch and ward."

"My father," said Susan sleepily. "My father . . ."

Later, when her mother brought her tea and toast in bed at eight o'clock, a special treat to celebrate her birthday, Susan had forgotten her earlier awakening, had forgotten she'd had the recurring dream again. But something lingered, she knew she'd dreamed . . .

She looked at her mother sitting on the end of her bed.

"I had an interesting dream last night. I think. Only I can't remember what happened. It seemed important. . . ."

"It's good to dream," said her mother, who lived much in a dream herself. She ran her fingers through her long, luxuriantly black hair, streaked here and there with the white of grief, not age. Jassmine never let anyone cut her hair; she became very agitated when Susan suggested she do more than trim the ends, which she did herself. "Most of the time . . . but there are bad dreams, too. . . ."

"I think my dream . . . I think it was somehow about my father?"

"Oh yes? More tea?"

"Are you sure you can't tell me who my father is, Mum?"

"Oh no. It was a different time. I wasn't the same person. He . . . did you say yes to more tea?"

"Yes, Mum."

They drank more tea, both lost in their own thoughts.

Eventually, Susan said with some determination, "I think I'll go up to London early. Get acclimatized. There's bound to be pub work I can get. And I . . . I'll try to find my dad."

"What was that, darling?"

"I'm going to go up to London. Before I take my place. Just find some work and so on."

"Oh. Well. It's natural, I suppose. But you must be careful. He told me . . . no, that was about something else. . . ."

"Who is 'he'? What did he say to be careful of, or about?"

"Hmm? Oh, I forget. London. Yes, of course you must go. When I was eighteen I couldn't imagine being anywhere else. But I insist on postcards. You must send me postcards. Trafalgar Square . . ."

Susan waited for Jassmine to continue, but her mother's voice trailed off and she was staring at the wall, whatever thought had been about to emerge lost somewhere along the way.

"I will, Mum."

"And I know you will be careful. Eighteen! Happy birthday, my darling. Now, I must get back to my painting before that cloud comes over and ruins the light. Presents later, okay? After second breakfast."

"Presents later. Don't miss the light!"

"No, no. You too, darling girl. Even more so for you. Be sure to stay in the light. That's what he would have wanted."

"Mum! Who's 'he'. . . come back . . . oh, never mind. . . ."

CHAPTER ONE

>-I-<>-O-<>-I-<

A clerk there was, sinister gloved
Dexter scorning, his sword well-loved
Wielded mirror-wise, most adept
Bookes and slaughter, in both well kept

>-I-<>-O-<>-I-<

A SLIGHT YOUNG MAN WITH LONG FAIR HAIR, WEARING A PRE-OWNED mustard-colored three-piece suit with widely flared trousers and faux alligator-hide boots with two-inch Cuban heels, stood over the much older man on the leather couch. The latter was wearing nothing but a monogrammed silk dressing gown, which had fallen open to reveal an expanse of belly very reminiscent of a puffer fish. His fleshy face was red with anger, jowls still quivering with the shock of being stuck square on his roseate nose with a silver hatpin.

"You'll pay for this, you little f—" the older man swore, swiping with the cut-throat razor that he'd just pulled out from under one of the embroidered cushions on the couch.

But even as he moved his face lost rigidity, flesh collapsing like a plastic bag brushed against a candle flame. The young

—-•-•-

man—or perhaps it was a young woman who was dressed like a man—stepped back and watched as the tide of change continued, the flesh within the pale blue robe falling into a fine dust that ebbed away to reveal strangely yellowed bones poking from sleeves and collar, bone in its turn crumbling into something akin to the finest sand, ground small over millennia by the mighty ocean.

Though in this case, it had not taken an ocean, nor millennia. Merely the prick of a pin, and a few seconds. Admittedly a very special pin, though it looked like any other pin made for Georgian-era ladies. This one, however, was silver-washed steel, with Solomon's great spell of unmaking inscribed on it in letters too small for the unaided eye to see, invisible between the hallmarks that declared it to have been made in Birmingham in 1797 by Harshton and Hoole. Very obscure silversmiths, and not ones whose work was commonly sought after, then or now. They mostly made hatpins, after all, and oddly sharp paper knives.

The young man—for he was a young man, or was tending towards being one—held the silver hatpin in his left hand, which was encased in a pale tan glove of very fine and supple cabretta leather, whereas the elegant fingers of his right hand were free of any such covering. He wore a ring on the index finger of his right hand, a thin gold band etched with some inscription that would need close examination to read.

His gloved left hand was perfectly steady as he slid the pin back into its special pocket in the right sleeve of his suit, its head snug against the half sovereign cuff links (1897, Queen Victoria; the jubilee year, not any old half sovereign) of his Turnbull & Asser shirt. His *right* hand shook a little as he did so, though not enough to make the hatpin snag a thread.

The slight shake wasn't because he'd disincorporated crime boss Frank Thringley. It was because he wasn't supposed to be there at all and he was wondering how he was going to explain—

"Put . . . put your hands up!"

He also wasn't supposed to be able to be surprised by someone like the young woman who had burst into the room, an X-Acto craft knife in her trembling hands. She was neither tall nor short, and moved with a muscular grace that suggested she might be a martial artist or a dancer, though her Clash T-shirt under dark blue overalls, oxblood Doc Martens, and her buzzed-short dyed blond hair suggested more of a punk musician or the like.

The man raised his hands up level with his head. The knife-wielder was:

1. Young, perhaps his own age, which was nineteen;
2. Almost certainly not a Sipper like Frank Thringley; and
3. Not the sort of young woman crime bosses usually kept around the house.

"What . . . what did you do to Uncle Frank?"

"He's not your uncle."

He slid one foot forward but stopped as the young woman gestured with the knife.

"Well, no, but . . . stay there! Don't move! I'm going to call the police."

"The police? Don't you mean Charlie Norton or Ben Bent-Nose or one of Frank's other charming associates?"

"I mean the police," said the young woman determinedly. She edged across to the telephone on the dresser. It was a curious phone for Frank Thringley, Merlin thought. Antique, art deco from the 1930s. Little white ivory thing with gold inlay and a straight cord.

"Who are you? I mean, sure, go ahead and call the police. But we've probably only got about five minutes before . . . or less, actually—"

He stopped talking and, using his gloved left hand, suddenly drew a very large revolver from the tie-dyed woven yak-hair shoulder bag he wore on his right side. At the same time the woman heard something *behind* her, something coming up the stairs, something that did not sound like normal footsteps, and she turned as a *bug* the size of a small horse burst into the room and the young man stepped past her and fired three times *boom! boom! boom!* into the creature's thorax, sending spurts of black blood and fragments of chitin across the white Aubusson carpet and still it kept coming, its multi-segmented back legs scrabbling and its hooked forelimbs snapping, almost reaching the man's legs until he fired again, three more shots, and the huge, ugly bug flipped over onto its back and spun about in frenzied death throes.

As the deafening echoes of the gunshots faded, the woman realized she was screaming, and stopped, since it wasn't helping.

"What . . . was that?"

"*Pediculus humanus capitis*. A louse," replied the young man, who was reloading his revolver, hitching up his waistcoat to take rounds from a canvas bullet belt. "Made bigger, obviously. We really have to go. Name's Merlin, by the bye."

"Like Merlin the magician?"

"Like Merlin the *wizard*. And you are?"

"Susan," said Susan automatically. She stared at the still-twitching giant louse on the carpet, then at the pile of reddish dust on the lounge, contained by the pale blue robe. The monogram "FT" was uppermost, as if pointing out who the dust used to be.

"What the hell is going on?"

"Can't explain here," said Merlin, who had gone to the window and was lifting the sash.

"Why not?" asked Susan.

"Because we'll both be dead if we stay. Come on."

He went out through the window.

Susan looked at the phone, and thought about calling the police. But after a single second more of careful but lightning-fast thought, she followed him.

CHAPTER TWO

A left-handed bookseller I did spy
In a wood one darkling day
I durst not ask their business, why
Best not to know, I do say

THE WINDOW OPENED ABOVE THE ROOF OF THE CONSERVATORY, which ran from the back of the house to the fence. Beyond that lay the dark mass of Highgate Wood. Merlin was walking out along the steel ridgeline of the conservatory, Cuban-heeled boots notwithstanding. The flat ridge was no wider than his hand, with long sloping panes of glass on either side. But he acted as if they were of no account, though if he fell he'd smash through them and be cut to pieces.

Susan hesitated and looked back. The monstrous bug was still writhing, but there was something else happening now. A dark fog was flowing up the stairs. It looked like thick black smoke, but it moved very slowly and she couldn't smell burning. Whatever it was, she instinctively knew it was wrong, something inimical. She shivered suddenly, bent down, and crawled out onto the ridge of the conservatory, moving swiftly on hands and knees.

"There's a weird black fog coming up the stairs," she panted as she reached the end. Merlin was standing in front of her, but as she spoke he jumped, clear across to a branch from an ancient oak that overhung the garden fence.

"How can you do that in those heels?" gasped Susan.

"Practice," said Merlin. He held on to a higher branch with his right hand and extended his left. "Jump."

Susan looked behind her. The extraordinarily dense, dark fog was already coiling out the window. It didn't move like normal fog at all; in fact, one broad tendril was coiling out towards her specifically. Reaching for her. . . .

She jumped. Merlin leaned out to her but Susan didn't need help, landing close to the trunk and immediately steadying herself by wrapping her arms around it.

"Down," said Merlin, climbing quickly. "Fast!"

Susan followed him, jumping the last five feet, her Docs splattering hard into the leaf mulch and mud. It had been raining most of the day, though it had eased off at nightfall. Now, past midnight, it was simply clammy.

The wood was very dark. All the light was behind them, spilling out of the houses and streetlights onto Lanchester Road.

The black fog was streaming over the conservatory, flowing down the panes on either side of the ridge. Spreading and extending, blending into the night once it moved outside the fall of light from the houses and street.

"What *is* that?"

"More to explain later," said Merlin. "Follow me. We have to get to the old straight track."

He led off, almost jogging, zigzagging between trees. Susan followed, hands up to ward off snapping-back branches and saplings. She couldn't see anything clearly. Merlin was a dark shape ahead; she had to trust he could see where he was going and try to stay right behind.

A few minutes later she almost ran into Merlin's back as he came out onto a path. He hesitated for a moment, looking left and right and then up at the cloudy sky, and the very few visible stars.

"This way! Come on!"

He was running now. Susan followed as best she could, fighting the feeling that they would both run into something and really hurt themselves, balanced against the feeling that something even worse would happen if they didn't outpace the black fog that she was sure still followed, flowing faster in the darkness, tendrils reaching out to either side, looking for her. . . .

Merlin stopped.

"We're on it," he said. "We can walk slowly now. Stay close, stay on the path."

"I can't even see the path!" gasped Susan.

"Keep right behind me," said Merlin. He was walking slowly. The sky was lighter above, here, and there was more open space about the path, the trees not crowding so close.

Susan looked behind her, eyes wide as they'd go, trying to

see. The dark seemed to be of different tones, different shades.

"That fog," she whispered. "I think it followed us."

"Yes," said Merlin. "But it can't come onto the path."

"Why not?"

"It's an old thing, and obeys old custom," said Merlin. "Anyway, it's not so much the fog itself we have to worry about, it's the Shuck."

"The Shuck?"

"The fog is what you might call a companion effect," said Merlin. "It disorients and distracts, and it's necessary for the thing that moves within the fog, once it's thick enough. That's the Shuck. Though it has other names, too."

He slowed, studying the ground in front. The path was veering off to the right and there was a copse of young beech trees straight ahead. "The new path isn't following the old straight track. We'll have to turn around and go back."

"Go back!"

"Yes. Backwards and forwards till dawn, if necessary."

"But the . . . the Shuck thing . . ."

"It can't touch us on the true path, either," said Merlin. "Turn about. Don't step off!"

Susan turned on the spot, and started walking slowly back the way they had come, following the path as best she could.

"I can't see," she whispered after only a few steps. She could hear the loose gravel of the path under her feet, different from leaf mold and mud. But it was too easy to wander off in the darkness, lose the way.

"If you don't object, I'll hold your shoulders and direct you," said Merlin. "Walk slowly. It'll be fine."

She felt his hands come down on her shoulders, a light touch. But even so, his left hand felt odd. She could feel a weird warmth from it, coming through glove and overall bib and her T-shirt, as if he had some sort of warming device in that hand. He pushed slightly on the right, redirecting her.

"On the positive side," Merlin said after they'd slowly walked thirty or forty yards, "no one else will dare come after us now they've loosed the Shuck."

"They won't?"

"It's not very discerning," said Merlin. "Hopefully, the rain earlier will have ensured no one else is in the wood tonight. Slow down. Damn!"

"What?"

"The path at this end veers away as well and trees have grown up. Why couldn't they follow the old track? Stop. We'll turn around again."

They turned around. For the first time, Susan realized there was something else disturbing her. Besides all the obviously disturbing things like "Uncle" Frank turning into dust, the giant bug, the black fog.

"I can't hear the traffic. Or the trains. Or anything except us. Why is it so quiet?"

"It is two a.m."

"Oh, come on. I might be from the country, but I've been to London before."

"Ah. Which part of the country?"

"West Country. Between Bath and Chippenham. Don't change the subject."

"I'm afraid the silence means we are now completely surrounded by the fog within which the Shuck roams. Speaking of which, it will probably try to scare us from the path, so be ready. Hold my shoulders and stay close."

They walked on, the only sounds coming from the gravel and snapping twigs beneath Cuban heels and Doc Marten air soles and Susan's breathing, which still hadn't slowed down.

"Moon's coming out of the cloud," said Merlin.

"Is that good?" asked Susan.

"Not always. Good for us tonight. A new moon is kinder to the younger folk, meaning humans, for the most part. And it makes it easier to see the path as well."

It did make it easier to see the path. In fact, the mix of gravel and leaf mold and mud was now luminous, not simply reflecting the soft, pale light of the moon but seemingly kindled by it.

The moonlight also made the black fog more palpable. It was all around them, walling them in, making the path like a narrow, dangerous alley. Every now and then tendrils and wisps edged in, recoiling as they reached the path, rolling back into the mass.

A few paces farther along, Susan's nose suddenly wrinkled and she felt bile rise in her throat.

"I can smell something really horrible," she whispered. "Like rotting meat and . . . foul water. . . ."

"It's the Shuck," said Merlin. He didn't lower his light, tuneful voice. "It's probably been summoned from the stretch of the Fleet that took away the offal and blood from the Smithfield Market, and so hates mortals all the more for defiling its water. Don't look. It's pacing us, a little behind and to the right."

The smell grew stronger, and the hairs on the back of Susan's neck rose and she felt a shiver between her shoulder blades, as if the point of an impossibly sharp tooth rested there, waiting to be driven into her flesh.

"Let's play twenty questions," said Merlin easily. "Take your mind off . . . er . . . things."

"That yes-no thing always drives me crazy," said Susan. It took an effort for her to speak normally. She was acutely aware that there was something behind her, something huge and horrible whose breath reeked of carrion. "How about we actually *answer* each other's questions."

"Sure," said Merlin. "We're coming up to where we need to turn around again. Keep your eyes down. If you do see the Shuck, don't look directly at it."

"Okay," replied Susan. "Uh, when I say actually answer questions, this isn't one of those situations where if I know too much you have to kill me, is it?"

"You already know too much," said Merlin. "But you're not at risk from me. Or mine. Though I'm afraid your *life* might never be the same."

"Oh," said Susan.

"Some of it might be an improvement," said Merlin carefully.

"Depending on your actual relationship with your 'uncle' Frank. Eyes down, turn around."

Susan tried to keep her eyes down, but even so she did catch a very fleeting glimpse of something terrible within the fog, a massive, misshapen, twisted thing with eyes like open wounds and a vast, constantly dripping maw—

"Eyes down! Keep walking!"

"I am, I am," Susan said, shuddering.

"It's dropped back. And it really can't get us on the path," said Merlin. "Let's imagine we've met . . . er . . . somewhere . . . and we're having a chat. So, what were you doing in that house?"

"Frank was one of Mum's friends from years ago," said Susan. She opened her eyes again, a little, looking through slitted eyelids. "I thought he was a boyfriend . . . he always sent me presents at Christmas, signed 'Uncle Frank.' I never actually met him until I came up to London today. I mean yesterday. I knew straight away that I'd made a mistake. Coming to see him, that is. I was about to sneak out when I heard you come in . . . what did you do to him, anyway? And why?"

"To cut to the heart of the matter, I touched him with a silver object inscribed with Solomon's spell of unmaking Harmless to mortals . . . humans . . . but Frank was what we call a Sipper. A blood drinker—"

"A vampire!"

"No, they don't exist, though almost certainly Sippers are the basis for the legend. They do bite, but nearly always at wrist or ankle, not the neck—because they don't want to kill—and they're very small bites. They let the blood flow and sip it. No big hollow teeth nonsense; they lap it up like a cat. Triangular-pointed tongues. One of the signs that gives them away."

"And you hunt and kill them?"

Merlin sighed.

"No. We usually leave them alone, provided they behave themselves. In fact, there's a Sipper who works for us in accounts, and . . . uh . . . our infirmary. Sipper saliva has powerful healing properties."

"So why stick Frank with your hatpin?"

"You recognized it as a hatpin?"

"I'm an art student. Jewelry is one of my things, though I'm mainly a printmaker. Or I will be an art student, when term starts. That's why I'm looking for my dad now; I have about three months before I have to buckle down, as Mrs. Lawrence says."

"Who's Mrs. Lawrence?"

"My sixth-form school art teacher. She helped me get my place, and says I'm not to waste it."

"Which art school? Get ready to stop and turn around."

"The Slade."

"You must be good, then."

"My etchings, I believe, are worth coming up to see, as they say. And I can *draw*. Though it's not really the rage at the moment. Being able to draw, that is."

"It must be satisfying to make things. Turn."

They turned. Susan caught a strong waft of the carrion stench and almost gagged, but she also realized that talking was distracting her. Quickly, she gabbled out the first question that came into her head.

"If we're safe on the path, can't we sit down?"

"No," replied Merlin. "It only has the virtue of the old straight track if we're moving on it. If we stop, it's simply a patch of ground, and both the fog and the Shuck will have us."

"So," said Susan. "Are you actually a wizard?"

"Well, I'm mainly a bookseller."

"What?!"

"Really. A bookseller. I handle incoming deliveries for the most part, unpacking, shelving. Not a lot of the actual *selling*. The right-handed generally do that."

"The right-handed?"

"It's a family business, of sorts. Perhaps *clan* would be a better word. We're either right-handed or left-handed. Though it can change. 'One for the books, one for the hooks,' as we like to say."

He held up his gloved left hand, stark in the moonlight.

"As you can see, I am of the left-handed moiety."

"But what does that mean? What's the hook business?"

"It's obscure, to be honest. I mean, we've never really used hooks. Swords, daggers, hatpins . . . but the left-handed St. Jacques—"

"Sanjucks?"

"San Jark. The family name. French. Though we're not French and it's not really our name, it's something pinned on us by the first Elizabeth; she was confused, and it kind of stuck. Anyway, we left-handed types do most of the active stuff, running about, fighting, and so on. The hook part might be a bitter reflection that, back in the seventeenth century, a number of us ended up strung up on hooks by various religious parties."

"But what . . . I mean, this Sipper thing . . . and the Shuck and the fog . . . *what is going on?*"

The last few words burst out of Susan almost like a scream. She'd managed to hold in the bizarre mixture of panic and puzzlement but it was threatening to break free.

"Yeah, I realize it's a shock. But your best chance of survival is to stay calm and stay with me. Ah, how can I put this? The world you know, the 'normal' human world, is the top layer of a palimpsest—that's a many-times overwritten parchment—"

"I know what a palimpest . . . palimset . . . I know what one is even if I can't say it."

"Well, there is another world beneath the everyday human one, and under certain conditions or at particular times, the Old World comes to the top, or elements of it become the primary world, as it were. And there are . . . environments and creatures or individuals who exist on multiple levels at the same time, either due to their nature, or because of some—I guess you'd call it magical—intervention. We booksellers fall in the latter category, both left- and right-handed, and for various reasons we've ended up . . . policing, I suppose . . . the interaction between the various more mythic levels, collectively known as the Old World, and the New World—the prosaic human world—what you might fondly call 'reality.'"

"But what does bookselling have to do with all this?"

"We have to make a living."

"What!"

"Most of the old mythic levels are sequestered and most Old World entities are bound, or the ones that aren't behave themselves anyway. We rarely have to intervene. In between, we sell books. There are some other reasons, too; it's rather complicated. . . . You ready to turn?"

"Uh, yes, I guess."

They turned about again. This time Susan didn't bother shutting her eyes, though she kept looking straight down. She could tell from the disgusting drain smell that the Shuck was close, but it bothered her less now. Merlin's calm, light conversational tone had somehow cut through the fear, as had the rhythmic tramping up and down on the path.

"Uh, I have another question," said Susan. "Only it's a bit intrusive. . . ."

"I am human," said Merlin. "A human male at the moment, as it happens."

"At the moment?"

"We are somewhat . . . shape-shiftery . . . I guess you could say," replied Merlin. "I was born male, but I have been pondering if I should change."

Susan didn't answer for a moment, digesting this.

"You get to change that easily?"

"Oh, it's not easy," replied Merlin. "But much more possible for us than—"

He was interrupted by the sudden sound of a horn, not very

far away, from deeper in the woods. Not a car horn, but the deep, long, drawn-out bellow of some large medieval instrument.

"What's that?"

"The Shuck being called off, sent back to its source," said Merlin. He had tensed; Susan could feel it through his shoulders. "The fog will dissipate, too. It's an odd move; there's still hours before dawn. I wish I knew who summoned it in the first place. It can't have been Thringley."

"What do we do?"

"Keep walking, but be ready to run, along the new path. Hear that? The fog's clearing."

The sounds of the city were coming back. Traffic; the deep, distant rumble of a train; indistinct voices on the wind. It was lighter, too, particularly back towards Lanchester Road, and intermittent flashes of blue light were coming through the trees.

"The police!"

"At your 'uncle' Frank's house. They'll have responded to the gunshots, at the least," said Merlin. He was looking left and right and up into the trees. "I hope not too quickly, for their sake. Okay, the Shuck's gone. Get ready—"

All of a sudden he pushed Susan violently to the ground. She heard something whoosh above her head as she struggled to get up and then a sudden harsh slap as Merlin's left hand intercepted something, and he was pushing her back down again with his right. She rolled away and began to sit up, lying back down immediately as a white-fletched, red-shafted arrow whisked past and buried itself deep in the tree behind her.

Merlin batted another arrow away, his left hand moving so fast she could barely see it, his lithe body dancing to avoid another. But he couldn't move fast enough to avoid the third, which struck him high on the right shoulder with a sound Susan wished she hadn't heard. He spun around and fell on one knee, his yak-hair bag with the revolver falling from his shoulder. Without any conscious thought, Susan crawled for it, to get the revolver and fire back in the direction the arrows were coming from.

But Merlin hadn't *fallen* to one knee. He'd knelt on purpose, hitching up his trouser leg to draw a small automatic pistol from an ankle holster. This one he fired right-handed, while his left hand continued to deflect arrows up and away, protecting both himself and Susan.

The smaller pistol's shots were much quieter than the big revolver, which Susan was still trying to extract from the bag. Almost like a sharp dog's bark, but the flash was bright and Merlin fired fast, eight shots in quick succession. After his fifth shot, there were no more arrows.

Susan got the revolver out, holding it in two hands. She'd fired shotguns, and ironically was a fair archer, but she'd never fired a handgun before. Still, it seemed simple enough.

"No, no . . . put it down," said Merlin. He put his back against a tree trunk and his left hand gripped the shaft of the arrow. "Police'll be here . . . any minute . . . from Frank's . . ."

"Who fired the arrows?"

"A Raud Alfar warden . . . I guess awakened by the Shuck . . .

ah . . . intrusion. That's why Shuck . . . called off . . . should have . . . have thought of the Raud Alfar . . . propitiated them with gifts. . . ."

"Did you kill . . . er . . . this warden?"

"No . . . gunfire drives . . . off. Sometimes. Machine sounds . . ."

Susan left the revolver on the bag for easy access and crawled over to Merlin. In the moonlight she could see the arrow was embedded below his shoulder bone, and his shirt and the mustard-colored coat were already sodden with blood. She hadn't looked at him up close until now, but she didn't have time to dwell on how handsome he was, because he was much paler than he should be and his breath was coming in short, controlled gasps.

"I need . . . your . . . help. A silver vial in my left . . . waistcoat pock . . . get . . . good . . . open it . . . swish and hold in your mouth . . . yes, I know. . . and hold . . . I'm going to break arrow, push it through. Soon as I do, spit into . . . wound."

Whatever was in the vial was disgusting, but Susan swished it from cheek to cheek and held it. Merlin snapped the shaft easily with his left hand, letting out a small gasp, his face twisted in pain. He gasped again as he started pushing the shaft through, and tears welled up in his eyes.

"Pull . . . pull it through . . . and spit. . . ." he whispered, fainting, and fell forward, the bloodied arrowhead thrust clear out of his back.

Susan clamped her lips on a sob. Holding the precious fluid in, she reached over and pulled both halves of the broken arrow out, front and back. Throwing them away, she bent down close and spat into the wound. Pale blue-green light spilled from her mouth, like burning brandy on a Christmas pudding, but without heat, the cold flames licking about the hole in the coat before sinking into the flesh beneath.

Susan sat back and wiped her mouth, but there was no light in her saliva now. Whatever the strange fluid had done, it hadn't brought Merlin back to consciousness. As gently as she could she laid him down and stripped off his coat. Taking the pocket square from it, she folded a pad and held it against the exit wound on his back, while she kept direct pressure with the palm of her other hand against the hole in his chest.

It was hard to see, but she thought he was still bleeding, and she couldn't tell if his chest was moving.

She bent closer, hoping she would catch the sound of breathing, but instead she heard heavy footsteps behind her, and the white beam of a flashlight suddenly lit up the area, sending her shadow across Merlin's body.

"Stop! Armed Police! Show me your hands!"

CHAPTER THREE

No sorcerer can compare
For such magic strange and rare
As in the glov'd bookseller's lair
But secrets, nay, they will not share

HALF AN HOUR LATER, SUSAN WAS UNDER THE HARSH FLUORESCENT lights in an interview room at Highgate Police Station, having at first been arrested for suspected murder by a rather excited armed constable and then five minutes later informed by a passive-aggressive sergeant that maybe that wasn't right but now that it had been done they had to go through the motions at least, which apparently was her fault as well. At least they'd taken the handcuffs off before the short walk to the station, and once there had let her wash the blood off her hands, and given her tea and biscuits.

The uncertainty about her status centered around Merlin, as far as she could tell from the muttered conversations that started once the sergeant got a look at a black leather case from the elegant young man's suit pocket, which contained an identification card that sent the sergeant straight on the radio to higher authorities. Merlin was being worked on by two ambulance attendants at that stage, and Susan was relieved to hear them talking as if he was still alive and, surprisingly, not too seriously injured.

"Hello, you all right, then? Need another tea? Biscuit?"

This was the constable who'd arrested her, popping his head around the door. A large, black-haired young man in his middle twenties, with a surprisingly lighter-colored moustache, his relaxed face looked quite different from the stressed, super-hyped visage she'd seen over his Smith & Wesson as he'd ordered her to show him her hands, edge on her knees away from Merlin, and then put her hands behind her—upon which she'd been cuffed by his partner and everyone had relaxed slightly.

"I'm fine," said Susan. "But what's going on? Am I still arrested or what?"

The constable blushed.

"No, sorry, that was my mistake. We're waiting for Inspector Greene now, to sign you out."

"Inspector Greene?"

"Special Branch. You're Box 500, right? Do you normally work with someone else?"

"I don't . . ." Susan started to say, but then stopped, as her weary and rather disturbed mind caught up. Being signed out sounded a lot better than being arrested for murder. "Um, can I get my backpack from the Frank Thringley house?"

"Oh, I'll check with the local jumbos. I'm not from *here*. I'm D11."

He said that proudly, as if it meant something significant. Belatedly, Susan realized he was trying to impress her; this was some weird kind of flirting.

"Speaking of firearms, that Smython .357!" He whistled. "I didn't know what it was; Sergeant Bowen recognized it. Very tasty. Not that I want to say anything against that little Beretta of yours, miss. Easily concealable, I'll give you that."

"Yeah, right," agreed Susan. She was suddenly feeling very, very tired. She looked at her watch, one of the very new new-fangled plastic ones called a Swatch that her mother had bought her as a going-away present. It was a few minutes to six, so probably only just light outside.

"Well, if you need anything, knock on the door," said the constable. "Sorry we have to keep you in here, but out of sight, out of mind, hey?"

"Hey," replied Susan. She let her head fall forward, cradling it on her arms, and went to sleep.

Inspector Greene was a woman. Which was a little surprising to Susan, though it shouldn't have been, since it *was* 1983. But the Metropolitan Police, more than the regional forces, had always been one of the great holdouts against gender equality, right back to the postwar reforms of Prime Minister Clementina Attlee's radical government. Paradoxically, Britain's second woman PM was now in power, but Margaret Thatcher was an old-school Tory and was working hard to roll back many of the changes brought in by Attlee and later Labour governments, equal opportunity legislation being on her hit list.

Susan, like almost everyone under thirty who wasn't a banker or hereditary lord, disliked Thatcher and her government. The previous year's war over the Falklands had turned that dislike into near hatred, while boosting Thatcher's popularity with far too many older people, and like all her friends, Susan had a permanent sick feeling in her stomach at the likely outcome of the forthcoming election in a few week's time, the first in which she was old enough to vote. She'd already put in her postal ballot, for the Social Democrat candidate, but the Conservative, Chris Patten, would almost certainly win in the Bath electorate.

According to Susan's Swatch, she'd slept for an hour when Inspector Greene tapped her on the shoulder, not very gently. The police officer was thirtyish, tough-looking, and dressed like Sergeant Carter in *The Sweeney*—the television show, not the real Flying Squad—leather jacket over shirt and jeans. She even looked a bit like Denise Waterman—a subcontinental version of her, anyway.

"Miss Arkshaw. Time to go."

"Go where?" asked Susan muzzily. "Who are you?"

"Mira Greene, inspector with Special Branch. I handle liaison with your *bookselling* friends."

"Uh, they're not . . . um . . . is Merlin okay?"

"I believe so," said Greene. "They came and retrieved him from Whittington Hospital half an hour ago. I wouldn't worry.

The left-handed types are very, very tough. But I guess you already know that."

"Uh, no," said Susan. "I only met Merlin last night. It was all an accident. I don't know anything."

"You know more than's probably good for you," said Greene. "Luckily for you, with anything involving those booksellers, the official unofficial policy is that the less everyone knows—or heaven forbid, writes down—the better. We act as if they're from the security services and sweep it under the carpet."

She swung her car keys around her finger and said, "Where do you want to go?"

"Go? Uh, I need to get my backpack from—"

"Already in the car. How about Paddington, train back to Bath? We'll buy you a ticket. Go home to mum, lie low."

Susan was tempted for a moment. She had three months until the Michaelmas term started. Her student accommodation wasn't available until a few days before the start of term, so she had nowhere particular to go and a limited supply of money to find a place to live.

But she had come to London early for a reason, and though it had started badly, and become very strange indeed, she wasn't going to give up.

"No, thanks," she said. "I'll find somewhere to stay. I can go to a youth hostel to start, I guess. Or some cheap . . . very cheap . . . hotel. Till I get a job. In a pub or whatever. I am eighteen."

Greene stared at her. Her eyes were fierce, penetrating. She looked like she might favor the *Sweeney* school of physical interrogation as well, and was definitely someone Susan wouldn't like to cross.

"Seriously, you'd almost certainly be better out of London. Not that you'd be entirely safe back home. But somewhat safer."

"What do you mean?"

Greene shut the door behind her and sat on the desk.

"You've been in the Old World. You've been seen and marked by things from the Old World," she said slowly, and with emphasis. "You'll find yourself there more easily now, or it will come to you. But geographically speaking, word travels slowly in the Old World; there are many borders to cross between Highgate Wood and the entity that lives in the spa waters of Bath, or any of the other . . . things. Or so the booksellers tell me, because to be honest I know sweet FA myself. If you go home it could be years before anything else weird happens, if ever. Stay here, everything you've already met is much closer."

"I want to stay," said Susan. "I've got something I need to do."

Greene stared at her for a moment longer, then got off the desk and paced around, pausing to loom over Susan. "Okay. Remember this. Nothing you think happened last night happened. If you talk about it to anyone, anywhere, but particularly the newspapers, the best that can happen is you'll be locked up in a mental asylum and we'll throw away the key."

"I understand you're threatening me," said Susan slowly. She'd been arrested—though not ultimately charged—with her mother twice at CND antinuclear demos. She knew what was going on. "But I know my rights—"

"No, you obviously *don't* understand," said Greene. "This isn't a police thing, it's not a legal matter, it's not part of British law. All the ancient weird shit, the living myths and walking legends and so on, they're restricted, bound, held down, contained within boundaries by agreements and oaths and bindings and rituals and custom. And some of these can be broken or unraveled once people become aware of them, decide to reenact a bit of harmless old folklore or whatever. So we try to nip anything like that in the bud, stop people even thinking this stuff might be real. Usually, in minor cases, we put people away in a mental hospital, convince them they went gaga for a while, and everything works out. But you're a special case, you're already in too deep. We'd have to hand you straight over to the booksellers."

"That doesn't sound so—"

"Capital punishment doesn't exist in the United Kingdom anymore, but the booksellers have an exception," said Greene bleakly. "When they deal with someone who's delved too deep, no one ever sees them again. And I understand from the booksellers that even that's a better option than some of the things that happen to people who get in too far."

There was silence in the room, save for the annoying hum of the fluorescent tubes overhead.

"Okay, I do kind of understand. . . . I mean, I get there's stuff I don't understand," said Susan wearily. "I know I was lucky to survive last night. I have no intention of talking about it to anyone."

"All right. You're being sensible. Cooperative. So I'll help you out, too. If you're positive you're going to stay, there's a boardinghouse, not exactly a safe house, it's simply somewhere we keep a bit of an eye on. We'll put you up there—paid for by HM government—until you go to your student housing. The house is in Islington, so pretty handy for everything."

"You know about my place at the Slade?"

"I'd like to think we know everything about you," said Greene. "Since I've had five officers scouring all possible records since I got the call about 'some of your MI5 agents' rampaging about the North London shrubberies. But I'm sure there are things we missed. That's the nature of it and one of the reasons I'll be happier if you're staying with Mrs. London in Islington. In case we find out something we should already know."

"Mrs. London?"

"Yes. It is her real name, though she's from Glasgow originally. God knows why she moved here. We have a deal?"

"What's the place like?"

"Bedsit, but quite big. Gas ring if you want to cook, though Mrs. L does meals. Bathroom each floor, you only share with two others," said Greene. "Place is hardly ever full anyway, so you might get lucky with the bathroom. Better than anywhere you could afford."

"You've seen my bank account?"

"Like I said. Five officers. Two hundred and sixty-two pounds, fifty-five p as of close of business yesterday, and your bank manager was as cross as fire at being woken up too early in the morning to look that up for us, till I said we'd send him a letter of commendation from the deputy commissioner. Anyway, two-hundred-fifty-odd pounds is not a lot to last until term starts. Did I say breakfast is included at Mrs. London's? And not skimped, none of your two Weetabix and half a cup of powdered milk. She does a fry-up and all."

Susan was suddenly ravenously hungry. But then, she realized, she'd only eaten two slightly stale biscuits since lunch yesterday. "Uncle" Frank had invited her to dinner, but she claimed to feel unwell, planning to sneak out at the first opportunity. Though he'd been pleasant to her, she'd figured it was better to stay in her room and keep her door locked.

"What was Frank Thringley involved in?" she asked.

"What did the bookseller tell you?" asked Greene.

"No, I don't mean . . . him being a . . . what did he call it . . . a Sipper . . . I mean as a criminal," said Susan. "I saw some of his . . . minions . . . I guess. One of them had a sawn-off shotgun in a Sainsbury's bag. I mean, it was obvious, it stuck out."

"Why didn't you leave then? Back off and run away?" asked Greene. "Why were you still there last night?"

"I wanted to ask Frank some questions about his relationship with my mum, and about her other friends at that time," mumbled Susan. "Frank told me he'd tell me in the morning, offered me the spare room for the night; it had a lock and everything. I didn't have anywhere to go, and the guy with the shotgun left. Frank himself didn't feel threatening, to me, anyway. It seemed . . . well, not safe . . . but not immediately dangerous.

But then I changed my mind, I was going to leave, but I heard the commotion upstairs and . . . went to look."

"Must have been some pretty important questions," said Greene. "Looking for your dad, right?"

"That obvious?" asked Susan. "Not that it's any of your business."

"Maybe," replied Greene. "But I reckon you knew it wasn't Frank straight away."

"I felt he couldn't be," said Susan. She frowned. "I don't know why. . . ."

"Because he was a Sipper," said Greene. "Humans instinctively feel there's something 'off' about some of the mythic types like a Sipper. Handy for criminal bosses, makes it easy for them to put the frighteners on people."

"But I still thought Frank might have known my dad; he could have told me something useful. What kind of criminal was Frank?"

"The usual," said Greene with a shrug. "Protection, drugs, stolen goods. You name it. He was the boss of a big territory, everywhere north of Seven Sisters Road to the North Circular."

"Why did Merlin turn him into dust?"

"Ah, now you're asking," said Greene. "I wish I knew. The booksellers usually tell us if someone . . . something . . . from the Old World is causing problems with ordinary people and that they're going to deal with it. Particularly if there's an overlap with ordinary crime."

"But they didn't."

"Nope. You ready to go?"

"Yes," said Susan.

"Forget all this," said Greene. "Put it behind you. Move on."

"I'll try," said Susan as they went to the door.

"But if some weird shit does happen, don't forget to call," added Greene, handing her a business card. "Our duty officer's on the first number, twenty-four hours a day, seven days a week. The handwritten one is my home number. I hope that after I drop you at Mrs. London's you go on to have a nice, normal life. But just in case . . ."

"Okay," said Susan. "What exactly do you mean by weird shit?"

The constable with the strangely pale moustache was in the corridor outside, loitering as if he wanted to say something. But before he could open his mouth, the expression on Greene's face—as if she'd spotted a dog turd a step away—made him turn around and flee.

"You'll know," said Greene quietly. "Believe me, you'll know. There is also a chance . . . slim, in the opinion of my colleagues over at Serious Crime, that you might be contacted by your 'uncle' Frank's entirely human criminal associates, since some of them will know you were there on the night of his . . . well, let's call it death. But provided you stay out of seedy pubs and betting shops north of Holloway, you should be safe enough. Most ordinary criminals steer clear of the weird shit. There are the Death Cults, but . . . I trust you'll never need to know about them."

Susan nodded slowly. She didn't want to be involved in anything to do with anything Greene had mentioned.

"What about the whatever-handed booksellers?"

"They should leave you alone, too," said Greene. "But stay away from their shops."

"They have actual shops?" asked Susan in disbelief.

"Two in London. Big one in Charing Cross Road for new books and a smaller one in Mayfair for the collectors," replied Greene, opening a side door to the car park and going out ahead of Susan. She paused to look carefully around and then beckoned. "Watch the steps."

CHAPTER FOUR

Most strange dreams I had, and
Waking, had them still
Of storied creatures, good and ill
Under the bookseller's right hand

MRS. LONDON'S BOARDINGHOUSE WAS INDEED FAR BETTER THAN anything Susan could have afforded by herself. A four-story early Victorian town house on Milner Square, it was clean, immaculately maintained, and everything worked. Susan was even allowed a choice of rooms and took one at the top, which—though she didn't say so—was considerably larger than her bedroom in her mother's very old and rambling farmhouse. It was certainly cleaner and tidier and it came furnished. Even the bed was more comfortable.

But it was being paid for by Special Branch, and that meant not only being observed—Susan had a very jaundiced view on what Inspector Greene's "keep a bit of an eye on" actually meant—but also beholden to the police. This made Susan feel more than uncomfortable and she wasn't prepared to put up with it for long. She told herself it would only be until she could find a job and some doubtless far worse accommodation that didn't come with strings attached.

Susan presumed that her comings and goings would be recorded by the apparently uninterested Mrs. London, and quite possibly all the other inhabitants of the house would be watching her as well. She expected questioning at breakfast, and possibly a handsome young man (or woman) strangely keen on showing her the city or something like that and being a bit too curious about her life, but was surprised to find that there were only three other inhabitants, two women and a man, all much older and all very much dedicated to keeping to themselves. There was hardly any talk at breakfast, and after the barest introductions—and those with patently false names—Susan was left entirely to her own devices.

Surveillance was another possibility, so she spent some time examining the light fittings and a couple of minor bumps in the wall plaster for microphones, but they seemed innocuous as far as she could tell, and besides, what could she do about it anyway? There was only the one phone for the residents, in the entry hallway. That was undoubtedly bugged, but as so far she had only called her mother, it didn't seem likely there would be anything of interest for the police to record.

Susan's mother, Jassmine—the extra *s* added only a few years before, courtesy of a short-lived relationship with a numerologist—had been curiously uninterested in the demise of Uncle Frank, though Susan had not gone into any details and certainly had not said anything about Merlin, giant lice, or the Old World. In fact, Jassmine wasn't particularly interested in anything Susan had to say, her bemused tone typical of one of her periods of detachment the psychologists blamed on her use of LSD in the sixties, when she had been heavily involved in the music scene. Jassmine herself, when she returned to a more alert plane, did not think it was to do with drug use and claimed to have taken "very little" acid, despite hanging around with people who did. Susan wasn't sure whether to believe her but had long since gotten used to her mother varying between being somewhat unreliable and completely so.

"The bedsit sounds good," Jassmine had said vaguely. "Do send me a postcard. Trafalgar Square or somewhere nice."

"I will, Mum," replied Susan. Why Jassmine thought Trafalgar Square was nice, she didn't know, but it was a place they always visited on their trips to London, which, though they usually coincided with Susan's birthday, never seemed to have a particular point or object to them. In fact, the only regular part of these excursions was a visit to Trafalgar Square, where Jassmine would sit beneath one of Sir Edwin Landseer's bronze lions for a while and then suggest going somewhere—anywhere and nowhere in particular—for cake.

Jassmine's early life was a mystery. Like much else, she either wouldn't or couldn't talk about it, so Susan only had snatches of information gleaned from occasional comments, never answers to questions. The fifteenth-century farmhouse near Bath was the only home Susan knew. It had apparently "belonged to the family forever," but it had been a holiday house until Jassmine moved there sometime before Susan was born. Jassmine herself had grown up somewhere in central London, evidently to a family with money, since the farmhouse sat on three acres and had been extensively rebuilt at least twice in the last hundred years.

But Susan had never met a living relative. There was only she and her mum.

Given Jassmine's general stonewalling on the past, it was a minor miracle Susan had managed to extract some names and other fragments of information about the men who could possibly be her father. One look at Frank Thringley had given her a visceral sense he was *not* her father, later confirmed by Greene's explanation about the usual sense of wrongness from a Sipper.

Thringley had been the easiest of the names to investigate, because of the Christmas presents and a definitive current address. For the others, she had some first names; possibly misremembered or misspelled surnames; a reading room ticket, presumably for the British Museum, that looked like it had been through the wash, with the name written on it faded into oblivion; and a silver cigarette case engraved with some sort of emblem or perhaps heraldic device, which might or might not have any relevance to the past owner.

But before she could start investigating, Susan needed a job. She was used to working in cafés, restaurants, and pubs (since the age of fourteen, illegally, though no one paid any attention to that in the country), but with the country falling into recession, jobs were not easy to find, even casual pub work. But Susan was lucky, and on her first day, after only fourteen attempts, she walked in as a barmaid walked out to go home to Australia. She and the owners immediately got on, and so Susan was employed at the princely cash-in-hand rate of 60p per hour for a casual but regular shift at the Twice-Crowned Swan, which was on Cloudesley Road, less than half a mile from Milner Square.

The Swan was a good pub, as they went, Susan considered. It was clean and well-run and the publican and his partner—Mr. Eric and Mr. Paul, as they insisted on being called—were both former circus performers; they'd done a strongman/acrobat routine for twenty-five years where they threw each other up in the air and spun about and also threw enormously heavy items at each other and juggled them. Both could still do a standing backflip and lift a keg under each arm. No one messed with either of them, so the drunken anger-management issues that had marred some of Susan's previous pub work experiences tended to be few and short-lived.

Mr. Eric and Mr. Paul were control freaks, but she didn't mind that, once she'd learned they really were particular about the *exact* angle to hold a glass when drawing a pint, or that the tonic bottle had to go on the *left* side of the gin glass, and change had to be counted back, no reading it off from the cash register.

After starting at the pub, Susan didn't have much time to think about what had happened in Highgate Wood, or to do much else. Her shift was from eleven in the morning to half past eleven or midnight, depending on the clean-up time after last drinks at ten thirty. The pub was closed between three and half past four, but there was always work to do, cleaning or sorting or helping Mr. Paul in the kitchen.

But after a week at the Twice-Crowned Swan, Susan had her day off coming, and her subconscious took advantage of this approaching treat by deciding to process what had happened at Highgate Wood. As this resulted in waking up terrified at four a.m. from a dream about the black fog streaming in through her windows and the Shuck coming up the stairs, she was grateful work had kept her occupied or exhausted for so long. If she'd had the dream on her first night, she would have woken screaming, rather than only choking in panic.

Even so, she got up and turned the light on, and checked her door and window. Both were shut and locked. No one was in the street or the square's garden. The moon wasn't up, the sky was clouded, the only light came from the streetlamps at the front.

At first it seemed nothing in particular had triggered the dream.

Then she looked out the smaller rear window of her room, which provided a view onto the very long, narrow garden at the back of the house. Most of it was laid down to lawn, with a vegetable patch on the right side, and there was a wooden shed with a shingled roof right at the back, by the fence.

Something was on the roof of the hut.

A lump of darkness and shadow, with shining green-blue eyes.

An urban fox, Susan told herself. Or Mister Nimbus, the landlady's cat.

But it was much bigger than a cat or a fox, and the eyes weren't reflecting light from the house because there weren't any lights on out the back. They were lit within, by some banked-down fire of intense turquoise. . . .

Suddenly, the eyes and the shadowy body disappeared. Not sliding away like a fox, or a cat.

It was gone. Vanished.

Susan checked the window. It had a solid bolt as well as the latch on the sash. Both were locked shut.

Nothing could get in. Or not easily, anyway. Not without breaking the window entirely.

Somehow, this did not fill Susan with confidence. She got dressed, in her well-worn Clash T-shirt and faded black overalls, hesitated over bothering with shoes but decided she should put on her Doc Martens before going downstairs to the kitchen to borrow Mrs. London's rolling pin. An old one, a cylinder of solid, iron-hard wood, tapered at each end. Then she sat in her single armchair where she could watch the door to her room, the big street-side window, and most important the smaller one at the back, and stayed up the remainder of the night.

In the morning, she ate her full English breakfast, without black pudding—which Mrs. London now knew to leave off her serving—and thought about going back to bed. The other lodgers disappeared to their work or study or whatever they did, with Mrs. London offering her usual incomprehensible Glaswegian farewell that probably meant "Have a nice day" as everyone left the breakfast table.

Susan had thought about starting her search for her father, but the shadow on the shed in the night had changed her mind. She had to talk to Merlin, and that meant finding one of the bookshops Inspector Greene had mentioned.

Half an hour after breakfast, she left the house. She had just shut the door when she realized someone was on the steps: a glamorous young blond woman in a white cowboy hat, a leather biker's jacket over a blue cotton sundress, and Docs very similar to Susan's, though black. This ensemble was completed by a tie-dyed yak-hair shoulder bag, at which point Susan did a double take and stared.

"Merlin?"

"Susan!" said Merlin with a ravishing smile. He . . . she . . . came up the steps and delivered a sort of half bow, half curtsy salutation.

"Um, have you changed?" asked Susan doubtfully. "Into a woman, I mean."

"No," said Merlin. "That kind of shape-shifting takes some time, and we have to go to Silv . . . go somewhere special to do it. But I like to wear a nice dress from time to time anyway."

"I was going to look for your bookshop today, to try and find you," said Susan. "How did you know?"

"I didn't," said Merlin. "I only got off the sick list this morning, and the first thing I'm told by the powers that be is to fetch you in for a bit of a chat."

"Uh, when you say 'powers that be,' do you mean, like, actual power—"

"No, I mean my great-uncle Thurston and probably great-aunt Merrihew as well," replied Merlin. "Why were you coming to see me?"

"I . . . I saw something last night," said Susan. "I mean, early this morning. In the garden, watching my window. Sort of like a fox, but bigger, with glowing eyes."

"What color?"

"Sort of green-blue. Turquoise. And it disappeared. I mean, I was looking straight at it and then it wasn't there. It didn't move, or jump away."

Merlin raised an eyebrow.

"This was in your garden? Here, behind the house?"

"Well, on the roof of the garden shed. What was it?"

"I'd better have a look."

Susan still had her latchkey in her hand. She opened the door and saw Mrs. London standing in the hall, looking slightly flustered, only a few steps back as if she'd suddenly retreated when the key clicked in the lock. Merlin, who was close behind Susan, called out a cheery greeting and waved his white-cotton-gloved left hand.

"Good morning, Mrs. L! How are you?"

"None the better for your asking," sniffed Mrs. London. "Which one are you? Only I have to write it in the book."

"Which one . . . which . . . I am heartbroken, Mrs. L. Merlin, of course."

"Thought you were your sister. You and your shenanigans."

"It's easy to tell us apart now, Mrs. L," replied Merlin easily.

"She's gone right-handed."

"What do you mean you have to write in a book?" asked Susan. "You mean for the police?"

"For the inspector," said Mrs. London dourly. "Not quite the same thing."

She looked at Merlin suspiciously.

"What do you want anyway? Inspector said Susan should be done with your lot."

"Sadly, it seems otherwise," replied Merlin. "I need to take a look in your garden, Mrs. L. Something was there last night. On the shed, at least."

"I wondered why Mister Nimbus was sniffing about the shed this morning," said Mrs. L. "Go on, then."

"Thank you!" beamed Merlin, proceeding past the landlady at speed, with Susan close behind. Once through the kitchen and out the back door, he leaned in close and whispered.

"Who's Mister Nimbus?"

"Her cat," replied Susan.

"Really? He's new. . . . I wonder what happened to Terpsichore, her old cat. Useful types, cats. You know what they say: 'The cats and the owls and the better type of raven, know more of what is doing than any human maven.'"

"Who says that?"

"I read it somewhere," said Merlin. He proceeded along the edge of the lawn, bending over to look at the bricks laid along the edge. "Do you like this dress, by the way?"

"Um, sure."

"Do you like me better in a dress or in trousers?"

"I haven't really thought about it. . . ." mumbled Susan, who had thought about it.

Merlin smiled wickedly and ran his left hand over the paving stones that demarked the end of the lawn, with the shed on the other side.

"The wards are intact."

"What does that mean?"

"The wards are magical lines of protection, boundaries that something inimical cannot cross. This house and the gardens are strongly warded and, as far as I can tell, no one has tried to interfere with them."

"As far as you can tell?"

"It's more of a right-handed thing," said Merlin. "But they haven't been obviously broken. You look good in overalls, by the way."

"Uh . . . thank you," replied Susan.

"I look good in overalls, too," mused Merlin. "When I can get some that fit."

Susan found herself nodding, and stopped.

"Fancy a drink later? Or a movie?" asked Merlin.

"Are you asking me out?"

"Yes," said Merlin. He sounded a little surprised himself, as if he hadn't meant to ask her at all.

"I hardly know you," said Susan as dismissively as she could manage. She was attracted to Merlin—who wouldn't be—but she didn't like that he was all too aware of it. He seemed to be the sort of beautiful person who had to test their charms on everyone they came in contact with, and she wasn't going to fall for it.

"We have saved each other's lives," said Merlin. "That's a real icebreaker. Tell me—"

"What about this creature on the shed?" interrupted Susan, keen to get the conversation back on track. "And you taking me to your bookshop . . . and anyway, I have someone back home."

"Really? But you broke up when you left, right? It wouldn't be fair, otherwise. What's her name? Or his? Anyway, with the boundary wards intact, the Kexa couldn't get closer than the shed."

"The what? And his name's Lenny. He plays the French horn."

Even as she spoke, Susan regretted offering up this detail, though Merlin restrained himself from more than the faintest lift of one eyebrow.

"Kexa. Or hemlock cat, if you prefer. A cat beast of the darkest hours of the night, whose breath is poison. Sent by someone to have a poke around, or maybe breathe on someone. I suppose this confirms it."

"Confirms what?" asked Susan. She was feeling both slightly flustered and a little bit annoyed. Merlin had no right to be so attractive, mysterious, and annoying all at once.

"It confirms that Great-Uncle Thurston is right, which to be fair does happen occasionally when he stirs himself. The Greats do need to see you. Come on, the cab's waiting."

He turned about and started to walk back along the lawn,

but stopped as Susan grabbed his shoulder.

"Ow!"

"Oh, I'm sorry! Does it still hurt?"

"Of course it does," replied Merlin. "I'm on light duties for two weeks. No unpacking books, no tidying shelves. Marvelous."

He started to turn away again, but Susan spoke very sharply and sternly, and he stopped.

"Merlin! Why do your relatives want to see me? And who sent the . . . the—"

"Kexa."

"Kexa. Inspector Greene warned me I was at risk from the Old World if I stayed in London—"

"Yes," said Merlin. "Far more so than we thought initially, if a hemlock cat is prowling about the place. That's why you need to come in to the shop."

"Greene told me not to have any more to do with you and the booksellers, either."

"That was good advice. Then."

"What do you mean 'then' and why are you interested now?"

"Well, *personally* I like you and—"

"Merlin—"

"There's a Kexa after you, but that aside, my esteemed elder relative has got the idea that the Raud Alfar warden in the wood wasn't shooting at me. Admittedly, I gave him that notion, after I'd had time to think about what happened."

"What do you mean? You were the one who got hit!"

"Yes. I put myself in the way. But the warden was aiming at you."

"Me?!"

"And the Raud Alfar don't shoot regular mortals. Not usually. So my sainted great-uncle—technically great-great-great-times-something-great—has consulted with my sainted great-aunt, likewise times whatever, and they have asked themselves, What does that make you?"

"It doesn't make me anything," protested Susan.

"Your mum was friends with a Sipper," pointed out Merlin. "Who else did she know, back then?"

"That's what I'm trying to find out," said Susan. "And how can you be sure the Raud Alfar warden was shooting at *me*?"

"I am sure. But Great-Uncle Thurston checked; he had Cousin Norman look back."

Susan opened her mouth to ask another question, but Merlin took pity and answered before she had to speak.

"Norman's one of the right-handed, and a seer, of sorts. A reverse oracle, you might say. He can look back at things that have already happened. And yes, before you ask, there are other right-handed who can look forward, but it's much more difficult to make sense of what they see. So no fortune-telling, as such."

"I wasn't going to ask about my future," said Susan indignantly. "Only . . . if Norman can look into the past, maybe he could see my dad, which would make everything so much easier."

"Hmm. The further back it is, the more difficult it is to discern anything in particular," said Merlin. "Particularly for Norman, who's a bit dim, to be honest. Come on, like I said, cab's waiting."

"Really?" asked Susan, following him back inside. "You are extravagant. I can't afford to even catch a taxi, let alone leave one waiting."

"Oh, I'm not paying!" exclaimed Merlin. "I work in a bookshop, remember? The pay is execrable. I never have any money to speak of. All my clothes, wonderful as they are, are from Oxfam. Or nicked from relatives. No, we've got three cabs; Aunt Audrey and Uncle Jerome drive two, and various cousins take turns with the third. They won't let me drive, worse luck, because I crashed Emilia's Jensen that time, taking no account of the fact I did it on purpose to stop a . . . well, never mind. Great-Aunt Merrihew got the idea to use cabs from that old TV show, the spy one. You know, with the swinging light bulb that gets shot, da-da-dum, da-da-da-dum, da-da-dum, da-da-da-dum, pow!"

"*Callan*," said Susan. "I've seen it. I suppose it makes sense, to blend in. Though I'd have thought it was quicker to take the Tube most of the time."

"We can't take the Tube," said Merlin. He went out the front door but paused on the bottom step, resting one hand on the low iron gate. Susan shut the door behind them and stood on the next step up from Merlin, waiting for him to go on. But he didn't move, instead looking up and down the square.

"The mythic palimpsest concept I mentioned to you—well, the layers are very thick and close throughout London in general, but particularly below. There are lots of things under us that are bound or forgotten, and best left undisturbed. And others, wakeful, but not roused to action. Our presence disturbs them. We only take the Tube when we absolutely have to."

"Inconvenient," muttered Susan. "What about the bus?"

"Oh, we can take buses all right," said Merlin. "But one of our taxis is better. I was lucky they let me have one this morning. Either you're really interesting or they're feeling for me in my weakened state."

"I'm sorry I grabbed your shoulder," said Susan. "I should have remembered."

"Didn't feel a thing, to tell the absolute truth, but don't let anyone else know," said Merlin. He was still looking up and down the square. "Where has Aunt Audrey gone with my cab?"

Susan looked, too. There were plenty of cars parked up all around the square, but no black cabs.

"She's taken a fare, damn it!" swore Merlin. "She's always tempted by a short run, bit of extra pocket money. She wouldn't dare do it for the older cousins. And it's going to rain."

"So we have to get the bus after all," said Susan. She looked up at the clouds gathering above. It *was* going to rain, in defiance of a brief promise of the spring becoming an early summer even earlier, with blue sky and sunshine between approximately 8:20 a.m. and 9:13 a.m. "Um, where are we going, by the way?"

"The New Bookshop," said Merlin, who was still studying the cars on their side of the square. "Mayfair. Stanhope Gate."

"Oh. I thought Inspector Greene said you sold new books at a big shop in Charing Cross Road. I've been to Foyles. Is it near there?"

"The New Bookshop sells old books, collectibles, and rarities," replied Merlin, who still hadn't moved off the step. Following his gaze, Susan saw he was intent on a green Ford van with two men sitting in it. "The Old Bookshop sells new books in Charing Cross Road. About a hundred yards up from Foyles."

"That's confusing," said Susan. "Are those the actual names of the shops?"

"Yes," said Merlin. "The New Bookshop, in its current form, was built in 1802; the Old Bookshop was built in 1729. Hence New and Old. Have you seen that green van before? In the square?"

Susan looked. It was a very nondescript green panel van, at least a decade old. It had faded "Greater London Council" lettering on the side.

"I don't know," she answered slowly. "I don't pay much attention to cars."

The men in the car saw her looking, turned to each other, and had a very brief conversation, ending in mutual nods. Doors opened, and they got out. Two ordinary workmen in overalls. Though the balaclavas and hammers were a bit unusual. . . .

One of them pointed at Susan.

"You, Susan Arkshaw. Come here!"

"Go inside and tell Mrs. London to press the button," said Merlin easily, opening his tie-dyed bag. His gloved hand went in and came out holding the very large revolver. A Smython .357, Susan recalled as she fumbled her key into the lock and pushed the door open.

"Mrs. London! Merlin says press the button!"

Outside, Merlin was speaking in a conversational tone.

"Drop those hammers and hold your hands up . . . very high."

Mrs. London came down the stairs at a trot, Mister Nimbus at her heels.

Susan couldn't quite hear what one of the men in balaclavas said, but it was something along the lines of "Pretty girl . . . that gun's too big for—"

Followed by the boom of a gunshot, a scream, the sound of hammers clattering on the road, and Merlin calmly issuing some more instructions.

"Booksellers!" spat Mrs. London, hurrying over to the "Stag at Bay" print in the gilded frame that hung in the hall above the shared phone on the wall. She pushed a corner to tilt the painting, revealed a recessed push button in the wall, and pressed her thumb firmly against it for a full second.

Susan stood aside as the landlady surprised her even more by drawing a small, blue-finished automatic pistol from her apron pocket and going to the partly open door, where she stood off to one side and looked out, holding her pistol with both hands down by her thigh in what seemed a very professional manner.

"Hmph," she said. As Susan moved closer, she added, "No. Stay there."

Merlin was saying something else to the men. Susan tensed, half expecting another gunshot. But none came. In the distance, she heard multiple sirens.

"What's happening?"

"Two very stupid men are lying facedown in the road, one of them likely missing half his foot," said Mrs. London.

The phone rang. Mrs. London left the door partly open but kept watching it, backing up to pick up the handset with her left hand.

"London. Yes. Secure. Two assailants down in the street, one GSW foot, ambulance required. One LIBER MERCATOR SPECIAL outside, a young . . . woman, blonde, blue dress, leather jacket, with revolver. I'll tell her."

Her Glaswegian accent had entirely disappeared while talking on the phone, Susan noted.

Mrs. London hung up and shouted out the door. The accent was back again.

"Merlin! Two D11 response cars minutes away, and the Tolpuddle panda. Hold up your warrant card."

"Will do," Merlin shouted back. "And here comes Aunt Audrey, looking abashed, as well she might. And where were you, Auntie?"

"Send her inside," called out Mrs. London.

A few seconds later, a cheerful, short, black-haired, dark-skinned, fortyish woman in jeans, T-shirt, corduroy jacket, and one battered brown leather glove on her left hand came inside. In her bare right hand, she clutched a steaming roll of foil that smelled delicious.

"Wotcher, Mrs. L," she said. "I only went to get a kebab because Merlin was taking so long, and I missed breakfast. Hello, you must be Susan. I'm Audrey."

"Uh, hello, Audrey," said Susan as Mrs. London gave a kind of grunt. The sirens were much closer now. "Uh, will I have to go to a police station again?"

"No," said Audrey and Mrs. London at the same time.

"Inspector Greene will want to talk to you, though," said Mrs. London.

"Got to come with us first," said Audrey. "You recognize those two lads, Mrs. L?"

"No," said Mrs. London. "No one local. Had to be, not to know what this place is. Or really stupid, I suppose."

The sirens reached a crescendo outside, accompanied by screeching tires, which suddenly stopped and were replaced by the sound of numerous slamming doors. Blue light washed the hallway through the partly open door.

"Armed Police! Armed Police! Don't move!"

Audrey unwrapped the end of her kebab and bit off a large mouthful. Mrs. London put her pistol back in her apron.

"Give 'em five minutes to clean up and we'll be orf," said Audrey indistinctly, her mouth full.

CHAPTER FIVE

⪢─⟡─⪡

Below the street in darkness deep
The goblins of the fair do sleep
Their mischief done until tomorrow
When they bring a new day's sorrow

⪢─⟡─⪡

"YOU'RE VERY QUIET," SAID MERLIN IN THE BACK OF THE TAXI. HE
sat opposite Susan, on the fold-down seat, eyes flickering left
and right, watching the cars behind and adjacent to them as
they slowly drove up Euston Road. The traffic was horrendous,
as per usual, and it had started to rain in a halfhearted way.

"I'm an art student from the country," said Susan. "I came
to London to study, and find my father. Not . . . not be part
of . . . whatever the hell is going on. It was bad enough with the
weird shit, as Greene calls it, but with those thugs as well . . .
I mean, why me?"

"Good question," said Merlin. "I'd like to know, too."

Susan glared at him, but didn't say anything. No further
conversation occurred until they were going past Broadcasting
House on Portland Place.

"The BBC," pointed out Merlin, with the air of a townsperson helping out a yokel.

"I know," said Susan impatiently. "I told you I've been to London before. We used to come here every year for my birthday until quite recently."

"Ah," replied Merlin. "Just making conversation. You were very quiet—"

"Why did you stick Frank Thringley with a silver pin?" interrupted Susan. "You never did say."

Merlin glanced over his shoulder at Audrey. The hatch in the glass partition between the passenger and driver compartment was open.

"Good question, luv," said Audrey. "Why did you, Merlin?"

"He wouldn't answer my questions," said Merlin stiffly. "I asked him very nicely, too. And then he tried to razor me."

"You're lucky Thringley did have a go, and that he was up to no good," said Audrey. "I mean, our-neck-of-the-woods no good, what with that giant louse and all. Otherwise, you'd be hoeing the cabbage rows out back of Thorn House."

"I know," replied Merlin testily.

"What are you talking about?" asked Susan crossly. "And you still haven't properly answered my question. What were you trying to find out?"

"Thorn House is one of our places in the country," said Merlin. "Dorset. They grow a lot of vegetables there. You'd probably be at home. Whereas I wouldn't be, making it a suitable place to send me for a punishment."

"Growing up in the country doesn't make me a farmer," said Susan. "What were you trying to find out?"

Merlin sighed.

"My mother was killed six years ago," he said quietly, looking down at his hands, the bare right laid over the gloved left. "A shotgun blast. An accident, supposedly, one of those 'wrong place, wrong time' things. She interrupted a robbery in Sloane Street. Three armed men rushed out of a jeweler's as she came out of her favorite florist's, next door. She put the robbers down, but there was another one in a car on the street, with a sawn-off shotgun. She got both barrels in the back.

"When I turned eighteen and was fully inducted, I got the file from Scotland Yard. Call it morbid curiosity, I suppose. But once I'd read it, I thought it wasn't an accident at all. I'm sure those four men were sent to kill my mother. The jewelry heist was cover for it. So, for the last year, off and on, I've followed things up."

"Despite being told to leave it alone," interjected Audrey. The traffic had seized up again at Oxford Circus, so she could turn around and talk through the hatch in the glass partition. A strong waft of beef kebab and onions came with her words. "There was no evidence of it being a planned murder."

"Nothing except the unusual imbecility of the perpetrators," snapped Merlin. "I interviewed them all in prison. Well, all except Craddock, the shooter—Mum lived long enough to *stop* his heart—and they were all near morons. I'm sure their minds had been tampered with. And they all had the same story to tell."

"Maybe it was true," suggested Audrey, but her heart wasn't in it. "Lots of criminals ain't too sharp. Hang on, we're orf again."

The cab clicked into gear and lurched forward, Audrey expertly exploiting the narrow gap that had opened between a white Ford transit and a bus before the van could close it up and deny any crossing of Oxford Street for another ten minutes.

"No criminals ever tell *exactly* the same story," said Merlin. "Not over and over again, across years, word perfect. They get things wrong, or forget. This was burned into their minds, and a lot of other stuff burned out. So I had to dig around, look deeper into their records, their associates and so on. To find some common connection, something that put them together for this job."

"And you found sod all," said Audrey, swinging the wheel for the sharp right into Hanover Street. "And got told to leave it alone. Again."

"Yes, I didn't find anything conclusive," admitted Merlin.

"What about your cousin?" asked Susan. She'd been thinking about him ever since Merlin had mentioned what he could do. "The 'reverse oracle.'"

"The wot?" asked Audrey.

"A term I used to try to explain to Susan what Norman does," said Merlin loftily. "As a matter of fact, Norman did have a look for me. But by then it was five years, and he's really only good for a month or two back. But there are . . . entities . . . who can help unravel the past or look towards the future, give clues to help work out what went on. So I went to one of them."

"Against regulations," said Audrey.

"It's a gray area," said Merlin.

"Is that right?" commented Audrey dryly. She swore as she had to swerve to miss a man who stepped out into the road. One of a stream of pedestrians trying to get past a huddle of workmen who were eyeing a partly dug hole in the pavement as if it was something unfamiliar and might move if they didn't watch it.

"Anyway, what . . . it . . . told me was as follows."

Merlin took a breath, pushed himself back against the partition, and intoned in a strange, flat voice:

Seek the Sipper, blood-lapper
Purse-cutter, goods-taker
Chieftain of outcasts
in the north
in the north
of the city of the moon
He knows, he knows, he knows
But is silenced, held fast
By vows and oaths
And will not speak

"Bit of a clue, there," said Audrey. "The 'will not speak' part, I mean."

"Oracles being notoriously unreliable and deceptive," said Merlin, "I chose to consider there was an unspoken 'unless' at the end of that little ditty, or—as may in fact be proven to be the case, finding the chap referred to would give me some other lead. 'City of the moon' means 'Luan-Dun' or London, by the way. So I looked around for North London Sippers who were also criminals, and talked to two—who were not exactly chieftains, I mean one is a bookie and the other a pickpocket, but they led me to Thringley, who definitely was a chieftain of outcasts. I talked to the first two Sippers *perfectly peaceably*, and I would have continued that way if Susan's 'uncle Frank' hadn't gone for the razor—"

He abruptly stopped talking and leaned forward to stare over Susan's shoulder through the back window, and then twisted about to look out the front. The taxi was making very slow progress along Curzon Street, had passed Bolton Street, and there was not only a lot of traffic but many pedestrians, a high proportion of them obviously tourists.

"Audrey!" snapped Merlin. "Urchins!"

"I see 'em," said Audrey in a disbelieving tone. "What's got them out under the sun?"

Susan peered through the rain-dappled side window, trying to see what Merlin and Audrey were disturbed about. Everything looked normal to her, a sea of cars and vans and motorbikes on the road, and spilling onto the road from the footpaths, a confusing, multidirectional tide of pedestrians under umbrellas of all shapes, colors, and sizes; those without umbrellas ducking and weaving between those with, trying to move faster to keep out of the rain, or to avoid an umbrella spoke in the face.

"There is no sun," she said. "And what are you—"

"Figure of speech," said Merlin. "Urchins don't usually come out in daylight at all. . . . I've counted three, Audrey. . . ."

"Four," replied their driver. "Five . . . curse this traffic! Six! Seven! Go, no, you idiot!"

They jerked to a complete standstill, thanks to a delivery van reversing ahead, where there was no room for it to do so. The traffic behind closed up immediately, and they were stuck.

"Stay or go?" asked Merlin urgently.

Audrey peered through the windscreen, and then left, right, and behind.

"They're ringing the cab for a May Dance," she said grimly. "Cold iron *might* anchor us. I dunno, this is a new one to me. I've never seen so many, and as for 'em trying anything like this in daylight, forget it! We'd better go!"

"Right," said Merlin. "You break east? We'll go west?"

"Yeah," said Audrey.

"You got something suitably ancient to hit them with?"

In answer Audrey pulled a blackthorn stick down from above her head, where it had been clipped above the sun visor. A yard-long length of gnarled, knobby, iron-hard wood, without ferrule or adornment. Two of the natural thorns had not been cut or ground off the stick, forming a kind of hilt. She pushed it through the hatch.

"You take it," she said quickly. "It must be Susan they're after."

"Thanks," said Merlin.

"If you make it, turn out the guard," said Audrey.

"You do the same," said Merlin.

"Ready?" asked Audrey. "Go!"

"What?" asked Susan. She was still looking out the window. Everything appeared to her to be entirely normal. At that moment, a child popped up, close to the glass. An odd, pinch-faced child of five or six, bright-eyed and red-cheeked, wearing an oversized, bright scarlet, badly ripped shirt, like a clown who'd gone through a wind tunnel.

He started to caper up and down, adding to the clown impression, then suddenly grinned widely, showing a blackened, destroyed mouth, save for two very sharp and long incisors of yellow-streaked white.

Susan jumped back. Merlin grabbed her hand and swung open his door, leaping out, as Audrey did the same in front.

A dozen flamboyantly dressed, misshapen children were dancing around the taxi, holding hands, but had not quite closed the ring. Merlin swung the stick left-handed to smash down two reaching arms, made a gap, and dashed through. Susan followed as closely as she could to avoid having her arm pulled out of its socket.

Merlin stayed on the road, running alongside the car ahead, but stopped suddenly as even more of the weird, frightening children poured into the street, gyrating and tumbling and leaping about.

At that moment, Susan realized with horror that all the other pedestrians had vanished, all the colorful umbrellas were gone, the turned-up collars on sensible coats, the fast-moving coatless optimists. There were only dozens and dozens of these children, who were clearly not children, a great crowd of them dancing closer and closer, reaching out to join hands. But their hands had only three fingers, their thumbs were in the wrong place and bent backwards, and their nails were horribly long, all in all more like the taloned foot of a hawk than a human hand.

The dancers had already formed a second, wider handfast ring around the empty cab, Merlin, and Susan, this one made up of forty or fifty dancers, all moving in a counterclockwise direction. They made no noise save the shuffle of their rag-wrapped feet, though their mouths were open to show their fangs and rotten gums, and their breath was fetid. Around and around they went, shuffling and capering, shuffling and capering. . . .

Merlin drew Susan close, his right hand tight on her left, and held the stick down at his side.

"Too late," he said. "They've got us in a May Dance. Don't let go."

"Where did everyone . . ." Susan started to say, but she stopped, staring around in bewilderment more than fear. Beyond the circling ring of urchins, not only had all the ordinary people vanished, but now the street and the cars and buildings were fading away as well, replaced by open fields to the north, and close to them, a huddle of tents, shanties, barrows, and stands. Even the clouds and rain had disappeared, the sky was a vivid blue, and it was hot, like a prime August day, though it was—or had been—only the nineteenth of May.

"Don't accept anything anyone gives you freely," warned Merlin. "Particularly food or drink."

"But there's no one—" Susan started to say, but she stopped as suddenly there were people, a great crowd of them. People dressed in medieval clothes, jerkins and smocks and hose, boots and simple leather shoes. Sound suddenly came back as well, sellers calling out their wares, people talking and laughing, musicians in the distance, pipes warbling above a constant drum. Smells wafted across—sweaty, unwashed people stink and earthy farmyard stench, overlaid with cooking meat and fat, and smoky, burning smells.

The circling dancers stopped, laughed in unison, and suddenly broke apart, individuals racing off in all directions through the crowds, ducking and weaving to disappear among the larger people.

"Where are we?" asked Susan. She blinked several times. There was something wrong with how everything looked, but she couldn't quite work out what it was. . . .

"The May Fair," said Merlin shortly. "Or more precisely, a mythic resonance of the fair that was held here for centuries, with the obvious lending of its name to the place later. It's a trap. The urchins . . . who you might know better as goblins . . . have danced us here. Which is extraordinarily unlike their usual behavior. They're tricksters, but usually fairly harmless. They never kill, for example, not on purpose—"

"Give us a kiss, darling," roared a drunken man clad only in a rough smock hitched too far above his knees. He leaned in close to Merlin, who dodged aside and smacked him across the back of the knees with the blackthorn stick, sending him crashing down to the muddy ground. Holding Susan's hand all the tighter, the bookseller led her away as the man lay in the puddled track that had been Curzon Street, laughing his head off as if he had wanted to land there all along.

"They're real," said Susan, aghast, as she was brushed by the corner of a tray of small steaming pies being carried past by a woman whose face was transformed by the most delighted smile. "And all weirdly happy."

"It's real for us, for now," said Merlin. "They're happy because, like I said, this is an idealized version of the best days of the fair. The urchins have trapped us here. But they have to follow tradition and give us a chance of getting out—"

He jerked aside to avoid a skipping child—a human one, not one of the pinch-faced, sharp-canined urchins—and Susan had to jump after him to avoid letting go of his hand.

"Like the Shuck, the goblins have to follow the rules of the legend. Apart from the two of us, there'll be something here that doesn't fit, that isn't right. They have to show it to us three times. If we don't claim it, we'll stuck here forever; we'll forget who we are, become archetypes, caught up in the mythic fair."

"Something that doesn't fit?" asked Susan slowly. She was distracted because a bear was ambling towards them along the right-hand alley between the closer tents. A glossy-furred bear on a flimsy chain, dancing as if it was enjoying itself, the bear ward by its side mimicking the bear steps, in a way that made it look as if they were happily dancing together.

"It could be an object, a person, anything that looks wrong, out of place," said Merlin. He pulled on Susan's hand, dragging her out of the way of the bear, in front of a sausage table heavily laden with pyramidal piles of different kinds of fat sausages below a cloud of flies. Dozens more were cooking behind on a grill laid over a charcoal firepit.

"Sausages! Best sausages! Fit for a king . . . or for a queen!" roared the vendor. A small woman with a very loud voice, she bowed low before Susan and extended her cooking fork, a section of sausage steaming on the end. "Try a taste, Your Highness!"

The cooking sausages did smell wonderful, overriding any distaste for the unsanitary conditions. Susan's mouth watered, and she felt extraordinarily tempted. But before she could reach out, Merlin dragged her on, past three jugglers and an eel-diving contest with the contestants leaping into the largest barrel Susan had ever seen, to a narrow space between two wattle-and-daub huts that got them out of the immediate rush of fairgoers.

"Eat nothing, remember!" snapped Merlin. "That would fix you here. I wish Vivien was with us."

"Who's Vivien?"

"My sister. Right-handed. Very good at puzzles and so on. Seen anything so far?"

"How would I know what's out of place?" protested Susan. "I've never been to a medieval fair before! Even a modern re-creation of one."

"We'd better walk around," said Merlin. "Keep your eyes open, and don't let go of my hand."

"The happiness is unsettling, all the smiling and laughing," muttered Susan as they proceeded along the narrow lane that led to a much broader one, in the heart of the fair. "I mean, it's kind of more unnerving than if they were scowling."

"The other side of the fair will be here, too, somewhere, or will come along. The dark doings and despair, the thievery and murder hidden by the glitter and fun. We need to get out before it turns into *that* fair. But I can't see anything out of place!"

At the next intersection of alleys, Susan paused to stand on tiptoe and have a good look around. She was taller than almost everyone anyway, which she wasn't used to, but it helped. A group of dancing musicians was coming towards her: several drummers, two lutenists, a bunch of others playing recorder-like instruments, and one something that looked like an oversized set of bagpipes. But as the two lutenists pirouetted apart, she saw a young girl behind them with a huge basket of flowers, and Susan realized what was out of place, and what had been bothering her all along.

"The flower seller!" she exclaimed, sliding between a group of gawping, sack-clothed country folk, red-faced and doubled up with laughter at the antics of two stilt-walking jesters who were mimicking some sort of failed amorous coupling, possibly of insects. This time, she dragged Merlin after her, instead of the other way around.

"What?"

"Everything's in brighter color than it should be!" explained Susan, ducking under a tray of pies that might have been swung across to slow her down, Merlin slinkily following. "It all looks like a Super 8 film! Supersaturated, brighter than life. But the flower seller, she's got a flower that has no color at all. There she is!"

The flower seller was walking away from them, and the crowd between grew thicker. Everyone in the fair had suddenly turned around and was streaming back to the intersection ahead, their intention obvious—to prevent Susan and Merlin from reaching the girl, without actually stopping them—bending the letter of whichever ancient law said they had to be given the opportunity to escape.

Merlin moved in front again, swinging his blackthorn stick. People swerved away from it, as if fearing the touch of the wood, but when he did make contact, they showed no pain, continuing to smile and laugh.

The flower girl turned to go down one of the narrower lanes, and as she did so, Susan saw the flower again, and this time, so did Merlin. A tall rose, a translucent flower that might have been made of glass, save that its stem bent and petals trembled as the flower seller walked.

"Second sighting!" snapped Merlin. "Come on!"

He pushed the stick between the legs of an eel carter, sending the woman and the tub of eels she carried on her head sprawling, the eels sliding every which way, people slipping over them and falling down in a confused mass. All still smiling and laughing, as if it was an experience they'd paid to enjoy.

Merlin and Susan jumped over the writhing trail of eels and ran after the flower seller, who was only a dozen paces ahead, walking briskly down a much narrower alley between the backs of a row of small theaters, two- or even three-story affairs of painted canvas over timber frames.

As they ran, a shadow caught up with them overhead, clouds obscuring the sun and the blue sky, and there was a sudden chill in the air.

"Oh, play fair!" shouted Merlin. He accelerated, and managed to touch his blackthorn stick to the flower seller's back, the lightest tap. She stopped, and turned to face them. She'd looked like a pretty, smiling girl when Susan had spied her across the crowd, but now her face had narrowed, her skin was lightly scaled, and her mouth was broken-toothed and decayed save for the sharp canines of a goblin, and she had shrunk a foot or more.

"We are not of this time or place, and nor is the rose," declaimed Merlin. "Deliver it to—"

A growl was the only warning Merlin had of sudden attack. Spinning in place, he rammed his stick across the mouth of an enormous shaggy dog that lunged out of the shadows between the shacks. Its sheer weight drove him back several steps, and since he wouldn't let go of her hand, Susan was dragged with him, falling sideways into the mud onto her hip. She saved herself from worse by putting her free hand down, but it still hurt. A lot.

"Bad dog!" she shouted, more from instinct than anything. "Bad dog! Drop that at once!"

Much to everyone's surprise, perhaps not least the beast itself, the dog did drop the stick.

"Sit!" commanded Susan, standing up. She was furious:

furious at falling in the mud, furious at being dragged into the mythic shenanigans, plain furious about everything.

The dog sat. Susan looked at the flower seller.

"And you! Urchin, goblin, whatever you are. Hand over the rose."

The flower seller plucked the colorless rose from amidst the riot of colored posies in the basket, and passed it to Susan, going down on one knee as she did so.

Susan took it.

The May Fair disappeared like a fast-forwarded video of an ice sculpture melting, the vibrant colors replaced by the drabber, grayer reality; the medieval stench by vehicle exhausts; and the human hubbub of the May Fair by the sound of twentieth-century Mayfair.

They were on the footpath, on Curzon Street, near the laneway entrance to Shepherd Market. The rain was coming down harder, a drop splashing right in Susan's eye. Two young Americans, clearly tourists, were standing nearby.

"Did you see those little kids?" one of the tourists asked her friend. "The ones that ran through a second ago?"

"What? Sorry, I kind of phased out there for a few seconds. Must be jet lag. Hey, look down this cute alley! A real British pub."

"They're in for a shock," said Susan. "Room-temperature pints of real ale and young Americans do not go well together—"

"That was actually a *wolf* biting my stick, you know," said Merlin. He frowned and inspected the deep tooth marks in the bog oak, sighed, and brushed some flecks of mud off his dress, smearing them into streaks that somehow looked punky, intentional, and cool. "So now I really wonder who . . . or what . . . you are."

"I'm me," said Susan slowly. The rose was in her hand, but it was only glass now, rigid and fragile. "I've always had a way with dogs."

"Have you now?" asked Merlin cheerfully. He put his stick over his shoulder in best Gene Kelly style and skipped through a puddle, sending his dress swirling as he spun about to look back at Susan, who was motionless, lost in thought. "Come on, it's not far to the bookshop now!"

CHAPTER SIX

It is not music that soothes those savage hearts
Our soldiers, left-handed, of many parts
Stories and tales leech their wrathsome blood
The beast is calmed, embanked the flood

THE NEW BOOKSHOP HAD ONLY A SMALL BRONZE PLATE BY THE front door of the imposing five-story Georgian town house to announce that it was, in fact, a shop of any kind. As the front door was itself shielded by a columned portico, it was unlikely anyone who wasn't already looking for the shop would ever step inside.

Unusually, there was a kind of vestibule beyond the front door, a short hallway that was closed off by an inner metal door of antique bronze, etched with the figure of two bearded giants raising nailed clubs, their eyes large inset crystals that looked like diamonds but were far too big to be actual gems. As Merlin ushered Susan inside, the outer door swung shut behind him and clicked heavily as it locked itself.

"We have unwanted visitors from time to time," explained

Merlin. He stepped past her and pressed the bell button next to the inner door. "We won't have to wait long."

"That's beautiful work," said Susan, looking at the giants etched in the door.

"Gog and Magog," said Merlin.

The giants' crystal eyes suddenly lit up, making Susan start and step backwards.

"The door was made by the 'Great Rondelhyde, Magic Artificer' in 1899," said Merlin. "One of the right-handed. His real name was Ronald Biggins. Amongst other things, he made apparatus for stage magicians in the last half of the nineteenth century, disappearing cabinets and so on. He loved this kind of stuff. Our customers enjoy it, too."

"Does it do anything?" asked Susan. "I mean, is it actually a magical door?"

"No," said Merlin. "The eye lights are electric and mainly to make sure we can clearly see who's waiting. It is a very solid door, though, two-inch bronze on a steel frame."

Susan looked up. There was an odd-looking mirror set into the ceiling.

"One-way glass," she said.

"Oh no, that is magical," said Merlin. "Two handfuls of water from . . . let's say a sacred lake . . . cupped in the same moment from different shores. If it was big enough you could walk through to the other side, though as that is just the tea room here, it would be disappointing. Here we go."

With considerable creaking and rumbling, the bronze door

began to open. It got halfway, with one of the two giants sliding out of view, and then stopped. Through the gap, Susan saw a charming, comfortable book room lit by bright electric chandeliers above six rows of glass-door bookcases full of old tomes bound in green and red and blue and black leather or buckram; or more exotic materials like animal hides and even metal. Each row of shelves was bookended with a well-worn leather chair, for the most languid book-browsing experience.

Straight ahead there were two long mahogany tables stacked with more old books, and in the aisle between them stood a bright-eyed, middle-aged bookseller with a surprisingly long beard, which had been plaited into three braids. He wore a green apron with numerous pockets over his untidy, shiny-at-the-elbows blue suit; a checked shirt; and a limp, pale green bow tie. He wore a white cotton glove on his right hand and Susan noticed his apron had a scabbard pocket for very long, thin paper knife.

"Door's stuck again," he said. "At half Gog, as we like to say. Welcome back, Merlin. Practically everyone from both shops is out looking for you."

"Audrey got here, then?"

"She did, with her surprising and rather disturbing news," replied the man. "No one can recall the urchins daring such a dance, at least to one of us. Oh, please forgive me. You must be Susan. My name is Eric. Can I offer you a towel, perhaps?"

Susan looked down at herself. So much had happened so quickly she hadn't had time to take in that she was soaking wet and her Docs were muddied to the ankle. Merlin was drenched, too, but he somehow looked glamorous, as if he'd gotten wet on purpose.

"Uh, yes, please," she said, correctly interpreting Eric's quick sideways glance that he was really concerned she didn't drip on any of the books.

"Come straight along between the tables here and out to the staff washrooms," said Eric. "And then they're expecting you upstairs, Merlin."

"Both Greats?" asked Merlin. "Merrihew came in?"

"Yes, they're both here today," said Eric. He hesitated, then added, "Good luck."

Merlin grimaced and handed him the blackthorn stick.

"Give that to Audrey, will you, when she gets back?"

Eric nodded, and popped it into a tree stump umbrella stand by the door, complete with sawn-off roots, which held several similar sticks, two ivory-handled black umbrellas of some antiquity, and a two-handed sword with a bronze entwined dragon hilt that was longer than he was tall.

"Would you like me to take your glass rose, too?" asked Eric.

"Uh, no, I'll keep it," said Susan. She wasn't sure why, except that she wanted to look at it more closely when she got the chance. She'd seen it swaying and bending, the petals fluttering, and even though it was now stiff and solid glass, it had a naturalistic feel and looked like a work of very fine art, not something from some factory mold.

Susan followed Merlin between the tables towards a door at

the back of the showroom, trying not to turn her head too quickly to look at interesting books and shower them with droplets of water. Because the books were old and most didn't have dust jackets, it was hard to see what they were while rapidly passing by, particularly without turning her head, but she did manage to read the gilt or silver embossed type on some as she went past, noting titles and names she knew like *The Tempest* and *Ivanhoe* and *Persuasion* and *Wuthering Heights*, Shakespeare and Walter Scott, Austen and Brontë. Several shelves contained only Bibles, some of them obviously very old indeed, and there was a special display case between two bookcases where she paused for a moment, awed by its contents: William Blake's *Poetical Sketches*, a first edition of *Seven Pillars of Wisdom* by T. E. Lawrence, and the crowning presence of a Shakespeare *First Folio*.

Next to the rear door, there was a very large glass-fronted bookcase, where the books were not in rows, but face out on stands. Susan stopped as she recognized childhood favorites, made much easier because many of these were of a later era than those on the other shelves and did have dust jackets. There was John Masefield's *The Box of Delights*; and the C. S. Lewis Narnia books; and Patricia Lynch's *The Turf-Cutter's Donkey*; *The Winter of Enchantment* by Victoria Walker; *Black Hearts in Battersea* by Joan Aiken; several of Rosemary Sutcliff's historical novels, including Susan's favorite, *The Silver Branch*; *Power of Three* by Diana Wynne Jones; *The Weirdstone of Brisingamen* by Alan Garner; *Five Children and It* by E. Nesbit;

and many others. Most were editions she knew from the library, but in much better shape, the dust jackets kept pristine under protective clear wrappers.

"Children's writers," said Merlin. "Dangerous bunch. They cause us a lot of trouble."

"How?" asked Susan.

"They don't do it on purpose," said Merlin. He opened the door. "But quite often they discover the key to raise some ancient myth, or release something that should have stayed imprisoned, and they share that knowledge via their writing. Stories aren't always merely stories, you know. Come on."

Susan tore herself away from the children's books and followed Merlin through a cramped rear office that contained two rolltop desks, an old wooden six-drawer filing cabinet, and a rifle rack containing six Lee-Enfield .303s, their 1907 Pattern Sword bayonets in a smaller rack below, and a slightly battered green ammunition case beneath that, with stenciled yellow type: "300 Cart. .303 Ball."

Merlin led Susan out through a door at the rear of the office, into a narrow wainscoted corridor with two doors on the left and a broad staircase on the right. The left-hand door had a stylized bonnet drawn on it in gold, and the right-hand a top hat.

"Which bathroom do you want to use?" asked Merlin. "Towels inside, and there'll be clothes, too; you can get changed if you want. Only boiler suits, I'm afraid, and mostly too big. I think we bought all Winston Churchill's old ones. At least they'll be dry."

"Are you getting changed?" asked Susan suspiciously. She couldn't picture Merlin in an oversized Churchillian boiler suit.

"Later," said Merlin. "I'm only suggesting it because you really are *very* muddy. . . ."

Susan looked down at herself, noted this was accurate, and went in through the door marked with the bonnet. She figured the women's toilet would be more salubrious than the men's. Cleaning toilets in pubs had made her well aware of the difference.

When she emerged ten minutes later, Merlin was waiting. He had somehow cleaned and dried his blue dress, and the towel wrapped around his head in a turban didn't look stupid, but like some sort of new fashion he'd started.

Susan didn't feel too jealous. Despite Merlin's comment, she'd found a blue boiler suit exactly her size, and it still had a belt, which the ones she'd seen in charity shops had always long since lost. With the belt pulled in, the suit had some shape, and numerous useful pockets made up for the rough feel of the heavy cotton. She'd tied her own clothes into a bundle and felt rather like an unlikely hobo from a 1930s film, a bit too shiny and clean.

"How did you get one that fits?" asked Merlin. "I've looked in both bathrooms tons of times! They're always way too big! Were there any more that size?"

"No," said Susan.

"Typical," muttered Merlin.

"What's with all the boots in there?" asked Susan. As well as shelves of carefully folded blue boiler suits, there were racks and racks of highly polished heavy black boots in the expansive bathroom, which was more like a locker room at a big school than anything you'd expect out the back of a bookshop. Very large, cumbersome, and doubtless uncomfortable boots.

"Old ceremonial stuff," said Merlin, with a shudder. "Which we are forced to wear occasionally. Come on. Great-Uncle Thurston and Great-Aunt Merrihew are upstairs."

Susan took two steps up, and paused. The central staircase was older than the rest of the house. It was medieval, not Georgian, with black oak banisters and rough-planked treads. She looked up the stairwell and saw it extended at least six floors, which was one more than she'd counted from outside. Looking down, the stair disappeared into darkness after three or four flights; there were no electric lights down there, not even the dull, antique lamps on the staircase above.

"Yes, there's a kind of penthouse that can't be seen from the street," said Merlin breezily. "And the stairs go down a long way. The place was built around the remnants of an older one, and above an older structure still. Come on."

"I've had a lot to take in," said Susan mulishly, sitting on the bottom step. "By rights I should be sobbing in a corner and demanding to wake up from this terrible dream."

"Really?" asked Merlin. He started back down the steps. "Uh, are you in fact okay?"

Susan paused to think, then nodded.

"Yes," she said. "I wonder if it's delayed shock. Later I'll be talking gibberish."

She hesitated, then added, "In a way, it even felt . . . not unexpected."

"Being danced by goblins into a mythic May Fair?"

"Yes . . ." replied Susan. She frowned. "Maybe I don't know enough to be properly frightened."

"Maybe," said Merlin. He seemed to be about to say something else, but didn't, instead clattering on up the stairs. "Top floor! Come on!"

Susan stood up, and followed, but she stopped dead on the first landing. The arched doors leading off to left and right here were eight feet tall and painted with scenes from Shakespeare's plays. The left-hand door depicted the witches and Macbeth gathered around a huge iron cauldron, which looked oddly out of scale, being as tall as the women. The right-hand door featured Prospero and Miranda from *The Tempest*, with Caliban lurking in the darkness behind them, in a cave by the sea.

Susan recognized the paintings immediately, or rather recognized they were much larger versions of paintings by an obscure eighteenth-century artist called Mary Hoare, who Susan only knew about because Hoare was one of the favorites of her art teacher, Mrs. Lawrence.

"These are by Mary Hoare!" exclaimed Susan, leaning in close to look. "But much bigger . . . and in oils. Does anyone know you have these?"

"I hope not," said Merlin. "Mary Hoare was one of us, right-handed, you know. Lots of visual artists among the right-handed; we left-handed tend more towards poetry and music. I believe

Miranda there is a self-portrait, of sorts. And the cauldron is . . . um . . . also based on . . . never mind."

Susan paid no attention to Merlin's sudden reversal on whatever he was going to say about the cauldron. She leaned closer to look at the painted door.

"If these are original," she said, "they were painted in the . . . sometime around 1800?"

"Seventeen ninety-six," said Merlin. "We do need to get a bit of a move on—"

"I love them!" exclaimed Susan. She started up the stairs. "Are there more?"

"Uh, no," replied Merlin. "I mean, no more by Mary Hoare. Slow down. . . ."

Susan was taking the steps three at a time, but she slowed as she reached the next landing, and Merlin heard her disappointed sigh. The doors there were gray-painted steel, riveted along the edges, and would not have looked out of place on a ship. Which was actually where they had come from; they were armor-plated doors from the magazine of the World War One dreadnought HMS *Benbow*.

"Those are from a battleship," said Merlin, following Susan as she continued on up the stairs. "There have been a number of people in charge of interior decoration over the years, and since we practically never let visitors past the actual bookshop, there's never been a push towards uniformity—"

"You practically never let visitors in?" asked Susan. "What about me, then?"

"You're an exception," said Merlin. "Evidently. Now, I wonder if you can tell me the artist responsible for the next set of doors?"

Susan stopped again as they reached the landing of the third floor.

"No . . . they're beautiful. German, I think?"

The doors here were very old, and each leaf was set with nine deeply carved limewood panels, depicting scenes of medieval life in a late Gothic style. There were peasants reaping a field, merchants weighing coins, knights at a tourney, monks in a scriptorium, a wagon at a tollgate . . . and several showing booksellers amongst their wares, but with swords hidden behind the books, and odd creatures, even a dragon. All beautifully represented, the carving incredibly detailed.

"You're good," said Merlin. "They're by Tilman Riemenschneider. A fifteenth-century sculptor. In Würzburg for the most part, though he carved these here."

"One of the right-handed?" asked Susan.

"Oh no, not one of us at all," said Merlin. "But he owed a debt to a family member, and made us these panels. I'm afraid the doors on the next two floors are perfectly ordinary, but we do have quite a quantity of artwork throughout the house, and elsewhere. I could show you around sometime, perhaps. Before we go out to dinner or whatever. People do tend to give us things when we help them out, and the right-handed are inveterate collectors of art."

"Points for *inveterate*," said Susan as they continued upstairs. She chose to ignore the implication that they would definitely be going out somewhere together. "I've never ever heard anyone actually say that."

"We live among books," said Merlin, with a shrug.

"Do the left-handed collect anything?" asked Susan as they passed the doors on the next landing, which were very disappointing, and would not have been out of place at Susan's 1950s-built school.

"Weapons," replied Merlin.

There were three doors on the fifth-floor landing, where the main staircase ended. Those to the left and right were the same as the previous floor, dull factory-made things and only notable because they looked much newer than the rest of the building, things of ugly postwar painted plywood.

But there was also one door straight ahead, which, while not adorned with artwork, had the impressive, dusky sheen of very old, highly polished mahogany. There was no doorknob or handle, but a knocker in the middle, a ring held in the mouth of a lion, whose bronze mane spread impressively for at least a foot in every direction.

Merlin went up to the door and knocked three times.

"Don't worry," he said, looking back over his shoulder. "You'll be okay."

"What?" asked Susan, who hadn't been worried about not being okay. Not until Merlin mentioned the possibility. "What do you mean?"

"I'm on your side," replied Merlin, stepping back as the door opened. There was no one there, only a narrow stair between roughly plastered stone walls. The steps were thickly carpeted in red with bronze stair rods, and lit by gas lamps, which Susan could actually hear hissing as they climbed up.

"Why do I need someone on *my* side?" asked Susan. "And why the gas lamps?"

"The Greats are old; they like familiar things," said Merlin. "Affectation, I suppose. We are all a little prone to it."

Susan stared after him, wondering how long it was since any house in London, or anywhere in the United Kingdom, had been lit by gas. But as Merlin showed no sign of giving further explanation or slowing down, she followed.

The stair went up a long way, and as they climbed, the plastering disappeared, and the stonework became more obvious.

Finally, after what seemed to Susan to be an ascent equivalent to three or four floors, they came to another door, of rough-hewn wood. Merlin knocked again, with his gloved left hand, and it was opened immediately by a tall, elegant, very dark-skinned woman who looked to be around thirty or so, with long black hair in a gilded hairnet, wearing an ankle-length silk dress of vibrant red, and canvas jungle boots. She was backlit in the doorway by sunlight and made a very striking impression.

She was holding a blue enameled fountain pen in her right hand and a notebook in her left. For a moment Susan thought she wore a single glove of brilliant silver cloth, before she saw it was her actual left hand that was shining silver and she wasn't wearing a glove at all.

"Cousin Sam!" exclaimed Merlin. "I didn't know you were back. Writing a poem?"

"Indeed," said Sam. "Compulsorily returned for restorative

reading and therapeutic poetical composition, post my contretemps with the Rollright stones and the Silver-Eyed One. Only to be dragged from my study to do a spot of light bodyguarding for the Greats, since there seems to be something of a flap going on."

"Sonnet? Villanelle? Chanso?" asked Merlin.

"Limericks," said Sam gravely. "Thematically linked limericks."

"I look forward to the next poetry night," said Merlin. "Do you—"

A slightly querulous, Scottish-accented woman's voice from somewhere behind Sam interrupted him.

"Sam! Is that Merlin and the girl? Hurry them along, I haven't got all day!"

Sam stood aside, and gestured. Susan followed Merlin, up into a very large open-plan penthouse that had huge floor-to-ceiling windows on every side. She could see Hyde Park to the west, the houses on the southern side of Stanhope Gate and the Dorchester to the north, but they were all curiously below them, though she could have sworn the hotel at least should be much taller than the bookshop. It had stopped raining, and the sky was sort of blue, though it didn't come close to the perfection of the May Fair sky the goblins had taken them to.

Sam sat down on a chair by the door, lifting her book. There was a scabbarded sword leaning on the wall by her side, next to that an AK-47 and a canvas ammunition bag holding three curved magazines, and next to that a blackthorn stick very similar to the one Audrey had in the taxi. Susan tried not to look at Sam's faintly glowing silver hand, and after two or three gawping seconds, succeeded.

Looking across the room, Susan noted a life-sized bronze sculpture of a man that was either *The Age of Bronze* by Rodin or more likely a copy, since it looked rather battered and was being treated in a very cavalier fashion, with an old Burberry trench coat and some sort of waterproof cape hanging off its head. Apart from the sculpture and a broad and very faded Persian or Turkish carpet, the large room was very sparsely furnished. There was a 1920s art deco–ish lounge and three club style leather armchairs of older vintage facing it in the middle of the room, and between them, serving as a coffee table, a large cut-down whisky barrel with a glass top, the barrel staves marked in fading six-inch-tall red letters: "Milltown 1878."

Two seventyish or maybe older people put their books down and rose from their chairs to greet them. A silver-haired, craggy-faced man, massively shouldered, who had to be close to seven feet tall, clad in a well-worn tweed suit, a brown leather glove on his right hand; and a much shorter, slighter woman, still beautiful though very lined, her pure white hair pulled back and tied with a black ribbon. She wore a very eccentric outfit: a fisherman's green vest replete with colorful flies hooked onto loops above the pockets, over a black, sleeveless cotton dress that showed off her surprisingly muscled, if wrinkled, arms, complete with a very faded tattoo of a long dagger with three drops of blood on her left forearm. She wore a rubberized gardening glove on her left hand.

"Great-Uncle Thurston and Great-Aunt Merrihew," said Merlin. "This is Susan Arkshaw."

"And about time," said Merrihew, her Scottish accent very clear. "As you know, this is very inconvenient, Merlin. Come closer, young woman. We won't bite."

"I won't anyway, lass," rumbled Thurston. "There's nowt to fear."

He had a broad Yorkshire accent. Susan walked over to the chairs, glancing from one to the other, noting that Thurston was reading Barbara Tuchman's *A Distant Mirror*, in which he'd carefully placed a bookmark before closing it; and Merrihew had simply put her Penguin paperback of *The Tiger in the Smoke* by Margery Allingham open facedown on the whisky barrel table.

But it was their voices she noticed most. Susan hadn't really thought about it till now, but Merlin had a kind of posh, public-school voice. Audrey was definitely a Cockney. Sam by the door sounded maybe Canadian or some kind of softer American. And now a Scotswoman and this great Yorkshire farmer type. It was very confusing to her, as it would be for anyone British, who initially, at least, sorted people into social classes according to their accent, whether they consciously wanted to or not.

"There is always rather a lot to fear, as a matter of fact," said Merrihew. "It's possible we should even be afraid of *you*."

CHAPTER SEVEN

⊱⊰⊱⊰⊱⊰●⊱⊰⊱⊰⊱⊰

In London a bookseller feller
Wore one glove surprisingly yeller
Matched with a new suit of dark blue
Stuffed with a pistol or two
That well-armed bookseller feller

⊱⊰⊱⊰⊱⊰●⊱⊰⊱⊰⊱⊰

"AFRAID OF *ME*?" ASKED SUSAN, TAKEN ABACK. "WHY WOULD *YOU* BE afraid of *me*?"

"Well, that's merely an example. We don't know if we should be afraid or not, because we lack information," said Merrihew. "Would you care for some tea?"

"Uh, yes, please," said Susan. "Look, I don't understand. I mean, anything, really."

"Sit ye down, lass, sit ye down," said Thurston, gesturing to one of the chairs with his massive gloved right hand. "What Merry is getting at is that we were puzzled by the Raud Alfar warden shooting at you, as if you represent some threat to them, and then there was quite an attempt to prevent you coming here today, what with some thugs and then, of all things, May Fair goblins in daylight!"

"One question being, are you responsible for both actions?" asked Merrihew. "Were both these apparent kidnappings staged? To try to avoid us?"

"What!" exclaimed Susan, almost getting back out of the chair she was about to sit on. She looked at Merlin, who gave her a sheepish smile. "I never knew anything about the Old World or any of this stuff before I met Merlin. I'm an art student—well, almost one. And I want to find out who my father is, that's all."

Merrihew looked at Thurston, who nodded. He sat down himself and began to rummage in his waistcoat for something.

"Aye, aye, she speaks truth, inasmuch as she knows herself," he rumbled. "Our apologies, Miss Susan. Where's that tea?"

"I'll go see, Great-Uncle," said Merlin, fleeing the scene, pursued by a dirty glance from Susan. She was surprised to see him disappear into an alcove she hadn't noticed before, where someone's hand came out and drew him in. A slim, feminine hand, a right hand, gloved in satin. With buttons up the wrist.

Susan felt the slightest pang of jealousy and had to firmly push the feeling away. Once again she reminded herself that Merlin was not good boyfriend material; he was obviously more in love with himself than he ever could be with anyone else. His interest in her would doubtless not last beyond the consummation of the chase, and she wasn't interested in that kind of relationship. Her mother had too often fallen for just such a trap.

It did pass through her mind that Merlin was also much more fascinating than poor Lenny. Who had always been something of a stopgap boyfriend anyway. He did play the French horn beautifully, and had very dexterous fingers and lovely curly hair, but there was something missing. . . .

"Now, why don't you tell us about your encounter with the goblins," said Merrihew. "We heard from Audrey you'd been danced away. How did you escape the fair? Was it Merlin who noticed what was out of place?"

"No, no, it was me," said Susan, bringing her mind back from an invidious comparison of Lenny and Merlin. She held up the glass flower. "This glass flower . . . only it was alive, transparent, where everything else was very much in color."

"Ah, the left-handed aren't so good with that sort of thing," said Thurston comfortably, opening the leather pouch he'd taken from his waistcoat to take out a pinch of tobacco, while simultaneously searching his other pocket for a pipe or papers. "Give them something to stand up and fight, none better, of course. So from the beginning, when those pesky goblins danced around, what went on?"

Merrihew sniffed but didn't comment.

Susan told them, as best she was able to recall. She noticed Merlin was leaning in from the tea-making alcove, listening.

"Hmm, that's interesting," said Thurston. "And the dog let go the stick when you said, eh? I'm thinking we might be needing to know who your father is, too, lass."

"Why?" asked Susan bluntly.

"Well, the Raud Alfar think you're someone who's dangerous to them," explained Thurston, dropping wisps of tobacco as he waved his hand around to punctuate his words. "And those two ruffians who came after you, we've heard from Inspector Greene she can't get a peck of sense out of them, they're right mazed, which suggests someone from our neck of the woods has been interfering with mortal minds. They were from Birmingham, members of the Milk Bottle Gang. Neither Greene nor ourselves know of any connection between that gang and the Old World, here or there. Indeed, it is a rare thing for organized gangsters to have dealings with the mythic, and vice versa. Some mortals are drawn to serve malign entities, the so-called Death Cultists, but not your garden-variety criminals. Oh no."

He paused, possibly for dramatic effect but more likely to prevent his pinch of tobacco from entirely escaping his grasp.

"When we additionally consider the relatively few personages or entities who are capable of forcing or enticing the May Fair goblins to snatch two mortals away in broad daylight, and one of them a bookseller . . . eh . . . something must be up. And what connects all these things? Susan Arkshaw. And what is most interesting about Susan Arkshaw? Her unknown father."

"It's my business," said Susan indignantly. "I didn't ask for anyone else to pry into my family history."

"Nor do we particularly want to," said Thurston. "In fact, it's quite inconvenient—"

"*Extremely* inconvenient and likely inconsequential," interrupted Merrihew impatiently. "Where is that tea?"

"Coming!" called out Merlin. There was a confirming rattle of cups and saucers and silverware from the alcove, and some muttered conversation.

"As I was about to say," continued Thurston. "We can help you find out who your father is . . . or was . . . far more swiftly than you could by yourself. Or even with anyone else's help. Ah!"

He found his pipe in an inside coat pocket and pulled it out. With its curved stem and rather enormous bowl, it looked like he'd stolen it from a hobbit, thought Susan, who was a big fan of Tolkien. He started stuffing the pipe with what remained of the pinch of tobacco he'd been waving around.

"I hope you're not planning to light that monstrosity," said Merrihew as Thurston put the pipe in his mouth and started patting his waistcoat pockets again. "Remember? Strictly no smoking in the bookshops now. Not since last year. We all agreed."

"Ah, yes," grumbled Thurston. He removed the pipe and looked at it sadly.

"Tea's up," said Merlin.

Or, in fact, not Merlin. Someone who sounded like him, but with a lighter, smokier voice. Susan looked around and saw a young woman who looked very like Merlin as she'd first seen him, in a suit. In this case a pale blue pinstripe through navy blue, over a powder-blue silk shirt, with a half-undone tie striped in some school or university pattern that would mean something to those who cared about such things. She was a little more rounded than Merlin, and at least an inch taller, even though she wore brogues to his current Docs. A pale blue buttoned satin glove covered her right hand, which was holding a black-and-white-spotted porcelain cow creamer. Merlin, next to her, carried a silver tray with cups, saucers, sugar bowl, and spoons.

"You must be Vivien," said Susan.

"Regrettably, my younger sibling and I do look alike," replied Vivien, waiting a moment for Merlin to put the tray on the whisky barrel coffee table before she also set down the cow-shaped milk jug. She offered her hand to Susan, who stood up and shook it, before both sat down.

"Welcome to the New Bookshop," said Vivien. "And thank you for coming to see us. I think we kind of missed that part, didn't we?"

"Hmph," snorted Merrihew, while Thurston waved his hand around in a gesture that might mean anything, but was perhaps agreement and also a kind of weak implied apology.

"Vivien got all the airs and graces in our extended family," said Merlin. He sat down and picked up the teapot. "I'll pour, shall I?"

"Very steady tea pourers, the left-handed, I will say that," said Thurston.

"Thank you, Great-Uncle," replied Merlin. "Milk, Susan? And su—"

"Biscuits," interrupted Merrihew suddenly. She got up and headed for the alcove. "I specifically said biscuits were to be brought up."

"Great-Aunt Merrihew is *extremely* fond of McVitie's Jaffa Cakes," said Merlin. "But as a matter of self-control, only eats them when we have visitors. Which, as I mentioned, is a very rare occurrence."

"No sugar, thank you," said Susan, taking her cup. She lifted the cup to admire the pattern. It wasn't one she knew, a pink color scheme with floral panels, so she flipped over the saucer. But there was no maker's mark. Ceramics were one of her interests, a field she thought she still might possibly pursue. Mrs. Lawrence had gently tried to channel Susan's many artistic enthusiasms into a mere several or perhaps even two fields, but she had not succeeded.

"H and R Daniel," said Vivien. "Eighteen thirty. Not the cow creamer, of course. M and S, I think, from about five minutes ago."

"So, your father," said Thurston, looking intently at Susan over the rim of his cup, which he then upended, draining it in a single draft. "Ahh! Now that's a good cup. Too small, but good. Your father. What do you know?"

Susan looked at Merlin, who raised one eyebrow. Vivien leaned over and patted Susan on the shoulder.

"You are going to have our help whether you want it or not," she said. "I'm sorry about that, but there are very good reasons for it. The Old World can be extraordinarily dangerous, and the greatest danger is not knowing what you're dealing with. Please let us help you."

Susan took a deep breath and they all sat silently for a few seconds. Thurston poured himself another cup of tea and muttered something about the superiority of mugs. Merrihew did not return from the alcove, from which a rustling sound was emanating, suggesting work upon a packet of biscuits.

"I don't suppose I have a choice," said Susan eventually. "But I hope . . . I hope I'm not going to get dragged into any more . . . weird stuff. I want to find out who my father is, work through the summer, and start my course. That's all."

"Well, one step at a time," said Vivien, which was not at all comforting. "I know you went to see Frank Thringley as a possible parental candidate. What led you there, and what other information do you have?"

"Frank was the easy one," said Susan. "He sent us postcards at Christmas, with his address and everything. But even before I saw him . . . and felt his strangeness . . . he was a long shot. Mum's always been kind of dreamy; apparently she took a lot of acid back in the sixties, though she says she didn't, and she said Frank was 'one of her friends' but in a slightly different tone than the others, if you know what I mean."

"Your mother's absentminded, rather dreamy?" asked Vivien. "Sort of disconnected from what's going on?"

"It comes and goes," replied Susan defensively. "But you could describe her that way."

Merlin poured Susan more tea. Merrihew returned from the kitchen nook with a plate of her favorite chocolate-and-orange biscuits and sat down, balanced the plate on her knees, picked one up, and started eating.

Vivien and Thurston exchanged glances.

"What?" asked Susan.

"Well, the dreaminess, lass . . . for some mortals, this might be a sign of extended contact with the Old World. Time spent somewhere like the May Fair you were taken to, or with entities that are out of step with our world. Or even deliberate interference with her mind."

"Oh," replied Susan. She blinked back a tear, thinking of her mother's difficulties. "I see. I suppose that makes sense. She always said she didn't do drugs, though she hung out with lots of bands before I was born . . . the Stones and the Kinks and everyone, taking photographs—she's a photographer, and a painter—I should have believed her. . . ."

"What are your other clues?" asked Merlin gently.

Susan took a tarnished silver gilt cigarette case out of one of the many pockets of her boiler suit. She carried it with her everywhere, since her mother had given it to her on her twelfth birthday "from your dad" but then denied having done so later, and said she'd never seen it before. The case was also convenient for carrying the other scant clues she'd gleaned over the years.

"This case was apparently my father's," she said, pressing the catch to open it, revealing a folded piece of paper and a washed-out rectangle of printed cardboard. "Mum gave it to me on my birthday. We were here in London, as a matter of fact. She said something or someone reminded her of him, but she couldn't think what it was, and then she gave me this—but she wouldn't talk about it afterwards, not ever. So it hasn't been very helpful."

"Is that a crest or badge, engraved on the front of the case?" asked Vivien eagerly.

"Maybe . . ." replied Susan, angling the case so they could all see the faded engraving.

"I suppose it *could* be an animal head of some kind," said Thurston. "Rather abstract, all those straight lines. Not a boar, horse, or lion . . . hmm . . ."

"I took it in to *Antiques Roadshow* when they came to Bath a few years ago," said Susan. "But they weren't very interested. Their silver specialist confirmed something I'd looked up before; she said the hallmarks are wrong, and dismissed it as a fake.

"It has the anchor mark for Birmingham, and the sterling lion and a date mark for 1962. But there's also a hand, which usually means Sheffield, but of course it can't have been made in Sheffield *and* Birmingham. And the hand is back to front anyway. The expert couldn't identify the maker's mark, either. It's a kind of rune, but not Norse or like one of Tolkien's. I didn't get on the show, needless to say."

"Birmingham? And an extra hallmark, is it? Well, well," mused Thurston. "May I see?"

He took a loupe out of his waistcoat and screwed it into his eye. Susan took the papers out and handed over the case.

"The card has been through the wash," she said, putting it down on the table. "But you can still see it says 'Reading Ticket' and part of a number, 'something, something seven three,' but the name was written on in blue ink and it's almost completely gone. I thought it might be for the British Museum reading room."

"It isn't," said Vivien immediately. "Wrong design and shape. It's for one of the private libraries. We can easily find that out, and we might be able to restore the number, maybe the name as well."

"With magic?"

"No," said Vivien. "We'll try more usual means first. Our conservation workshop is over at the Old Bookshop, which of course makes no sense because all the old books are here at the New Bookshop—"

"Happen there's more room and better light over at the Old Bookshop," said Thurston, looking up from the cigarette case. "There's method there, young Vivien."

"Anyway," continued Vivien. "Aunt Helen and Aunt Zoë are considered among the best paper conservators in the world. Lots of museums send books and papers for us to investigate, repair, and conserve. I'm sure we can find out where it's from, and maybe even retrieve the name."

"And as I thought," said Thurston, handing the case back to Susan. "Harshton and Hoole, our right-handed silversmiths. Sterling silver, Birmingham, 1964. The reversed hand mark indicates it was a pact gift. Given to encourage some kind of agreement or alliance between mythic entities who must have been in human form at the time. Though I can't say I recall anything of that nature in the early sixties. Or cigarette cases . . ."

"We can probably look it up," said Vivien. "Though 1964 . . . Harshton and Hoole had a fire that year, didn't they? Or was it 1963?"

"They did, in 1964," rumbled Thurston. "Electrical. The whole place should have been rebuilt after the war—it was damaged during the Blitz—and we ended up having to do so anyway in 1970. But very little was lost in that 1964 fire. Their papers are archived to the mine with everyone else's."

"It's not so far back; the silversmith who made it is probably still working," said Vivien. "I'll write a note to inquire."

"And be lucky to get a reply before the solstice, knowing them," complained Thurston. "So the case, a reader's ticket . . . and what's on yon piece of paper?"

"A list of names," said Susan. "Mum would never come out and tell me a complete name, or she couldn't, but at various times she'd mention people and things that happened or who she did something with, and I've been keeping a list of the men who she mentioned multiple times. But I don't know which first names line up with the surnames. Except for Frank Thringley, who I knew from the Christmas cards, and like I said, Mum never talked about him in quite the same way as these others."

"So what do you have?" asked Vivien.

Susan unfolded the sheet of paper and smoothed it out on the table. Everyone peered in, except Merrihew, who was busy demolishing her third biscuit and, if she leaned, might lose the plate.

"So you see I have John, Magnus, Edwin, Rex. But only three surnames came up more than once, and I couldn't link them up to any particular first name or the events she was talking about. They're Smith . . . yes, I know, completely useless; Asher or Usher; and Liston or Biston, or maybe something else -iston."

Merrihew made a noise. It might have been a comment, but it couldn't make its way past a mouthful of Jaffa Cake.

"Oh, give those biscuits over, Merry!" exclaimed Thurston

in a booming aside. "You'll make yourself sick."

"Yes, yes, I know," said Merrihew testily. She took one last biscuit, her fourth, and put the plate on the table. "But we haven't had a visitor here for years!"

"There's not a lot to work with, these names," said Vivien. "But we might be able to do more with the mundane stuff. I know Inspector Greene has already checked you out, and we have that file coming over. Again, I apologize, I know it seems intrusive—"

"It is intrusive!"

"Yes. I . . . we apologize. But it has to be done. As the file isn't here yet, for my notes, if you wouldn't mind . . . your date and place of birth? I'm presuming you have a birth certificate, but it doesn't list your father?"

"Yes, father unknown and May first, 1965," replied Susan. "Why do you keep looking at each other?"

"I'm reet sorry, lass," replied Thurston, his Yorkshire accent growing stronger. "It's the May Day birthday, it's significant. The Old World comes closer to the New at certain times, and that's one of them."

"May first," said Vivien thoughtfully. "Do you know the time you were born?"

"Dawn," said Susan. "With the sun, Mum always said. Maybe encouraged by the name of the pub where it happened."

"What was that name, and where was this pub?" asked Vivien.

"The Sunne in Splendour, in a village a couple of miles outside Glastonbury. Mum was visiting some of her musician friends who lived near there in what she says was 'decayed grandeur,' and I came early. She was going to the hospital but only got as far as the pub."

"Glastonbury," mused Thurston. "The Vale of Avalon . . ."

"You said before you used to come to London on your birthday," said Merlin eagerly. "May first. Were you here, in London I mean, on May first, 1977?"

"My twelfth birthday," replied Susan. "Yes."

"Do you remember where you stayed, where you went?" asked Merlin. He held up his hand as Vivien tried to interrupt.

"Where we always stayed, this very run-down hotel near Victoria Station. I think Mum knew the family who owned it; they gave her a good deal. It isn't there anymore—they knocked it down and built an office block. We stopped coming here when it closed, that was three years ago. Why?"

Merlin looked at Vivien.

"Mother was killed on May Day 1977, less than a mile from Victoria Station. We never found out who she was getting the flowers for . . . and she was attacked by thugs whose minds had been tampered with, like the two who came to snatch Susan today. It has to be connected somehow!"

"Coincidence!" snapped Merrihew. "There's no evidence of anything else."

"It is a very slight similarity," said Thurston. "When you've been on this earth as long as I have, Merlin, you'll see many things are simply coincidence, or accidents."

"I want to investigate," said Merlin with determination.

"Not on the firm's time," said Merrihew.

Thurston sighed and rubbed the bridge of his beaky nose with his gloved hand. "Merrihew governs the left-handed, but you're entitled to follow it up in your own time. Right now, finding Miss Susan's father is something we probably need to do sooner rather than later. Vivien, you can lead on that research. Merry, you agree?"

"I suppose so," said Merrihew, dabbing crumbs from her mouth with a black handkerchief. "It's very annoying that this should come up now, when the old carp is rising in the quarry pond. But it seems this girl is a focus for *something*, so I suppose more information is needed in order to deal with her appropriately."

"You're a very rude person," said Susan stiffly. "I'm not 'this girl.' I have a name. And what does 'deal appropriately' mean?"

"I am a rude person," agreed Merrihew.

"Happen we'd best set someone to watch over her," said Thurston. "Until we know what's what."

"Is that really necessary?" asked Merrihew.

"Yes," said Merlin.

Merrihew looked at Merlin.

"You're on light duties, aren't you? I suppose you can look after . . . Susan."

"What? By myself?" asked Merlin. "I need at least four of us for round the clock—"

"Everyone's busy," interrupted Merrihew. "You can stay at

Mrs. London's until we get this sorted out. I'll square it with Greene."

"You said there was a Kexa prowling the warded perimeter at the Milner Place house last night?" asked Thurston, his voice dubious.

Merlin nodded.

"That might also be a coincidence," said Merrihew dismissively. "But in any case it can't get through the wards."

"Other things might," said Merlin. "And there is the criminal angle."

"That is somewhat unusual," said Thurston. "Though such things are sometimes attracted by the mere presence of any magical protections."

Merlin did not look convinced.

"I'll have whoever's driving the cabs tonight swing past when they can," said Merrihew, waving a dismissive hand. "That should prove more than sufficient."

Merlin nodded unhappily. Clearly, he thought this was not enough.

"You think there's going to be . . . more's going to happen?" asked Susan.

"Nay," said Thurston, pouring the last dregs from the teapot into his cup.

"No," said Merrihew, shoving another biscuit in her mouth.

"Yes," said Merlin.

CHAPTER EIGHT

▷┤◇┤○┤◇┤◁

Old, old it was, and keen
Keen as a blade
Blade-thin and thirsty
Thirsty for blood
Blood for its drinking

▷┤◇┤○┤◇┤◁

"THE YOUNG ONES WILL FRET," SAID THURSTON TO SUSAN, IGNORING Merlin. "But likely as not, there's nowt to worry about and we'll track down your dad in due course. So off you go—"

He stopped speaking suddenly and stiffened up, like a dog catching a scent, tilting his massive head to the side as if he were listening to someone or something that no one else present could hear.

Susan looked at Merlin, who lifted his hand slightly, gesturing to wait.

After ten seconds or so, Thurston sighed, straightened his head, and spoke again.

"It seems you youngsters need to introduce Susan to Grandmother."

"What?" asked Merlin. "Grandmother? Now?"

"Aye, now," replied Thurston. "She may recognize Susan's family, you see."

"Is this really something Grandmother needs to be involved in?" asked Merrihew. "It seems routine, to say the least."

"She thinks so," said Thurston. "You disagree?"

Merrihew sighed. "Which one is it?"

"I don't know," said Thurston. "But she's spoken."

Merrihew grimaced. "If she's spoken, she's spoken."

"How will your grandmother recognize my family?" asked Susan, but no one answered. There was a long pause before Vivien spoke, and it was to her great-uncle and great-aunt.

"How is Grandmother?"

"Much as ever," said Thurston. "I would suppose."

Vivien looked expectantly at Merrihew.

"I don't know," snapped Merrihew. "I haven't visited for simply ages. Let her rest, I say."

"Has *anyone* seen her recently?" asked Merlin. "Great-Uncle Thurston?"

"I popped down a few years ago," said Thurston. "Or mebbe it was five or six years. There hasn't been anything to bother herself with."

He heaved himself out of his chair and took the coats off *The Age of Bronze*, handing the cape to Merrihew and shrugging on his own trench coat.

"It'll be fine!" he said. "Off you go."

"What . . . what's with your grand—" Susan started to expostulate.

"I'll explain," interrupted Merlin. "Come on. We'll see Grandmother and then Vivien will take us out to lunch somewhere nice."

"No I won't," said Vivien crossly. "Firstly, because I will be working on finding out who Susan's father is, and secondly because I'm broke. Borassic. A veritable pauper. Not least because you owe me fifty pounds, Merlin. Remember?"

Merlin looked guiltily away.

"Well, sandwiches in the lunchroom here, then," he said. "After we see Grandmother."

"Very good. You carry on," rumbled Thurston. He surprised Susan by opening a hatch in the muscular abdomen of Rodin's bronze young man to take out a telephone handset. The tight coil of telephone cord dangled rather obscenely in front of the statue's groin.

"Thurston here. We're leaving now. I'll be back in receiving shortly; they'd better not have started unpacking without me. Have Neil bring a cab around for Merrihew. She's off to—"

He looked at Merrihew. She had a plastic waterproof watch pinned high on her fisherman's vest, like a nurse. She flipped it up to read the time.

"Straight to Paddington," she said. "I might make it in time for the 12:47 that stops at Ledbury."

"Not since 1965," replied Thurston. "Beeching cuts, remember? Earliest you'll catch now is the 2:26 to Hereford."

Merrihew shrugged crossly. "I might as well go to Paddington now, anyway."

"Merrihew's to Paddington," said Thurston into the phone.

He replaced the handset, closed the hatch, and beamed at Susan.

"I look forward to having you all sorted out soon, Miss Arkshaw. Goodbye."

Susan nodded, repeating the action as Merrihew waved and followed Thurston to the stairs. There, the guardian cousin Sam had stopped writing limericks and had already slung on her ammo bag, buckled the scabbarded sword to her belt, and was holding the AK-47, her left hand now gloved, the silvery skin hidden. She preceded the two Greats down the stairs. The blackthorn stick remained behind, leaning against the wall.

"Want a Jaffa Cake?" mumbled Merlin, his mouth full.

"No thanks," said Susan. She leaned forward and rested her head in her hands. "How long is this all going to last?"

"What do you mean by 'this' exactly?" asked Merlin.

"Me being guarded by you and thugs and goblins attacking me," said Susan.

"Well, the May Fair goblins won't do anything," said Merlin. "They've shot their bolt; I doubt they'll have the strength to do even a nighttime May Dance for a few years."

"You're not answering my question," said Susan.

"It's not an easy question to answer," said Vivien. "There are several possibilities. One is that we will quickly discover who your father is or was, and that, in turn, will lead us to working out who or what is interested in you and then we can deal with that situation. Presuming this can be handled satisfactorily, then you will be no more at risk than any other mortal who has had some chance contact with the Old World."

"And I suppose the other possibilities are a lot less good for me," replied Susan, rather bitterly. She looked at Merlin. "I wish I'd never met you!"

"If you hadn't, you'd be dead, I think, or a prisoner at least," said Merlin. "You chose to seek out Frank Thringley."

"I was about to leave when you turned up," said Susan.

"I don't think so," replied Merlin. "The only way in and out of that house was the upstairs window. I wondered why the doors had been so carefully locked and warded. I conclude that it was to keep you in. At least until Thringley handed you over to whoever or whatever he answered to."

"Really?" asked Susan.

"He's telling the truth," said Vivien. "We can nearly always tell. A right-handed thing, you know. 'Verum ponderet dextrum.' The right hand weighs the truth."

"And like I said, you saved my life later," said Merlin. "Clearly, we are meant to be together."

Vivien snorted.

"Don't fall in love with my brother, whatever you do," she said. "The left-handed are not reliable in matters of the heart."

"Oh, come on, Vivien! You were left-handed until last year—"

"But I'm not now, am I? What is it with you lot and Jaffa Cakes? If you've stopped stuffing your face we should take Susan down to see Grandmother. Better to do it now, while the sun's shining."

"It isn't down there," said Merlin.

"The sun affects things, even if you can't see it, as you well know," said Vivien. "Just as with the moon. Come on!"

Susan planted herself more firmly in her chair, hands gripping the armrests.

"I'm not going anywhere until you tell me where we're going and why you are both so obviously nervous about going to see your own grandmother."

"The where is the easy part," said Merlin. "Downstairs. I suppose you might say the sub-subbasement. Below the air raid shelter from the war. There's a Roman temple, a mithraeum . . . Grandmother . . . Well, let's see how to put it—"

"She's not simply our grandmother, as such. She's, uh, *all* our grandmothers. They're sort of spiritual remnants that inhabit the place," interrupted Vivien. "They go back a very long way, and you can never be quite sure which particular . . . er . . . grandmother you'll get. She changes."

"So they're ghosts?" asked Susan.

"We don't use the term; they're what we call Shades, mythic relicts of strongly magical once-living entities—"

"Ghosts," repeated Susan firmly. "Are they dangerous?"

"Yes," said Merlin as Vivien said, "No."

"And no," continued Merlin. "It depends."

"Grandmother is only dangerous if she forgets we're related, or one of the dogs decides they don't like your smell."

"Dogs! What dogs?"

"Well, there's always been a tradition of the elder women of the St. Jacques clan keeping dogs, and so there are Shades of their dogs as well as themselves."

"What happens if they do forget you're related or the dogs *don't* like how you smell?" asked Susan.

"We run away, of course. The trick is to stay near the gate. And wear sensible shoes. You're okay on that point."

"But I'm *not* related to begin with," said Susan.

"Yes, but you'll be with me," said Merlin. "I'll hold your hand. Like in the fair."

"I hope not," said Susan. "My shoulder still hurts from being dragged all over the place."

"Actually, you know what?!" exclaimed Vivien. "We can put Grandmother in a good mood straight away. Whichever one she is."

"How?" asked Merlin. "Do they ever have good moods? I've only met her once and she was cranky as anything. Besides, how would you know?"

"I've been down three times and, unlike you, I study. She . . . all her incarnations . . . like gifts. You give her your glass rose, Susan," said Vivien. "Goblin work, from the May Fair. She can probably even touch it. She'll love you then."

"I was going to keep it," said Susan.

"It won't last past sunset anyway," said Vivien. "It's goblin work. Made under the sun, it'll disappear at dusk."

"Oh," replied Susan. She shrugged and got up. "All right. I didn't realize. Typical. Your grandmother . . . grandmothers . . . might as well have it."

"If only we had a goblin bone as well," muttered Merlin. "For the dog. I hope it's not that horrendous wolfhound, Nebrophonus. Or are they all like that?"

"Shut up, Merlin," said Vivien. She smiled at Susan. "It'll be fine. Come on."

Susan took one last look around before they started down the stairs. She still couldn't figure out how they were so much higher than the other buildings, but apart from that, everything looked perfectly normal. The steady flow of traffic on Park Lane, people wandering around Hyde Park, the contrails of jets headed to Heathrow in the sky above.

On the way down the narrow stair to the building proper, Merlin went ahead and Vivien behind.

"Is your life always like this?" Susan asked, while Merlin opened the lower door. "I mean, are there constant problems with Sippers and Shucks and goblins and all that?"

"Oh no!" laughed Vivien. "Gods! That would be unbearable. No, the Old World is mostly dormant these days; we've been in a very quiet period since the early sixties. Every now and then something happens to stir things up, everyone has to rush about doing stuff, and then it's quiet again and we can get on with our everyday work. Very peaceable. Like the rest of today will be, I hope."

"So what do you do when you're not . . . um . . . involved with the weird shit, as Inspector Greene calls it?"

"Me? I work at the Old Bookshop three days a week," replied Vivien as they filed out and spread into a line to go down the main stairs together. "And I'm halfway through my second degree, at London Business School."

"You're studying business?" asked Susan doubtfully.

"I'm doing a new thing," replied Vivien. "Called a Master's in Business Administration, part-time."

"Plutocrat," said Merlin, semi-affectionally.

"What about you?" Susan asked Merlin. "You seem to do more 'rushing about.'"

"It's my dynamic personality," said Merlin. "The left-handed do more of our visible work, as it were, since we're the field agents. And there's training, too. But like Viv, at least half the time I work in the bookshops. Generally moving things around, I hate to say. No one seems prepared to let me deal with customers, despite the fact that I would undoubtedly double sales."

"You had a tryout," said Vivien. "You doubled the amount of time spent talking to attractive customers without selling them anything."

"I sold that copy of *The Ashley Book of Knots* no one else could sell," protested Merlin. "A fifty-quid hardcover!"

"Selling a single fifty-pound book in two weeks is far less use than selling two or three hundred two- or three-pound books in the same period," replied Vivien. "And I heard you didn't manage to sell anything when they tried you out front here, and given the bibliophiles who frequent the place, that's quite a non-achievement."

"All the customers were old," said Merlin. "And Eric or Alison always took the good ones."

"The prosecution rests," said Vivien.

"Maybe they can put me in special orders," said Merlin. "That would be better than the stockroom."

"You would get cross checking *Books in Print* and destroy the microfiche reader," said Vivien. "Which is why it's a right-handed job."

"Are all your staff, um, special-handed booksellers?" asked Susan. They were back at ground level now, but they kept going. The stair became darker, as there were no lights, only the spill from those higher up.

"Not all, but most," said Vivien. "Wait a tick."

They stopped, two levels below the ground, though the stair continued down. Vivien ran her hand along the wall, found an industrial-sized light switch, and rotated it to the on position. A faint light flickered above them, barely bright enough to show the faded letters painted in stark white on a rusting steel door: "Air Raid Shelter, Cap. 39 persons."

It also lit up a wooden fruit crate on the floor. Vivien knelt and rummaged in the box, removing three candle stubs melted onto chipped china saucers. She handed one each to Merlin and Susan.

"Hold it out," she instructed Susan, and blew on it, with a faint whistle. A spark left her mouth and the candle flared into life and almost went out again as Susan dropped and caught it in one motion. She held it steady and the flame strengthened.

"Sorry," she said. "I didn't know you could do that."

"It's easy here," said Vivien. She lit her own candle with

another pursed-lips exhalation, and then Merlin's. "There's a lot of mythic power, more and more as we get closer to the old temple. And Grandmother."

"And other things," said Merlin.

"What other things?" asked Susan. She found herself whispering, though she wasn't sure why.

"Oh, don't worry," he answered. "Grandmother keeps them in order. Not far now."

It grew colder as they descended, and the walls were no longer plaster or worked stone but rough-hewn, pale gray rock, with rivulets of water winding their way down and drips coming from the ceiling. After what seemed to Susan rather farther than it should have been to go down only two floors, they reached a large cavern, most of it impossible to see in the candlelight, save for the massive marble gateway on the other side, the stones pale in the darkness and the open gateway seeming to be even darker than the edges of the cavern. The marble was carved with what Susan thought were battle scenes, but it was hard to tell.

"We mustn't take more than three steps beyond the gate," whispered Vivien. She moved up close to Susan on her right side, and Merlin shuffled in from the left. "Stay in line. Don't move ahead of us."

They moved together through the gate, candles flickering, and stopped. Susan had no sense of what they'd entered. She could see nothing beyond the narrow pool of light around them, and their footsteps had echoed on the imperfectly smoothed stone, as if they were in some much larger cavern or chamber.

It was much colder again, and her breath fogged out, making her notice that she was breathing too quickly. She forced herself to hold a breath in, and exhaled very slowly, counting to six. She didn't want Merlin or Vivien to think she was afraid, even though she was.

"Gods," muttered Merlin. "It *is* Nebrophonus."

A huge, gaunt, ice-white wolfhound came slowly stalking out of the darkness ahead, stiff-legged and growling.

"Don't move," whispered Vivien. She shifted even closer to Susan, their shoulders touching, as Merlin slid his right hand around her elbow.

The wolfhound edged closer, sniffing, lifting his huge, shaggy head, lip curled to show massive teeth.

He didn't look like a ghost, or a spiritual remnant, or whatever Vivien had said. He looked very real. Susan had been entirely accurate about being good with dogs; they nearly always obeyed her. But part of being good with dogs was knowing when to leave the clearly dangerous ones alone.

"We brought a friend, Grandmother," called out Vivien. "A friend with a gift for you. It's me, Vivien, and my brother, Merlin."

"Antigone's children," added Merlin. "Daughter of the fourth Henry, and him the son of Theresa, the one nicknamed Mintie, and her the daughter of Serena."

"And Serena the daughter of Claude, the second of his name, and him the son of Sophia and her the daughter of the fifth Guinevere, the first to use the name St. Jacques, in the true line all back to the beginning," added Vivien.

There was a whistle in the darkness. Nebrophonus turned his head and then ever so slowly, like an ocean liner turning, curved away in front of them, retreating once more into the dark from whence he came.

A moment later, a woman appeared in front of the apprehensive trio. A short, businesslike old woman in an unadorned pale gray high-waisted dress, a snow-white fichu pinned at the neck, a faded blue bonnet over her silver hair, and one white glove, on her right hand. She had deep-set dark eyes that were immediately troubling. She looked to Susan very much like a well-known slightly mad old man in Bath, who wandered the streets dressed as Jane Austen whenever he could escape from his family.

Vivien and Merlin curtsied, dragging Susan down with them.

"Vivien and Merlin, is it," said the woman. It wasn't a question. Her voice was soft and scratchy, and weirdly menacing. "Come to visit their old granny. But you want something . . . you always do. . . ."

Vivien didn't answer that. She shuffled half a pace forward and spoke brightly.

"This is our friend Susan Arkshaw, Grandmother. She has a present for you."

Merlin gave Susan a little push and let go of her elbow.

Susan took an even shorter step than Vivien's and held out the rose, instinctively lowering her head and bending her knee.

The Grandmother took it from her, and as she did so, the

glass flower became real again, though still transparent, the stem bending. Petals shivered as the old lady lifted it to her nose and inhaled deeply.

"Ah," she said wistfully. "It's been long and long since I smelled the scent of a rose. I make you welcome, Susan Arkshaw."

Susan felt more than heard Vivien's sigh of relief, which was cut off as the Grandmother lowered the rose and peered over the top of the flower, her eyes bright with mischief.

"But it has no color. It should be red, my dears. Red is the color for roses. Roses and blood. The left-handed one, Merlin. You've a knife or two upon you, dear. Use it."

Susan glanced at Merlin, who was looking aside a little. At Nebrophonus, who had reappeared and was staring back at him, his jaws roughly at groin height and only a foot away.

"Susan has the guest-right of the St. Jacques," said Vivien. She spoke confidently, but her right hand was trembling in its glove. "Bread and water . . . well, tea and biscuits, freely given."

The Grandmother laughed, a kind of choking, coughing laugh. Susan resisted the urge to turn and run. The wolfhound would be on her back straight away if she did, and Merlin and Vivien hadn't said anything, or given a sign to flee.

"Oh, you silly children," said the Grandmother. "I only need a few drops. You want to know who Susan's people are, do you not? A drop of color for the rose, a drop for me to see what's what, a drop for Nebrophonus as a treat. That's all."

"Three drops of my blood," said Susan. "And you can tell me who my father is?"

"Your people," said the Grandmother. "I can't say a name in particular."

"Is there a catch?" asked Susan bluntly.

The Grandmother laughed again.

"Sometimes it is better not to know such things," she said. "That's all."

"Vivien?"

"It should be okay," whispered Vivien, bending her head near Susan. "We do give blood ourselves sometimes . . . it makes Grandmother more connected to the New World, more able to speak and so on. The older ones in particular."

"They're incomprehensible otherwise, the really ancient ones," whispered Merlin, leaning in close to Susan's other ear. "Weird dialects of Latin and so on. Worst relatives you could have."

"I heard that," said the Grandmother. "I won't brook at punishing disrespect, young Merlin."

"I'm sorry, ma'am," said Merlin hurriedly. For once, he sounded like he meant it.

"I haven't got all day," said the Grandmother. "Or rather, this rose has no more than the day, and I'd like to enjoy it fully. What's it to be?"

"You may have the three drops, ma'am," said Susan. Some innate caution and memory of fairy tales made her add, "But no more, and in return you will tell me who my people are, and that is all there will be between us."

She held out her hand, palm uppermost, and extended her forefinger. A thin, very sharply pointed blade appeared in

Merlin's left hand, as if from nowhere. He held Susan's wrist lightly with his right hand, and with a sudden stab, pricked her finger. A drop of blood welled up and hovered there.

"First blood to Nebrophonus," said the Grandmother. She gestured, and the wolfhound approached and with his great sandpapery tongue lashed Susan's finger, taking the drop of blood. As he turned away, his tail wagged slightly in satisfaction.

More blood welled to the surface. The Grandmother extended the rose, touching a petal to the next shivering droplet. The blood ran into the flower, spreading through the petals, which bloomed a glorious red, but even the stalk took on color, too, a darker shade that was a kind of green-black.

The Grandmother raised the flower and sniffed it again, her piercing dark eyes momentarily hooded, a smile passing across her thin-boned face like a glimpse of some small, colorful bird darting between dark and brooding trees.

"And one for me, to tell your bloodline," said the Grandmother. Susan started as the old woman took her hand, because the old lady was no insubstantial ghost. Her flesh was solid, and colder even than the room.

The Grandmother raised Susan's hand to her mouth and in a matter-of-fact way, like tasting a spoonful of soup, licked off the blood. She dabbed her mouth with the back of her hand and frowned.

"Oh," she said. "It's old, old . . . too old for me. . . ."

She turned around on the spot and suddenly was a different old woman, this one taller and quite majestic in a jewel-encrusted burgundy gown over a black kirtle, all typical of the fifteenth century, her hair under a bifurcated veil that fell down her shoulders to left and right. She wore a doeskin glove on her right hand, with a massive emerald ring over the glove, on her third finger.

Nebrophonus was gone, too, replaced by a much smaller, Scottish terrier type of dog, lying on a cushion, who gave the visitors an uninterested glance and yawned mightily.

"Nay, it is older than I, Nan," she said gently, and turned as if in a courtly dance, one hand raised to an invisible partner.

Now there was a true ancient, a woman bent over a blackthorn stick, in simple homespun, with colored ribbons at neck and cuffs and a leather gauntlet on her left hand. Her dog was at her side, some long extinct or absorbed breed, yellow in color, with broad, floppy ears and curly hair and a self-satisfied, none-too-bright expression.

This grandmother spoke in Latin, inclined her head, and turned about as well.

Susan glanced at Vivien with a questioning look, rapidly turning back as she saw Vivien staring at the next Grandmother.

This one's face was hidden beneath the hood of a white robe that was vaguely reminiscent of a Roman toga, and both her hands were in gloves, mulberry-colored gloves set with fragments of tesserae, so they sparkled in the candlelight. She sat on an oaken tree stump that hadn't been there a moment before, and the dog at her feet was another wolfhound, very much like Nebrophonus, but a rich chestnut brown rather than white.

She spoke a few words in Latin, stopped, and pushed back her hood. She was not so old as the others, perhaps fifty, her hair pale not from age but from always; she was a strawberry blonde. She smiled, seemingly more friendly than the other grandmothers, and continued in strangely accented English, the emphasis within each sentence not where it would be expected.

"This will be easier for you, no?"

"Yes, thank you," said Susan.

The Grandmother licked her lips.

"Old indeed," she said. "No less than the blood of the Old Ones, the Ancient Sovereigns, the Oath-Makers, the Vassal-Takers, the line of the High Kings and the High Queens. Diluted with mortal essence. Yet still potent, most potent. Be careful, my children, for if this one comes into the power of her sire, she could bind even such as you, with salt and iron and blood enough."

With that, Grandmother, dog, and stump were gone, and all three candles blew out with a rush of wind, leaving the trio entirely in the dark.

CHAPTER NINE

⊱❧⊰

Once I was young, as you saw me then
A bright fire, no moment's spark
Bright as the sun, but that was when
It was early morn, as said the lark

⊱❧⊰

"SO, WHAT DID THAT ALL MEAN?" ASKED SUSAN AS SHE WAS USHERED into Audrey's taxi, with both Vivien and Merlin joining her in the back. She noted the blackthorn stick had been returned to its position above the sun visors, and Audrey winked at her in welcome. "And I thought we were going to have lunch in your staffroom?"

"We'll get something somewhere," said Vivien, who had hurried them up from the subterranean regions and out through the bookshop proper, pushing Susan past Eric and another bookseller, a woman, who had both attempted to make conversation. "They always have terrible sandwiches here. Anchovy paste, that sort of thing."

"Awful," said Merlin. "Look, I need to get changed; why don't we stop by my place and have something sent up. I think

I can stand the doings this once."

"Have something sent up? The doings?"

"Merlin lives in a hotel," said Vivien. "We own it, but it's room only, any meals are strictly charged. Northumberland House; it's near the Old Bookshop, and very necessary for the young left-handed, who are almost without exception domestically useless—"

"Oi!" exclaimed Audrey.

"I said almost without exception, you being one of them," replied Vivien. "Besides, you never lived there, did you?"

"Not to mention, not all that young," whispered Merlin to Susan.

"Always lived with my ma on Grove Road, reckon I always will," said Audrey, ignoring Merlin's barb. "Except for Wooten, of course, and when I was up at Durham."

"The university? And what's Wootton—is that from the Tolkien story, 'Smith of Wootton Major'?" asked Susan. "I thought you were all one big extended family, living in a haunted house or something—but you all have different accents. . . ."

"Go on, Viv, explain; you're the right-handed one," said Audrey, accelerating madly to exploit a momentary opportunity to insert the cab into the continuous artery of traffic pulsing along Park Lane. "Yeah, I did two years of history at Durham, dropped out to join a band; I'm a drummer, see? Northumberland House, is it? I hope there's no trouble with the lions in Trafalgar Square."

"What!" exclaimed Susan, leaping forward, almost thrusting

her head through the hatch, causing Audrey to brake and the cab close behind to swing around them with a blare of the horn, narrowly missing their rear bumper. "The lions? The statues?"

"A joke," said Audrey, the cab clicking as she accelerated to get back in the flow. "What with those urchins having a go at you and all. The lions don't walk in daytime, and never in May."

"But they do walk sometimes?" asked Susan, sitting back as Audrey swung the cab off Park Lane and into the lane by the rather ugly 1960s London Hilton, to cut through to Piccadilly and avoid the traffic choking to a halt as it fed into the Hyde Park Corner roundabout. "It's only . . . my mother . . . she always made us visit Trafalgar Square, and she'd lean against a lion and tell stories . . . what I thought was make-believe, fun for a little girl, about the lions coming awake."

"The statues don't actually animate or move," said Merlin. "The things we call the lions were there long before the statues, or the square, or the city. They don't really look like lions. But they're fierce, and hunt in prides, and roar. And they like raw meat. Not fun for anyone. But they sleep deeply, and do not rouse of their own accord."

"I think Mum must have known something about the Old World—"

"To answer your question about us being one big extended family," interrupted Vivien quickly. "We are more of a dispersed clan. We all have one non-bookseller parent, you see. It's rather like being an extreme Catholic, because when you marry in, you have to agree to the children being raised a particular way.

Which means going to school at Wooten Hall—spelled with one *t* and an *e*, not like the Tolkien story, but I reckon he must have got wind of it somehow. Fantasy writers, they're the bane of our existence! Wooten Hall is in Gloucestershire; we board there from age seven. That's why we have different accents; they're all pretty much fixed by the time you're seven, and of course, we'd go home in the holidays and reinforce it. Though some people, and I name no names . . . cough . . . Audrey . . . like to ham their natural ones up a bit more."

"Bit of Cockney's good for a massive tip from the Americans," said Audrey. "You wouldn't Adam and Eve it, how they part with the bees and honey—"

She stopped, chuckling, as a unanimous groan filled the car.

"I don't know how you make time to take normal passengers," said Vivien. "Or find the gall. What'll you do if Merrihew finds out?"

"Split the takings," said Audrey promptly. "Merrihew's a pirate at heart. Long as I don't mess up anything operational, of course. Which I'd never do."

Susan was digesting the information about the booksellers' parents, but also what the Grandmother had said. She had noticed Vivien didn't want to talk about that, or about her mother, which meant Susan's parentage overall. At least not in the Old Bookshop, and not in the taxi. Which suggested she didn't want Audrey or any other booksellers to know.

"So, talking about fathers—" she started, a little mischievously. As she expected, Vivien interrupted her immediately.

"Let's not have lunch at the Northumberland," she said. "The food is generally pretty bad. There's a quiet pub I know nearby—"

"I thought you were broke," said Merlin.

"I am," said Vivien indignantly. "You can pay."

"We can get some burgers sent to my room," said Merlin. "Won't have to settle till the end of the month."

"I'll pay, provided no one goes overboard," said Susan. "I got paid yesterday."

"Oh good," said Merlin, while Vivien said, "You will not! Merlin has money, but he doesn't want to spend it."

"Anyway, I wanted to ask about your father," said Susan as Merlin muttered something about sisters, but did not deny that he might, in fact, have some money. "Who is he?"

"He's an archaeologist. Met Mum on a dig where . . . things went wrong . . . she saved his life, they fell in love. But it's hard to be married to one of us. They kind of drifted apart, and of course once we went away to school . . ."

"We see him every now and then," said Merlin, with a complete absence of filial devotion in his voice. "Richard Upbright's his name; he's quite a well-known archaeologist. He's professor of European prehistory at Cambridge."

"Merlin Upbright," said Susan, experimentally.

Merlin shuddered. "Don't, please."

"It's no worse than Arkshaw," said Susan. "Better, even. I wonder what *my* father's surname is—"

"We'll find out," interrupted Merlin.

"What did your grandmother mean—"

"Oh look, a brewery dray! I love shire horses."

A very slow-moving, rather enormous cart emblazoned with Greene King brewery signs was taking up one and a half lanes, effectively stopping all the traffic behind it. The team of four blinkered Clydesdales drawing the dray could be no more oblivious to the occupants of the frustrated cars behind them than the smock-wearing drivers.

"I don't," said Audrey. "Horse-drawn vehicles shouldn't be allowed in the city; it's right out of order. The roads are slow enough already, and they're not even really delivering beer. Hosses shouldn't be allowed . . ."

As Audrey continued on her diatribe concerning all the ills of London traffic, Susan leaned in close to Vivien and whispered in her ear.

"Why don't you want to talk about what your grandmother told me in front of other booksellers?"

"But what gorgeous horses—I never mind dawdling behind them!" exclaimed Vivien loudly, and then very quickly, looking down at Susan's shoulder so her mouth was not visible in Audrey's rearview mirror, she hissed vehemently, "Later, okay?"

"I mean, changing the guard is one thing, if you go down the Mall you expect it, but they're regular, scheduled, not hosses popping up whenever, wherever . . ."

Susan nodded and sat back. Audrey continued to talk about the intrusions of horses and other livestock and/or wild animals onto London roads, segued into pedestrians who didn't have a clue and then somehow on to a monologue about one of her favorite books: *The Mystery of a Hansom Cab* by Fergus Hume. Which was apparently from the nineteenth century and surprisingly was about a hansom cab driver in Melbourne, Australia, so Susan wasn't sure why Audrey saw it as a kind of taxi driver foundation myth for someone driving in London. But in any case, Audrey's dissertation upon it, interspersed occasionally with reactions to the current driving environment, provided all conversation until they passed the southern side of Trafalgar Square, darted across into Northumberland Street, and pulled up outside a huge but rather run-down Victorian-era hotel.

As they piled out, a harassed family of two parents and three children between three and six, with numerous bags piled on the curb, began to get in, with the mother declaiming loudly in a Midwestern American accent, "We have to get to Heathrow real quick, driver."

"No problem, missus! We'll be on the frog and toad in half a mo!" called out Audrey, popping out to help with the bags and an action that might be described as an ironic tugging of the forelock.

"Come on up while I get changed," said Merlin.

"You need to be 'real quick,'" said Vivien. "I'm starving."

Susan followed Merlin into the hotel, which was very busy. The lobby, which like the exterior was grand but run-down, was crowded with a horde of people checking in for some sort of conference. About seventy percent men—for other nations were still catching up on the postwar egalitarian reforms the

United Kingdom had enjoyed—they all knew each other, apparently, despite the variety of accents and appearances from all over the world.

"Dentists," said Merlin gloomily. "Five hundred of them, I believe. The bar will be unbearable tonight."

Susan noticed a couple of teenagers lurking by one of the massive fake stone columns that broke up the lobby. They were dressed in New Romantic style, a kind of cross between Boy George and Adam Ant, with ruffles and lace and eye makeup, but both also wore white gloves on their left hands.

"Are they more of your lot?" she asked Merlin as they weaved their way through the crowd of dentists, who seemed a lot less serious than dentists ought to be while attending a major professional event. Many of them were wearing Hawaiian shirts, for one thing.

"No," scoffed Merlin. "I'd say they're confused about their music idols, can't decide whether to be Michael Jackson or someone from Duran Duran. Our people *work* here. See that porter? That's Cousin Heather."

"But she has gloves on both hands."

"She's a porter! Got to protect your hands. Terribly wearing, handling luggage."

"'Billie Jean' has been quite helpful, in terms of disguise," said Vivien, reverting back to the style-conscious teenagers. "Everyone thinks we're simply Michael Jackson fans now. Hardly anyone asks me about wearing one glove since the song came out."

"Why don't you wear them on both hands and avoid questions altogether?"

"But then people would always be asking why we wear gloves," replied Vivien, as if this answered the question.

"Come on, we'll take the stairs," said Merlin. The queue for the two curiously undersized lifts was immense, made worse by dentists coming out or going in stopping to greet each other, with lots of shaking hands and hugs, while the lift doors fruitlessly tried to close around them.

"What floor are you on?" asked Susan, who was already tired of going up and down stairs, though at least in this hotel she presumed they would not lead to such strange spaces as in the New Bookshop. In fact, she was tired in general, she thought. What with no sleep since the Kexa showed up, and then everything else . . .

"Sixth," said Merlin. "Come on! I'll race you."

He sped off and ran up the grand staircase, looking rather like Diana the Huntress, turning quite a number of both male and female heads. Neither Susan nor Vivien ran after him, instead continuing to walk at the same pace. Or possibly even slower.

"Is he always like this?" asked Susan.

"Only two settings, off or on," said Vivien. "But the quicker he gets there, the less time we'll have to wait while he changes clothes."

Something in the way she said that made Susan raise an eyebrow.

"You'll see," said Vivien. "Merlin and clothes . . ."

Vivien was right. When they pushed the door to room 617 open, Susan's first impression was that it was an extensive walk-in wardrobe, until she saw a narrow bed hidden among the serried ranks of racks of clothes. Wheeled racks, which had clearly been purloined from various clothes shops or fashion warehouses. There were men's and women's clothes of all kinds, ranging from evening wear to sundresses with one rack entirely of denim, in all its glorious variations of trousers and jackets, from standard Levi's to multiply patched, holed, and worked-on objets d'art that had probably once graced a catwalk.

To make the small room even more crowded, there were piles of books under the racks. Nearly all orange-spined Penguin paperbacks, as far as Susan could see, arranged alphabetically by author in piles of six or seven. They looked fairly new, but obviously read, some with ordinary bookmarks poking out, and one—*The King's War 1641–1647* by C. V. Wedgwood—was on the bed and kept open with a clothes-peg about halfway through.

Merlin was nowhere to be seen, at least until a door previously hidden from view swung open, pushing a rack aside to reveal a very small bathroom, with a shower cubicle perhaps two-thirds of the size necessary for an adult human to stand up, and no bath. Merlin stood in the doorway, in black leather pants, frilled white shirt, and a burgundy leather waistcoat. He had also acquired a large moustache, a drooping thing that looked like a hairy blond slug stuck under his nose.

"I am ready!" he declared. "Susan, help yourself if you want to get changed into something else."

"I like this boiler suit," said Susan.

Vivien grimaced. "Merlin, that moustache . . . really . . ."

Merlin stroked his new addition.

"Good, isn't it? A friend from the D'Oyly Carte gave it to me with a bunch of other stuff when they shut down last year. This was the Major-General's from *The Pirates of Penzance*."

Susan nodded, relieved that he hadn't grown it in a matter of minutes. He had talked about being "shape-shiftery" and she'd thought this might be an example.

Merlin cleared his throat and began to sing in a powerful baritone:

> *I am the very model of a modern Major-General,*
> *I've information vegetable, animal, and mineral—*

Vivien leaped upon him and put her hands to his throat. The siblings swayed to and fro, sending clothing racks scudding on their casters, until Merlin managed to weakly get out, "Enough! Okay, I won't sing."

"Good," replied Vivien. "Let's go eat. I'm starving."

But Susan didn't move. She shut the door behind her and leaned back on it.

"Why do I have to keep doing this? I'm not going anywhere and I'm particularly not buying anybody lunch until you tell me why you didn't want any of the other booksellers to know what your grandmother said about my ancestry," she said firmly. "I'm clearly deep in an absolute sea of shit and I want to know what direction to swim in to get out of it."

"I think the adjective should be with shit, not sea. It should be a sea of absolute shit—" started Vivien.

"Answer the question!"

Merlin blinked and raised his eyebrows. Vivien frowned.

"She needs to know," said Merlin to his sister.

"I know! Look, Susan, according to Grandmother, you're not entirely an ordinary mortal."

"Go on."

"I think Merlin has explained to you that the mythic landscape is layered, and usually quite local. Entities and environments are generally confined to a particular geographic area and often also to particular times of day or night, phases of the moon, that sort of thing. Even weather, as with the things that come out after rain, or only when it snows. And they are bound by custom and lore to behave in certain ways, to do certain things, and of course these days are mostly dormant anyway.

"But above these local entities, which number in the tens of thousands, there are around nine hundred or so greater beings, who can command all the lesser ones within far larger bounds, which might be geographic, seasonal, temporal, or defined in other ways. Again, they're generally dormant, but the potential is there. Perhaps most important, if they are somehow awoken, they have the power to bind new vassals to their service, magically ensuring near-absolute loyalty. We call them Old Ones, or the Ancient Sovereigns, or sometimes High Kings or High Queens of Faerie."

"Like Oberon and Titania?" asked Susan.

"Shakespeare knew too much," muttered Merlin.

"Well, sort of; there are two such Ancient Sovereigns who have been called by those names, though they are not as depicted in *A Midsummer Night's Dream*. Their power is immense, over a large part of what we now call England, but only within the bounds of a single day, the summer solstice. And those two have not risen to the present world for at least six or seven hundred years."

"But what have Ancient Sovereigns got to do with me?"

"Your father must be one," replied Vivien bluntly.

Susan's mouth fell open, and did not close.

"Quite a number of mythic entities can take mortal form, and wander in the world, albeit in a generally reduced, more vulnerable form," added Merlin hurriedly, noting Susan was temporarily unable to speak. "When in mortal shape it is possible for them to have children with ordinary people. According to Grandmother—who is very rarely wrong—you're one of these children."

Susan exhaled slowly, suddenly aware she'd been holding her breath, and also shut her eyes and her mouth while she counted to three before continuing.

"And this is a problem because . . ."

"It doesn't happen often, and usually the parent isn't a significant entity, so we don't worry about it," said Vivien. "But if they are significant . . . you see, the most powerful of the Old Ones can bind practically anyone or anything, of the Old World or the New. Including us. The St. Jacques, the left- and right-handed booksellers."

"So a child of an *Ancient Sovereign* is big, bad news," said Merlin.

"And in the past our general policy when one of these children is discovered was to . . . um . . . execute them," said Vivien.

Merlin bent down and picked up his yak-hair bag. His left hand rested on the top, and Susan was acutely aware of the revolver inside, and the weapons he doubtless had elsewhere on his person.

CHAPTER TEN

A most humble bookman of yore
Held authors in considerable awe
But it was all just an act
For as a matter of fact
He hated every writer he saw

"AT LEAST, THAT'S WHAT WE WERE TAUGHT AT SCHOOL," CONTINUED Merlin. He rummaged in the yak-hair bag, found a tortoiseshell comb, and carefully began to groom his oversized moustache.

"There haven't been any mythic-mortal offspring for a long time," said Vivien. "Recorded by us, anyway. The last one was in 1818, if I remember correctly. I'd have to look it up."

"So," said Susan. "Are you going to kill me?"

"Heavens, no," said Vivien. "Those were simpler times, and we had more leeway. Imagine the fuss now. Besides, if you had the power of an Old One, I'd feel it. And you don't."

"I don't kill my friends," said Merlin. "Not on purpose anyway."

"But Thurston and Merrihew are not only very old, they are very *old-fashioned*, and perhaps even more important, very bloody lazy. They'd probably want you locked up at the least because that would be the easiest thing, and they might even go for the traditional solution to the problem," said Vivien. "So it's better they don't know about your lineage for as long as possible. Which by my estimation will be about two days, since Merrihew has gone back to Wooten, ostensibly to take charge of the school but in practice to fish; and the New Bookshop has bought Sir Anthony Blunt's library, so Thurston will be busy cataloging and gloating for at least that long, possibly longer. Both of them are far more interested in their ordinary pursuits than they are in our more esoteric responsibilities."

"Which is why they should retire and let more competent people take charge," said Merlin. "But that's another story. Anyway, we have around forty-eight hours to find out exactly who your father is."

"How will that help?" asked Susan. She felt very detached as she spoke, as if it wasn't really her in this situation. Too many things had happened, too quickly, and now there was the threat of being killed by people she had supposed to be a force for good. It was as if Inspector Greene had calmly announced that the police had orders to shoot her on sight.

Then there was the news about her father.

A mythic being, not even human . . .

"Well, some of the Ancient Sovereigns are far more malign than others," said Vivien. "Many are passive, and there are even some that are benign. The Oath-Makers, for example, so-called because they affirm oaths made by others, rather than enslaving lesser entities or people."

"Oath-Makers often inhabit stones or the like," offered Merlin. "Which would become confused with their singular property, so to swear upon Fingael's Stone, for example, would be known to make an unbreakable oath, because Fingael . . . er . . . resides, I suppose is the best way to put it . . . in the stone."

"Are you saying my father could be a stone?"

"Well, mythic entities usually have a primary physical locus: a stone, a hill, an ancient tree, a section of river, a spring or well . . . all that sort of thing. . . . Obviously, your father wouldn't be only a stone or a pool or whatever, since he would have to take full mortal shape to . . ."

Merlin's voice trailed off as Vivien gave him a scathing look.

"I'm still not sure I understand how finding who my father is will help," said Susan. "I mean, if he's one of the bad ones, that'll make matters worse, won't it?"

"Not necessarily," said Vivien. "Knowledge is power, as they say. And we generally prefer to come to agreements with mythic entities, rather than taking harsher action."

"Besides," added Merlin. "It's not only about your father. I'm sure he . . . and you . . . are somehow connected to the people who murdered our mother."

"Merlin—" Vivien started to say, but Susan forestalled her.

"You might be right. I've been thinking about those trips to London. That one in 1977, when I was twelve, it was different. Mother was excited about meeting someone—I'm pretty sure not a man, because she would have behaved differently—and then she was sad when it didn't happen. And . . . I'd forgotten till you talked about the florist . . . we got a truly amazing bunch of flowers at the hotel that afternoon, and the desk clerk was impressed it came from such a famous florist in Kensington, one that was all the rage back then. I never knew who sent them, but I guess . . . I guess it could have been from your mum."

"What!" exclaimed Merlin. "But there was nothing in the police report . . ."

"She was coming out of the florist's," said Vivien, her eyes fixed on the far wall, avoiding Susan's. "But she wasn't carrying flowers. She must have ordered them to be delivered to someone else."

"Those incompetent flatfoots," said Merlin savagely. "They never investigated it properly as a murder, right from the start."

"Six years ago," said Vivien. "I doubt the florist would have any records now. But I'll check with them. I don't suppose your mother would remember?"

"Probably not," said Susan. "But it's impossible to know what she will or won't recall. I'll call her tonight or tomorrow, and ask."

"The question is, why would your mum be meeting ours?" asked Merlin.

"Was she left-handed or right-handed?" asked Susan.

"Both," said Vivien. "Yes, it's possible. Unusual. Mum was one of the even-handed, but at that time she mostly worked with the right-handed, not out in the field."

"Do you know what she was working on, or interested in?"

"We were at school," replied Vivien. "So no."

"When I started to look into everything last year, I asked around," said Merlin. "But no one wanted to talk about it. I mean, the Greats thought I was wasting my time, and everyone took their lead from that. But Cousin Onyeka did say that mum liked to work alone; she enjoyed 'teasing out mysteries.'"

"We all like to 'tease out mysteries,'" scoffed Vivien. "That's practically a definition of being one of the right-handed."

"Not alone, though," said Merlin. "I mean, you all love your intellectual one-upmanship, destroying each other's theories. Not to mention all the actual collaborations. Is there anyone right-handed in either bookshop now or any of the out-stations who's doing anything someone else doesn't know about, is involved in, or wants to interfere with?"

"Yeah, you're right," said Vivien. "No one works entirely solo. I hadn't really thought about it. Mum never talked that much, though. She was a very reserved person."

"So say she found evidence of a child of an Ancient Sovereign, born at dawn on May Day, near Glastonbury," said Susan. "She'd want to follow that up, wouldn't she?"

"Absolutely. But what evidence?" asked Vivien. "What could have led her to learn about your existence, Susan, and who your mother was?"

Susan couldn't answer.

"If we can find out exactly who Susan's father is, that might tell us," replied Merlin. "And then we might also be able to work out who in the crime world—or from the Old World but who is working with criminals—wants Susan out of the picture."

"Out of the picture?" asked Susan.

"I didn't want to say dead," said Merlin, with a bright smile. "Besides, I don't think whoever it is does want you dead, or they'd have shot you from a distance or something like that. Those two thugs, the van, that was an attempted kidnapping. And the goblins . . . maybe that was to put you on ice, or it might have been a temporary prison, before they handed you on."

"What about the Raud Alfar you say was shooting at me? That was to kill."

"That's separate, but it makes sense. The Raud Alfar are fiercely independent. They would fear the child of an Ancient Sovereign—you might claim their allegiance and make them serve you. So the opportunity to kill you before you came into your powers—and that's another interesting question, the nature and extent of whatever your potential powers are—would be welcome to them."

"So the Raud Alfar of Highgate Wood must know who you are, and thus who your father is," said Vivien thoughtfully. "I wonder how?"

"You could go ask them," suggested Merlin.

"I value my life too much, brother," said Vivien. "You know Midsummer Eve is the only day we'd not be met by arrows, and that's too far away."

"So we're back where we were before," said Susan. "We need to find out who my father is. The only thing that's changed is that now you might have to kill me once we do."

As she spoke, she felt a realization crystallize in her head. She needed to not only find out *who* her father was, she needed to *find* him. Whether the booksellers wanted her to meet him or not.

"That's about it," said Merlin cheerfully. "Let's go and have lunch and we can work out how to identify your father and *not* have to kill you. Oh, and I found this so you won't even have to pay."

He reached into his waistcoat pocket and pulled out a crumpled twenty-pound note with a flourish, waving it in front of Susan and Vivien.

"After you," said Vivien. She leaned back to whisper to Susan. "Told you. He always has money squirreled away somewhere. Never pay for him. He'll get used to it."

"I heard you, dear sister," caroled Merlin. He opened the door and stepped out into the corridor but then immediately leaped back inside and slammed the door shut.

"What?" asked Vivien.

"I don't know," said Merlin woodenly. His left hand was inside his tie-dyed bag. "Something's not right."

Vivien approached the door, wrinkling her nose. Susan sniffed the air, too. There was a faint hint of something she couldn't identify.

"Scent of laurel," said Vivien sharply.

"Maybe someone's keen on Aleppo soap," suggested Merlin weakly.

"And a hint of amaranth," added Vivien. "It's not some

vigorous over-soaper. Overlaying a faint but definite whiff of putrescent flesh."

"But there aren't any of them anymore. There hasn't been for over three hundred years!" exclaimed Merlin. "And if there were, how would one get past the wards?"

"I don't know," said Vivien. "But the smell, that's textbook. . . ."

"I should take a look," said Merlin, but he didn't open the door again. Instead, he took his hand out of his bag and reached between two Burberry trench coats on the closest clothes rack to draw out a sword, an old light cavalry saber with a curved gilt-bronze guard, sharkskin grip, and bronze lion head pommel. "You'd better call downstairs, Viv."

Vivien nodded and looked around.

"Behind the PVC raincoat," said Merlin.

Vivien shifted a rack aside and lifted a bright pink raincoat, revealing a telephone on a bedside table some distance from the bed. She lifted the handset and dialed "0," the familiar *click-click-click-click* of the dial returning to its position somehow now strange and ominous to Susan.

"What is it?" she asked. Merlin had not seemed so apprehensive before, not even in the fog, with the Shuck stalking them. And Vivien was clearly rattled.

"From the scent, a Cauldron-Born," said Merlin. "They smell of funerary flowers and death . . . and I felt a peculiar kind of wrongness, nothing I've ever sensed before."

"Um, what is a Cauldron-Born?" asked Susan.

"Someone dead who's been reanimated by sticking them in a magic cauldron," said Merlin very matter-of-factly, clearly keeping a lid on his own reaction. "Incidentally causing them to be very, very hard to make dead again. They have to be hacked into little pieces, and the pieces burned. So guns aren't much use. Oh, and they're completely under the control of the master or mistress of the cauldron, in fact becoming a kind of puppet, an extension of the Cauldron-Keeper's mind."

"Uh . . . a magic *cauldron*?"

"Yes," said Merlin. "You know, a giant pot. Big enough to stand up in. You saw one, in the painting on the door at the New Bookshop."

"And they can make dead people alive again? Like zombies or something?"

"Considerably worse than the classical zombie of fiction," said Merlin. "Because like I said, they are controlled by the Cauldron-Keeper. So they're smart. And if the corpse is fresh enough when they go in, they don't even look dead."

Susan thought about this for a few seconds. "Have you got another sword?"

Behind Susan, Vivien was speaking urgently to the front desk.

"There's one under the bed," said Merlin. "Do you know how to use a blade?"

"I fenced for four years in the lower school," said Susan. "Saber and foil. So I can hack at . . . things . . . at least."

"Okay," said Merlin. "Saber? You take this one, then."

He handed her his saber, hilt first, and rummaged under

the bed, pulling out a much older, straight-bladed sword. Its narrow, flattened oval guard was solid bronze, the grip inlaid with ivory strips, and there was a rough emerald in the pommel.

"Does anyone know you have that?" asked Vivien, hanging up the phone.

"I signed it out," said Merlin. There was something slightly evasive in his tone that Susan noticed but Vivien didn't.

"Okay, I don't think Cousin Armand believed there's anything to be concerned about based on the smell alone," said Vivien. "But he's playing it by the book. There's only three left-handed here right now but they'll cover the fire stairs, Armand the foyer, and the response team is on its way from the Old Bookshop, led by . . . Aunt Una."

Merlin made a face.

"What's the problem with Aunt Una?" asked Susan.

"Generational difficulties," said Vivien. "She doesn't think any of the left-handed under sixty are any good, or have a clue. Merlin, being one of the youngest left-handed, gets an extra serving of that attitude. I guess to be fair she also thinks Merrihew's past it and should let her take over."

"We'd better have a look in the corridor," said Merlin. He spoke as if he had to talk himself into it. Susan suppressed her own shiver. If *Merlin* was scared . . .

"On the bright side, if it is a Cauldron-Born, it must be under control or it could never have got up here," said Vivien.

"You mean they can get out of control?" asked Susan.

"I only know what I learned at school; I haven't done any

advanced reading on the subject. But I understand the more Cauldron-Born you control, the more difficult it is, because you have all their senses and perception coming in at once, as well as your own. Historically, that was often how they were dealt with, when an overambitious Cauldron-Keeper tried to command too many and lost control."

"What happens then?" asked Susan. "Do they freeze up or flop down dead again or anything useful like that?"

She settled her feet into the proper pose and flexed her knees before testing the weight of the cavalry saber with some slight cuts and a stop thrust in slow motion. It was considerably heavier than a fencing saber and balanced differently. There was something written on the blade in a curlicue script about it having been used at Waterloo by Cornet someone someone, of the something or other regiment of hussars. The names were so worn and the script so ornate it was indecipherable.

"We wish," said Vivien. "They lose the guiding intelligence of the controller, to become—"

"Mindless, ravening beasts," said Merlin. "Who hate, hate, hate everyone and everything else, so they turn on whoever or whatever is closest. Including each other, which is a small blessing. Ready?"

Vivien nodded.

"Don't you want a sword?" asked Susan, thinking three swords would be better than two when dealing with undying monsters that needed to be hacked into many pieces. "I bet Merlin's got another half dozen squirreled away here."

"The right-handed don't fight with physical weapons," said Vivien. "We have the left-handed for all that."

"Stay a bit behind me," Merlin instructed Susan. "If there is a Cauldron-Born, chop at its left side and I'll hack at the right. Go for the knees, get it down on the ground first. And don't hit me."

"Okay," said Susan.

"Viv, you pop its eyeballs or do whatever you can do," said Merlin.

"I'll try," said Vivien. "Depends who's inside its head, doesn't it?"

"That's what's worrying me," said Merlin quietly. He hefted the old sword in his left hand and pushed down the door handle with his right, easing the door open.

The hotel corridor looked no different from how it had on the way up, emanating a sad and faded grandeur with its oft-patched-up wallpaper of bluish lilies and pinkish crowns on beige, and a once royal-blue carpet faded to commoner status, so worn in the middle there was almost no pile left, with the warp beneath showing through. It was in the kind of perpetual twilight that is the default of a class of hotels that only ever replaces half the light bulbs in the public areas.

"It's gone," said Merlin.

"Where? Into a room?" asked Vivien. She sniffed the air. "The scent has almost faded."

"Maybe it went back to the lifts," said Merlin. "If it was dressed up properly it wouldn't be too noticeable, at least to ordinary—"

A door suddenly opened three rooms along the corridor behind them, and the trio spun around, but it was only an elderly couple who shuffled out, shrugging on raincoats and hefting umbrellas.

Susan looked at the sword in her hand and held it close against her body. She glanced at Merlin, who didn't bother, slanting his weapon back so the blade rested on his shoulder, making it very obvious indeed.

"Won't they see the swords?" hissed Susan.

"That's what Vivien's for," said Merlin. "She'll cloud their minds."

"Stand against the wall and be quiet," instructed Vivien.

Merlin and Susan obeyed, backing up against the wall. The old couple were coming closer, weaving slightly and muttering to each other about the kettle in their room, which wasn't big enough to fill a proper teapot. They had brought their own with them, and the last time they'd stayed, for the Queen's coronation thirty years ago, the kettles had been bigger, the room cleaner and brighter, and everything had been better.

"Quiet," whispered Vivien. She took in a deep breath and held it as the duo came up to them. They walked past without even glancing at Merlin and Susan or their swords. They got to the lifts and the man slowly and regularly pressed the call button three times, neither of them looking back along the corridor.

Vivien exhaled and shook her head, as if to clear it.

"I'm going to call Armand. Warn him the Cauldron-Born might have gone back down in the lift."

"We'd better go back and wait for Aunt Una's team anyway," said Merlin. He touched his upper lip. "And I think perhaps this moustache *is* a little too . . . too vigorous. It has to go."

They retreated to Merlin's room, where he immediately sidled into his bathroom, but he left that door partly open.

Susan did not relinquish the saber. She felt better with its heavy weight in her hand. Vivien picked up the phone and dialed the front desk.

"Armand? Merlin thinks it may have gone into the lift. No sign of anything? What about the wards being compromised? A side door, something like that?"

She listened to the response, then hung up. Merlin came out of the bathroom, minus the moustache.

"Armand hasn't seen anything," said Vivien, frowning. "And no one's come down the stairs. Maybe it *was* someone binging on an unusual perfume."

"I don't think so," said Merlin grimly. "I felt a presence. Something indefinably wrong."

"Then how did it get past the wards?"

"Do the Cauldron-Born have to be invited in, like vampires?" asked Susan.

"There are no vampires," said Merlin and Vivien together.

"Sippers don't count," added Merlin.

"This hotel . . . all our buildings . . . are warded against inimical creatures, and that would definitely include the Cauldron-Born. The boundaries are traced and the wards renewed twice a year, May Day and All Hallow's Eve. I suppose one could have miscast, or even broken with fresh blood and mercury, but surely someone would have noticed—"

The phone rang. Vivien picked it up before it got to the second ring.

"Yes. It's Vivien. Merlin felt it first, then I caught the scent. Definitely laurel and amaranth, over rot. We think it went into the lift. I've asked Armand to check the wards . . . yes . . . yes . . . the one taken by the Mayfair goblins . . . yes . . . she is . . . no, we'll stay put."

Vivien put the phone down.

"Aunt Una wants us to stay here. They're going to quarter each floor. She's called it in to Thurston but Merrihew is still on the train."

"Do you think Una believes us?" asked Merlin.

Vivien thought for a moment, and shook her head. "No, but she's a stickler for doing things right."

Merlin sat down on his bed, rested his sword point-first on the floor, where it tore the already threadbare carpet, and rested his hands on the pommel and his chin on his hands.

"Maybe we shouldn't wait around," he said slowly.

"What?" asked Vivien. "Aunt Una was very specific. A direct order."

Merlin frowned.

"There is that. But I'm thinking about the Cauldron-Born. If there is one, how was it made, and by whom?"

"Hmm," said Vivien. She recited from memory: "The Stone Cauldron was broken by Corabec of the Folk of Ishur, the pieces given to the sea in the four quarters of Britain; the Copper Cauldron was lost, in the time of Antoninus Pius, and never seen again; the Bronze Cauldron was melted down as idolatrous in the first year of the Commonwealth of Cromwell; the Iron Cauldron is ours, and under the Grail-Keeper's hand."

She paused and added, "That's what the standard history says, anyway."

"The last Cauldron-Born came out of the Bronze Cauldron, in 1643, right?" asked Merlin.

"Yes," agreed Vivien.

"But the Bronze Cauldron's gone, melted down by Roundheads. The Stone Cauldron likewise gone. No one's seen the Copper Cauldron since Hadrian built the wall. What does that leave?"

Vivien shook her head. "Ours. The Grail. But there's no way—"

"Hang on!" interrupted Susan. "You have one of these cauldrons? You as in the booksellers?"

"Yes, the Iron Cauldron, but we call it a grail," said Merlin. "Makes it sound more respectable."

"And we don't put dead people in it to reanimate them," said Vivien.

"What do you do with it, then?" asked Susan.

Merlin and Vivien looked at each other.

"It's a secret, of course," said Merlin. "But you'd probably figure it out anyway."

"The cauldrons aren't simply for making monsters," said

Vivien. "In fact, that's not what they were made for at all. It's a perversion of their purpose. They are enormously powerful mythic relics that greatly amplify all kinds of magic, and they have many different uses. Each of the cauldrons has or had unique powers in addition to their usual properties—"

"Oh, tell her, Viv," said Merlin impatiently.

"Our hands are dipped in it when we turn seven," said Vivien. "It's what makes us what we are, though no one can tell whether we'll initially be left-handed or right-handed."

"Why only your hands?"

"Because if a living person is entirely immersed in the cauldron, it will shatter, its power gone forever," said Merlin. "Oh, and the person dies."

"So someone could be using your cauldron, grail, or whatever you call it to make Cauldron-Born?"

"No," said Vivien.

"It's not impossible," argued Merlin.

"It's very, very unlikely," said Vivien firmly. "The Grail-Keeper wouldn't . . . no . . . it's much more likely we're mistaken and there is no Cauldron-Born. Some coincidence of scent; I mean you mentioned Aleppo soap, that has laurel oil in it, maybe I imagined the amaranth, someone's bad BO—"

"I definitely felt a malign presence," said Merlin. "It was like being hit by a sudden icy wind, deep inside. I had to stop myself shivering."

"Maybe you're getting a cold."

"But what if there is one—" Susan started to say, but she

stopped as there was a sharp knock at the door.

"Who is it?" called out Merlin.

"Room service bringing you a bloody bottle of champagne, who do you think!"

"Aunt Una," said Merlin and Vivien together. Merlin opened the door.

A biker clad top to toe in black leather with a fluorescent vest emblazoned "Urgent Book Delivery" loosely worn over the jacket strode in like an avenging Valkyrie, shaking her long black hair loose, her helmet decorated with a fluoro skull and crossbones under her arm. She appeared to be in her thirties, was brown-skinned and very attractive. She looked like a West Indian model channeling Suzi Quatro in an advertisement for Harley-Davidson. Or very expensive rum. Or both. Except she wasn't smiling; she looked quite cross.

She had biker's gauntlets on both hands, but the one on the right was plain black leather, and the left was reinforced with bands of interlinked rings across the knuckles, like medieval mail.

"I expect you to waste my time, Merlin," she said, ignoring Susan. "But I don't expect it from you, Vivien."

"We're not wasting your time, Aunt Una," said Vivien evenly.

A walkie-talkie at Una's belt squawked. She grabbed it and held it some distance from her ear. A male voice crackled out.

"Yeah, can't find what you said."

"Okay," said Una. "What about you, Darren?"

Another, softer voice answered in the negative.

"Diarmuid?" asked Una.

"Nah, nothing of note. We're going up on the roof."

"Sabah?"

"Nothing here."

Una clipped the walkie-talkie back on her belt.

"And you're sure you're not wasting my time?"

"I smelled laurel and amaranth, over decaying flesh," said Vivien. In the face of Una's disbelief, she didn't sound quite as confident. "And Merlin felt a presence. Who have you got checking the wards? That's a right-handed job."

"Uncle Jake," said Una. "What? He was available."

"It's not his area of expertise," said Vivien.

"Does he even have an area of expertise?" muttered Merlin.

"Yes, he does," replied Vivien. "An encyclopedic knowledge of novelists in the period 1920 to 1950, English and in translation."

"I meant . . . oh, never mind," said Merlin.

"Uncle Jake is perfectly capable of gauging whether a ward is compromised or not," snapped Una. "So you smelled something, Merlin felt something, and you leap to the conclusion that it is a Cauldron-Born, when there haven't been any for more than three hundred years. Now why would a Cauldron-Born even be here? And who would have made it and been directing it?"

Merlin shrugged. Vivien frowned.

"It's been a very unusual day," she said. "The goblins danced Merlin and Susan into the mythic May Fair. And before that, two ordinary mortal thugs, but whose minds had been adjusted, tried to abduct her. So if there was a Cauldron-Born, it was probably here for Susan."

"Why?" asked Una. She gave Susan the kind of suspicious glance a chef might give a butcher about to hand over a piece of rabbit masquerading as chicken.

"We don't really know yet," said Merlin hurriedly. "Susan's father is a person of interest. The Greats have told us to find out who he is."

"Then you should get on with it," said Una. Her walkie-talkie screeched; she lifted it and said, "What?"

"Nothing found. We're all back in the lobby, zero on any floor. Uncle Jake says all is copacetic. Which I guess means okay."

"Back to the shop, then," said Una. "And Jake is not riding pillion with me; you take him, Diarmuid."

"Why me?"

"Because I said so. Out."

"I'm going to take a look at the wards myself," said Vivien. "Jake can't have checked all the entrances. What about the kitchen?"

"Good idea. You waste your time instead of mine. See you later."

She spun on her heel and stalked out, like a cyclone reversing direction after the passage of the eye.

"I guess it wasn't a Cauldron-Born," said Vivien. "We're . . . jumpy."

Merlin didn't answer. Then he spoke, slowly and thoughtfully.

"I can't exactly remember the lesson on this, but wasn't there something about Cauldron-Keepers using dead rats or birds sometimes? What happened with them?"

"Same as a human," said Vivien. "Birds *were* used, more than rats, though both were apparently harder to control than humans. Different senses. And flying."

"The thresholds of the doors and windows in this building are warded," said Merlin. "But what about sewer pipes and so on? Rats can swim up those."

"The water mains are, and I suppose any big pipes," said Vivien. "But some could have been missed."

"A Cauldron-Born rat would be a perfect spy. Sent out to track someone down, for instance."

"We still come back to who, why, and with what cauldron," said Vivien. "Look, I think we *are* simply getting jumpy. Let's have lunch, then go to the Old Bookshop and get the aunts to look at Susan's library card. If they can identify it, we follow that up. All right?"

"I guess so," said Merlin. He looked at Susan.

"Can we take the swords?" asked Susan.

"I'll find a bag," said Merlin immediately, as Vivien started to say, "No," but then thought better of it.

"I can't cloud lots of people's minds at once," she warned. "So don't go waving those pigstickers around unnecessarily."

Merlin produced a vintage leather cricket bag adorned with the cryptic gold monogram "PDBW," unstrapped it, and opened it up to receive the swords, replacing them in their scabbards before he put them carefully inside. Susan was interested to see her saber went into an entirely iron scabbard, lined with wood, whereas Merlin's was heavy, ancient leather, banded and tipped in greenish bronze. It looked like it had been preserved in a peat bog for a thousand years.

"If you wouldn't mind carrying this," he said, giving the bag to Susan. "I think I should keep my hands free."

"Happy to," said Susan. She stuffed her bundle of clothes into the bag as well, and swung it experimentally. The bag would make a reasonable weapon in itself, even without getting the swords out in the first place. A violent swing from the heavy bag could easily knock someone down.

"At least a Cauldron-Born rat would be easier to hack apart," said Merlin. He opened the door and added, "Harder to spot, though. And if it tried a surprise attack . . ."

He hesitated, then said, "You know what? Though their lunchroom is as awfully provisioned as the New Bookshop's, why don't we go straight to the Old Bookshop and eat something there? Skip the pub. If we hurry, we can probably cadge motorbike rides with Una's lot. Always fun. Provided you don't fall off the back."

"And strength in numbers," said Vivien. "You really do think a Cauldron-Born of some kind was here, don't you?"

Merlin didn't answer, instead hurrying to the lift. Susan and Vivien hadn't waited for his reply, and all three moved swiftly down the hallway. When they got a few paces away, they all rushed to press the call button, Merlin's left forefinger getting there first.

CHAPTER ELEVEN

⪼⊶⊙⊷⪻

Be a writer, if you will
Or don't, no one will care
Order your shelves, or not
Kill or kiss your darlings
Simply write

⪼⊶⊙⊷⪻

RIDING PILLION ON A HONDA CB400N SUPERDREAM BEHIND AN evidently deranged left-handed bookseller-cum-courier—whose idea of getting through traffic owed a lot to embroidery, threading in and out and around slower or stopped vehicles, always at high speed—was fun, as Merlin had promised. Made slightly scarier because it was still drizzling and the road was wet, and Susan found falling off the back rather more likely than expected, since she was holding the cricket bag under her left arm and so could only hold on with her right.

Susan, Merlin, and Vivien made it to the Old Bookshop in a three-minute sprint up Charing Cross Road. Sabah chirped "Off you get" to Susan at the curb out the front, allowing about five seconds for her to dismount before roaring away with Una and the others down a side alley to some unseen garage or loading dock around the back of the building.

The Old Bookshop was another six-story Georgian edifice, with the addition of what looked to be a Victorian-era turret on one end, but it was entirely different from the New Bookshop in Mayfair. The ground floor facing the street was all floor-to-ceiling high windows, with a wonderful display of Umberto Eco's *The Name of the Rose* complete with a cardboard castle to the left of the central revolving door, and a selection of new release thrillers and mysteries built up in series of pyramids in the window to the right, including John Le Carré's *The Little Drummer Girl*, Jeffrey Archer's *First Among Equals*, and Ken Follett's *On Wings of Eagles*. Smaller displays at the far end of each window showcased some nonfiction, as if to ballast the made-up stuff in-between, including A. N. Wilson's *The Life of John Milton*, a biography of Frida Kahlo, and *Adventures in the Screen Trade* by William Goldman, which caught Susan's eye because as far as she could tell she was one of the few people in the world to have read *The Princess Bride*. No one she talked to had ever heard of it. Her mother had bought the book because William Goldman had written her favorite film, *Butch Cassidy and the Sundance Kid*.

Unlike the New Bookshop's discreet brass plate, the Old Bookshop sported a three-foot-high green neon sign proclaiming "The Old Bookshop, All New Books Today" and beneath that a smaller neon sign that announced in brilliant orange "Complete Penguin Bookshop."

Also unlike the other bookshop, it was busy with customers,

and there was a steady column of people moving in and out through the central revolving door and the smaller door to its side, both watched over by two small, middle-aged women who had to be twins. They were cheerfully checking bags and casting the eye of disapproving shame on a student in an enormous greatcoat stuffed with stolen books who'd made the mistake of thinking he was in Foyles and was now suddenly intent on returning all the books to their correct shelves without a word spoken, somehow sensing the inherent threat in the twins' single-gloved left hands and their smiling good humor.

Susan, Merlin, and Vivien got nods and smiles from the twins—Aunts Kristen and Kersten, Vivien muttered—as they were flung out of the revolving door into a large, brightly lit acme of bookshops, with well-ordered and well-labeled shelves in all directions, pleasant staff asking "Can I help you?" and comfortable chairs in strategic corners, all occupied by readers.

"This way," said Vivien, heading past the central payment desk, where a trio of right-handed cotton-gloved assistants were selling books to a steady line of customers queuing with innate British ease alongside a rack of current magazines and newspapers. The afternoon papers were being put out, all with similar headlines, again catching Susan's eye.

The *Sun* said "Gangsters Gunning to Kill!"; the *Daily Mirror* "Gangland Death Spree!"; *The Times* "Organised Crime Violence Peaks"; and the *Guardian* "Several Underworld Murders."

None of the staff spoke to them, but Susan noted Merlin got smiles from everyone, and Vivien serious head inclinations that could not be described as simply nodding. Susan thought some glances of curiosity were directed her way as well, but that was all. Being with Vivien and Merlin and clearly on a mission from their rapid movement, no one paid her any other attention.

Vivien turned left at the "New Fiction" shelves, along an aisle for "New Nonfiction," and continued towards the rear of the ground floor, where a broad fake marble staircase with bronze banister rails was visible going up and down, and an old wooden-stepped escalator clanked up next to it, beside a sign pointing right "To the Lifts."

An illuminated sign with the Penguin logo in black and a red arrow pointing down flickered above the stairs. Vivien and Merlin followed this direction, clattering down the stairs for a few steps before, as if by second nature, they both sat up on the smooth bronze banister and slid down.

Susan had paused momentarily to look at the directory board by the escalator, noting there were three floors above, including a children's department, Maps & Atlases, and Technical Books. There were two floors below, first the Complete Penguin Bookshop on Lower Ground One and then Bargains, Remainders & Records on Lower Ground Two.

When Susan looked away from the board, Merlin and Vivien were sliding down the banister, already going faster than she could take the steps, so she followed suit. But she had to hold the cricket bag across her body, which made it much harder to balance, and she almost fell twice as she wobbled down to the next floor and sprang off the end to land with a stagger in a large, extremely orange room, narrowly avoiding a collision with an oversized cutout penguin of the bird variety, which was holding a sign proclaiming "The Complete Penguin Bookshop Stocks All Penguins in Print."

Even though many Penguin books now had pictorial covers, their spines were still mostly orange, and the sheer quantity of books on the shelves here meant few were face out, explaining the extraordinarily dominant color, though there were also a few sections of green-spined mysteries, blue-spined nonfiction, and so on.

This part of the bookshop was busy, too, though the active shoppers were outnumbered by browsers and a few dedicated readers who were obviously intent on reading entire books in the shop. The right-handed bookseller here raised his eyebrows and mouthed something to Vivien that Susan couldn't catch as they breezed past, towards a door at the rear of the shop marked "Strictly Staff Only."

"My favorite part of the store," said Vivien with satisfaction. "Very advanced. Every night we ring the Penguin warehouse in Harmondsworth with a list of the ISBNs of the books sold that day and we get replacement stock within two or three days, instead of the paper order forms and the weeks the other publishers take. Very efficient."

"Unpacking new releases is the best," said Merlin. "Particularly when you don't know what's been ordered, so it's a surprise what's in the box."

"It is very therapeutic," agreed Vivien.

Merlin looked at Susan. "That's one of the other reasons the St. Jacques are booksellers. Or mostly booksellers. Books help us anchor our souls. Or re-anchor them. Particularly for us, the left-handed, given the things we have to do."

"Writing helps, too," said Vivien. "Poetry in particular. We are all poets, after a fashion."

She knocked on the door at the back with her right hand. It opened without apparent human intervention, revealing a long, dimly lit corridor that was half closed off with stacked cardboard book boxes emblazoned with the logos and names of various publishers: Penguin, William Collins, Hodder & Stoughton, Pan Macmillan, Oxford University Press, Victor Gollancz Ltd, and others.

Vivien led them along the corridor to a steel door that had an additional "Strictly Staff Only!" sign. She knocked again. A judas window slid open so an unseen viewer could check who it was, followed a moment later by the sound of a heavy bolt being withdrawn, and the door was swung open by Darren, one of the left-handed bikers who'd been with Una's response team.

The steel door led to a large open warehouse area dominated by high metal shelves stacked with boxes of books and a long sorting desk piled high with books, and beyond that a sunken receiving dock and ramp lined on one side with half a dozen motorbikes and a blue Jensen Interceptor leading up to a lorry-sized roller door that was closed. A smaller metal gate next to it was open. One of Una's bikers stood by it, a slung L1A1 SLR on his back, the kind of rifle Susan recognized as being the same as the ones used by UNIT in *Doctor Who*.

The other bikers from the response team were at work at the sorting table, along with four more young left- and right-handed booksellers. They were opening boxes, checking off stock, and putting books in shopping baskets ready to be carried to the appropriate part of the store, or wrapping orders to be dispatched outwards to mail order or phone customers.

Una herself was sitting in a folding aluminum deck chair on the side of the loading dock, reading *Heat and Dust* by Ruth Prawer Jhabvala and drinking tea from a large blue mug. She had a sword similar to Merlin's on the floor next to her, alongside a sawn-off double-barreled shotgun. She looked up from the book at the new arrivals, sniffed, and went back to her reading.

"I didn't realize how big this bookshop is," said Susan. "It must be even bigger than Foyles."

"And it is much better," said Vivien. "We are all *professional* booksellers. Come on."

"Foyles has a charm that Vivien does not perceive," said Merlin. "I like all kinds of bookshops myself, not just ours."

Vivien looked at him scornfully and turned left, and they crossed the warehouse to yet another door, marked "Fire Exit," and then up five flights of fire stairs to what Susan warily thought was the top of the building, though if it was like the New Bookshop, possibly not. The fire door here opened into a charming atelier, under a Victorian iron-and-glass roof. It was still raining in a desultory fashion, drops plinking on the glass and sliding down in slow rivulets. On a sunny day it would be beautifully bright, but today the natural illumination was assisted by a line of very large and unusual art deco light bulbs that ran along under the peak of the ceiling.

The floor was of warm, old oak planks, many of the individual planks extraordinarily long, as if sawn from the mast of a tall ship. There were two working tables in the middle of the room, and around the walls were located a binder's press, with its tall screw; a camera stand; an industrial sewing machine; a gluing cabinet with exhaust hood; a guillotine table and cutting board; a TRS-80 computer and dot matrix printer on a narrow mahogany desk that might have come from a boat; a partner's table topped in green leather and gilt edging on which resided no fewer than six typewriters, ranging from a 1920s Underwood to a very recent all-plastic Brother machine; a mid-eighteenth-century highly polished flame mahogany map cabinet of twelve drawers; and a French Second Empire grandfather clock with an intricately carved headpiece. There were also several other small worktables of less obvious purpose, complete with racks of tools and shelves of papyrus, vellum, paper and cardboard, and other writing materials.

At the closest table, a fiftyish woman with dark curly hair

tinged with silver was examining a page in a giant medieval Bible bound in leather and iron, complete with chain. She wasn't wearing gloves, and *both* her hands shone with the silver luminosity Susan had seen in the New Bookshop, with Cousin Sam.

The woman at the next table was perhaps a decade older than the first. She sat in a lightweight wheelchair with chromed rims. She was entirely white-haired and slighter, and was engaged in delicatcly separating stuck-together leaves of some impossibly thin paper with what looked like a small ivory or bone spatula and long tweezers. Like the other women, she was dressed in a well-cut white pantsuit, almost like a navy tropical uniform. She also didn't wear gloves and her hands were silvery and beautiful.

"Yes," whispered Vivien. "They're both even-handed."

Something in the way she said it told Susan that Vivien would like to be one of the even-handed.

"Aunt Zoë, Aunt Helen!" called out Merlin.

Both women continued their tasks for several seconds, and then at exactly the same time, they leaned back and turned their heads to look at the visitors.

"Hello, my dears," said the closer woman. "We had a note from Thurston to say you were coming over with a little puzzle sometime. But we're quite busy now. Could you come back—"

"No, I'm afraid we can't," said Vivien. "I'm sorry, but I think it's more urgent than Great-Uncle Thurston realizes. Um, this is Susan Arkshaw, by the way. Susan, our aunt Helen and behind her, our aunt Zoë."

Aunt Helen blinked and pushed the magnifying lens up her forehead, like a knight lifting a visor. Aunt Zoë pursed her lips and leaned forward, eyebrows lifting in anticipation of something interesting.

"We think it might be related to what happened to Mum," said Merlin quietly.

"Poor Antigone," said Helen. Behind her, Zoë nodded. "Well, what is it you want us to look at?"

"A lending library card," said Vivien, pushing Susan forward. "I don't know which library it's from, and the name of the person it was issued to is gone. Then there's a 1964 Harshton and Hoole cigarette case, I know it's silver, not paper, but there's something about the design on the front . . . I'd like your opinion on. It reminds me of something. . . ."

"Let's see it!" declared Helen, wheeling out from the table to hold out her shining right hand. Zoë stood up and came up to stand behind her cousin.

Susan took the cigarette case from the pocket of her boiler suit, popped it open, and handed it over. Helen took out the library card and held it up to the light, flipping it over several times. Zoë watched closely, then took the card herself, Helen handing it over her shoulder without looking around.

She examined the cigarette case next, and smiled immediately.

"Oh, they have such cunning artists up at Harshton and Hoole," she said. "I can almost forgive them forsaking books in the great split of 1553."

"You know what that is, then?" asked Susan.

"I will shortly," said Helen. She pushed her wheelchair over to one of the smaller tables and rummaged in the boxes upon it. "Heelball, heelball . . . ah . . . here we are."

"Oh!" exclaimed Susan. "A rubbing! I should have thought of that."

Helen held up a ball of inky black material and took it and the cigarette case back to her table. Placing the case on a heavy wooden chopping block branded "Fortnum & Mason" in pokerwork in the corner, she laid a piece of paper over it and rubbed it with the heelball, a black image forming as she rubbed. At first it seemed no more than many small lines, but within a few seconds, the lines made sudden sense, though were still somewhat abstract.

"It's a mountain," said Merlin. "Or a hill. With clouds."

"Yes," said Helen thoughtfully. "Very simple lines, the lesser ones are almost invisible in the silver, hence the need for a rubbing to see it clearly. It reminds me of something, some part of a broader landscape, a painting or drawing . . . I daresay it will come to me. . . ."

"Thank you so much," said Susan. "That's already incredibly helpful. If I . . . we . . . can work out where this mountain is—"

"It's not a very distinctive mountain," muttered Merlin.

"What about the library card?" asked Vivien.

"The where is easy," replied Zoë, surprising Susan, because she had an American accent, a notable Western twang. "It's from the Robert Southey Library, one of the smaller private libraries that sadly hasn't lasted. It closed down in 1967, and the collection was sold to the London Library, which also absorbed the membership."

"And the name?" asked Susan. "I thought perhaps it starts with an O."

"More likely a C, I think," said Zoë judiciously. "With this sort of thing, the surname was often written first; I think the trace of the comma separating the names is visible. The good news is even though the ink has almost completely faded, we can probably bring up the name with a photographic technique, using ultraviolet light."

"Thank you," said Susan. "I'm very grateful."

"But we don't have the UV lights here; a friend at the museum does that kind of specialized work for us," said Zoë. "When she can fit it in."

"I think it really is urgent," said Vivien.

"I'll call Jocelyn and see if she can do it tomorrow morning," said Zoë. "We've put in to get fluorescing UV light for the darkroom here in the annual stipendiary requests, but it never gets approved. I think Thurston won't sign it off because the globes come from America now; the local manufacturer went out of business a few years ago."

"Made in Britain," muttered Merlin.

"Now, now, dear," said Helen. "You were made in Britain, after all. We still make many fine new things, and who but us know the value of the old so well?"

"I know," sighed Merlin, giving his aunt a smile so bright and charming Susan felt she had to look away or go weak at the knees. "I guess I'm . . . I don't know . . . on edge."

"And hungry," said Vivien. She looked at the grandfather

clock. "It's after four and we still haven't had any lunch!"

"They've got stargazy pie in the canteen today," said Helen brightly.

The others all shuddered.

"And corned beef and Branston pickle sandwiches."

Susan brightened at this, suppressing an urge to lick her lips. Merlin did not seem cheered.

"I'm sure Jocelyn at the museum will help as soon as she can," said Helen. "What's this about, anyway?"

Susan looked at Merlin, who looked at Vivien.

"The case and the card were probably my father's," said Susan awkwardly. "We're trying to find out who he is because . . . um . . . well, a Raud Alfar warden shot at me, and both criminals and the May Fair goblins have tried to abduct me. All of which seems to be about my father."

"What did Grandmother say?" asked Zoë. "Thurston said you saw her this morning. Which one was it?"

"The eldest, in the end," replied Vivien. She hesitated. "Ah . . ."

"We won't tell Thurston or Merrihew," said Helen. She looked at Susan. "Yes, I can read minds a little. And I see our old granny told you something that scares you."

"She did," said Susan slowly. "Apparently, my father is of the oldest blood, one of the Ancient Sovereigns."

"That would do it," said Helen. She wheeled over, close to Susan, and held up her luminous hands. "May I touch your face, child? It won't harm you."

"Uh, I guess so," said Susan uncomfortably. She leaned

forward. The older woman gently laid her hands on Susan's cheeks, cradling her as she might some grandchild. She held her breath for a long, long minute, the room silent, Susan hardly daring to breathe herself. Then she exhaled, sat back, and folded her luminous hands in her lap.

"There *is* a spark of some great and ancient power within you," she said. "Only an ember . . . but embers can flare into mighty fires. Did you have a significant birthday recently?"

"May first," said Susan. "I turned eighteen."

"I don't know what the power is or where it comes from," said Helen. "Or whether it will grow. But it seems to me to be the promise of something to come. . . ."

She hesitated for a moment, before quietly continuing.

"I do not wish to give you sad news, but I suspect . . . only suspect, mind, I cannot say for sure . . . that you would not have this small spark within you if your father is still present in either the Old World or the New. It smacks of a gift given in inheritance, some small portion of a far greater magic that is no longer here. "

"You mean my father's dead?"

"The Old Ones do not precisely die," said Helen. "Most sleep, perhaps never to awaken, but they are here. Some have faded almost to imperceptibility. But a few have been . . . removed, I suppose you could say. Utterly destroyed. If that is the case with you, I am sorry."

"It's okay," replied Susan evenly. "I always thought he must be dead. Otherwise, you know, he would have . . . I don't know . . .

written to me at least. I have my mum, a happy childhood home. I'm lucky."

"And I bet super hungry," said Vivien. "Can we leave the library card with Zoë and Helen? Let's eat and then get you home."

"Yes," said Susan. "I am hungry. And tired. I'd forgotten I was up half the night, after I saw the Kexa watching me from the roof of the shed."

"A Kexa, too?" asked Zoë. She frowned. "Thurston's note didn't mention half of these things. Only the May Fair goblins."

"There was a Cauldron-Born in Northumberland House," said Merlin suddenly.

"What!" exclaimed Zoë and Helen.

"We can't be certain. I felt it, and Viv smelled laurel and amaranth and decay," said Merlin. "But Una and her team didn't find anything, and Uncle Jake checked the wards, which were apparently intact."

"Have Thurston and Merrihew been informed?"

"Una said she called Thurston; Merrihew's probably still on her way back to Wooten."

Helen and Zoë exchanged a look, which the others correctly interpreted as an indication of lack of confidence in the current leadership of the booksellers.

"We'll make sure to follow this up," said Helen.

"I wonder if they've told the Grail-Keeper," mused Zoë. "I think under the circumstances that needs to be done."

"I doubt it," said Merlin bitterly. "Great-Uncle Thurston is in raptures over a library purchase, and Merrihew's going after that giant carp in the old clay pit lake. Again."

"Hmm," said Helen.

"Besides," continued Merlin. "If there was a Cauldron-Born, how was it made? Who has a cauldron besides us?"

Helen and Zoë shook their heads.

"No, Merlin," they said together. "The Grail-Keeper would never allow it."

"But—"

"No," said the two older women together, very firmly.

"We will inform the Grail-Keeper, even if the Greats have not," said Aunt Zoë. "I can nip into the Serpentine tomorrow."

Susan looked at her blankly but didn't have the opportunity to ask what on earth that meant as Helen asked her a question.

"Are you staying with Merlin at the Northumberland, Susan?"

"No," said Susan. She could feel herself blushing.

"She's at Mrs. London's; you know, the place Special Branch keep for us to park the oddbods," said Merlin. "Though they've been naughty and put in a couple of Soviet defectors and I'd say some sort of ex-peace group infiltrator who's been found out as well."

"Is that who they are?" asked Susan, who had been mystified by her housemates. Their desire to not discuss who they were or why they were there was even greater than her own.

"Is it sufficiently secure?" asked Zoë. "You mentioned a Kexa?"

"It has the usual wards," said Vivien. "It's on neutral ground.

As much as you can get in London, anyway. No known entity of the Old World resides there, or claims it; it doesn't fall under the suzerainty of any Ancient Sovereign."

"And I'll be there with Susan," said Merlin.

"In the house, generally," added Susan. "Not in my room or anything."

Merlin nodded, as if nothing else had been implied. Maybe nothing else had been implied, Susan thought. She didn't know what was worse. He wasn't as self-obsessed and vain as she'd thought, but no less attractive. . . .

"While it is not uncommon for some of the lesser entities and minor human dabblers to also be criminals in the ordinary sense," said Helen, "this sort of directed activity by goblins—who most certainly would not answer to any mere mortal instruction—in combination with gangsters is very unusual. It can't be a coincidence. And you think this connects with what happened to your mother?"

"I don't know, but I think it's worth finding out," said Merlin.

"It certainly is," said Zoë. "If Jocelyn can't do the photographs at the BM tomorrow, I'll find someone who can. Either way, I'll have the job done by midmorning. Call me."

"I'll drop in," said Vivien. "I'll be here anyway. I have a shift tomorrow, front counter."

"Oh!" exclaimed Susan. "I have to work tomorrow, too. I'd forgotten, what with everything . . . but I guess I'll be safe at the pub?"

"I'll be with you," said Merlin cheerily. "Like a remora stuck to a whale . . . no . . . something rather nicer, like a strawberry in champagne—"

He oofed as Vivien struck him sharply in the stomach, and subsided.

"Be careful, children," said Helen. She spun her wheelchair around, back to her desk.

"Yeah, be very careful," said Zoë. "And don't eat the godawful pie they have downstairs!"

CHAPTER TWELVE

Short stories are brill
Novels can thrill
A play's just the thing
But poems can sing

SUSAN AND MERLIN FINALLY GOT BACK TO MRS. LONDON'S CLOSE TO seven, because after their very late lunch, which vehemently did not include stargazy pie, they had to go first to Northumberland House to drop off Vivien, who wanted to look at the wards there, and to wait for Merlin to pack and close a ridiculously large leather suitcase that boasted numerous straps. At Merlin's insistence, aided by Vivien's diplomacy to actually make it happen, they traveled in one of the bookseller's cabs, this time driven by the very silent, focused Cousin Wendover, not Audrey.

Susan was exhausted, wanting only a bath and bed, but this was denied her, for as they walked in the hall, the door to what Mrs. London called the common room swung open to reveal Inspector Greene, wearing the identical clothes she'd been in the week before when she'd brought Susan from Highgate Police Station to this house. A definite look.

"About time you got here," she grumbled, making a beckoning gesture. "Come on, then. Let's be having you."

"Can't we talk tomorrow?" asked Susan. "I am totally knackered."

"No, because I need to know what the hell is going on," replied Greene, standing back to let them into the room. "As does my colleague from Organized Crime, who has graced us with his presence. Susan Arkshaw, Merlin St. Jacques, allow me to introduce Chief Superintendent Holly."

"Reg Holly!" cried the older, heavily built, once-handsome ex-boxer type in a charcoal three-piece double-breasted suit, bright white shirt, club tie, and chunky silver-braceleted watch peeking out from under his French cuff, with gold yacht club links that made him look more like a banker than a police officer. "Call me Reg."

Merlin looked from Holly to Greene.

"This is bookseller business," he said. "No one outside of your unit is cleared, Greene. None of the regular police. You know that."

"Don't fret, lad," said Reg. "I was in Greene's job once upon a time, until I moved on to greener—ha ha—pastures, career-wise I mean, something I've suggested to young Mira here, because it's a dead end working with you booksellers. And look at me now, chief super and in charge of what I like to call incompetently organized crime."

"The chief superintendent has a historical clearance that has not been revoked," said Greene evenly.

"And I called up Merrihew to make sure it was kosher for me to stick my head in," said Reg. "Fine, she said. So here I am."

Susan flopped down into an armchair. Merlin remained standing, looking at Holly suspiciously.

"So you must be Susan . . . Arkshaw," said Holly, looking intently at Susan. He had small, cruel eyes, she thought, and looked away. "A newcomer to all the sort of things the booksellers get into."

"Ms. Arkshaw has nothing to do with anything in your area of responsibility," said Greene. "Sir."

"What I'd like to know," said Reg, ignoring Greene, "is what your arrival and the . . . uh . . . departure of our dear and unlamented friend Frank Thringley has to do with a bunch of Brummagen boys trying to take you off the doorstep here?"

"Sir, I will be advising the deputy commissioner—" Greene tried to interrupt, but Holly pressed on.

"Birmingham mob, organized crime, that's *my* bailiwick," he said, almost snarling at Greene, though when he looked back at Susan his face was placid again. "So I have to ask what the arrival of one Susan Arkshaw has got to do with the demise of Frank Thringley, North London mobster *and* Sipper, and then those gits turning up here for you *and* the sudden outbreak of violence between and within a number of usually quite-well-behaved gangs in London, Birmingham, Liverpool, Manchester, Leeds, and Newcastle. Or in other words, the whole of bloody Britain that matters, since the Scots and the Welsh—or ninety-nine percent of them—are apparently sailing on oblivious."

"What?" asked Susan. "It's nothing to do with me."

"Now, as there's nothing written, no statements as is par for the course with you lot, I only got to know this morning from *informal sources* that you even existed and you were present when Frank Thringley was knocked off by Mr. Merlin St. Jacques here—"

"You have no operational involvement in this and you should not have been informed of either—"

"Shut it, Greene. I told you, I talked to Merrihew and she said I can talk to whoever I want."

Again, the attack dog disappeared as he turned back to Susan. She frowned, wondering why on earth he bothered, as if she wouldn't notice how rude he was to Greene. He could be as nice as pie to her and she'd still know he was a total arsehole.

"Now that was a week ago, so maybe I might think this outbreak of argy-bargy isn't all connected. But this morning, two of the Milk Bottle Gang show up here, try a snatch and get their comeuppance, not counting on your Mr. Merlin being at the front door with a damned hand cannon. Why were they here? What's the connection?"

"Why don't you ask them, *Reg*?" suggested Merlin, though he already knew the answer.

"I did ask them, after Greene's lot had a go, and their minds were like a plate of mushy peas. They didn't know where they were, what they were doing, or who they were doing it for. They'd been interfered with, I reckon, by someone you booksellers are supposed to make sure can't do that sort of thing, or maybe by your lot themselves. Who's out there messing with the gray stuff of my ordinary mobsters, that's what I'd like to know?"

"We'd like to know, too," said Susan. "Me particularly, since I don't fancy any more attempted kidnappings."

"And you don't know anything you can tell me?" continued Reg. He put on what he obviously thought was a kind, pleading face, but his cauliflower ears and broken nose made him look like a slightly demented pug.

"I don't know anything about gangs in London or anywhere else," said Susan. She looked away from Holly, not wanting to meet his eyes. She'd caught something there, a momentary flash. For a second he'd looked at her the way a particularly cruel cat might look at an injured bird.

"What about you and yours?" Reg asked Merlin, his expression once again all police officer, bland and impersonal. "Anything you can tell me?"

"No," said Merlin, very shortly.

"You must have something!" protested Holly. "Look, I've been in this job eighteen years, everything peaceable as you like. Sure, there's crime, the gangs do what they do, but orderly like and to each other, or if it's not, it's to do with lowlifes anyway. Hardly a murder or even a beating involving honest members of the public. Nothing to make the papers or the TV. I retire in six months. My record was perfect and then today everything gets flushed down the crapper. You must know something. Miss

Arkshaw, you're Thringley's adopted daughter or something, aren't you? Come on, I need help."

"I am not Frank Thringley's daughter, adopted or otherwise!" said Susan. "He was an old friend of my mum."

"Oh, I must have got that wrong," said Holly. "Who's your dad, then? I've only got your mum's name. She lives down near Bath, doesn't she? Lovely town, beautiful countryside."

Susan wondered if he meant that as a threat of some kind. There was nothing in his tone of voice, and the words were innocent enough. But she felt it was somehow. In any case, she'd had enough of Chief Superintendent Holly.

"I can't help you," said Susan firmly. "I'm really tired and I'm going to have a bath and go to bed."

"All right, all right," said Reg, throwing up his hands. "Throw an old copper on the rubbish heap. But if you're really worried about more kidnapping attempts, you'd best help me out. I can help you. In fact, how about I lend Mira Greene a couple of officers to keep an extra eye on this place? I'm not saying anything against Unit M, but if a bunch of your real London thugs come all tooled up to have a go . . . well, I don't like your chances."

"We've got it managed, thank you, sir," said Greene. "And it would be strictly against *direct orders* from the commissioner for any of your junior officers to be aware of the booksellers and matters concerning the Old World."

"I reckon it's the criminals of this world you should be worried about, Miss Arkshaw," said Reg to Susan, ignoring Greene. "But you dig your own grave. If you change your mind, here's my card."

Neither Susan nor Merlin reached out to take it, so he dropped it on the coffee table and stalked out. Greene turned on her heel and followed him, and they heard the two police officers talking on the way to the front door.

"I didn't know you were retiring, sir. Costa del Sol?"

"Fuck off, Greene. Have your laugh. You know I'd stay if I could; they're forcing me out. And it'll be the Costa del Cumbria most likely, on my pension. And I don't appreciate you suggesting I'm bent. Costa del Sol indeed!"

"Good luck, sir."

The slamming door cut off most of Holly's strident "Get f—!"

Greene came back into the room a few seconds later.

"Sorry about that. Holly's a zombie, hardly going through the motions. The reason the gangs have been so quiet for so long is because he lets them get away with so much! He's a lazy sod who's always away on courses or sick leave or whatever. And I reckon he is bent as well; no one could be as ineffectual as he is accidentally. The only surprise is it's taken so long to give him the boot. Now tell me what the hell is going on."

"It's bookseller business," said Merlin.

"And where that crosses over with police matters, it's my business, too," said Greene. "I wish there was someone else to talk to with your lot other than Thurston. Or Merrihew, who's never in either shop, and when I call her in the country it takes half an hour to get her to the phone and costs a fortune. I had to call Thurston *three* times today and kept getting told he was too busy to answer my questions."

"He is *very* busy," said Merlin. "Unpacking the personal

library of Sir Anthony Blunt. Former sir, I guess, since they took away his knighthood."

"The traitor? Are the *Soviets* connected—"

"No, of course not," snapped Merlin. "Sorry. Thurston . . . irritates me as well. There's no connection. It's simply that Blunt had an amazing library, full of first editions and collectibles. They're all going gaga over it at the New Bookshop and Thurston can't spare a brain cell for anything else. I wish he'd retire."

"Uh, will he ever?" asked Greene. "I only have very limited records and what I've been able to find out myself, on the job, but Thurston and Merrihew seem to have been running the St. Jacques operations since 1887."

Susan started in surprise. "Eighteen eighty-seven?"

"Yeah, that's about right," said Merlin wearily. "For Thurston. Merrihew's been in charge of the left-handed for even longer. Since 1815, a few months after Waterloo. Some of us live a long time. If we don't get killed, that is. Look, it really is better if you don't know what might be going on. I mean, despite the job and all, you're still a mortal, and generally the more you know the more you are at risk."

"That's my line," said Greene. "Is Ms. Arkshaw at risk?"

Merlin hesitated, then said, "I think so, though the Greats don't. I'm going to bodyguard her for a while—I'll stay here tonight—and the taxis are going to drive by regularly."

"Mrs. London told me something tried the wards last night," said Greene. "You apparently called it a Kexa. Unsurprisingly, my predecessor never mentioned one to me in what I laughably refer to as my training, and I couldn't find any other reference. What is a Kexa?"

"Mrs. L has got very superior hearing," complained Merlin. "A Kexa is a hemlock cat. And you could look it up in *The Golden Bough* ... no, wait ... you're right, it's not in the version that made it to print. Anyway, a Kexa is a summoned servant called from the sacred burial urn of a pharaonic cat; a few were brought here from Egypt by the Romans, but we've collected most of them over the years. Not all, clearly. A very dangerous creature, but it couldn't get in, and it can only prowl at night, when it's clear, and the moon is neither new nor full."

"Like tonight," said Greene. "Can a Kexa be shot? I mean, will bullets kill one?"

"Theoretically yes," said Merlin. "But they're very hard to hit, because they move between this world and somewhere else that isn't ... er ... here. Though I suppose it might be easier than fighting urchins. . . ."

"Why?" asked Susan.

"You need something old to strike goblins. Cold iron or steel— and preindustrial steel at that—more than three hundred years old. Or stone or ancient wood. Like Audrey's bog oak stick."

"Are any members of the public likely to be at risk because of whatever or whoever is after Susan? Speaking of goblins, I understand there was some sort of unusual event in Mayfair this morning?"

"No members of the public were at risk," said Merlin. "The urchins only wanted us; they took us out of time and clouded the minds of those nearby for the few seconds it took to do that."

"Except for that one American tourist," said Susan, with a yawn. "But I think she thought it was a kind of jet lag illusion or something."

"Is the situation with Ms. Arkshaw—"

"Call me Susan. You did before."

"Is the situation with Susan, whatever it is, likely to be resolved in the near future? The very near future?"

"I don't know," said Merlin. "But, as your lot like to say, inquiries are proceeding."

"Maybe everything will settle down," said Susan hopefully. "And I can look for my dad. . . . Anyway, I have to get upstairs. I can't stay awake."

"I'll check in on you later," said Merlin. "Uh, don't forget your cricket bag."

"Oh, right," said Susan. She picked up the cricket bag with the swords and her clothes, ignoring Greene's inquiring and somewhat disbelieving gaze, and left the room. She narrowly missed Mrs. London wielding a pink feather duster, where she was pretending to spruce up the hallway. Mister Nimbus was on the stairs, a very distinguished black cat with white socks. He looked at Susan with narrowed eyes. Not suspicious exactly, but wary, as if the cat thought she needed both eyes kept upon her, not one.

"Good night, Mrs. London," said Susan. "I'm turning in early."

"Very wise," said Mrs. London. "Do you want me to bring you a cup of tea?"

"No, but thank you. I'll have a quick bath and then go straight to bed. I reckon I'll be asleep before my head hits the pillow."

"Come sleep, O sleep, the certain knot of peace," recited Mrs. London, surprising Susan.

Susan was in bed when Merlin knocked on the door.

"Susan? It's me, Merlin. Can I come in?"

"Um, yes," said Susan, a little flustered, and annoyed with herself for being flustered. "I'm in bed."

Merlin opened the door and ran his hand along the edge, found the bolt, and slid it back and forth a few times. Not suggestively.

"Don't lock your door unless I tell you to," he said. "And keep your clothes and boots handy. In case we need to leave in a hurry."

Susan, who'd been feeling nicely relaxed after her bath and perfectly safe in bed, struggled upright. She felt a brief pang at thus revealing she wasn't sleeping in one of her cool band T-shirts but in a massively oversized one featuring a photo of the Wombles, furry suits and all, but told herself she wanted to put Merlin off anyway. Or did she? A small voice inside told her to take a chance; what was the worst that could happen? Her mother's experiences with very handsome men did not have to be her own.

"What! You mean . . . you think more is going to happen? Here?"

"No, I want to be prepared," said Merlin. "Baden-Powell and all that. And . . . and . . . uh . . . Vivien called. One of the wards at Northumberland House *was* compromised. Not a pipe or a sewer. A ward meant to stop evildoers entering a service door to the plant room for the air-conditioning. Someone poured fresh blood mixed with quicksilver—that's mercury to you—under the door, which will dull a lesser ward—"

"Fresh blood!"

"Um, yes. Someone must have been killed minutes before and very close by, though we haven't found a body yet. Anyway, the ward *was* breached, so someone with malevolent intent could get in. Which at first didn't seem to be a problem because the plans showed no connection from the plant room into the hotel proper, but Viv found a crawl space inside that allowed access to the laundry, so . . ."

"There could have been a Cauldron-Born."

Susan was out of bed in a flash, opening the cricket bag to get out the sword she already thought of as hers.

"Yes. That's probably a good idea," said Merlin, and took up his own sword.

Susan leaned the saber against the bed, the hilt close to hand, and got back under the covers. Her boots and discarded boiler suit, and embarrassingly the day's underwear, were already in an untidy pile at the foot of the bed, easy enough to put on in a hurry if circumstances so required.

"The boundaries of this house have superior wards and are also alarmed against more usual intruders," said Merlin. "Vivien's coming over to check the wards. Inspector Greene has decided to stay as well, and there will be extra police patrols in the square. I'd prefer her not to stay if there is going to be anything *I* need to deal with, but then again if there is some sort of attack by gangsters she's apparently pretty handy. I'm in the next room, by the way, and Mira will be across the hall—"

"So she's Mira now?" asked Susan. Surely the inspector was too old to fall for Merlin's charms? She had to be thirty, maybe even mid-thirties.

"We are on first-name terms, upon occasion," said Merlin gravely. "But it's a professional relationship, you understand. Anyway, that's it in the house, apart from Mrs. L. The Russians and the CND turncoat have been relocated for the time being."

"What, too risky for them?"

"Yes," replied Merlin. "And they weren't supposed to be here anyway, according to our agreement with the police. Special Branch trying a sneaky little budget saving at our expense. It'll be fine. Get some sleep. What time do you start work, by the way? And . . . uh . . . where exactly?"

"Eleven," replied Susan. "The Twice-Crowned Swan. Cloudesley Street."

"Well, I'll see you at breakfast at, say, a civilized eight thirty," replied Merlin. "Would you like a good-night kiss, by the way?"

"I don't think so," said Susan, after a moment's hesitation. Caution still had the upper hand, though it took considerable exercise of willpower and common sense. "I have a feeling your good-night kisses might lead to a distinct lack of sleep."

"Another time, perhaps," said Merlin. He smiled, and exited.

Sometime later, there was another knock on the door. Susan woke with a start, the room dark, only partly lit from the spill of light from the square outside, creating numerous menacing shadows.

"Susan? It's Vivien. Can I have a quick word?"

Fuddled with sleep, Susan sat up and wiped the corners of her eyes. Without even really thinking about it, her hand trailed across to the hilt of the saber by her bedside.

"Yes. Come in."

The door swung open, and Vivien stood there, backlit by the hallway light. She had changed from her suit into dark blue jeans, a khaki shirt, and a dark brown vintage bomber jacket with a lambskin trim, and for a moment Susan thought she was actually Merlin pretending to be Vivien for some reason.

"I'm sorry to wake you," said Vivien. "Are you okay?"

"Yeah," said Susan, wiping her eyes again and waking up more completely. "What about you?"

Vivien didn't answer that directly, nor move from the doorway.

"I've checked the wards around the house and they are all strong," she said. "But . . ."

"What?" asked Susan. She was feeling rather irritable at being woken up.

"We . . . the right-handed . . . often have premonitions, some of us even visions," she said. "Of the possible future and of the past. Like Cousin Norman, who I believe Merlin idiotically described to you as a reverse oracle."

"And?"

"I've had one. Not exactly a premonition. A strong feeling

that I should give you something, only I'm not sure it's the right thing to do."

"What is it?"

Vivien frowned. Susan had never seen her so indecisive. Like Merlin, she always appeared omnicompetent. Now she was standing on one foot on the doorway, hovering and hesitating.

"Come on. You've woken me up now. What is it?"

Vivien grimaced, as if suffering a momentary pang of agony, then finally walked forward and held out three paper sachets of salt from Wimpy and an old bone-handled butter knife.

"Carry these with you," she said. "The knife is good Sheffield steel and it's been sharpened a bit, so you can draw blood."

"Uh, why would I want to?" asked Susan. She didn't take the offering. "Oh, what your grandmother said . . . salt and steel and blood . . . but what does that mean?"

"It's one method by which Ancient Sovereigns and others bind people . . . things . . . to their service," said Vivien. "One of the surest and easiest ways for you, if you come into that power. Mix a little of your blood and salt on the flat of the knife; ask them to ingest it, if they're willing. Or smear it on an open wound, or stab them, if they're not willing. Your blood and salt and steel will bind whoever or whatever you need to, with some exceptions. You'd need to give them a command at the same time. Something along the lines of 'You will serve me' or 'I am your master,' you know, that sort of thing."

"'I am your master'? I don't want to bind anyone or anything to my service!" exclaimed Susan with revulsion. "I mean, what happens then? Do they follow me around forever, wanting to help and tugging their forelock . . . forelock equivalents?"

"No," said Vivien. "You can release them again. That's simple; lay your hand on their head—or whatever approximates a head—and say something like 'By my blood and salt and steel, I release you.' Or you can order them to go and live their lives until summoned, or sleep until you need them, or whatever you like, really. And the binding will weaken over time, if it is not renewed or some other method employed to strengthen it."

"I could do this to anyone? That business about smearing on a wound, I could scratch someone in their sleep and dab on the mixture, for example?"

"Yes. If you do inherit the power of your sire," said Vivien. "You might not."

"That is awful!" burst out Susan. "I don't want to be able to bind people, or entities, or anyone!"

"It might all be purely theoretical. And even if you do gain the power, you don't have to use it," said Vivien. "But I think you need to know about the possibility—"

"I don't want it," snapped Susan. She lay back and pulled the covers over her head. "I don't want the knife, or the stupid salt! Go away and let me get back to sleep!"

"Okay," said Vivien. "Sorry."

She turned to go, and trod on the discarded boiler suit at the foot of the bed. She hesitated for a moment, then bent down and put the salt packets in a side pocket and slid the knife into the long, thin pocket made to hold a ruler. Vivien's mouth quirked at that. A ruler . . . Susan might well become one, no matter how she felt about it.

Vivien left the room, quietly shutting the door behind her.

Merlin was in the hall. He'd changed into dark pants, black tennis shoes, and a black turtleneck sweater under a black ballistic vest with "Police" on the front and back. He had the old sword belted on his right side and the Smython in a holster on his left, butt forward like an old-style gunslinger. All of which added up to the fact that he clearly expected trouble, no matter what anyone else thought.

"How did she take it?"

"She didn't," said Vivien. "But I put the knife and salt in the ruler pocket of her boiler suit."

"I still don't know how she got a suit that fitted," said Merlin.

"I hope I haven't made a very bad mistake," mused Vivien.

"Your premonition average is running about eighty percent," said Merlin. "Remember when Dad almost caught us three years ago when he came back unexpectedly when we were stealing that special bottle of champagne from his cellar? If you hadn't sensed he would, there'd have been no end of uproar."

"The 1959 Dom Pérignon," said Vivien, with a sigh. "We didn't appreciate it."

"Speak for yourself," said Merlin. "But to the matter at hand. Do you have a *specific* feeling for why Susan will need salt and steel? Anything definitive?"

"No," said Vivien. She shivered. "But I do have a presentiment of danger."

"Yeah. But when, and where?"

"I don't know. Maybe I should stay here, too," said Vivien. "I was going to go back to the New Bookshop to check through the Harshton and Hoole records, see if we've got anything at all about that cigarette case. A mountain design, and a gift to seal a treaty or bargain, that can't be very usual. There might be some correspondence on it. Which means the microfiche, since everything prior to 1979 has gone to the salt mine."

"Sooner you than me," said Merlin.

Vivien held up her right hand.

"Obviously. So should I stay or go?"

"Go. The wards are extant. Barlow is here, as well as Mrs. L, and we have the alarms. All three cabs are checking in through the night, and there's an extra shift of D11—two cars—working out of Tolpuddle tonight, if it is gangsters we have to worry about, like that Superintendent Holly reckons."

"Who?"

"Chief Superintendent Holly. Head of Organized Crime, but he had Greene's job years ago. He was around earlier, asking questions."

"That's unusual," said Vivien. "Unprecedented even."

"Greene says he's lazy and about to retire, only going through the motions. He's upset because there's a surge in gang violence and he thinks it's related to Frank Thringley. And Susan. Because she was there, and those Brummy gangsters tried to lift her."

"The gang connection again," said Vivien. "I think I'll look up Holly's record while I'm at it."

"Reg Holly," said Merlin. "You'd better be careful; don't ask for his file through the usual channels. Greene says he's influential. And he seems to get on with Merrihew."

"Okay. I'll see what I can dig up, and I'll duck in here early tomorrow morning, before I go to work in the shop. Are you planning to sleep at all?"

"Maybe not," said Merlin.

"Look after yourself, stupid brother," said Vivien, heading down the hall. At the top of the stairs she stopped and looked back. "And take care of Susan. I like her."

"Me too," said Merlin. He frowned, wondering why this was so. Susan wasn't at all like anyone else he'd been involved with before, in looks and background and behavior. She was certainly attractive, but there was more to it than that. He liked how she moved, and how she talked, and the way she'd taken everything that had happened in her stride, no matter how fantastical it had to be to someone who'd never encountered the Old World before.

Whatever he was beginning to feel for Susan, Merlin realized, it didn't feel *casual*. But casual was his mode; he didn't want anything else. Or at least he never had before. . . .

CHAPTER THIRTEEN

A shadow creeps along the wall
More shadows sweep across the hall
Many shadows leap and dance and fall
But shadows need both dark and light
No shadows crawl in blackest night

SUSAN WOKE AGAIN, DEEP IN THE NIGHT. FOR A MOMENT, SHE DIDN'T know what had woken her, before she became awake enough to recognize a ringing bell, a very loud bell like a fire alarm, though somewhat muffled. It came from somewhere lower in the house.

Two seconds after that realization, Merlin knocked on the door. Harsh and very loud.

"Susan! It's me. Get up and get dressed!"

He came through the door a moment later and rushed to the rear window overlooking the garden, raising a hand to shield his eyes as the back was suddenly flooded with harsh white light. The clangoring bell was louder with the door open.

Susan leaped from the bed and into her underwear without bothering to take off her giant Wombles T-shirt, almost levitating into bra and underpants, and then she hauled the boiler suit up over everything, tucking the T-shirt in.

"What's happening?"

"Perimeter alarms tripped in the rear, triggers the lights for the back, and a bell in Mrs. L's room," said Merlin, who was at the side of the window, tilting his head cautiously to look out. "Stay low, don't come closer."

Susan concentrated on lacing up her Docs.

"Shit!" cried Merlin. He ran from the window, back out through the door, to shout down the stairs.

"Greene! Don't shoot until they're well on the property! Don't—"

The *crack-crack-crack-crack* of four rapid shots interrupted him. Merlin came back and looked through the window again.

"Damn! Clever. Susan, get your sword and lock the door."

"What's happening?"

"Stalking horse. Two gunmen, tricked out in vests holding quicksilver. Greene's shed their blood on the boundary; blood and mercury will negate even those wards briefly and . . . I thought so . . . it is a Cauldron-Born. Lock your door!"

He exited, stripping off his glove, his left hand silver-bright.

Susan grabbed her saber, unsheathed it, and went over to lock the door, before returning to the window, her heart beating faster than it ever had before.

She copied Merlin and stayed to one side, leaning out cautiously to take a look. A man in a blue hospital gown flapping open at the back was walking slowly across the lawn, stark in the floodlights. He seemed like a lost drunk at first, someone concentrating too hard on walking steadily, till she noticed his head sat strangely on his neck, and then, with a terrible shock, that the shadow trailing behind was not human at all, instead a mass of smokelike, writhing tendrils that only connected to the man at his heels and did not mimic his upper body or movements at all.

Susan gasped as more shots rang out. Someone—Greene or Mrs. London—was shooting from the back door. She saw the rounds' impact, fragments of flesh and bone spraying out where they hit in head and chest, but there was no blood and the Cauldron-Born barely staggered, as if he'd encountered a gust of wind, no more.

Then Merlin was there, with his old sword. He ran past, incredibly swiftly, striking at the Cauldron-Born's knees. But it suddenly accelerated, leaping over the scything blade and twisting, almost managing to grab Merlin as he sped past and turned himself and then there was a sudden exchange of sword strokes and clawing hands, very fast. The sword hewed pieces from the Cauldron-Born but it was like striking chips from hard wood, and Susan gasped again as the Cauldron-Born almost managed to grab hold of Merlin's arm. She knew instinctively that once it had him in its grip, it would never let go.

Merlin backed off towards the garden shed. He was trying to draw the Cauldron-Born away from the house, Susan realized. But it was fixated on its task. The creature took one step after the bookseller, then suddenly spun about and ran for the back door, only to be met by Mrs. L wielding a two-handed sword, a crude Glaswegian gangster's copy of a claymore. She chopped diagonally at the Cauldron-Born's shoulder, but she didn't have a left-handed bookseller's speed. The Cauldron-Born ducked under the blow and punched her aside, flinging the woman into the vegetable garden, where she hit hard and lay still.

But Mrs. London had slowed it down, perhaps at the cost of her own life. Merlin came up behind, and spinning on the spot, struck a titanic two-handed blow at the thing's neck, where its head was already somewhat detached from whatever had killed the man originally. The blow decapitated the Cauldron-Born, the head flying off to strike the fence.

Even so, the headless body turned about and groped towards Merlin. Susan watched aghast as Merlin chopped and chopped and chopped at its legs and arms, switching sides and stepping back so it couldn't grab him. Over by the fence, the dismembered head thrust out its tongue and worked its jaw back and forth, trying uselessly to pull itself around so it could see, its eyes half-buried in garden soil.

A noise in the room made Susan whip around. A soft *tock*, like a single muffled drumbeat. She couldn't see anything in the dim light, but she heard another soft *tock*, quite close.

Something fell on her face. Her hand snapped to the place. She felt liquid, and looked up, her mind flashing through possibilities. It hadn't rained that much, the roof had never leaked before—

A large circular section of plaster and lathe from the ceiling suddenly crashed down near the door, plaster dust blowing up in a cloud. Blood, as Susan now knew it must be, gushed down from where it had been splashed to break the protective wards on the roof. It was followed a moment later by the body of a dead or dying man. Even in the dim light Susan saw his throat had been slashed from ear to ear. Mercury slowly ebbed from a kind of life vest he wore, which had also been slashed. Bright silver trails flowed ponderously through the faster-spreading blood.

Susan lifted her sword and readied herself, shouting with all the breath in her lungs and every muscle in her throat, "Merliiiiin! Merliiiiiiin!"

Goblins dropped through the hole, lots and lots of them, two or even three at a time, a torrent of goblins who landed on top of each other, rolled and jumped and giggled—but it was weirdly soft and distant giggling, as if smothered under pillows. They were physically like the Mayfair urchins, twisted children with pinched faces and red cheeks, but these were dressed only in leather aprons that flapped up as they fell and tumbled on the floor, showing their sticklike legs, which joined straight to their torso, without a bum, and they had no genitals. Like foreshortened, wizened Barbies or Action Jacksons, made rude flesh.

Susan cut at the first one, steeling herself for the impact, the spray of blood, the horror. But the blade passed through the goblin, leather apron and all, as if parting smoke. Meeting so little resistance, Susan was swung off balance, almost turning around herself.

In an instant, the goblins were on her, and their grasping hands had no difficulty gripping her flesh. Susan dropped the sword, the metal not old enough to touch these faery invaders, and lashed out with fists and boots.

"Help! Help! Goblins!"

The goblins hung on Susan's arms and legs, forcing her down. As soon as she was on the floor, they gagged her with her own pillow slip and wrapped her ankles and wrists with leather cords, immobilizing her, and then immediately lifted her up over their heads, as if in a weird parody of crowd surfing. More goblins jumped down through the hole and formed a pyramid, many goblins deep. Susan was transferred to them and they lifted her up and up, through the hole in the roof space. It was open to the sky now, the tiles above removed, a section of rafters broken. There was another dead man nearby, a young skinhead, only a teenager, his throat slashed, blood used to break the wards. An empty bottle of mercury lay next to him, the skull and crossbones of the laboratory warning label uppermost.

The goblins lifted Susan up onto the roof. She tried to arch her back to break free, to force a fall down into the roof space, but at least a dozen goblins held her, six on each side. They walked easily despite the slant of the roof, taking her over to the next town house in the row. Coils of cut concertina wire that had previously barred the way had sprung to either side.

Susan kept struggling and managed to work her mouth out of the gag, which had been tied on in a great hurry. But her mouth was dry and she had no breath. The goblins rushed on, swift and sure-footed, over the neighboring roof and onto the next, and the next, all the way to the rooftop of the house at the end of the row. There was a rope ladder there and they swarmed down it to the garden, Susan shutting her eyes as they carried her with them, thinking they would drop her for sure. But the goblins were immensely strong for their size, and dexterous. They gripped the rungs with their four-toothed jaws and one hand, while keeping Susan tightly gripped in the other hand, four of them in a line.

They laid her down in the middle of the garden and stepped back, before suddenly running off in all directions, like cockroaches frightened by a light.

For a moment, Susan thought Merlin must have come to the rescue, before she managed to roll over and look up to see the dark outline of a truly massive wolf. It was the size of a minibus, taking up most of the rear half of the garden. Its eyes, larger than the square's streetlights, were a dull red like the raked-down coals of a firepit. Its mouth was open and cavernous, its teeth forearm lengths of yellowed ivory, its tongue a writhing length of darkness.

"Merlin!" shrieked Susan, finding her breath. She wriggled away from the massive wolf like an inchworm, but it put one great paw on her and held her in place and bent its head down, huge jaws opening. Susan lifted her bound-together feet and kicked it at the point of the lower jaw. But the attack did not meet fur and flesh. It was more like jumping into cold water from a height, giving but shocking at the same time, and there was a sudden flare of pins and needles through her feet up into her calves.

The wolf lowered its head still more, jaws closing on Susan's middle, but it pressed down without closing, snout digging into the prize turf of the lawn, positioning its mouth so it could pick up Susan with the least dangerous part of its maw. Susan stopped wriggling as she saw what it was doing, and the wolf slowly worked its nose deep to get a safe grip on her. If it was going to eat her, she thought, it would simply gulp her up, careless of the damage.

Susan was right. The wolf worked its lower jaw under her, and slowly lifted her up, with her head and feet dangling outside its mouth. Again, it didn't feel like she was in the mouth of a living creature. While she was held securely, it felt very strange, as if the wolf's teeth weren't always entirely there or completely present in the real world. Susan had the unpleasant sensation of floating on something like oil, far more buoyant than water, with enough pressure that she could not get free.

She lay still as the wolf slowly angled its head, making her slide a bit farther back to be securely settled directly behind its great canines.

"Susan!"

It was Merlin's voice. From the sound of it he was on the roof of the house. Susan turned her head and shouted, but the wolf was already moving, spinning about. It tensed to leap, there was a kind of meaty thud, the wolf gave a shuddering whimper that Susan felt as much as heard, then it jumped and it was Susan's turn to cry out as the landing jarred her, despite the weird cushioning effect of the wolf's otherworldly jaws.

The jump took them to Waterloo Terrace, fifty or sixty yards away. The wolf accelerated immediately into a swift lope, but it held its head as still as possible so Susan was not hurt. She saw streetlights rushing past and could not guess at their speed, but it felt fast. They overtook a car and then another as the wolf turned north onto Upper Street.

There was a long line of cars and trucks there, but the wolf ignored the steady line of traffic, moving around each slower vehicle, using both sides of the road and even jumping over cars when necessary. The drivers did not see the creature, or react to its presence. There was no swerving or emergency braking. Susan shut her eyes at some of the overtaking procedures, when the wolf almost miscalculated an oncoming vehicle's speed. Even if the humans couldn't see the monster, it was avoiding possible collisions, which was some relief to Susan. It might survive a head-on at speed. She knew she wouldn't.

The wolf didn't stop for red lights. It ran so fast, and the angle she was held at was so confusing with buildings and lights flashing by, that it was impossible for Susan to work out where they were going, until they took the sharp turn at Highbury Corner and she got her bearings.

The wolf was taking the A1, going up Holloway Road. Back towards Highgate and Frank Thringley's manor, thought Susan. Back to where everything had begun.

Susan slowly moved her wrists to try to find a sharp piece of tooth to saw the cord against, but there was nothing like that. She could see the giant teeth very clearly, she knew she was held between them, but when she moved her bound hands against the surface of the tooth under her, she felt only the weird soft resistance. Her hands sank in a little and then rose back, and all she got was pins and needles for her effort.

Susan stopped the sawing motion and tried to angle her head to get a better view of where they were going. At first it was all nondescript London street and traffic, but then she saw the great arched viaduct of Archway Road, confirming her guess about their destination, only to be confounded a little later when the wolf did *not* turn onto Muswell Hill Road, but kept on up the A1.

And on, and on, towards the M1.

Northwards, always north.

Merlin swore as the Fenris jumped away with Susan in its mighty jaws. His sword was deeply embedded in the wolf's left haunch, but he'd aimed for the back of the creature's head. The wound would slow it down, but there was no sign of that happening quickly, and the weapon had embedded itself so deeply it had also sealed the wound, so there would be no obvious blood trail to follow.

Obvious to one of the right-handed, Merlin hoped, since he didn't know himself how to track the spilled ichor of a mythic being who both did and didn't exist in the contemporary world at the same time.

He ran back across the roofs and dropped through the hole into the roof space. The dead man there was a skinhead, safety pins in his ear, chains down his trousers. Probably a local who had no idea he was being set up to be a sacrifice to get the goblins past the roof wards. The hard men who died in the back garden, shot by Inspector Greene, probably hadn't known, either. Though they must have wondered why they had to wear the strange tubed vests that had been filled with mercury. Merlin wondered about that, whether Greene really didn't know not to shed blood on the wards, or whether she was part of a conspiracy he was fairly sure was at work. Though perhaps whoever had planned this had been prepared to shoot them from behind anyway, in order to spill both quicksilver and blood, and Greene had beaten them to it.

He lowered himself into Susan's room, noted the dead man also wore a mercury-filled vest. He was middle-aged, had a holster for a pair of heavy wire cutters on his belt and rings tattooed around his fingers, indicating he was a sworn follower of a malevolent entity. One of those termed "Death Cultists" by the St. Jacques. This one would have known what the vest was for, and had offered himself as a willing sacrifice. He'd probably killed the skinhead on the roof before going on to his own purposeful death.

The alarm bells were loud in the hallway, and Merlin could hear multiple sirens approaching.

He ran down the stairs and found Greene on the phone and her radio at the same time, alternatively barking orders into one and listening to the other. She looked at Merlin.

"Bookshops been notified?" asked Merlin.

"Yes," snapped Greene. "First thing. Your response teams are en route."

"I'm going to pack up the Cauldron-Born," said Merlin.

"What—"

Merlin was already gone. The bookseller went into the kitchen and threw open cupboard doors until he found the saucepans. Taking out a giant soup pot, with its lid, he went out into the garden.

Greene had sat Mrs. London up with her back against the rear wall of the house, her pistol in her lap. She had no obvious wounds, but blood trickled from the corner of her mouth, and she was very pale.

She was conscious.

"Ribs busted, into my lungs, too . . . probably everything else inside," she gasped as Merlin looked at her.

"Ambulance is on the way," said Merlin. He hesitated. "Did you ever brief Greene on the wards? And what fresh-spilled blood would do, with mercury?"

"No," she gasped. "Thought she knew. Always a problem . . . in this job . . . no one knows what anyone . . . already knows . . . or is meant to know."

"That's true," said Merlin with a sigh. "Um, is there anything I can—"

Sipper saliva could not be applied to internal wounds, unfortunately. And the right-handed had healing powers.

But he was not right-handed.

"One short sleep past, we wake eternally . . ." she whispered, and shut her eyes.

Merlin left her and walked across the lawn to where various

pieces of the Cauldron-Born were wriggling and writhing, trying to reach each other and piece themselves back together. But Merlin had chopped it up into a great many small parts and stomped them into the damp grass, so they hadn't gotten far.

The head he'd left intact, because he knew the right-handed would want to talk to it. It was still in the vegetable garden, but had managed to pull itself some distance through the earth using its chin. Merlin bent down and scooped it into the pot and held the lid down as the head used chin and tongue to bang itself against the stainless steel sides. He carried the pot back towards the house, treading down the pieces on the lawn again in a strange, capering dance.

Near the door, he noticed Mrs. London was no longer breathing and her head had lolled to the side. A great deal more foamy, bright blood was dribbling from her mouth.

"And death shall be no more; Death, thou shalt die," he whispered. He set the pot down and sat on it, leaning forward to gently close Mrs. London's eyes with his luminous silver hand.

CHAPTER FOURTEEN

⊱┈◇┈◯┈◇┈⊰

In the spring green shoots
Small signs of renewed triumph
Death's grip is broken

⊱┈◇┈◯┈◇┈⊰

VIVIEN ARRIVED AT THE MILNER SQUARE HOUSE FIVE MINUTES AFTER the response teams from both bookshops and, it seemed, every possible other emergency vehicle. The entire length of the square in front of the safe house was jammed with two police Rovers, a police armored Land Rover, a police van, two police motorbikes, two ambulances, a paramedic motorbike, and two fire engines, one a ladder truck, its turntable ladder being extended to the rooftop of the third town house in the row along from Mrs. London's. There were uniformed police officers outside almost every house, sending people back inside, who kept ducking out to see what on earth was going on. The short stretch of cross street on the northern end of the square's garden was blocked by two of the bookshops' taxis and a dozen motorbikes from the Old Bookshop response team.

Vivien was in the third taxi, driven by Audrey, who said, "Lord love a duck" and parked up on the curb at the southern corner of the garden. Vivien was out of the cab even before Audrey had turned the engine off.

Two edgy armed police officers in the street outside the safe house raised their H & K MP5s but lowered them as Vivien held up her warrant card, and they let her proceed to the unarmed constable by the front door, who was recording names of personnel as they arrived. He looked at her card for a few seconds, made a face, and waved her in without writing anything down.

As she went up the front steps, a group of paramedics came out with a body on a stretcher and she had to stand aside. A green blanket was pulled over his or her face, but Vivien noticed the shoes, and stopped, shocked into stillness.

Mrs. London's sensible square-toed shoes, from some nursing supplier that had somehow survived into the twentieth century. Florence Nightingale shoes.

"Goodbye, Mrs. L," whispered Vivien, and went inside.

Greene was on the hall phone, standing almost at attention and listening to someone who liked the sound of their own voice. Vivien—who, as with all the right-handed, had extraordinarily acute hearing—could make out most of it, particularly as the one word *deniability* was vehemently repeated. The inspector cupped her hand over the receiver and said, "Merlin's out back."

Vivien rushed past. Merlin, his left hand in a paisley oven mitt rather than a glove, was standing on the floodlit back lawn, talking earnestly to Una, who for once was listening intently.

The younger bookseller had his foot on a cooking pot, which was rattling and thudding. The other left-handed members of the response team were picking up . . . wriggling bits of meat . . . from the lawn and garden, using forks and barbecue tongs and dropping them into half a dozen smaller saucepans, sorting them in some fashion because they didn't drop them into the closest pot. Three of the right-handed booksellers from the New Bookshop response team were taking notes and making drawings of the pieces, while another two were on their knees, inspecting the wards at the back of the garden.

There were two bodies near them, right on the boundary, men in workmen's overalls with pig-face plastic masks, sprawled in pools of drying blood and ever-lambent mercury. One still held a sawn-off shotgun, the other lay sprawled near a Sterling submachine gun. Three SOCOs—scene-of-crime forensic officers—in their blue nylon suits and slippers were standin.g together in the far corner, waiting their turn and pointedly not looking at what the various booksellers were doing. They had all donned elbow-length gloves and were fingering their gas masks nervously.

Vivien could hear the SOCOs whispering something about MI5, biological and chemical weapons, and Porton Down and distrusting the assurance they were safe, but she paid them no attention.

"Cauldron-Born," said Vivien quietly behind Merlin, working it out. "Different pots for different bits so it can't put itself back together, right? And I guess the head's in that pot."

Merlin turned. He looked terrible.

"Vivien. They've got Susan."

"What? Who?"

"This was all to kidnap her. Men killed here and on the roof, fresh blood and mercury to break the wards. Then they came in through the ceiling of Susan's room. Islington goblins, you know, the leather apron crew. They took her to a garden a few doors down and a Fenris carried her away. I threw my sword at it—hit it—but from the way it jumped it can't have been badly wounded."

"A Fenris? Which one?"

"I don't know!"

"There are only seven in England," said Vivien. "Did you see any distinguishing features? Silver hairs along the snout? Extra toes? The wider tail?"

"No, no, it was dark and it was a huge bloody wolf, so I didn't take the time to check its identity!" said Merlin. "I was on the roof, it was preparing to jump, I threw my sword like a spear and you know how hard that is. I missed the head, got it in the haunch. I thought that might stop it for a second, it was deep, but the sword stayed in the wound and it took off."

"The sword? *That* sword! You've lost it as well?"

"I haven't lost it, it's stuck in a Fenris heading north," said Merlin. "And as soon as I'm finished here I'm going to find the wolf, Susan, and the sword."

"You are finished here," said Una. "But you can't simply hare off north. The Greats will want to see you as soon as possible.

Merrihew's even cadged a helicopter ride from Hereford *at night* and you know she hates that."

"The Greats can wait," said Merlin. "I'll phone from somewhere along the road."

"How are you going to find out where the Fenris has taken Susan?" asked Vivien. "And what if the sword falls out along the way?"

"I'm not worried about the sword!" said Merlin tensely. "It will find its way back to the Grail-Keeper if necessary; it always does, doesn't it? It's Susan I'm worried about. Who would—or could—go to all this trouble to kidnap her, and why? Four . . . five . . . mortals dead, the Islington goblins scared enough to take Susan even though they know they'll be on our shit list for years, one of the seven sacred wolves of England forced to become a kidnapper. . . ."

"Yes," said Vivien. She hesitated. "It may be her own father, of course."

"What?" asked Una.

"Need to know," said Merlin hurriedly, with a swift look at Vivien.

"Yeah, well, I think I do need to know," said Una dangerously. She pointed at the jiggling pot Merlin had his foot on. "A *Cauldron-Born*, attacking a safe house we maintain with the Metropolitan Police? I'm the senior left-handed here. Tell."

"It's because there was a Cauldron-Born I want to keep this information very close," said Merlin.

"What?"

Merlin took a deep breath.

"Who has a cauldron?" he asked, very softly, so Una had to lean in. "And who goes to Silvermere most often?"

"The Greats . . ." Una started to say, then stopped. "You don't seriously think . . ."

"I don't know," replied Merlin uncomfortably. "But I want to focus on getting Susan back with as few people as possible knowing that's what we're doing, okay?"

Una was silent for a long three seconds.

"We have told Aunt Helen and Zoë," said Vivien. "They don't think Merlin's suspicions are well founded, but they're going to consult the Grail-Keeper, whether Thurston and Merrihew do or not."

Una nodded slowly. She looked at Merlin, very intently.

"Vivien's going with you?"

"Of course," said Vivien swiftly.

"You'll telephone from the road, at least once every two hours," said Una. It wasn't a question.

"Yes," said Merlin.

Una raised her left hand and fluttered her fingers.

"Get going, then," she said. "Be clever."

Merlin lifted his foot, spun about, and stalked away. The pot rattled vigorously, Una put her foot on it, and when she looked up Merlin and Vivien had gone inside the house.

The older bookseller took a deep breath and looked over to one of her compatriots.

"Darren, give me your belt."

"Why?"

"To tie around this bloody saucepan."

"But my pants will fall down. You've got a belt."

"Yeah, but I don't want *my* pants to fall down. Oh, don't make that face. Go and see if you can scrounge up some string or rope. Or some warning tape. The coppers will have tape. Get that."

Merlin and Vivien hurried upstairs. Merlin picked up his glove and swapped it with the oven mitt, repacked his yak-hair bag with the Smython and other items, and got his suitcase, while Vivien looked at the hole in the ceiling. The two SOCOs—a man and a woman—who'd been looking at the body that had come down the hole turned their backs, and whispered to each other. One of them thought Vivien was cute and he didn't even mind when the woman warned him off, describing the right-handed bookseller as "one of those *really* weird spooks."

On the way back out, they first had to skirt Mister Nimbus, who was crouched in the hall, his fur up all along his back. He was watching the door with narrowed eyes where Mrs. London's body had been carried out, and now Chief Superintendent Holly was trying to come in, with Inspector Greene intent on keeping him out.

Though it seemed unlikely he'd been out running at three o'clock in the morning, the superintendent was currently wearing runners and a dark blue tracksuit with a caricature of Bruce Lee on the left breast over the inscription "Enter the Copper," and he had a black towel around his neck. He looked younger, less bulky, and more efficient than he had earlier, in his three-piece suit.

"You shouldn't be here, sir," said Greene, very firmly. "You know the procedure. No senior officers to be identifiably present at a LIBER MERCATOR SPECIAL incident. We've got a cordon around the square but there might be someone with a telephoto lens gets a photo, or one of the householders chances a snap to sell to the papers. You're well known. You need to leave at once."

"I'll be off once I have a bit of a shufti around the place," said Holly. "You've got some bodies, right? Tooled-up local lads? I can probably identify them, straight off, save a lot of time."

"No, sir," replied Greene. "I spoke to the deputy commissioner minutes ago. She has confirmed I have operational control. You must leave at once or I will have you removed."

Greene looked past Holly to the two officers outside the door, whose steely expressions wilted slightly at the prospect of having to manhandle a senior officer.

"You need to leave, sir," repeated Greene.

Holly chuckled and held up his hands. His tracksuit sleeve slid back enough to reveal part of the chunky silver watchband Merlin had noticed before, at least subconsciously.

"Okay, okay, you're right. But as soon as you know who the dead intruders are, I want it called through. I need to find out what is causing the current gang fracas, and the sooner the—"

He caught sight of Merlin and Vivien, swiftly lowered his arms, and lumbered out the door, muttering "better."

Greene watched him go.

"He's up to something," she said very quietly to Merlin and Vivien, her voice hard to hear with the background noise of people talking, radios squelching, the engines of the vehicles running in the street, and there was now even a helicopter clattering in slow rotation overhead. "I don't know what."

"He's definitely more current in our business than I would have expected," said Vivien, as quietly. She glanced at Merlin. "You see his watchband? Some sort of charm. I don't know what for, though. Or where it's from."

"I noticed the watchband," said Merlin. "I didn't know what it was. It caught my attention, somehow."

"Maybe he got it from us when he had your job," said Vivien to Greene. "Probably some sort of defensive charm. He wasn't in the job for long, though. Nineteen fifty-nine to sixty-four, and then he went to CID for a year as a DCI, moving over to gangs as a superintendent in 1965, promoted to chief 1979."

"You looked him up," said Greene. "Is there something else I need to know? I mean on top of absolutely everything else I don't know?"

"Merlin thought he was suspicious," said Vivien. "That's all. And it's unusual for someone who's not active in our neck of the woods to wear a charm. Why's he so curious now?"

"I don't know," muttered Greene. "He's never interfered before. Like I said, he's known to be the laziest chief super in the Met. It's the last thing I need. He's a very senior officer, connected across the board. At least he's retiring soon."

"He said he had Merrihew's permission to stick his nose in," said Merlin. "That must be true. Too easy to check. But why would Merrihew okay him interfering?"

No one answered him, but Vivien gave him a long-suffering look.

"Yeah, probably couldn't be bothered saying no," said Merlin. "Gone fishing, and the old carp rising . . ."

"What did you say that monster you had to cut up is called?" asked Greene.

"I didn't," replied Merlin. "A Cauldron-Born."

"Are . . . are there are any more like that around?"

"I sincerely hope not," said Merlin. "But it is now entirely possible."

"I suppose we could pick up a job lot of machetes from an army surplus store or something. . . ."

"You'd do better to borrow swords and poleaxes from the Royal Armouries; they've got plenty at the Tower," said Vivien. "Old steel is best."

Greene looked at her. "You're not joking."

"No. I'd start getting that organized now if I were you."

Greene groaned and made a face. "And you still say you don't know what's going on?"

"We *really* don't know what's going on," said Vivien.

"But it does all seems to hinge on Susan," added Merlin.

"Who's been eaten by a giant wolf," said Greene. "Yeah, I went after you, Merlin, only slower because I'm not bloody half elven or whatever. I saw what happened from the window of her room. I should have *insisted* she go home immediately after we picked her up—"

"She hasn't been eaten," interrupted Merlin. "The Fenris took her somewhere, and made a great effort not to hurt her, so I'm presuming that means whoever wants her, wants her alive and unhurt. We are going to find out where she is and rescue her. Half elven, hey? I didn't take you for a Tolkien fan. Or much of a reader at all, to be honest. All action, no reflection. No offense."

"I have to visit your bookshops often enough," said Greene. "I read. And you know 'no offense' means 'I am about to be or have just been fucking offensive.'"

"Yeah. Sorry."

"I think I like C. S. Lewis a bit more than Tolkien," said Greene. "The White Witch reminds me of some people in the Met. Good luck finding Susan. And as soon as you can tell me something . . . tell me. Okay?"

She turned back to the phone, where a different very superior voice from the earlier one had started ranting, asking her what was happening and could they plausibly blame everything on the IRA?

Merlin and Vivien slid outside, past the recording officer and the armed police. There was no sign of Chief Superintendent Holly, though the taillights of a receding Jaguar Series III XJ probably marked his departure out the northern end of the square, since it was let through the police cordon. It was still very noisy, with idling vehicles, the helicopter circling low overhead, the neighbors being constantly told to go back inside, and other bystanders trying to come into the square being turned back from barricaded checkpoints set up at the north and south entrances, and also across Almeida Passage, the almost hidden pedestrian lane in the corner.

Audrey was waiting by her cab, watching the sky and smoking. She ashed her cigarette as they approached, her face somber. She could tell from their expressions whatever had happened was not good.

"We need your cab, Audrey," said Merlin.

"Sure. Back to the New Bookshop?" asked Audrey.

"No, I mean we need to take it farther afield, out of London," said Merlin. "Though you *can* drive us, if you like."

"Whoa! Hang on," said Audrey. "What's going on?"

"They were attacked here by a Cauldron-Born, with Islington goblins, and a Fenris has taken Susan," said Vivien. "We need to follow it. North."

"What!" exclaimed Audrey, spitting out her cigarette stub. "Have you called Thurston? What did Una say?"

"We haven't called Thurston. Una said go," said Merlin. "Look, something's a bit rotten in the state of Denmark. We don't know who is involved. But we do need to get Susan back, and that means going after the wolf without anyone else knowing we are."

"Something rotten . . . but you can't mean—"

"Maybe not rotten, maybe torpid, you know what we mean," soothed Vivien. "We aim to get Susan back and then reconvene. But we don't want to tell Thurston or anyone at the bookshops because there is definitely a leak somewhere. Intentionally or not."

"So why are you telling me?"

"Because we trust you. Now can we have your cab?"

"Una said okay? And you're both going?"

Vivien nodded as Merlin grimaced.

"What is this? Does no one trust me on my own?"

"Not really," said Audrey. "Bloody hell, Merrihew will probably kill me. . . ."

She hesitated for a few seconds, then swore quietly to herself.

"Go on then, keys are in the ignition. You know how to use the two-way?"

"Yes," said Merlin and "No," said Vivien.

"Control won't be able to receive once you're past the M25 or thereabouts," said Audrey. "Uh, I guess if you're going incognito, as it were, I'd better call in now? Tell Uncle Desmond I'll be here for the foreseeable?"

"Good idea," said Merlin. He was softly clicking the fingers of his right hand, which Vivien knew was a sure tell for impatience and anxiety.

Audrey opened the door and leaned in. They heard the click and buzz of the two-way radio handset, Audrey's "Come in, Control" and Uncle Desmond's casual "Yeah, wot?" and Audrey's "This is three, Des, going to be a while here, I reckon. I'm going to lock up Nelly and go find myself a cuppa somewhere."

Audrey leaned back out as Desmond's voice crackled out an uninterested acknowledgment.

"Reckon I might as well do what I said," she told them. "Be careful, yeah?"

Merlin and Vivien nodded. Merlin quickly put his suitcase

in the back, threw his ballistic vest and the empty sword scabbard on top of the suitcase, and climbed into the driver's seat, putting his yak-hair bag down next to him for easy access to his revolver. Vivien got in the back and sat in the middle, to make it easier to talk through the hatch in the partition.

Audrey pretended to do a double take at Merlin taking the driver's seat, but didn't put much effort into it before wandering towards Almeida Passage, lighting up a cigarette again as she walked away

"So have you got a plan?" Vivien asked Merlin, leaning forward to talk through the partition. "Like how we are actually going to find Susan?"

"No, apart from presuming you have one," replied Merlin. "You do, don't you? I saw it on your face when I was talking to Una."

He took advantage of the cab's incredible turning circle to do a U-turn across the mouth of the square, narrowly missing yet another police Rover 3500 that was accelerating through the twenty yards from the barricade as if they were first on the scene and seconds mattered. "I guess that is my plan, come to think of it. For you to have a plan. So come on."

"The sword was firmly stuck in the wounded Fenris?"

"Yes."

"So wherever the sword is, the Fenris will also be there, and—at least until she's delivered or collected—Susan."

"Yes."

"So find the sword, find the wolf, find Susan. And cold

iron—and that sword in particular—will slow the wolf, so we'll have a better chance of catching up."

"Yes . . . but . . . how do we find the sword?"

Vivien held up the scabbard so Merlin could see it in his rearview mirror. He started and swerved slightly, alarming the police officers at the barricade, who moved it out of the way a lot faster. Merlin waved at them guiltily.

"Of course. I forgot. Um, how does it work again?"

"Did you ever know?"

"Uh, no, actually," replied Merlin, swinging the cab into Theberton Street.

Vivien laid the scabbard across her knees and took off her glove. Her right hand was bright in the dim cabin, but she covered it with her left, resting them both on the scabbard. Very slowly, she inhaled for a good twenty seconds, held her breath for at least a minute, then exhaled as slowly.

"The sword is moving swiftly; it must still be in the wolf," she said. She thought for a moment. "But not as swiftly as it might; the iron must already be affecting the Fenris. It's about thirty miles nor'-nor'-west now. Take the A1 and pass Audrey's road atlas back here. Not the A–Z, I saw a proper whole of Britain one—yes, that's it."

"What do we do once we retrieve Susan? If we can?" asked Merlin.

"I don't know," replied Vivien. "I don't know. . . ."

CHAPTER FIFTEEN

O! Wolf of ravening jaw and fix'd eye
Stay thy slaughter, if thou will
I never wish'd thee any ill
No! Never hop'd that thou wouldst die
Come! Good Canis, by my hearth lie

THE WOLF'S LOPE GREW EASIER AS THEY REACHED THE M1 AND IT USED the hard shoulder, streaking past the traffic on the inside, which meant it was running at a speed of at least eighty miles per hour. Susan slowly moved her wrists and feet backwards and forwards, hoping to loosen the bonds, since there was nothing to abrade the cords against. The wolf didn't appear to notice, but as far as she could tell the movement had no effect on the cords.

She felt curiously calm about the fact she was held in a giant wolf's maw and was being taken at high speed to some unknown destination. It was probably shock, she thought, though she didn't think she'd been seriously hurt when the wolf first picked her up. Her back and shoulders were sore, and her neck and arms and legs ached, but not unbearably. She was a bit worried her circulation had been cut off, though she wasn't tied as tightly as she'd first feared.

She had no idea how long it had been since the wolf had taken her up. Everything had happened so quickly at first, and now it was all so strange. She thought more than an hour, but then again, perhaps it was much longer?

"Plan ahead," Susan whispered to herself. She'd had a stranger danger lecture at school more than once, but as that emphasized screaming and running away if someone tried to make you get in a car, it wasn't a lot of help. She couldn't remember any advice for when you were actually kidnapped. Stay calm, perhaps? That was the generic advice for everything at her school. Stay calm.

She was calm. Too calm. And the only thing she could think of doing was to keep slowly working her bonds, undoubtedly removing more skin than anything else. But if she could loosen them enough to get free, then she could do something when . . . if . . . the wolf spat her out or let her go. She'd have to be quick, because she was sure there would be someone waiting for her at the other end.

The wolf had been sent by someone, as the goblins had been, and the men who had been killed in order to break the wards. Someone from the Old World who could also command the criminal underworld of the New.

Susan thought about that. Wards that could be bypassed by spilling human blood on them didn't seem very useful. But from what Merlin and Vivien had said, the Old World and the New didn't have much contact as a rule, so killing mortals to break wards must be a very unusual occurrence.

"Oh my god!" she exclaimed, reflexively lifting her head

and tensing her body, enough to make the wolf tighten its jaws. "There must have been someone or something else there to kill those people! Merlin said goblins wouldn't kill."

The wolf growled, as if in answer, or to tell her to shut up. Susan obeyed, and tried to work out where they were. Blinded by the motorway lights and the onrush of air, it was hard for her to see the road signs, but every now and then she got a good glimpse. She was still on the M1, still speeding northwards.

After a while Susan shut her eyes, because the rush of wind was making them water and the overhead lights were too bright and too annoying. Soon, she fell into something that was not quite sleep, a kind of daze that was probably also shock.

Susan snapped into full consciousness when the wolf stumbled and almost fell, and its mouth closed on her, hard, its teeth suddenly feeling much more present and firm. She cried out and struggled for a moment, before the wolf's jaws eased open and the teeth became fuzzy and less solid again, enough to let her draw breath.

It was still night, but dawn was drawing near. There was more traffic, but mostly going the other way. The wolf was passing what little there was on their side, heading up a long hill. Susan spotted a road sign, but as all this said was "Junction 22, 3 Miles" this didn't help her, as she had never taken the M1 and had no idea where the major junctions were located.

But reading the sign had been easier than before, because the wolf was slower on the incline. Soon it became clear to Susan that it was having difficulties. For the first time, she realized it wasn't breathing, that it didn't breathe at all. There should have been a rush of air backwards and forwards over her; any wolf or dog would be panting under the current exertion. But there was no movement of breath at all.

Nor was there any saliva, Susan thought a moment later, which was a relief. But it was also disturbing. Her captor had the shape of a giant wolf, but what was it really?

The creature slowed more, and growled, this time in exasperation. It turned its head from side to side, looking back along itself. Susan craned her neck to try and see, and when it turned again, she saw what was troubling it.

Merlin's sword, the old sword, was sticking out of the wolf's left haunch, and there was a long trail of thick golden blood running from it all the way down the wolf's leg, as slow and viscous as honey.

That must have been the cause of the meaty sound she'd heard, and the wolf's yelp, thought Susan. Though it hadn't had any effect at first, it was obviously hurting the wolf now, and slowing it down. Things immediately looked rather less desperate, though Susan knew everything would depend on the timing. A rescue would need to happen before the wolf got wherever it was going and delivered her to whoever had ordered this kidnapping.

If the wolf got where it was going . . .

It started off again, but it was limping badly now, dragging that left rear leg. It didn't continue up the hill along the hard shoulder of the motorway, but left it altogether, stepping over a low fence to head across a field of early harvested clover, the bales of hay dotted about the stubble. From the field, the wolf took a narrow lane, moving quite slowly and cautiously now, still wary of a head-on collision. Once it had to jump aside to avoid a Land Rover, and after that, while it still followed the lane basically westward, the wolf tried to move in the fields on either side.

There were no more big road signs for Susan to see, and it was still too dark to read the old white signposts with the local road names even at the slower pace. Besides, she doubted they would mean anything to her anyway. She was puzzled by the wolf's sudden change of direction, because it had been so fixed on heading north. The departure from the M1 appeared to be sudden and unplanned.

In fact, the wolf seemed as lost as Susan, or at least was finding its way. It stopped at every small crossroads and nosed the air and the ground, an uncomfortable process for Susan, who was jostled around every time.

After a while, she became aware the sky was getting lighter; the sun was coming up. The light offered small comfort. She ached all over, and her bonds felt no looser, despite all her efforts.

The wolf left the road again, this time taking a bridle path into a wood, some sort of ancient forest, though Susan hadn't caught the actual name on the sign at the beginning of the path. Though the wolf was so large it had to squeeze itself between trees, bending branches back and shaking leaves like anything, curiously none of the branches actually broke and no leaves fell, so there was little sign of its passing.

It was still limping, but moved with greater surety, as if it had finally found what it was looking for.

The bridle path turned to leave the edge of the forest to climb up to the crest of a small, bare hill, but the wolf left the path to descend deeper into the ancient wood. The trees grew thicker here, so close Susan could have sworn there was no way for the wolf to pass, but it made it through, squeezing between oak and beech and birch. It was careful not to knock Susan against the trees, though it didn't seem to matter for itself.

Eventually, the forest thinned out again, the slope becoming less and less steep until they reached a flat area and the wolf emerged into a dell, a natural clearing at the heart of the wood. There was a small pool in the middle, about twenty feet in diameter, entirely ringed by low, mossy stones. A well, of sorts. Bluebells grew around it in profusion, and on some other day, arriving by some other way, Susan would have found it tranquil and beautiful.

The wolf bent its head and gently lowered Susan down next to the well, though she still felt the impact. It then drank briefly, backed up a few paces, and lay down, turning its head to lick the area around the sword, while being careful to not actually touch the weapon.

Susan wriggled and rolled a bit farther away to a softer patch of ground and tested the cord around her wrists. She felt part of it give way, possibly enough to squeeze one hand free, but the wolf also stopped licking its wound and looked at her. Susan lay still, and waited until it went back to its business before trying the cord again, this time more surreptitiously.

A male blackbird started a hopeful warble from a tree nearby, but there were no human noises. The ancient wood was as it had been for centuries, unspoiled by people, those who had lined the natural spring with stones long since vanished, and the way to it forgotten by all but the creatures of the Old World. There were people living within three miles of the wood, but no footpath or trail came near the dell, and even those who had walked in the forest all their lives would be astounded to hear of the existence of the well in the dell.

Susan was trying to ease her left hand up and out of the binding cord when the waters of the well began to froth and bubble. She heard it first, and had to roll on her side to see what was happening.

The waters of the spring were flowing over the rocks that lined the edges, and the surface was beaten to a froth, as if a fierce wind were blowing across the well. But there was no wind, the dell was as placid as ever, the surrounding trees quiet, leaves undisturbed. Sunshine was creeping in from the rising sun, banishing shadow. It looked like it was going to be a beautiful day, at least as far as the weather was concerned.

A hand of transparent, swirling water reached out from the well and gripped a stone, narrow fingers flexing, long nails of white froth digging deep. This was followed by another hand, there was a moment of scrabbling for a grip, and a woman of water emerged to stand at the edge of the well. She was near transparent, clear water swirling and eddying from toes to head. But her eyes were black and rusty like the spots on a brown trout, her mouth was two lines of green pondweed, and her hair looked like a wig, a mass of blue-green rushes that sat unsteadily atop all the swirling water.

Susan lay quiet, and looked from the water woman to the wolf. The latter whined pleadingly and lowered its head in submission.

"What brings the Fenris of Onundar Myrr to my well, with so strange a burden?" asked the woman, glancing at Susan. Her voice was ageless, soft and liquid, but somehow distant, as if it came from all around, not from her pondweed lips, which hardly moved at all. A minnow slid from her mouth as she spoke. She caught it on her palm, the fish splashing into her hand to swim away up the inside of her arm.

The wolf whined again.

The water woman left the well and traipsed across the turf, leaving not so much muddy footprints as a muddy swath behind her. She walked the length of the wolf, who lay with its snout down in abject misery, and ran one watery hand through the fur along its flank. She came to where the sword projected above the crusted trail of blood, and stopped.

"Sa! Sa! This is star-iron and not to be touched by such as you or I, Fenris. The sword must be withdrawn . . . yet I cannot do it."

The water woman looked back at Susan as she spoke. Though her face was transparent liquid, and only her eyes and lips had color, Susan thought she saw an expression there. A hint of a lifted eyebrow, though the woman had no eyebrows.

"I'll take it out," said Susan. "If you free me."

The wolf growled, but subsided as the woman touched one watery finger to its enormous snout.

"The Fenris will want to take you up again," warned the woman.

"I will have the sword, then," said Susan, though privately she thought this wouldn't count for much against a monster who must weigh twenty tons. "And it is wounded and weak."

The wolf growled again, and showed its teeth.

"She," corrected the woman. "This Fenris is a she-wolf. If the sword is left in the wound, she will . . . in your terms . . . die."

"I said I'll take it out. If you untie me."

"For a mortal you are remarkably unperturbed by my presence," said the woman. "Or that of the Fenris. Most mortals I have met are greatly frightened, and run screaming, or collapse and gibber."

"I'm . . . I'm only half mortal," said Susan. It felt very strange to say that, but she instinctively felt she should not show weakness. A slight tinge of memory made her add, "Besides, I've met someone like you before, I think. From the brook at home . . . funny, I always forget, and then I remember, and then I think it was a dream. . . ."

"Half mortal?" asked the woman. "You appear entirely mortal to me. . . ."

She drifted closer, never moving in a straight line, and knelt by Susan's side. Reaching out with one careful fingertip, she touched Susan's forehead, leaving a faint wet patch on her skin. "Ah. Some little magic of your own, over animals and suchlike. But the promise of far more to come, perhaps, from your mighty father. But not yet, not yet, Susan."

"You know my name! And my father? Who is he?"

"A being older and far greater than I," said the woman, not answering Susan's question. She looked back at the Fenris. "I know your name as I know the names of all living things about my well. Come, the she-wolf is aware I must offer aid to those who seek it at my spring, and you have the means to help me give it."

She leaned down again, and Susan shrieked as an eel suddenly erupted out of the woman's hand, its sharp teeth flashing as it bit through the cord around Susan's wrists and then her ankles, before twisting back inside the woman again, to vanish into the apparently empty crystal waters of her body.

"Ugh," said Susan, with a shudder. She tried to get up, but her legs were cramped and so stiff she had to crouch on all fours, sobbing with the pain.

The woman reached for her again, and Susan flinched. But no eels emerged from her hands, which she ran lightly over Susan, not quite touching. A faint mist fell from her fingers to speckle on boiler suit and skin. With the mist, Susan felt a cool touch, not cold like ice, more like a mother's hand on a fevered brow. Her legs unknotted, her back stopped aching, her hands moved without pain.

Susan stood up, and instinctively bowed.

"Thank you, um," she said. "What . . . who . . . what should I call you?"

"Long ago mortals called my waters Morcenna's Well," said the woman, bowing back. "Morcenna is as good a name as any. Will you remove the sword now? The star-iron is in the she-wolf's blood; every passing moment poisons her more."

"Yes," said Susan. She walked to stand in front of the wolf, quailing inside at the immensity of the monster, and particularly those jaws, those teeth. She hadn't seen the she-wolf clearly before, in the dark of the Milner Square back garden.

She addressed the wolf directly, speaking loud and clear.

"If I take out the sword, will you let me be?"

The wolf slowly shook her head. Her eyes were growing dull, and there was a yellow cast about her gums, and froth upon her tongue.

"She must obey the one who bound her to their will," said Morcenna behind her. "Will you take the sword or not?"

Susan nodded, not trusting herself to speak. She swallowed, and walked along the side of the wolf, trying to think. The sword was deeply embedded. It would be hard to pull out. But if she immediately ran for the tree line . . . she looked over at the thickest area, where the oaks gathered close. If she could get in there, the wolf might find it hard to winkle her out, she could hack at its nose . . . though it seemed to have no problem passing through dense woodland—

"Every moment the sword poisons her," said Morcenna.

Susan took a deep breath, grabbed the sword with both hands, and pulled as hard as she could. But there was no resistance at all; the sword came out as if it had been in a well-oiled scabbard. Susan careered backwards, tripped over one of the encircling stones, dropped the sword, and fell into the well, plunging completely underwater before her panicked strokes brought her back up again.

"Damn it!" exclaimed Vivien. "The wolf's left the motorway. Stop!"

Merlin pulled the cab off onto the hard shoulder, adjacent to a field of new-mown hay. The sun was rising, and the traffic was increasing, though there was a lot more heading south than north, over on the other side of the motorway.

"They're west of here, and close," said Vivien. "And the Fenris is much slower now. Your sword must be taking a toll. I'm going to have a look where it went into the field—I think it's only fifty or sixty yards back."

"Make it quick," said Merlin. "We shouldn't be stopping here. I don't want to attract attention. From anyone."

He got out and opened the bonnet of the cab, to make it look as if it had broken down, on the principle of giving people an obvious reason for something so they looked no deeper. Vivien climbed over the fence and went into the field. Though it had been recently cut, and there was little more than stubble between the rolls of hay, it was fairly obvious where the wolf had gone. Though by its nature it did not leave enormous paw prints, it did cause mysterious scuff marks that would be very confusing to any normal person. If the creature had laid down for a while, and the clover was high, it would have made a crop circle.

Vivien followed the tracks through the field for about a hundred yards, looking at the distance between prints. There were bloodstains, too, though they were not visible to any normal mortal's eyes, and were not as frequent nor as large as Vivien hoped.

She turned to go back to the cab as a police Rover 3500 drew up on the hard shoulder about twenty yards behind it, with blue light flashing, but no siren. The doors on either side opened and the police got out but did not move beyond the doors.

Merlin was standing in front of the cab, leaning into the engine bay. He didn't step out to greet the police officers but instead knelt down, and Vivien saw him pull out the little Beretta he had in his ankle holster.

Vivien looked back at the police officers, who had drawn revolvers and were aiming over the top of their splayed-open doors. She started to run, drawing in an enormous breath as she did so.

The softer bang of the .25 Beretta came a fraction of a second after the crack of the police officers' Smith & Wesson .38 revolvers.

CHAPTER SIXTEEN

> moonlight on rushes and still water
> the quiet of the night
> yet if you listen
> very carefully
> you might hear it
> crawling closer
> and closer
> clos—

MERLIN FIRED TWICE FROM THE LEFT FRONT OF THE CAB, DUCKED across to the right, and fired twice more. Glass shattered as the police officers' bullets blew out the back window of the cab and starred the windscreen, but didn't go anywhere close to Merlin.

After these initial shots, there were no more.

Merlin dropped prone and crawled along the side of the cab to take a closer look. He saw one police officer on the ground and crawled farther, ready to shoot if necessary. But the other officer was also down. Merlin got up and raced forward. He arrived at the same time as Vivien on the other side, who kicked a revolver under the car before kneeling down to give the officer first aid.

Merlin checked the police officer closest to him. She was lying on her back, with her hands clutched low on the right side of her neck, blood trickling between her fingers. She looked up at Merlin, a puzzled expression on her face. Not from pain, but bewilderment.

"What's going on?" she asked. "Why on earth are we on the *M1*?"

"You'll be okay," soothed Merlin. He had aimed for her right shoulder, not the neck. He moved her hands aside, pulled open her jacket, and tried not to show alarm. It didn't look good.

He pulled a vial of Sipper saliva out of the narrow pocket inside his sleeve, snapped the top off, swilled it around in his mouth, and spat it into the wound. The liquid glowed as it fell, bright rivulets spreading through the darker blood.

Vivien appeared with the first aid kit from the police car's boot. She opened it, grabbed a field dressing, and pressed it hard on the woman's neck, holding it on.

"Bandage!" she said.

"Why is the sky so blue?" asked the woman. "So blue."

"How's the other one?" asked Merlin. He lifted the woman's head so he could get the bandage around her neck.

"Dead," said Vivien. She peeled back the edge of her glove so an inch of silver skin was visible at the heel of her hand and held it against the wound, sucking in her breath. She held it for several seconds, then exhaled.

"Definitely dead?" asked Merlin in a small voice.

"A ricochet off the door frame into his eye and then the brain. Instant death."

"Shit," said Merlin. "Shit, shit."

"This one will live, I think," said Vivien. She took her hand away and pulled up the glove. "But as well as the wound, someone's interfered with her mind. I can't tell who, or whether it will last."

Cars were slowing down as the people in them gawked at the scene. Merlin looked up as he heard a car stopping behind the police vehicle and instantly picked up his pistol. The stopping car was a newish Vauxhall Estate, splashed with mud. A woman in Wellington boots and wearing what looked like green hospital scrubs leaped out the passenger side, her hands held high. The man in the driver's seat was hunched as low as he could go and still see out the windscreen.

"I'm a vet!" called the woman nervously. "Can I help? Please?"

"Yes," shouted Merlin. "Tell your friend to drive to the next emergency telephone and call an ambulance and the police! You can take over here."

The Vauxhall took off. The traffic had been increasing, there was a steady flow, but now all of them were slowing down to have a look, which would cause a tailback for miles and bring attention sooner rather than later. It was also possible one of those who'd previously gone past had already stopped at the next emergency phone and called for help.

The vet ran up, keeping her hands in the air. Merlin picked up the officer's .38 to remove any temptation for some sort of heroic intervention, and went around the other side of the car to lean in and check the VHF two-way radio, stepping over the man he'd killed.

"The other officer's dead," said Vivien to the vet. "Keep

direct pressure on. I think she'll make it."

As Merlin expected, the radio was still on the London general frequency, useless here in Leicestershire. If this had been any sort of authorized excursion, they would have already telephoned the local police and prearranged a frequency or at least tuned it to the general channel for the county. He got out, and gestured to Vivien. The vet had her hands on the pad over the gunshot wound, concentrating entirely on the patient, not looking at Merlin and Vivien.

The two booksellers walked quickly back towards their taxi.

"How did you know?" asked Vivien.

"It's a Met car, not Leicestershire Constabulary," said Merlin. "That made me suspicious, and then they moved strangely getting out. Reminded me of the thugs who came for Susan. That constable back there, she wasn't asking why she was on the motorway out of shock, she genuinely didn't know how she came to be there. Her mind had been messed with!"

"I know," said Vivien gently. "I told you."

"I didn't shoot until they did and damn it, I was shooting to wound!"

"I know," repeated Vivien. "Come on, we have to go."

Merlin slammed the hood shut and jumped in the driver's side. He had to wait a moment for a gap in the traffic, and he wondered if someone was going to try and stop them, ramming the car or something equally stupid. But the people who'd seen what actually happened had already been carried forward by the ceaseless tide of vehicles. All those passing now saw was a slightly incongruous London black cab—a relatively rare but by no means impossible sight on any motorway—leaving some sort of accident involving a police car.

"We'd better ditch the cab. The Leicestershire force will be on to it soon. It's the murder of a police officer, as far as they're concerned. It'll take days at the least to sort it out with London," said Merlin as they sped away. "I *wish* I hadn't had to shoot."

He was silent for a few seconds, before he took a breath and continued. "We'll have to steal another car. And telephone Thurston."

"Merrihew will be at the New Bookshop by now as well," said Vivien, not happily. She had the scabbard back on her lap. "They'll have activated the full operations room. First time since the early sixties, I think."

"Where's the sword? And, I hope, the wolf and Susan?"

Vivien concentrated, once again holding her breath. Her face did not go red, but her silver hand grew bright enough for a thin line of light to escape the top of her glove.

"West, about four miles. And I think . . . yes, they've stopped."

"We'll take the next exit," said Merlin. "Any unattended car we see, we'll swap over."

Both of them were quite expert car thieves, hot-wirers, house-breakers, and picklocks. It was part of the curriculum at Wooten. The left-handed did most of that sort of thing, but as swapping handedness was very common through adolescence into the early twenties, the school trained everyone as if they would be a field agent at least until they became definitely right-handed and usually grew less interested in that sort of thing.

Merlin glanced at Vivien in the rearview mirror. She looked extremely troubled.

"Those officers back there," she said. "Their vehicle. Registration index A163SUY. It was in the square, at the safe house."

Merlin examined his memory.

"Yes," he agreed. "Parked at the north end. With those officers in it."

"They must have been sent after us almost straight away," she said. "They could have caught up to us ages ago, stopped us."

"But they didn't do anything but follow," said Merlin. "Until we stopped . . ."

"So whoever instructed them kept it simple," said Vivien. "Follow until they stop, then shoot to kill."

"Who or what could put an instruction like that into mortal minds?" asked Merlin, thinking aloud.

"An Ancient Sovereign, in its own demesne," said Vivien. She hesitated, then added, "A Cauldron-Keeper, probably anywhere—the cauldrons have no geographic boundaries and they all grant powers over mortal minds, amongst their more specialized powers. And one of us could have done it. A powerful right-handed bookseller."

"We would have felt the presence of an Old One," said Merlin. "I mean, everyone would have. Una and the others from the response teams."

There was silence for half a mile, both of them thinking.

"Exit," said Merlin, veering to the left. "Head westwards, right?"

"Northwest," said Vivien. She looked at the open *Bartholomew Road Atlas of Britain* next to her on the seat. "Take the A50."

"Okay," said Merlin. "Who was with the team from the New Bookshop? I saw Silas and Rory . . ."

"Uncle Silas, Aunt Esther, Cousins Rory, Stewart, and Darius," said Vivien.

"Could any of them—"

"I don't think so," interrupted Vivien. "They're all competent, unlike Cousin Jake. But a compulsion to kill, maintained for hours . . . Thurston could do it, of course . . . Great-Uncle Feroze and Great-Aunt Evangeline at Wooten, Great-Aunt Sheena . . ."

"Who's Great-Aunt Sheena?" asked Merlin, frowning. They were off the M1 now, into a big roundabout. He took the exit for the A50, already looking for cars to steal. They had only a few minutes, he thought, before every police vehicle and officer in Leicestershire was hunting a London black cab.

"She heads up Harshton and Hoole in Birmingham," replied Vivien. "You've never met her?"

"Never had anything to do with the silversmiths. What about the even-handed? Could they place such a compulsion?"

"Any of them *could*," said Vivien. "But . . . I can't believe they would."

Merlin slowed as he spotted a Forte Travelodge with a large car park, and pulled in, aiming for a spot where the cab would be shielded from the hotel and the road by a lone, remnant patch of trees left in the middle of the expanse of asphalt for mysterious tree preservation reasons.

"What about that superintendent? He was there, he's suspicious."

"But he couldn't do it, no mortal adept could compel someone to kill. I mean, maybe in the moment, but not to last for hours," said Vivien.

"He bears looking into, though," said Merlin. "You said he moved from Unit M to CID before going to gangs. His name wasn't on the file, but I wonder if he was involved in the investigation into Mum's murder."

"I wish we were back at the Old Bookshop so I *could* look into things," said Vivien fretfully. "I'm not meant to be in the field anymore."

"Hasn't been that long since you were left-handed."

"Long enough. How about that Austin 1300, there?" asked Vivien.

"No," said Merlin. "We might have to drive *fast*. Besides, that one looks like the wheels might fall off."

Vivien sat up straighter and pointed. "That Ford Capri over there!"

"You want to be Bodie from *The Professionals*, don't you?"

"I like her," said Vivien. "So what? You like Raelene Doyle."

"Doyle's much the prettier of the two," said Merlin.

He stopped the cab and they got out, moving swiftly but not in an obvious hurry. Merlin collected his yak-hair bag and suitcase, Vivien scooped up his belt, scabbard, and the road atlas.

The clump of trees shielded them from everywhere except the last row of cars in the car park, but there was no one watching. They walked three cars up, Merlin put his case down, drew a short length of what looked like a metal tape measure from his boot, slid it down next to the window, and opened the Capri's door in three seconds. He jumped inside to unlock the other doors before starting to hot-wire the ignition. Vivien threw her stuff in the back seat, shoved Merlin's case in as well, and got in the front passenger seat at the exact moment the engine roared into life.

Forty seconds later, they were back on the A50, now in a silver Ford Capri 3.0 Mk 11 with a black vinyl roof, exactly like the one in the ITV series *The Professionals*.

"Is the sword still in the same place?" asked Merlin.

"I'm checking," said Vivien, who had to reach back to grab the atlas and the scabbard. "Keep heading west."

Susan emerged panting and spluttering, crouched on the stony rim of the well, and looked desperately for her weapon. But she'd turned around completely in the water, and swum to the wrong side. The sword was well out of reach, and the Fenris was up, already looking healthier. Her eyes were bright again, the froth gone from her gums.

The giant she-wolf stalked without any noticeable limp towards Susan, and opened her jaws.

"No," said Morcenna, standing in the wolf's way. She looked

very small in front of it, watery and insubstantial.

The Fenris growled, but it was a halfhearted growl, almost a drawn-out yelp.

"No. I will not allow any scathe to come to those at my well. You know this, and you have been healed. Now you must go."

The wolf bowed her head and sprang into the air, becoming a vaguely wolf-shaped flight of dozens of somewhat insubstantial ravens that flew as one into the sky above, already bright with the new day. As the ravens circled up, they turned and became even more insubstantial, as if vanishing into some unseen wind that carried them northwards.

"What . . . how . . ."

"She was only in this world as much as was necessary to carry you," said Morcenna. "The sacred wolves have many shapes, of varying solidity. She has taken to the air to more quickly carry word of her failure to whoever holds her in thrall."

"Who is that?" asked Susan.

"Some great power," said Morcenna, with a shrug. "You, too, are healed of the slight hurts you bore, and so I ask you to leave my well. Take the sword with you; I do not want its poison here."

"Uh, okay," said Susan. She stood up, squelching, and walked around the edge of the pool to pick up the sword. "Um, can you tell me how long I have until the Fenris gets wherever it's going?"

"It goes at the wind's pace, in the upper air," said Morcenna. "It could be anywhere within the ancient bounds of Britain in an hour, or two, or three."

"Right," said Susan. "Um, thanks. Why didn't you tell me the Fenris would have to leave me alone? I mean, before I agreed to take out the sword?"

"I wanted to see what you would do," said Morcenna. Her thin pondweed lips split to show rows and rows of tiny, highly disturbing fish teeth. "While it is true I must offer healing to all those who come to my well, and I allow no others to harm my visitors, it is left to me to decide what I do with them after the healing."

"Oh, right," said Susan nervously. "Thank you."

She hesitated, then bowed her head again. Morcenna did likewise.

"I'll . . . I'll go," said Susan. She looked around. The dell was surrounded by dense woodland on all sides, and there was no sign of a path. She pointed towards what she thought was east, back in the direction she'd come in. "Which way is out?"

"All of them," said Morcenna, and dived into her pool, becoming a stream of pure, clear water as she moved, ending in a giant splash, as if someone had poured her out of a huge, invisible glass.

"Right," whispered Susan. She looked at the sword in her hand. Though obviously ancient, its edge gleamed with what appeared to her to be visible sharpness, banishing the brief notion she'd had of somehow sticking it down the leg of her boiler suit, in order not to terrify the first people she came across. Thoughts of holding it behind her back were also banished, because that would be even scarier.

"Maybe no one will care," she muttered to herself. "Crazy young woman with punk haircut in boiler suit emerges from ancient woodland with sword. That's eccentric, not frighteningly insane. No sudden moves. Ask to use a telephone. It'll be fine."

Aiming for what looked like it might be a gap in the undergrowth, and for what she thought was east, Susan walked away from Morcenna's Well, into the wood.

"There's a phone," said Vivien, pointing to a familiar red box ahead, across from a roadside café. "We'd better call in; it's been more than two hours."

"After we get Susan," said Merlin. "What if they move off again? Or the sword's fallen out? We can't waste time."

"The Greats will be furious," said Vivien. "Particularly since—"

"I know, I know!" snapped Merlin. "I didn't want to shoot that poor police officer! Where do I turn?"

"Next right," said Vivien. "There's an ancient wood. I think the Fenris has gone to ground there."

"Maybe that's its home," said Merlin.

"You really have forgotten everything we learned at school, haven't you," said Vivien. "There's no Fenris lair anywhere near here. It must have come from farther north, though that still leaves several possibilities."

"So why has it stopped?"

"I don't know," said Vivien. Neither of them wanted to say

aloud that the sword might have fallen out and Susan and the wolf were long gone somewhere else.

"Police behind us," said Merlin quietly. "Two cars back. Local."

Vivien didn't glance around, but leaned in closer to Merlin so she could look in the rearview mirror.

"If it follows us around this turn, I reckon there's a good chance this car's already reported stolen, and they've linked it to the cab," said Merlin. "I really don't want to shoot any more innocents."

"They'd have pulled us over already, or tried to," said Vivien. "And this lot won't be armed *or* compelled to try and kill us. I can probably put them to sleep, if we have to. This is it. Spendborough Road. Turn here."

Merlin slowed and indicated in a very law-abiding fashion, and turned into the smaller, narrower road. The two vehicles behind him continued on the A50, as did the police car.

"Try the radio," said Merlin. "See if the . . . see if the motorway incident has made the news, or they've put out a warning or a call for witnesses."

Vivien turned the radio on. The car was immediately filled with Mike Oldfield's "Moonlight Shadow" at high volume. She dialed it down and punched one of the five preset buttons for another station, which was also part of the way through "Moonlight Shadow." She punched the next and got a dry, plummy voice talking about the habits of water voles; the fourth button produced Puccini's "Recondita Armonia" from *Tosca*; and the last a confusing interview with a vicar in Somerset about the forthcoming general election and flooding, which at least in his mind were somehow related.

"Put it back on 'Moonlight Shadow,'" said Merlin.

Vivien pressed the button and music filled the car again.

"I'm hungry," said Merlin a minute later. "Have you got anything to eat?"

"Nope," said Vivien. She looked in the glovebox, hoping for chocolate or a packet of crisps, but it only contained a half-empty packet of John Player Specials, a matchbox, and a torch with a flat battery.

"We should get another car after we find Susan," said Merlin.

"As far as I can tell, the sword is . . . they're . . . in the middle of the wood," said Vivien. "We'll have to walk in anyway."

"Luckily, I have suitable outdoor garments in my case," said Merlin. "For you, too, if you like. A charming tartan skirt and matching hat."

Vivien made a face.

"Or you can choose something else," said Merlin. "We need to change up how we look. Do you want the D'Oyly Carte moustache? I brought it. And a wig."

"No thank you," said Vivien. "But a hat's a good idea. You do realize we'll have to dump the suitcase sooner or later?"

"Sadly, yes," said Merlin. "I daresay it will give the police rather a surprise when they find it."

"The contents?"

"Perhaps. But the case itself is very special. It belonged to Noël Coward."

"Sure," said Vivien, with unrestrained skepticism.

"His initials are under the handle, and his personal label inside," insisted Merlin. "I paid twenty quid for it at the Portobello Market."

"Twenty quid? You should have got Paddington to do the bargaining," said Vivien. "Not that he'd have been taken in to start with. I'm kind of sad a fictional bear is smarter than my brother."

Merlin did not reply to this sally. After a minute or two, Vivien made a peace offering.

"You'll probably get the suitcase back eventually. Afterwards."

"Hmm," replied Merlin. "Your optimism is welcome. Do we keep going? There's a lane to the northwest coming up."

The road was heading into the outskirts of some nondescript Midlands town, all red brick and 1960s concrete, takeaways and small shops sprinkled among the houses on either side of the road.

"Keep straight on for now," said Vivien. "We don't go into the town, we'll be through this bit in a few minutes, there's a couple of roundabouts. Then we take a lane on the left, called Old Forest Way."

They drove on, accompanied by "Moonlight Shadow" and then "Sweet Dreams (Are Made of This)" by Eurythmics, turning into the narrow, somewhat sunken lane as the DJ told them what they'd been listening to and announced the next song was going to be "A Winter's Tale" by David Essex, at which point both Vivien and Merlin reached to turn the radio off, his left hand momentarily clashing with her right.

CHAPTER SEVENTEEN

▷ ┤ ◆ ┼ ○ ╍ ┤ ◁

A tree is strong
But the wind is stronger
A stone is strong
But the sea is stronger
The sun is strong
But sorrow is stronger

▷ ┤ ◆ ┼ ○ ╍ ┤ ◁

SUSAN WALKED FOR WHAT SHE ESTIMATED TO BE AT LEAST TWO hours, though she couldn't tell for sure since her Swatch had stopped at 2:16, roughly the time the goblins had grabbed her. She knew she had already walked much, much farther out of the wood than the Fenris had gone coming in, but she was also sure she hadn't gotten turned around. It was such a dense forest it was hard to get a good look at the sun, but every now and then there was a gap in the canopy enough to see it and get a reasonable idea which way was east.

She also hadn't remembered the uphill slope being so long. It wasn't very steep, but combined with having to make her way between great oak trunks and under spreading, scraping birch branches and bypassing thickets of hawthorn and holly, it was all quite exhausting and the wood appeared to go on forever.

There was no sign of the bridle path, either, but Susan remembered that it had turned up the ridge, at the point where the wolf had descended into this densely wooded, secret valley. So if she kept going uphill she would eventually come to it, and from there make it to the road, and eventually a phone to call for help.

Who exactly to call was a little puzzling. She supposed dialing 999 would be easiest, and the police would inform the booksellers. But she had a slight nagging doubt caused by Merlin's suspicions that one of the booksellers might actively be involved in whoever or whatever was trying to kidnap her. So it might be better to try to lie low.

Susan thought about this, and stopped to catch her breath and check her pockets. Her father's cigarette case was in the top left breast pocket, suitably buttoned down. She had about fifteen pounds and a handkerchief in her left lower pocket and . . . she felt something in the long ruler pocket, and drew out the butter knife. Checking the right lower pocket, she found a bunch of soggy, bloated, but not split packets of salt.

As she touched steel and salt, she felt a strange jolt inside her body. A sudden feeling of excitement and tension fizzed through her from toes to head, as the dormant power inside her quickened. Instinctively and very swiftly, Susan put the knife and the salt back in her pockets and lifted her hands, as if the farther away she held them the more she could avoid whatever was happening.

The sense of waking and anticipation ebbed away, but it didn't entirely disappear. A shivering, coiled-up feeling that something truly momentous was going to happen remained inside her.

"No," whispered Susan to herself. "I don't want it. Keep your powers."

The sensation ebbed further, like a baby settling almost off to sleep, being also ready to come awake and bawl at the slightest provocation. Which Susan was determined not to provide.

She pushed herself off the oak she was leaning against, and started walking again, setting her mind very firmly on her immediate predicament and not on whatever was happening within her. With only £15, hiding out didn't seem very possible. Susan tried to think how she might contact Merlin or Vivien without letting any other booksellers know. She could call the Old Bookshop, pose as a friend with a different name . . . but they probably wouldn't be there anyway.

Hopefully, they were looking for her, perhaps via magical means. But then so would whoever the Fenris reported to, and the she-wolf knew exactly where Susan had been, so they had the advantage. Therefore moving away was the first priority. She could worry about everything else once she was a good distance from the well and the wood.

At least Morcenna's healing touch had fixed up her aches and pains. Despite being rather damp, Susan felt surprisingly lively and well. She was alive, and free . . . and it was good to be out among trees, in clean air, with all the constant noise of London gone, replaced by the gentler sounds of birdsong and the rustle of small animals about the undergrowth, perhaps hedgehogs or rabbits. . . .

Susan stopped to think about this. *All* she could hear were natural sounds. No aircraft overhead, no distant traffic noises from the motorway or some closer road. Nothing. But the Fenris had only gone three-quarters of a mile at most from the road, and she had walked at least a couple of miles.

"Of course!" she muttered to herself. "It's a mythic wood. Far bigger than it should be, once you're in it. But how do I get out?"

She thought about that for a bit longer. The wood didn't feel like the May Fair; there was none of the supersaturated color or feeling of otherness. She hadn't seen anything that appeared out of place, and instinctively she felt that this would not be the answer to getting out of the forest.

Instead, she drew a deep breath and loudly spoke to the trees about her, but not shouting, using her best loud, very polite voice.

"Could you please let me out? I love this wood, but I need to leave!"

All the soft sounds stopped as she spoke, the rustling ceased, the breeze no longer played in the upper branches. Everything was absolutely still and quiet. But Susan felt something change; something flickered, for an instant, in the corner of her left eye. She turned slowly, ready to bring up her sword.

As she turned, the little noises came back. The breeze wafted through the upper reaches, lifting leaves and branches. Something small and furry whisked through the thick undergrowth. A blackbird called again, perhaps that same hopeful male from the dell, keeping her company.

Two overhanging beech trees, rimed with green, had fallen on each other to form a gateway, a rough path visible beyond that gate. Neither beeches nor path had been there a moment before.

Susan bowed, said, "Thank you," and took the path. Almost immediately the wood opened up. There were no longer thickets of brambles, the oaks were farther apart, the beeches between them shorter and less grasping. She could even see the sky and the sun. Which looked much higher than it had when she'd last seen it.

Only a few minutes later, she heard other noises up ahead. The crack of a trodden-on stick, the swish of branches pushed aside, the scuff of footsteps . . . there were people coming towards her.

Crouching low, Susan left the path—not without a moment's hesitation, in case it disappeared—and slid around the trunk of a vast oak, so she could peek around but still be hidden— though the forest was so dense this worked both ways, and she couldn't see very far.

There were at least two people, she thought. Maybe more. She heard them come closer, then they also stopped, and she caught faint whispers. Susan held her breath, removing even that faint noise so she could hear better. They were moving again, towards her, noisier now, with clumping feet and—

"Susan!"

Susan whirled around, instinctively lifting her sword. Merlin had silently crept up behind her, a dagger in his left hand. She didn't lower the sword, but he was already disappearing the dagger. Literally, she couldn't see where it went; it was gone in the space of a single blink. Possibly up the sleeve of his corduroy jacket, which Merlin clearly considered suitable for rural wear, combined with a cream blouse atop a subdued tartan skirt, green stockings and upmarket Hunter Wellington boots with side straps, and what at first glance appeared to be a kind of green beret with a bobble on top. His tie-dyed yak-hair bag still graced one shoulder.

"What is that on your head?" asked Susan. The look of relief on her face made it clear these words were an expression of how pleased she was to see him.

"It's a tam-o'-shanter, of course," said Merlin, as if she should already know. He held out his arms and smiled. Susan walked into his embrace, they hugged for a moment, and then both recoiled as if suddenly remembering pressing appointments.

"I was worried," said Merlin.

"Me too," said Susan. "Who is that stomping around?"

Merlin looked past Susan and called out, "Vivien! It's Susan!"

Vivien approached from in front, not bothering with her heavy "for the purpose of distraction" boot stomps. She was wearing jeans, a checked shirt, a wide-brimmed straw hat with a crushed crown that had been pushed out, and Adidas running shoes. A British Caledonian vinyl airline bag hung over her shoulder and she was carrying the scabbard for the old sword.

"Oh, thank heavens," said Vivien. "Where's the Fenris?"

"Gone," said Susan. She let out her breath and lowered the sword, her heart beginning to slow down. "Merlin's sword . . . you wounded it badly but it took a while to take effect. So she . . .

it was a she-wolf, diverted to get healing from Morcenna's Well, down there. Morcenna healed her, but wouldn't let the wolf take me. So the Fenris turned into a bunch of ravens and flew off to whoever she answers to."

"Morcenna?" asked Merlin.

"Has to be a water-fay with that name," said Vivien. She frowned. "Lucky she wasn't hungry."

"What?" asked Susan.

"The water-fay are rather arbitrary," said Vivien. "Kind of a fifty-fifty proposition for visiting mortals. Get helped, or get eaten. Not that they need to eat. But they like to from time to time."

"I saw her teeth," said Susan, with a shudder.

Vivien handed the scabbard to Susan, who gratefully sheathed the sword. When the blade was bare she was always uncomfortably aware of its presence and sharpness, as if it *wanted* to cut someone.

"Do you remember any details about the Fenris?" asked Vivien. "I might be able to identify her. Did she have distinct silver hairs in her snout, or—"

"Morcenna greeted her as the Fenris of somewhere that sounded like One-under Mere."

Merlin raised an eyebrow and looked expectantly at Vivien.

"Onundar Myrr," said Vivien. "Lake Windermere."

"Does that help?" asked Susan.

"It will, I'm sure," said Vivien, frowning. "But I'll need to check the references. I don't recall the Fenris of Lake Windermere being associated with any particular Old One . . . we need to call in, Merlin. Ask Thurston and the New Bookshop team—"

"I'm still not sure that's a good idea," interrupted Merlin. "But we certainly have to get out of here, anyway."

He pointed at a distant speck in the sky, or what was a distant speck to Susan at least. It took her a few seconds as it drew somewhat closer to recognize it must be a helicopter.

"Police helicopter," said Merlin. "Following the A50. Hopefully not looking for our new car yet."

"What time is it?" asked Susan, lifting her wrist to set her watch. It was going again, but clearly wrong. "I got kind of confused in the wood, and the sun looks much higher than it did. . . ."

"It's ten to twelve," said Vivien, not bothering to consult any timepiece. Susan accepted this as another right-handed skill, and set her watch. "I'm glad you worked out how to get out of the wood; we've been wandering the fringes for the last two hours trying to find a way in. Not having the appropriate reference with us to tell us how to placate or pressure the entity concerned."

"I asked the wood to let me out," said Susan. She ignored the swift glance between Vivien and Merlin. "Um, why do we need to get away from a *police* helicopter?"

"Merlin had to shoot a policeman," said Vivien. "Well, two police officers. But one was killed."

"What!"

"I didn't mean to kill him," said Merlin wretchedly. "But once shots are fired . . . anyway, they fired first. They were under a compulsion. Like those thugs who tried to abduct you, and the ones who killed Mum. Someone . . . something . . . messed with their minds."

"It's going to take time to sort that out, and we haven't been able to call in to the Greats to get that done," said Vivien. "In the meantime, the Leicestershire Constabulary and I guess every other force in the country will be looking for the two people who killed a cop on the M1."

"Oh," said Susan, and then, "Oh! If it's really ten to twelve, Morcenna said the Fenris would get wherever it's going within a few hours. The wolf will have told whoever was expecting me exactly where I was."

"So two reasons to move," said Merlin, visibly pulling himself together. "You haven't got a book on you, by any chance, have you, Susan?"

"No," said Susan.

"Pity."

"There's no time to read, Merlin," said Vivien gently.

"I know, I know," replied Merlin. "I thought a few pages, as we walked . . . it'll have to wait. I should have put some books in with my clothes. I wasn't thinking. Come on, let's go."

"Where are we going?" Susan asked Vivien, as Merlin typically zoomed ahead. "Why does Merlin want a book?"

"He killed someone," said Vivien. "And he's understandably very upset about it. The left-handed have great capability for violence, and they need to . . . counterweight it, I suppose . . .

with quiet reading, or writing poems. He'll be okay."

"And where are we going?" prompted Susan.

"That's a tricky question," said Vivien. "Away from here, for now."

"Yes, let's get some distance," said Merlin. He'd found the bridle path and stopped to let them catch up, and was now looking up at the sky. "If we can. Damn!"

The helicopter was flying back along the A50, west to east, heading away. But a few miles away to the north, a murmuration of starlings was rising from a distant field, thousands of the small birds moving together to form a dark cloud uncannily like an enormous hand, its fingers groping over the land below. The birds were erratically moving towards the center of the wood, in a series of turns and drifts upwards and downwards.

"Is that natural?" asked Susan.

"It could be," replied Merlin. "But I bet it isn't."

"Definitely an Old One's work," said Vivien. "And a Cauldron-Keeper to boot. Crossing too many mythic boundaries for it to be anyone else."

She stared in fascination at the moving cloud of birds. "I've never seen a murmuration before, whether perfectly natural or not. It's rather beautiful. Or would be if it wasn't looking for us."

"They'll be overhead in less than ten minutes," said Merlin. "Come on!"

They'd left the Capri in a lay-by on Old Forest Way where the bridle path started, but as they got closer, Merlin stopped and held up his hand. Vivien and Susan moved up next to him and crouched down. They were still in the fringe of the forest, but Susan caught a glimpse of a silver car through the trees.

"What is it?" whispered Vivien.

"Helicopter's coming back our way," said Merlin. "Wait for it to pass over."

Susan could hear the *whop-whop-whop* of the helicopter, but couldn't tell whether it was getting closer until all of a sudden the sound grew much louder and a few seconds later it flew overhead, quite low.

"If it keeps going, we're okay," muttered Merlin to Susan. "If not, the car we took is already reported stolen and they'll have linked it to the cab."

"The cab?"

"We borrowed Audrey's to chase after you," said Vivien.

The helicopter noise faded away. Merlin craned his neck, surveying what he could of the sky between the treetops.

"It's turned west again," he said. "Come on."

He started off again, moving fast. This time, Susan and Vivien pushed themselves to keep up with him. Merlin unlocked the car and started it, as Vivien opened the passenger-side door and put the seat forward so Susan could slide into the bench seat behind.

"Not a lot of room back here," she said, laying the sheathed sword down on the floor, with a slight double take at the presence of Merlin's suitcase.

"We had a limited selection of vehicles to choose from," replied Merlin.

"Based on the prerequisite that it had to make us feel like we were in an episode of *The Professionals*," added Vivien. "I'm Bodie and he's Doyle."

"So I have to be Georgina Cowley?" asked Susan. "Thanks."

"She's the boss, to be fair," said Vivien.

"Yeah, and thirty years older than the others," said Susan.

"Still tough, though," said Merlin. He blipped the engine, put it in gear, and eased out onto the road, craning forward to look up through the windscreen. "You see the helicopter or the birds, Vivien?"

"Can't see the helicopter," replied Vivien, who'd wound her window down for a better view. "The murmuration is heading for the middle of the wood."

"Okay," muttered Merlin. He put his foot down and the car roared in answer, fishtailing slightly as it left the lay-by and accelerated out into the road.

"Take it easy," said Vivien. "We don't want to attract attention."

Merlin slowed down to thirty, nodding.

"Where *are* we going?" asked Susan.

"First we need to find a phone and call in," continued Vivien. "I asked Cousin Linda to follow up on the silversmith records and Aunt Zoë should have got the library card UV photographs done. We need to know that information before we can work anything else out."

"Yes," said Susan. The strange fizzing, apprehensive but also expectant sensation inside her leaped up as she spoke. It was almost as if the power that was building up within her also wanted to know—needed to know—who her father was. A puzzle completed would lead her to . . . to completion.

"Thurston and Merrihew will cut in if we call," warned Merlin.

"I know," said Vivien calmly. "We have to risk it."

"Risk it?" asked Susan. "They must know about me by now, surely?"

"They may have known all along," said Merlin heavily.

"What do you mean?"

"Merlin thinks either Thurston or Merrihew may actually be behind the attempts to kidnap you," said Vivien calmly. "And therefore also the police officers who were compelled to shoot at us."

"What?!"

"But I have to say the latter event makes me think they're not involved, or at least not directly."

"I don't know—" Merlin started to say, but Vivien didn't let him go on.

"They're definitely both lazy and can't be bothered with their responsibilities anymore," continued Vivien. "I agree they should retire. And they may know more about Susan's father and whoever wants to grab hold of Susan than they let on. But that's a sin of omission, not commission. I can't believe either of them would compel police officers to kill us. Or that either would arrange for Mum to be murdered."

Merlin was silent for a few seconds, intent on the road ahead.

"I don't know. I think . . . I feel . . . suspicious. But I don't know. I get mad at them for not doing the things that need to be done. I suppose laziness or inattention is more likely than anything else. . . ."

"What about the Cauldron-Born?" asked Susan. She had a vivid memory of that strange, cricked-neck man crossing the lawn, his horrid shadow crawling behind him. "I know Helen and Zoë said they couldn't have come from your grail, but do you accept that?"

"Helen and Zoë know far more about our grail and the Grail-Keeper than I do," said Merlin. "Though I guess I'd like to hear it from the horse's mouth."

"The Greats are still going to be a problem," said Vivien. "Whether they're actively involved or not, they'll want to sweep things under the carpet, or even to apply the old-style solution to the problem Susan represents. We need to figure out what—"

"I think I need to go to my father," said Susan suddenly. She sounded surprised, as if this was a revelation to herself. She frowned, and repeated her words. "I need to go to my father."

"Uh, Cousin Helen thought he's probably . . . gone," said Vivien.

"And I'm pretty sure he isn't," said Susan. "I can't explain it, and I wish it wasn't happening, but whatever power my father has given me is kind of . . . waking up. And I have this over-whelming sense I need to find him, whoever and wherever he is."

"Do you have a sense of that?" asked Merlin. "The where, I mean? We're coming up to a crossroad. I've been heading away from those birds, but if you have somewhere more definite. . . ."

"North," said Susan. Her hand flashed up, and pointed. "North. That's all I know."

"If your father is still extant, it's possible he sent the Fenris," said Merlin cautiously. "I mean, that would make sense. An Ancient Sovereign securing his child."

"Why wouldn't he tell me?" asked Susan. "He could have phoned! Or come to visit Mum. I think whoever wants to abduct me is an *enemy* of my father, and so, of me."

"We really need to find a phone," said Vivien, shaking her head. "We need more information. That has to be our main objective."

"Keep watching the murmuration," said Merlin. "And the helicopter. And we need to change this car."

CHAPTER EIGHTEEN

The night wraps me in darkness
Clouds deny the stars and moon
I see nothing, hear nothing
Perhaps I do not even exist

THEY DROVE NORTHWEST ALONG A COUNTRY LANE, A NARROW STRIP of asphalt hardly wider than the car, bordered by flat, wire-fenced fields of clover and other hay grass, a rural vista of extreme dullness, certainly not a tourist's picturesque green and merry England.

Susan looked back at the murmuration of starlings through the rear window. The vast, constantly moving cloud of birds was over the wood now, dark, groping, fuzzy-edged fingers swooping down into the trees and up again, to rejoin the huge flock above.

"I think they've worked out I'm not in the wood anymore," she said.

As she spoke, the murmuration broke into four smaller versions of itself, each of these pulsing clouds billowing out to strike north, south, east, and west. Smaller tendrils of birds extended from each group, swooping over roads and fields, spreading the search in all directions.

"Ornithologists will be wetting themselves," said Vivien. "Can you see the helicopter? I can't."

Susan scanned as much of the sky as she could see through the rear window.

"No."

"There's a phone box," said Vivien.

Merlin shook his head, and drove past the telephone box that stood lonely and proud at the intersection of two country lanes. It was one of the new steel-and-glass ones, and looked rather like it had landed there from space.

"We're still too close to the murmuration. It's too isolated, we'd be too easy to spot," he said. "Let's get into the next decent-sized village, call from outside a pub or somewhere."

"Come to think of it, I am absolutely starving," said Susan. "Can we get something to eat?"

"We can't stop long, we need to get clear," warned Merlin. "But I'm hungry, too. . . . I guess you could get some sandwiches or anything that's ready-made. Vivien and I probably should stay out of sight as much as possible, though the police will be looking for a man and a woman, not two women. Or three, for that matter."

"I'm more worried about the murmuration," said Vivien.

"But the birds are way behind us now," said Susan, looking out the back again. "What can they do, anyway?"

"Kill or stun us quite easily, I'd think. Imagine getting hit by a thousand starlings at once, at speed. Besides, any entity who can raise a murmuration and send it searching around someone else's mythic wood can do other things as well," said Vivien. "I really need to talk to some of the senior right-handed."

"Whoever it is must have a cauldron," said Merlin. "Summoning a murmuration of starlings might be the least of the things that they can do. And whoever it is might have Cauldron-Born somewhere close by. I wish we knew which one it is."

"Presuming it isn't ours, it has to be the Bronze or Copper Cauldron," said Vivien. "Unless there are others our seniors haven't bothered to tell us about. There has always been speculation the Bronze Cauldron wasn't melted down after all, despite the firsthand accounts and Major Claypole's report. I wrote an essay about that in fifth form. And though the Copper Cauldron hasn't been seen since Roman times, it is only presumed missing. Maybe the Old One who has it simply went to sleep with it in some deep cavern, and now they've woken up."

"But why use the cauldron now?" asked Merlin. "And why try to kidnap Susan? I mean, she could have been snatched far more easily from her home, before we even knew about her. Why do it now?"

"Maybe whoever it is didn't know she existed," said Vivien slowly. "Until she turned up at Frank Thringley's."

"But Frank knew about me already," said Susan. "He sent Christmas cards every year, to 'Jassmine and Susan.'"

"Sure, but he might have kept it quiet for his own reasons," said Merlin. "An ace in the hole."

"There were other people at Frank's house, weren't there?" said Vivien. "When you first arrived. Did you introduce yourself as Jassmine's daughter, Susan?"

Susan thought back.

"Yes," she said. "One man answered the door, the one with the sawn-off shotgun in the shopping bag. I wonder . . . even then I wasn't as frightened as I should have been. I said I was Susan Arkshaw. And there was another man in the room when Frank talked to me, a bodyguard I guess. Oh, I'd forgotten . . . Frank asked how Mum was by name. He said he was pleased to see me . . . he said something about a 'good time to visit.'"

"Frank definitely answered to some higher boss, and his people probably did, too, or at least would have afterwards," said Merlin. "What if that boss was actually someone from the Old World, or somewhere farther up the chain there was a mythic entity involved?"

"It would be the first time one of the Ancient Sovereigns has ever involved themselves so much in mortal affairs," said Vivien. "I mean, Sippers and changelings, half fay of various kinds, a few entities that like taking on mortal form, they can get mixed up with crime. And there's the Death Cultists, I suppose, but I wouldn't call them criminals, more like terrorists. And they're usually only associated with the lesser or perhaps middleweight entities, the bloody ones, who seek human sacrifices. As far as I know, there's never been an Ancient Sovereign associated with mortal criminals. Why would they?"

"Advantage over others," suggested Merlin. "Mortals aren't

bound by the same strictures as those of the Old World. If you had both mythic entities and mortal servants at your beck and call, it would make you more powerful, right? I mean for things like breaking wards."

"Yes," said Vivien. "It's just so unusual. Or it has been, before now."

She didn't sound convinced, but at the same time, was clearly unable to dismiss the concept.

"It doesn't change our main objective anyway," said Merlin. "Which is to get the hell away from here, and then identify Susan's father—"

"And take me to him," interjected Susan.

"Maybe, maybe not," said Merlin.

"We *need* more information," said Vivien, looking back to smile at Susan, taking the sting out of Merlin's curt dismissal.

Susan wanted to say they *had* to take her, she felt the compulsion inside so strongly. But she kept her mouth shut, and thought about that. Maybe this feeling she had really was a compulsion. Perhaps her mind had been meddled with in the same way as the Birmingham thugs or the police who'd tried to shoot Merlin.

She didn't think so, because she otherwise felt fine and perfectly compos mentis. But she still worried about it.

The lane they'd been following had no traffic at all, but there was an intersection up ahead with a more significant road, with a steady stream of vehicles flashing across.

Vivien consulted the road atlas as Merlin slowed down for the stop sign. Susan looked across at yet another nondescript field, a new-mown expanse with rolls of hay. She was surprised to see a scarecrow on a cross in the middle of the field, since there were no crops to protect. She hadn't seen an old-fashioned scarecrow since she was little, and even then it had been made by a local farmer to entertain his children, not for any practical use. This one was a classic Worzel Gummidge type of scarecrow, straw stuffed into old clothes, with a partially decayed pumpkin for a head and oddly pink paper cups for eyes, the fancy kind with the ruffled edges used for making cupcakes. . . .

The scarecrow's head turned. Susan felt its gaze, those pink eyes meeting her own.

"Scarecrow!"

Vivien and Merlin looked over. The scarecrow lifted one stilt-like leg, pulling it out of the earth, and then it lifted the other and stepped forward, leaned down, and hunched over so it could also use its long, stick-straight arms to scuttle forward, all too like some horrible, frightening insect.

"Damn!" exclaimed Vivien, and Merlin gunned the car, sending it rocketing around the corner with a squeal of rubber and a blast of the horn from the car on the main road that'd had to slow down to let them in.

The scarecrow changed direction, leaping forward, but as Merlin overtook a slow Fiesta and accelerated again, it clearly realized it could not catch up. Instead it rose up to its full height, tilted its horrid, putrefying pumpkin head back, and let out a ghastly screech, audible even over the roaring engine.

Then it fell apart, sticks and straw and old clothes tumbling end over end in the direction it was scuttling, leaving a line of debris across the field.

"Watcher," said Vivien. "Why'd you look at it, Susan?"

"What? I was curious!"

"It felt your gaze," said Vivien. "It wouldn't have noticed us in the car otherwise."

"What are the birds doing?" asked Merlin. "We might be far enough away they didn't hear its warning."

"Still spreading out from the wood in all directions," said Susan. "I can't see any coming this way in particular."

"That scarecrow won't be the only Watcher," said Vivien. "If you see another scarecrow, don't look directly at it. Or at any strange sculptures or things like that."

"How am I supposed to not look?" asked Susan crossly. She was weary, and hungry, and still damp, and tired of being the center of inimical attention.

"You can look. But don't meet their eyes," warned Merlin. "Damn!"

He swore as a farm tractor towing a long trailer loaded with hay turned into the road about two hundred yards ahead of them, instantly slowing the three cars in front of Merlin's. It was doing no more than ten miles an hour.

"The starlings aren't on us, and the helicopter's not in sight," said Vivien. "We're good."

"I guess so," grumbled Merlin, slowing down to join the line of traffic behind the tractor.

A second later, a police Ford Granada came into view, coming towards them on the other side of the road. It cruised along, not in any hurry, and they could see the driver and the officer next to him looking at the cars behind the tractor and trailer.

"Sit up straight, Susan," said Merlin. "They're looking for two people, not three, remember."

The Granada drew closer, still at the same speed. It slowed down as it came level with the Capri. Merlin glanced over and smiled, Vivien looked, too, and Susan tilted her head up, wondering if, like the Watcher, she shouldn't meet their eyes.

The police car drove past, and there was a general sigh shared by Merlin, Vivien, and Susan. Followed a moment later by a similar shared, sharp intake of breath as the Granada screeched to a hard stop, began a swift three-point turn, and the blue light on top flashed on and the siren whooped into action.

Merlin put his foot down, the Capri lurched out into the opposite lane and roared down the wrong side of the road, swinging back in front of the tractor just in time to avoid a head-on with a Mini that veered off the road on to the muddy verge, unfortunately not blocking the police car, which was now in pursuit.

Merlin changed gear, the speedometer jerking from thirty to fifty and then seventy, which to Susan felt much, much faster than she'd traveled with the wolf even though it wasn't, because the narrow, badly surfaced country road was definitely not the motorway.

"They're onto this car," said Merlin grimly, working the

steering wheel as he lost traction on the back wheels around the next corner, a quite gentle veering that would have been fine at thirty miles an hour. "They'll have the helicopter back as well. Tighten your seat belts."

"Uh, there's no seat belt back here," said Susan.

"Brace yourself, then!" snapped Merlin. "Vivien, can you put them under when I stop? I *can't* shoot another innocent person."

"Yes!" said Vivien, who had tightened her belt and was holding on to the dash with both hands. The knuckles on her ungloved hands were white. "Stopping is good!"

"Get ready!" shouted Merlin.

There was a village ahead, with houses clustering close to the road, narrowing it even more, a blind bottleneck impossible to take at speed. But there was a gated track off to the right before that, leading into a field.

"Stopping!" yelled Merlin. He braked suddenly, dropped back several gears, dragged the hand brake on, and spun the wheel. The right side of the car lifted up off the road and for a heart-stopping moment it felt like it would go over before it thumped back down again and they were sliding backwards with a terrifying squeal of rubber. The Granada was coming straight at them until Merlin blipped the accelerator again and the police driver jinked his car to the left and kept going, while Merlin slowed the car's backwards progress enough that when the rear end of the Capri collided with the gate to the field it was not so much a full-on crash as an arrested stop, sending the gate flying in pieces and crumpling the back of the car.

Vivien and Merlin were out in a few seconds, kicking the pinched doors open, but Susan took longer to struggle free. She retrieved the sword and stood up in time to see the police Granada slide to a halt across the road. The doors opened but before the officers could do more than get out, Vivien was in front of the car, raising her arms and inhaling deeply. When she exhaled and lowered her hands, the two police officers fell, sprawled on the road.

From a distance, it looked like they'd been shot with a silenced weapon.

Merlin leaned into the car and grabbed Vivien's British Caledonian bag and his own yak-hair bag. "Come on! We have to move."

"Where?" asked Susan. The tractor and the cars behind it had stopped, and people were getting out to gawp—or possibly attempt to intervene; the farmer from the tractor was pulling out a metal star picket from the trailer, obviously intending to use it as a club.

"To that copse over there to start with," said Merlin, pointing to a cluster of birch trees on the other side of the field. But there were only perhaps a dozen trees, with fields all around; it didn't offer any serious cover. "Viv, can you cloud anyone observing so we can cut away back to the village after we leave the copse?"

"I can try," said Viv, but she didn't sound confident. The farmer was now advancing down the road, and there were a couple of other people following. One had a tire iron.

Merlin took the Smython out of his bag. Susan caught her breath, and almost cried out not to shoot anyone, but he pointed the revolver well off to one side and fired two rounds into the verge in front of the approaching good citizens. But the double boom, the flying earth where the bullets impacted, and the sight of the weapon had the desired effect. The farmer and his followers sprinted back to take cover behind the tractor.

"Run," said Merlin.

They ran for the copse, skirting a patch of deep mud in the middle of the field. Merlin led them behind the trees, where they were out of sight from the road, but there was nowhere to go beyond which they wouldn't be brought into view, only more open fields.

"You ready to hide us?" he said to Vivien.

"I can do two minutes max," warned Vivien. "What good will that do?"

"Enough," said Merlin. He pointed over towards the village, about fifty yards along a side lane from where the main road narrowed between the houses. There was a fairly unattractive pub, a 1960s brick building with a large black-and-white sign that said "Food" over the inn sign, which was too far away for Susan to make out the name. "You see the pub? We run for that. They'll have a phone, we'll call in, get the info on Susan's dad."

"But . . . but there'll be police swarming here soon," Vivien started to say. "Maybe we should surrender—"

"We'll have at least ten minutes," said Merlin.

"And we'll be stuck in the pub! What are you planning, a siege? We can't—"

"No," said Merlin. "There's a pond in the village green. See, look through the gap between the pub and the house next to it."

Vivien stared at him.

"How does that help?" asked Susan.

"One of the left-handed to open the way; one of the right-handed to follow the ley," said Merlin, looking straight at Vivien. "I know traditionally it's done by Thurston and Merrihew, but it doesn't have to be them, does it? We can do it."

"And take Susan?"

"Where?" asked Susan.

"Can you think of anything else?" asked Merlin, ignoring Susan's question.

"Like I said, we could surrender to the police."

"The murmuration is moving, there are Watchers in the fields, whoever is after Susan wouldn't hesitate to take her from a police station. And kill us if we got in the way."

"But she's the child of an Old One! What if we're wrong about her?"

"I'm right here!" protested Susan.

"We'll explain later," snapped Vivien.

"It's a last resort, okay?" said Merlin. "Come *on*, we can't waste time."

"Uh . . ." Vivien vacillated, then suddenly nodded firmly and took an extra-deep breath. Holding it, she raised her arms, turning her palms outwards. She brought them down slowly and put them together, silver light shining from the edge of her glove. She lifted her right hand and placed it on top of Merlin's head. Susan gasped as he shimmered and became transparent. Not completely invisible—she could still see a vague outline if she stared right at him—but close enough. Vivien touched Susan's head next, with the same result, and then patted herself on the head, and, without waiting, ran towards the pub, still holding her breath.

Susan followed, almost bumping into Merlin, who could obviously see her better since he swerved aside. Susan looked down at herself as she ran and almost fell over, it was so disorienting *not* to see anything.

They made it to the road in front of the pub—which Susan now could see was called the Ambrose Arms—when Vivien suddenly reappeared in front of Susan, stopped, and doubled over to vomit. That done, she drew in a series of racking breaths. Susan saw Merlin reappear and looked down, to see her own feet and legs coalescing into visibility again.

"Sorry," gasped Vivien. "Couldn't . . . uh . . . keep it up!"

"Well tried," said Merlin. "Guess we'll have to hurry a bit more."

He reached into his bag, took out the Smython, and rushed to the door of the pub. Susan followed, with Vivien more slowly bringing up the rear.

There was only one customer in the pub, a surprised-looking sixtyish man in crumpled work clothes and a flat cap who had picked up a cheese and Branston pickle sandwich and was about to take a bite of it when Merlin burst in.

"Out!" ordered Merlin, gesturing with the revolver. "Leave the sandwich."

The man put the sandwich down and hurried out.

"Here! What's all this?" cried the large, no-nonsense publican, coming out from behind the bar, flapping her apron as if Merlin were an errant rooster who'd somehow gotten inside. "You put that away and don't be stupid."

"I'm very sorry," said Merlin. He swapped the revolver to his right hand, stepped forward, and gripped the woman on the shoulder with his gloved left hand, his fingers finding and pressing key nerves. She shrieked and slumped down, knees suddenly weak. Merlin propelled her forward and pushed her out the door, as gently as he could.

"Lock it," he snapped to Susan. "Viv, find the phone. I'll make sure no one else is here."

He moved to the door behind the bar, listened there for a moment, then went in. Vivien scanned the room, didn't see a telephone, and went through the swinging door into the smaller parlor. Susan clicked the deadlock on the front door and pushed home the top and bottom bolts.

"Susan!" Merlin called out from somewhere within. "Look at your watch, tell me when five minutes is up. That's all we've got."

Susan looked. Her Swatch had stopped again. There were beads of moisture under the face, from Morcenna's well.

"It's stopped!" she called out.

Merlin didn't answer.

Susan shrugged. She went back into the main bar and sure enough, there was a clock there. She was setting her watch again in vain hope it would dry out when she saw a flash of movement through the window, causing a sudden blip of fear. She ran over to make sure the windows were all latched shut, and saw the publican and the customer who'd sensibly walked straight out. They were on the far side of the road, talking to a woman in a clerical dog collar who listened intently and then all three swiftly walked away.

"I think the vicar's gone to get help!" called out Susan.

"Traditional," replied Merlin, coming up behind her. "Someone's probably already used the police radio in the Granada. I should have disabled it. Don't worry about your watch—we might have a bit more time than I thought. Viv, you on the phone?"

"Yes!" came a cry from the other bar.

"There's a door from the kitchen," said Merlin. "We'll go out, through the car park, across the green to the pond. Give me the sword."

Susan handed him the ancient sword, and he buckled it on his belt.

"Why are we going to the *pond*?" asked Susan, frowning.

Again, Merlin didn't answer. This time it was because he was staring out the window.

Susan looked. The sky was darkening above the field to the east and she suddenly heard and felt a constant low vibration, the bass humming of thousands upon thousands of wings. . . .

"The birds," she said. "The starlings!"

The full murmuration had come together again and was swooping in over the fields, tendrils composed of hundreds of birds leaping out ahead of the thousands in the main body, almost touching the ground before gliding up again, looking into every dip and hollow in the ground and behind every tree and building.

"Viv! We have to go *now*!"

CHAPTER NINETEEN

>─◆>─◦─<◆─<

How far away lies Silvermere?
A thousand leagues and none
Where shall I find the hidden way
If you don't know, none will say

>─◆>─◦─<◆─<

MERLIN'S SHOUT ECHOED THROUGH THE PUB AS HE GRABBED SUSAN'S elbow and dragged her away from the window, then hustled her towards the door behind the bar.

Vivien came rocketing out of the parlor bar, but Merlin hadn't waited. He and Susan almost fell out of the back door, running across the potholed car park to the village green. The pond in the middle of the green was roughly round and only about sixty feet in diameter, its clear water edged with reeds. Susan had no idea why they were running towards it, but the swiftest glance over her shoulder confirmed what they were running away from: dense, questing tendrils composed of thousands and thousands of birds.

Merlin stopped at the edge of the pond, and knelt down. He looked back, too, and saw the probing fingers of the murmuration testing the windows of the pub, pushing down the chimney, battering at the doors. Birds stunned themselves, or broke their necks, and fell like crumbs around every searching tendril, but there were always more birds funneled down from the vast, pulsating mass overhead.

The hum had become a roar, growing louder and louder.

"I hope this works," he said, stripping the glove from his left hand. It shone pale silver in the sunlight as he extended his fingers and thrust them into the water, at the same time muttering something under his breath.

Behind them, the vast mass of birds swooped across the roof of the pub, cascaded down into the car park, and leaped up again, tendrils rushing towards the three of them in the pond. Hundreds if not thousands of birds seemingly intent on smashing straight into them. Many of them would die, fragile bird bodies crushed, but at speed so many small tough beaks and claws would be like grapeshot, or nails exploded in a lethal cone from an improvised explosive device.

The water parted under Merlin's hand, flung back to either side, and the bottom of the pond sank away, mud vanishing to reveal rough-worked steps cut into earth and then the totally incongruous sight of a familiar-looking door. A hotel door, with the metal numbers "617."

Merlin's room at the Northumberland.

Merlin ran down the steps with Susan and Vivien close behind, even as the leading finger of the murmuration reached the green, totally blocking the sun, the hum of all those beating wings now a roar, as if a waterfall cascaded down behind them.

Merlin flung the door open and reached back to grip Susan's left hand, pulling her in. Vivien followed, kicking the door shut behind her, accompanied by a sudden drumbeat like a machine gun as starlings smashed into it, dozens of small, feathery missiles.

Then there was silence.

"Where are we?" asked Susan, looking around. They were in almost total darkness, but she had a sensation of space about them and the air, though still, had the bite of frost in it; she felt it on her face. The only light came from the silvery glow of Merlin's hand, and a moment later Vivien's, as she took off her glove. But this was not enough to illuminate more than their faces, and the ground beneath them. Which, Susan noticed, was not bottom-of-a-pond mud but stone.

"Nowhere," said Merlin quietly. "Somewhere. An in-between place. Vivien?"

It was cold, and becoming colder with every passing second. Susan shivered.

"Vivien!" Merlin spoke more urgently, his breath a cloud of white.

"We are atop a low hill, in the spring, when the air is neither warm nor cool," said Vivien, gesturing with her hand, as if indicating a vista for them to gaze upon. "Under a crescent moon in a clear sky, so bright with stars we can see our way."

Susan blinked. The sky had lit up with stars, and a slim sliver of moon hung there, and in the sudden light she could see they were indeed standing upon a low hill, of purple heather and fallen stones. But beyond the hill and the sky there was intense darkness, a total absence of light and detail.

The intense feeling of increasing cold disappeared. Their breath was invisible now, no longer frosty billows of white.

"The old road follows the ley, the old road shows us the way," intoned Vivien, once again gesturing. Her silver hand was brighter now, as bright as the stars and moon, while Merlin's had dimmed to a faint glow.

A road sprang up ahead of them down the hill and across the dark void. A straight, welcoming road, of dirt and not enough gravel and numerous potholes, with wildflowers growing on the grassy verges. But to either side of the road there was nothing but the dark.

"Susan, keep holding Merlin's hand and stay close behind me," said Vivien. She stepped onto the road and began to walk, holding her hand up in front, as if she needed to feel the way or might come upon some unseen obstruction.

Merlin's right hand gripped Susan's left. She was comforted by his touch. His skin was warm, hers still icy. But she did not move.

"Where are we going?" she asked quietly.

Apart from their voices and footsteps, there was no noise here at all.

"Silvermere," said Merlin, his voice also low. "Where the Grail-Keeper resides. It can be reached through any body of water, but usually we pass through at the lake in the old quarry at Wooten, where Merrihew fishes for the ancient carp. The Greats open the way, and lead whoever's going there. Viv and I have never done it by ourselves before."

"How far . . . how long do we walk through wherever this is?" asked Susan. She tried to sound calm, but she wasn't. There was something eerie and deeply troubling about the space around them, beyond the road.

"It varies," said Merlin. Susan noticed his eyes kept flickering to either side, alert for something in that nothingness, beyond the narrow way.

"It won't be long," said Vivien, with confidence. She was only a few steps in front, but she didn't pause or turn her head behind to talk. "Remember to keep walking along the road, no matter what."

"Like the old straight track in Highgate Wood," said Susan to Merlin. "Does that mean there's something like the Shuck out there?"

"Not like the Shuck," said Vivien, momentarily reassuring Susan before she continued. "But there are entities entirely unrooted from the world, who might seek to return by using us as vessels," replied Vivien, her face set on the road ahead. "They cannot harm us if we keep to the way and do not respond to their beguilement."

"Uh, okay," said Susan. She sped up a bit, to keep closer to Vivien. The darkness beyond the road felt even more inimical now she knew there definitely were things in its dark reaches that might wish her harm.

"I need to tell you quite a lot," said Vivien. "We might not be able to talk in Silvermere. I'm not sure what will happen there. Time moves strangely and it's weird in other ways. When I've been before, some of the people I was with didn't seem to be there at the same time, even though we went together. And some came back separately as well."

"What do you mean?" asked Susan nervously. Her mind immediately leaped ahead to being left in this dark void alone. Would the sky be bright, and the road here, if it weren't for Vivien and her shining right hand?

"The Grail-Keeper decides what occurs in Silvermere, who may come and go, and on what terms," said Vivien. "Don't worry, we'll definitely get there and it is much easier leaving, the Grail-Keeper sorts that out. But we might not be able to all talk together and we might be separated coming back. So you need to know what I learned from Aunt Helen and Aunt Zoë; a great deal of information has finally come in, and even though I don't know what it means yet, at least we're finally getting to grips—"

"You got through, then?" interrupted Merlin. "Thurston and Merrihew didn't commandeer the call?"

"Thurston cut in right at the end, in a total flap, ordering us to surrender to the nearest police station and wait for 'older and wiser counsel,'" said Vivien. It was weird her speaking without looking back, thought Susan; it almost made her voice seem disembodied. "But I talked to Zoë and Helen first, and they have dropped everything to work on this. Susan, the library card was in the name of 'Coniston comma Rex.'"

"Rex!" exclaimed Susan. "So my dad's name *is* Rex?"

"Not exactly," continued Vivien. "As soon as she saw that, Helen remembered where she'd seen the drawing on the cigarette case. It's—look down!"

Susan obeyed. She had a split-second glimpse of a vast shadow blotting out the moon and stars, and two brilliant and strangely fascinating violet eyes before she refocused on the back of Vivien's shoes. She kept looking at them. The shadow withdrew, but she could feel a presence nearby, and a sheen of violet light persisted in her vision.

"Don't look and you'll be fine," said Merlin, close behind her. His words were somewhat belied by how swiftly he had drawn the old sword, which he held high in his left hand, and his right hand closed more tightly on Susan's.

"Keep your eyes down. As Vivien said, it can't touch us on the road, only lure us to leave it."

"What is it?" asked Susan. She hoped she sounded calm and conversational. She could feel the thing's presence, keeping pace with them, a vast shape of shadow that loomed as close as it dared to the road.

"Something ancient and forgotten, something banished long ago," said Vivien. "Pay it no attention. As I was saying, Helen recognized the etching on your cigarette case as a stylized work after J. M. W. Turner's *A View in the Lake District*."

"And?" asked Susan. She was finding it hard not to look aside; it took considerable effort to keep her gaze focused on

Vivien's back. There was something about those violet eyes that she wanted to see again. . . .

"Head down!" snapped Merlin.

Susan almost wrenched her neck looking down again. She hadn't realized she was starting to look up, which was deeply disturbing.

"So, Turner, *A View in the Lake District ,*" she said, talking more loudly to distract herself from the lure of the creature who stalked beside them.

"It's commonly believed to be a view of the Old Man of Coniston," said Vivien.

"Which is a mountain," said Susan.

"True," said Vivien. "But the Old Man of Coniston is also one of the Ancient Sovereigns. And 'Rex' means 'King' in Latin."

"My father is the *Old Man of Coniston?*" blurted out Susan. "That's almost as bad as being a stone."

But though she said that, there was something about the phrase "the Old Man of Coniston" that resonated inside her; she felt that fizzy, expectant sensation grow stronger, as if recognizing that its time drew ever nearer.

"He's not actually the mountain," said Merlin. "I mean, he kind of . . . um . . . inhabits it metaphysically; it's the locus of his power. Did the aunts have anything else to add?"

"Yes," replied Vivien. "I hadn't got very far with the microfiche copies of the Harshton and Hoole records when I heard about the incursion at . . . at the safe house. But I asked Cousin Linda to keep going, and to tell Helen what she found. Which was almost nothing, which is suspicious in itself. A very *selective* fire, obviously—"

"What did she find?" asked Susan urgently. She was having trouble keeping her eyes on Vivien's feet, and now she thought she could hear faint music coming from the darkness, lilting, soft music that made her want to turn her head to catch it better, to fix the melody in her mind.

"A carbon copy of a lockbox inventory at the main Birmingham workshop that included *two* silver-gilt cigarette cases, 'for purposes of propitiation,' and they were marked as delivered."

"What does that mean?" asked Susan loudly. She shook her head to try to get the music out of it. It was like the worst earworm ever, made more intriguing because she couldn't quite make all of it out. The urge to stop and listen and turn her head was intense, like an unbearable itch. Distraction was the only thing that kept her from pursuing that music, from looking at the eyes she knew were mere feet away, staring at her. . . .

"And *two*? Why two cigarette cases?" added Susan. "Two! Two!"

Behind her, Merlin started to sing Gilbert and Sullivan again, "A British Tar Is a Soaring Soul" from *H.M.S. Pinafore* in a gruff, very flat voice quite different from the tuneful baritone he'd employed back in the hotel. It was, Susan realized, more effective in blocking the siren call of the creature that accompanied them in the shadows by the road. The otherworldly music latched on to the true notes, but was repelled by flats and sharps.

"Nearly all mythic entities can be propitiated or distracted with gifts; it's in their nature," said Vivien. She had adopted a droning, boring lecture tone, again clearly a tactic to counter the siren call. "They love precious metals and jewelry, and fine weapons and so on, which Harshton and Hoole make to help us when we need to do deals."

"So the booksellers were trying to organize something between my father and . . . who?" asked Susan. She was almost shouting, but neither Merlin nor Vivien objected. It helped block the lure.

"I don't know," said Vivien, with great frustration. "But someone does. I mean, one of us."

"Thurston, I reckon," said Merlin. He took a breath and sang on, "'And his fist be ever ready, for a knock-down blow!'"

"Maybe," replied Vivien. "It might not even be one of the Greats."

"So my father is the Old Man of Coniston," shouted Susan. "The Old Man of Conisto-on-on-on-on!"

"It seems that is precisely so," droned Vivien. "Let me cast my mind back to the *Index of Ancient Sovereigns and Principalities of England*. I cannot entirely recall the entry on your father, because he is not listed as malevolent, and we only made a particular study of the malevolents, of which there are approximately six hundred and nineteen. As of 1926, when the last edition of the *Index* was published. A new one is somewhat overdue."

"'He never should bow down to a domineering frown!'" roared Merlin.

"How interesting!" shouted Susan. "Do go on!"

The alluring melody was growing stronger, too, attempting to break through the cacophony of Merlin's singing, Vivien's droning lecture, and Susan's shouting. It was beautiful, but incomplete, and every part of Susan ached to hear it properly, to give in and listen to the most beautiful song she had ever partially heard. But she resisted it, and the violet eyes, opening her mouth to make a soft coughing sound in time to Merlin's singing, and lidding her eyes so that all she saw were the backs of Vivien's heels.

"The Old Man of Coniston rules two leagues north and west of his eponymous mountain, and two leagues south and east of the lake."

"How far is a league?"

"A little under three and a half miles," said Vivien.

"'His nose should pant and his lip should curl,'" roared Merlin. "'His cheeks should flame and his brow should furl!'"

"Would that include Lake Windermere?"

"The western shore at least, in my considered opinion," replied Vivien, very dry and matter-of-fact. "Ah . . . the Fenris of Onundar Myrr. The Sacred Wolves of England do not come under any particular rule, but they could be bound for a time at least by a sufficiently powerful Old One."

"The Fenris that kidnapped me was most definitely compelled to do so," shouted Susan. "Merlin did think *Father* might have sent her! I don't agree."

"The extremely distinguished and knowledgeable even-handed

Helen thought it most likely your father is no longer extant," replied Vivien, still talking in her stilted, pedantic fashion. Susan had to struggle to hear her over Merlin's raucous singing and the melodious siren. "Or you would not have inherited whatever power has begun to stir within you."

"I think he's alive!" shouted Susan. "And I don't think I have any power. I sense something sort of waiting inside me, but nothing more than that. Except I feel very strongly I need to go to my father, which suggests he's still around. Maybe he did send the Fenris to fetch me. . . ."

"Your old man isn't an inimical one, and he has no power in old Luan-Dun," sang Merlin, continuing the tune of "A British Tar" but changing the words. "Wouldn't have killed the men, or born monsters from an old caul-dren."

"My colleague has a dismal rhyme but he makes an important point," droned Vivien. "Whether the Fenris was sent by your father or not, I believe that after we take counsel from the Grail-Keeper it may prove our most efficacious course *is* to go to the Old Man of Coniston and—"

Mid-sentence, Vivien vanished from the road ahead. A moment later, Susan felt the ground beneath her feet disappear. The alluring music stopped abruptly and the darkness and the violet-eyed shadow were replaced in that same moment by warm, golden sunshine, reflecting from the waters of a clear but reedy-edged lake.

Susan stood on the very edge, in two inches of crystal-clear water, with sand and pebbles underfoot and tiny silver fish circumnavigating her Docs. Ahead of her, there was a narrow strip of beach before the ground rose to a wooded island, or perhaps a peninsula, since she could not see whether it joined some mainland on the other side. The island was at least a mile long, the lake bending around it at either end. Whether that was south and north or east and west or something else Susan had no clue, because despite the pleasantly warm sunshine, she could not see the sun, no matter where she looked.

Behind her, the lake extended into a hazy distance, any terrain beyond invisible. Certainly she couldn't see any mountains or hills, and the lake was far too wide for it to be the Lake District of England. Besides, she instinctively knew this was somewhere else.

She saw a cormorant dive and come back up with a wriggling fish. The wind moved across the lake, but there were only small and gentle waves. In fact, it was impossible to imagine this place ever had any wilder weather, the lake becoming storm-tossed and dangerous.

Presumably this was Silvermere. Something about the perfection of the golden light and the warmth of the air, with the faintest touch of pleasant coolness from the breeze, suggested this was a fabled place. It fairly oozed with peace and calm and a deep sense of rest. In other circumstances, Susan would have happily taken off her shoes and waded in the shallows, basked in the sunshine, watched the natural world go by.

There was no sign of Vivien and Merlin. Or anyone else.

But there was a path ahead, a well-trodden way between

the alders that leaned over the narrow sand and pebble-strewn beach. The path then went on between two protruding gray stones into the forest of oak and beech, sweet chestnut and rowan, and there were bluebells peeking up amidst the grass between the trees. A wood warbler flashed by, a fleeting glimpse of white and green.

Susan stepped up out of the water, and onto the path.

CHAPTER TWENTY

>-+-<>-0-<>-+-<

I 'ave a bright new sixpence
I found upon a sty
And with this wealth I will go hence
You know the reason why

>-+-<>-0-<>-+-<

THE PATH ROSE STEEPLY FOR ABOUT TWENTY YARDS, WHERE THE ground leveled out and the wood thinned a little, still with gray upthrust rocks sticking out here and there. A little way ahead, a larger rock protruded, and a young girl sat on top of it. A brown-skinned, dark-haired, black-eyed girl of perhaps nine or ten, wearing a homespun smock of natural wool, her feet bare. In sharp contrast to her simple clothing, she had heavy gold bracelets on each wrist, beautifully made ornaments of many twisted gold wires wound together.

A small silver-gray hawk sat on her shoulder, talons piercing the smock but surprisingly not the skin beneath, for there was no blood. It looked at Susan with a fierce black-pupiled yellow eye, and launched itself into the sky.

The girl raised a hand in greeting. Susan stopped a good

distance away and eyed her cautiously.

"Hello," she said. "I'm Susan. Who are you?"

The girl stood up on top of the rock. Her knees were skinned and her feet were dirty.

"I am the Grail-Keeper," she intoned, making Susan jump backwards, because her voice was not that of a young girl, but a much older and deeper-voiced man.

"Oops," said the Grail-Keeper. She coughed a couple of times before continuing, her voice becoming higher, more gentle and childlike. "That didn't come out right. I thought appearing in this guise would make things easier for you. But it is long since I have walked in this skin, and I do beg your pardon."

"Sure," said Susan. A horrible suspicion entered her mind, which she had to banish immediately with a direct question. "Um, that hawk, it wasn't . . . Merlin?"

"A merlin, certainly," said the Grail-Keeper. "But not Merlin St. Jacques. Nor his sister, since I see you are concerned that might be the case."

"Where are they?"

"They are here."

"This is Silvermere?"

"Yes. The lake, the island, the house. All are Silvermere. Though like me, they may appear in different guises for different visitors. The St. Jacques, for example, have a common view of what Silvermere should be, and so it is," she explained chattily.

Susan listened to this adult explanation, coming from what

appeared to be an enthusiastic child, but which she knew was really some sort of ancient mythic entity. Perhaps an Ancient Sovereign herself. Or maybe the Grail-Keeper was some sort of hybrid of mortal and myth, as the booksellers were? And, Susan realized, as she was herself. . . .

"Similarly, they have shared expectations of the Grail-Keeper, and that is what they get. Come, walk with me."

She jumped easily down from the rock and smiled, a brief, mischievous smile. The kind that if she were the little girl she seemed to be might lead to some sort of innocuous trick, but given who she actually was, made Susan feel very nervous.

"You will be safe here," said the Grail-Keeper, her face serious, the smile vanished. Susan wondered if she could read her mind, or at the least, detect her fears.

"Safe from all your enemies. Until you leave, of course."

"All my enemies?" asked Susan. "Plural. As in more than one."

"Did I say that?"

"Yes."

"Do you know who they are?" asked Susan.

The girl nodded.

"Can you tell me?"

"I could," said the Grail-Keeper. That mischievous smile flickered across her face again. "But I won't. I'm not supposed to interfere in what goes on beyond Silvermere. So I don't, on the whole. Perhaps a little nudge, here and there, nothing of great moment."

"My enemies," repeated Susan. "Plural. I don't suppose you'll wink if I guess who they are?"

"No," said the girl. She paused to wink ferociously several times, alternating eyes, before skipping on again. Susan followed her, but her mind was elsewhere, thinking about "enemies" and their possible motivations.

The Grail-Keeper suddenly stopped skipping and skidded to a halt as the path ahead forked, though in both cases it continued through the wood and the two paths looked no different.

"Shall we take the left- or right-hand way?"

"I don't know," said Susan. "Where are we going?"

"Where do you want to go?"

Susan opened her mouth, shut it, and thought very carefully. One part of her simply wanted to go home and go to bed and pull the Moomintroll quilt her mother made her when she was eight over her head, and have Jassmine absentmindedly bring her cold cups of tea she'd made hours before. She even felt this might be possible, that this strange, fey little girl before her might be able to arrange that. But she also knew her mother's house would be only a very temporary refuge. Whatever had been set in motion would carry on to the end, whether she hid from it or not.

Then there were the booksellers. Though she had serious doubts about Thurston and Merrihew, she had total confidence in Merlin and Vivien, and the even-handed Aunts Helen and Zoë had impressed her. Perhaps if she could go to the Old Bookshop, she would be safe and the booksellers could sort out what was going on. . . .

But neither of these felt right. Susan knew where she really needed to go.

She opened her mouth again and spoke forcefully.

"I want to go to my father. I'm sure he isn't dead, or gone, or whatever it is Helen and Zoë think. I want to go to the Old Man of Coniston."

"Then you shall," said the Grail-Keeper. "In fact, both these paths will take you there. The question is, which one?"

"Where are Merlin and Vivien?" Susan asked again. She looked past the girl to the separate paths. Both looked essentially the same, well-trodden trails through the wood. "Are they at the end of either of these paths?"

"No," said the Grail-Keeper.

"But they're all right?"

"They're enjoying a rather good dinner," said the girl.

"Dinner," sighed Susan. Her stomach twinged and she felt momentarily faint, and a touch confused. She hadn't had breakfast or lunch, and it was already time for dinner? "They couldn't wait for me?"

"They have, for the moment, forgotten you are here," replied the Grail-Keeper.

"What!"

"The Silvermere of the St. Jacques is not for you, at least not on this occasion. You may pass through *this* Silvermere with me, but you may not linger, nor may you eat or drink, for you are not an *invited* guest. I have allowed Merlin and Vivien to bring you here, but not to stay."

"And I have to leave without them? Without Merlin and Vivien?" asked Susan. She tried to sound strong, but couldn't help a faint tremor in her voice.

The girl nodded, very solemn now.

"This isn't one of those things where one path leads to my doom and the other to redemption or something, is it?"

"Perhaps both paths lead to your doom," said the Grail-Keeper. "But either one will take you where you say you want to go."

"I'm not simply *saying* it's where I want to go!" protested Susan. She took a breath and repeated herself, slowly and firmly. "I *need* to go to my father. To the Old Man of Coniston. I'd love to have the help of Merlin and Vivien, because I do believe they are my friends. But I will go alone if I have to. And I will take the right-hand path."

"Good," said the girl. She winked and added, "It's a bit quicker."

They took the right-hand path and walked on through the pleasant wood, with great oaks and slim ash trees and here and there bright rowan trees caught between bud and berry, the white flowers not entirely fallen and the berries coming into their full color. The sunshine shone down to make a dappled light, and many flowers grew amongst the grass to either side of the path: a carpet of bluebells and bursts of celandine, wood sorrel, lords and ladies, and ransoms.

But Susan was too hungry, tired, and generally apprehensive to appreciate the beauty of this wood. She strode on behind the Grail-Keeper, who walked fast and occasionally began to skip, which was even faster. The fizzing, expectant sensation inside Susan was still there, even growing stronger, but it was counterbalanced by a heavy feeling of lonely dread.

The path began to climb a little, and they came to a grassy clearing. The girl crossed it and climbed upon a strangely flat-surfaced lichen-covered rock that thrust up out of the earth, the greater part of it buried. Though at first it seemed an entirely natural outcrop, Susan realized it was in fact a roughly worked and truly enormous obelisk, bigger even than Cleopatra's Needle, fallen on its side and buried, with only the last dozen yards projecting out of the earth.

"Come on!" said the girl.

Susan clambered up the sloping face of the great stone to the end and stood next to the Grail-Keeper. She was surprised to see they had come to the other side of the island; the shore had been screened by the trees. The stone projected out over the lake. Clear water lapped directly against the rocky shore of the island underneath, some thirty feet below where she stood. The water beneath looked very deep, the sunlight only illuminating the upper reaches.

The Grail-Keeper gestured below.

"There you are."

"What?" asked Susan. "Do I jump in?"

It was a long way down.

"You could dive, though I don't recommend it," said the Grail-Keeper. "If you walk forward here, you will walk forward there."

"There being somewhere close to the mountain? To the Old Man of Coniston?"

"Indeed," said the Grail-Keeper. "Off you go."

Susan hesitated, looking down into the dark water. She glanced at the Grail-Keeper, wondering if she should trust her.

"Yes," said the Grail-Keeper. She sighed in exasperation and added, "You should have jumped straight away. Now there's an unnecessary complication."

"What?" asked Susan, but the Grail-Keeper had disappeared. Susan looked down but the girl was not in the water, not on the rock or in the clearing. Nowhere visible.

But someone else was.

The left-handed bookseller Merrihew, dressed as she had been in the New Bookshop, in a fisherman's vest over a sleeveless dress, but this time she had on black Wellington boots rather than shoes. She looked cross, her face set in stark lines, and she was stamping her feet as she crossed the grassy clearing.

Merrihew saw Susan, and without hesitation, a small, bright knife appeared in her hand. She flicked her wrist and it flew straight at Susan's face, so fast there was no chance to do more than flinch as it sped straight at her eye.

But it didn't hit her. In one instant the knife was in the air, death imminent, and in the next it was held by a tall, balding but white-haired and white-bearded man very reminiscent of a portrait Susan liked of Charles Darwin, the one by Walter William Ouless.

But his deep black eyes and the gold bangles of wound wire on his wrists indicated who he was, despite the change of gender and the rumpled gray suit he wore rather than a homespun smock.

There was no doubt he was another aspect of the Grail-Keeper.

"I don't allow killing on Silvermere," chided the Grail-Keeper. "Not by others, at any rate. You know that, Merrihew."

"You do not interfere in the business of the St. Jacques, Grail-Keeper," said Merrihew. "That is the law."

"Beyond my borders, that is so," said the Grail-Keeper. She looked at Susan and smiled her enigmatic smile. "But here, my rule is absolute. You may leave us, Susan. Simply step off into the water; you will be where you want to go."

"And I will follow!" said Merrihew vehemently. "And do what should have been done earlier. She's the daughter of an Old One, and a clear and present danger to all of us!"

"Good title for a book," shouted Susan scornfully. "Someone should use it. You know I'm not a danger to the St. Jacques. You're not only rude, you're a traitor as well, and Merlin and Vivien know it. I bet you even killed their mum."

The Grail-Keeper sighed, a little girl's sigh, odd from the old man's mouth.

Merrihew's lips thinned to the merest line, and her eyes narrowed.

"How dare you! I would never do such a thing. It was a coincidence, or an accident!"

"Yeah?" said Susan. "I bet you knew. And what about those police officers sent to kill Merlin and Vivien?"

"What?"

"You know!"

Merrihew's hand sidled to a pocket of her vest, but stopped as the Grail-Keeper suddenly flipped the knife, to hold it by the hilt rather than the blade.

"You're nothing more than a minor complication in a long and successful operation," called out Merrihew. She took a couple of slow steps forward. "Which has delivered great benefits to us, and will continue to do so when you are no longer able to cause highly unnecessary trouble."

"I bet Aunts Helen and Zoë are onto you, too," spat Susan. "Whatever happens to me, you've had it."

"You have no conception of how we booksellers conduct our business," said Merrihew. She raised her gloved left hand, and stepped forward again. "I command the left-handed—and the left-handed are both executors, executioners and the executive. If I say something has to be done for the good of all the St. Jacques, then that is so. But perhaps I have been hasty. The Grail-Keeper will not allow me to harm you here. We should talk, more calmly."

Susan realized that having failed to kill her, Merrihew now wanted to slow her down, to stop or delay her leaving. She doubted this would be to her benefit.

"I'll give you a small head start," whispered the little girl, close to Susan's ear, even though the Charles Darwin–like figure still stood in front of her. "It won't be much."

"I apologize for throwing the knife," called out Merrihew, sidling closer again.

"Fuck you!" shouted Susan. She turned around and stepped off the rock into the air, lifting her arms and scissoring her legs in the approved safety jump method taught to her in the interminable school swimming lessons, when you absolutely had to jump into water of uncertain depth.

Merlin and Vivien had changed for dinner and looked more alike than ever in their black dinner jackets, boiled white shirts, and black bow ties over stiff collars, though Merlin had adopted a pale gray waistcoat and Vivien an eggshell-blue one. They had finished with the potato and leek soup, and were working on well-grilled lamb chops with mashed potato and peas, accompanied by a 1971 Bordeaux from an unknown vintner (the label having come off) with the certain knowledge of a dessert trolley's appearance in the near future. Vivien filled Merlin's glass and started to refill her own, then stopped suddenly, the bottle held at a dangerous angle, not quite pouring but quite likely to spill.

"Merlin! What are we doing here?"

Merlin was eating and reading, a green linen-bound hardcover of *Gaudy Night* by Dorothy Sayers propped up open against the silver-topped cut-glass salt and pepper shakers.

"Pardon?" he asked dreamily, looking up from the book.

Vivien repeated her question.

Merlin finished chewing on a piece of lamb. He looked at his sister, then slowly around the wood-paneled dining room, the six other tables with their snowy white tablecloths, silver and glassware set, but no one sitting at them. The familiar, enormous mahogany sideboard with the silver tureen in the shape of a vast oyster, the tall windows to the right, overlooking the woods, because they were on the third floor.

"Silvermere," he said vaguely. "The upper dining room. Having dinner . . . or is it lunch? We came to . . . um . . . we came to . . ."

"Susan," said Vivien slowly, trying out the name as if it were unfamiliar or she didn't know what the word meant.

Merlin paled and closed his book. He looked around again, more alertly.

"Susan," he repeated. "We brought Susan here, and we've *forgotten*! How long have we been here?"

Vivien slammed the bottle down and pushed her chair back.

"Not long," said Vivien. "We were starving, we came straight to lunch. But Susan . . ."

Merlin pushed his own chair back, put the book into his yak-hair bag, and swung it onto his shoulder.

"We need to find the Grail-Keeper," he said. His voice was even, but he was clenching and unclenching his fists. "Could . . . could Susan still be on the road?"

"The road isn't there if I'm not," said Vivien. "She *must* have come through. I mean, the alternative—"

"Sometimes I hate this place," said Merlin vehemently. "Not that I suppose I'll remember."

"You will remember if you want to," said the Grail-Keeper. She swung her legs out of the large dumbwaiter that could bring a dozen meals at a time up from the kitchen below, and stood up, brushing some crumbs off her matronly white tunic. As she always appeared to the younger booksellers, she looked like a middle-aged, kind but firmly in-charge sort of woman, a sort of nicer version of Margaret Thatcher. Her eyes were black and she had golden bracelets on her wrists.

"Where's Susan?" asked Merlin.

"At this moment, walking with me through the wood to the Stone of Departure," said the Grail-Keeper. "On her way to wherever she wants to go."

"But . . . but she needs to be with us," said Merlin, ignoring the multiplicity of the Grail-Keeper being in two places; this was a known part of visiting Silvermere and he remembered *that*. "She'll be starving, too, and we need to work out what to do!"

"As I did not invite her here, and she does not have the standing invitation extended to those of your family, she cannot stay."

"Oh, I . . . I . . . thought . . . thought it . . . it . . . would . . . would . . . be . . . be . . . okay . . . okay," stammered Merlin and Vivien together, in weird sibling stereo.

"It is, as you say, okay, this time," replied the Grail-Keeper gently. "In any case, I think Susan knows where she needs to go and perhaps even what she needs to do."

"No she doesn't," said Vivien. "We're still working out exactly what's going on."

"Do you need to know 'exactly'?" asked the Grail-Keeper.

"No," said Merlin. "Viv! We need to get to the obelisk before Susan tries to go anywhere."

"We need to know about the Cauldron-Born," said Vivien,

resisting Merlin's tug on her arm. "Was it made here? With our . . . your grail?"

"No. The grail has never been used in that way, and it never will be," answered the Grail-Keeper, very firmly.

"Do you know which cauldron was used? And who has it?"

"I do not," replied the Grail-Keeper. "I do know the St. Jacques knowledge of the cauldrons is lacking—"

She suddenly stopped talking and her hand flashed up. A small, bright knife appeared there, snatched out of the air.

"Now, there's an unnecessary complication," she said testily.

"That's Merrihew's!" snapped Merlin. "One of her leaf knives!"

"Merrihew," said Vivien. "Oh no!"

"Likes knives, does she?" asked the Grail-Keeper.

She spoke to the air, for Merlin and Vivien had run from the room, tearing their napkins off to flutter to the floor behind them like startled, overburdened doves.

CHAPTER TWENTY-ONE

>─┤◆├─◆─○─◆─┤◆├─◄

Roses can be yellow, violets may be white
Hate might turn to liking, love could change to spite
Nothing is fixed forever, even stars will die
All that we can ever do, is ask the reason why

>─┤◆├─◆─○─◆─┤◆├─◄

SUSAN NEVER HIT THE WATER, OR AT LEAST SHE DIDN'T THINK SHE did. One second she was falling, the next she was on solid ground and somewhere else entirely, no longer in Silvermere. Looking like an idiot with her knees bent and arms outstretched, on the shore of a tarn halfway up a mountain. A kneeling, bearded hiker stared at her over the top of his smoking Volcano stove, which had started to whistle. An enamel mug fell from his hand on to the stony shore, landed with a musical ding, and rolled away to end up against a wax-paper-wrapped sandwich.

"Did you come out of—" the hiker asked hesitantly, pointing to the tarn.

Susan didn't answer. She could feel a power coursing up through her entire body from the broken shale beneath her feet, joining that fizzy sense of anticipation that had begun to wake inside her on her eighteenth birthday. It was her power, she knew, and it was centered here, beneath her feet and all around. The small lake behind her was part of it, which she immediately knew was in these days called Low Water, and the long lake to the east was Coniston Water, though once it had been Thursteinn Waeter.

Most of all she knew the mountain she was already two-thirds of the way up, its peak rising to the south, the way there traced by a zigzag path through the broken gray shale and brown-green grass, the top shrouded in low cloud, which even as she watched rolled farther down the slope.

The Old Man of Coniston, wreathed in fog.

"You came out of the water," repeated the man. It wasn't a question now. "But you're not wet. . . ."

Susan looked at herself. Not only was she completely dry, her boiler suit was clean again; the tears from the goblin's sharp nails and the rumpling from the Fenris's jaws and the stains of wandering through the woods had vanished. Her Docs were polished to a high sheen, which they never were normally; she put dubbin on them and left them dull.

The Grail-Keeper had dressed her up for a visit to her dad. Like she was six years old.

"Yeah," she said, half in a daze from the sensation of power building up inside her. She looked past the hiker to the sun, which was climbing up, but still low in the sky. It was morning, probably only nine or ten o'clock, but it had been early afternoon when Merlin had led them to the door in the pond. . . .

She'd lost at least a day. Maybe more.

"Uh, and good morning," added Susan. She started up the path, walking fast. With every step she felt more of the power within the mountain coming into her, but it was only a fraction of what was there, and she also felt a kind of countercurrent, as if something opposed the flow of magic.

Someone was working against her taking up her father's power. Until she came into her full inheritance she would be vulnerable, even here. But this also puzzled her. She knew deep inside that her father lived; he had not faded away or dissipated or whatever happened to Ancient Sovereigns. Why was his power coming to her now? And who was holding it back?

"Hey, don't go up!" the hiker called after her. "The weather's turning! You aren't dressed for it!"

Susan suddenly remembered Merrihew would be coming after her. She wouldn't want witnesses.

"*You* need to get off the mountain!" she called. "Quick as you can."

The hiker reacted as if he'd been struck by an arrow. He stepped back and grunted, turned on the spot, and ran to the downwards path over broken shale and rocks, leaving his pack, the still-whistling Volcano, and his enamel cup.

"But be careful!" shouted Susan, aware that she had *commanded* the man. Even if she had not come into her full power, what she had already was sufficient to compel a mortal to do her bidding. At least within the demesne of Coniston Rex.

The hiker slowed in obedience, but did not stop or look

around. Susan knew he wouldn't until he reached the village below, or maybe not even till he hit the shores of the lake itself.

Susan wondered if she had the power to lift the fog on the peak above. She raised her hands and ordered the cloud to dissipate. Nothing happened and she didn't feel the strange, electric spark that had leaped through throat and mouth when she'd ordered the hiker to leave. The elements, it seemed, were more resistant to persuasion than people. Or that magic was another level of difficulty altogether.

She started up the track again, pushing herself to almost run, pressing down on her thighs as she came to the first section of rough steps. She was surprised she wasn't out of breath. Despite being reasonably fit, it was a steep climb and she was taking it much faster than she usually would. But the power that flowed into her from the stones beneath her feet also revitalized every part of her. She felt fresh and energetic, undaunted by the climb.

But as she reached the first wispy descending tendrils of the fog, she felt a warning twinge, a sense of wrongness. It dizzied her for a moment, because it came from both ahead and behind, before settling into a definite sense of something bad behind her. A threat.

Something or someone who should not be on the mountain, who wished her harm.

Susan looked over her shoulder. Down below, Merrihew stepped out of nowhere onto the shore of Low Water. She kicked the still-smoking Volcano stove over, and the faint whistle Susan had tuned out finally stopped.

The bookseller looked up at Susan and drew a small pistol—like the one Merlin kept in his leg holster—from under her fishing vest and took careful aim for a moment, then dropped her hand and began to run. Clearly, for even a left-handed bookseller, the range was too great for such a small pistol. But despite being probably ten times Susan's age, Merrihew ran much faster up the path.

Susan lunged forward, taking the steps almost on hands and knees, pushing herself even harder. She was panting and wheezing now, both from the effort and from fear. She felt her shoulder blades clenching together in expectation of being shot at any moment, and wished the fog would come down faster and get thicker, but there were still only the leading wisps from the greater cloud above.

Soon the path veered to the right and became steeper, but without steps, and it was much rougher and less distinct. Susan had to clamber up amidst tumbled stones and broken slate, and it slowed her down. But the fog did finally begin to thicken, and it became colder and darker. Granted a faint sense of security, at least for a moment, Susan eased up from the grueling pace she'd set and looked down through the shifting fog only to see the dim shape of Merrihew sixty or seventy yards below, leaping like a mountain goat up the section with steps.

The left-handed bookseller saw Susan slow, and whipped up her arm, firing four quick shots even as she continued jumping up multiple steps at a time. The first three shots missed, ricochets screaming off the rocks above and below Susan.

The fourth bullet caught her as she started to run again, scraping across the outside of her left thigh, an inch above the knee. She felt it first like a cube of ice dragged across her skin, a distinct but not intense pain, but then as she ran on, the pain blossomed. Susan screamed, once, but it was more a scream of rage than fear. She glanced at the wound, saw it had scored the outside of her leg rather than going through, that it was not fatal or perhaps even serious. She pressed on, as fast as she could.

She was close to the summit now, she felt it, and she knew her father was somehow there. Above all else, she had to get to him. But there was also that warning twinge, that sense of something not right. The Grail-Keeper had spoken of enemies, plural. One was behind her, that was for certain. She felt another enemy lay ahead. But she had no choice except to go on. Merrihew wanted to kill her and she did not know what her other enemy wanted.

It was only another twenty or thirty feet to the summit. If she made it before Merrihew got close enough to see her despite the fog, if she could reach her father, draw in more of the magic of the mountain, then perhaps she could do something to save herself. And she had the knife and the salt. She didn't want to bind anyone to her service, but if the alternative was death . . .

Susan took out the knife as she struggled over the loose rocks, and wiped it against her wounded leg, smearing it with her blood before sliding it back in the ruler pocket, out of sight. She pulled out one of the small packets of salt, but she didn't dare stop to try to open it, so she clutched it in her hand and continued to clamber up and over the broken ground.

Merlin and Vivien came out of Low Water to the sound of gunfire.

"Beretta .25," said Merlin. He paused for an instant to snatch up something from the ground and ran onto the path up the mountainside. He couldn't see who was shooting or at what; the fog was too thick, majestically rolling down towards them. "Has to be Merrihew's. Shooting at Susan, I suppose. But the fog . . . she'd be very hard to hit."

He spoke to reassure himself, but it didn't work for either him or Vivien, and they both increased their pace, only to slow after a few yards as their flat leather-soled dress shoes slipped on the stones and grass. Merlin suddenly stopped, sat down and tore away the laces, and ripped his shoes off, Vivien sitting to do likewise.

"Damn Silvermere!" cursed Merlin, and ran on again. A totally incongruous pair, in evening wear with bare feet, each with one hand shining silver, as they had not stopped to pick up their white gloves nor their top hats when they sprinted from the dining room.

Susan came to the top of the Old Man of Coniston warily, staying low. The fog was so thick she couldn't see more than a few yards past her face, but she knew there was a cairn on a platform ahead, as well as she knew the layout of her own home. Though she had never been here, this mountain and all the land about was etched clearly in her mind's eye. She inched forward, the fog parting around her, came to the cairn, and stopped.

Chief Superintendent Holly was sitting on the stone platform, his back against the cairn. He was dressed as a hiker now, his solid bulk crammed into a red anorak and ex-army winter camo trousers, with expensive Gore-Tex boots completing the ensemble. Two other men . . . or women . . . stood at each end of the platform. They were clad only in Arsenal F.C. hooded shell suits, rough woolen gloves, and Adidas knockoff running shoes. The hoods of the shell suits were done up unnaturally tight and close on their faces, almost hiding the blotched, blue-black skin beneath.

Susan caught the smell of amaranth and laurel from them, and the deep stench of rotting flesh.

Not people at all. Not anymore. They were Cauldron-Born.

"About time you got here," said Holly. "Was that Merrihew who winged you?"

Susan nodded slowly. Her father was within the cairn. Or the mortal expression of him was, she could sense it. And she could also feel that the opposition to her taking in the power of the mountain came from Holly. He had diverted it to himself somehow, and he was trying not to give it back.

"The old crow *knew* I need you alive," said Holly. He didn't speak or gesture, but the two Cauldron-Born moved suddenly. They leaped away, into the fog, like rocks launched from catapults. "So I can't have her shooting you again, can I?"

He got up himself from the platform, dislodging a couple of stones, and stretched, offering a yawn up to the cloud-shrouded sky. Susan saw the silver watchband, and here, coming into her power, recognized it immediately for what it was. Not a charm of protection, but one of disguise.

This was not a mortal policeman who stood before her, but an Ancient Sovereign clad in human flesh.

"I should have saved myself the bother of trying to fetch you here, shouldn't I, since you were bound to come anyway," said Holly conversationally. "I thought those old booksellers would off you straight away, so I had to act quick. Soon as I knew about you, that is, which was not soon enough, no, not by a long shot. I've got to hand it to your old dad, the cunning bugger."

There was a flurry of gunshots below them.

"Shame Merrihew hasn't got anything better than a popgun on her," said Holly. Susan noticed that his left eye was unfocused, presumably because that one was seeing through the dead eyes of his servant below. "I'd put ten quid on her dealing with one Cauldron-Born, but not two. Not without an axe or the like."

Susan didn't speak. She watched him, and let her right hand fall on the opening of the ruler pocket. With the left, she made a fist and raised it to her mouth as she looked down, ostensibly to cover a cough but actually to tear the end of the salt packet open with her teeth.

"I'll give it to you straight, Ms. Susan Arkshaw," said Holly. He stepped closer, flexing his powerful hands. "I bound your dad and took his power when he was carrying on with your mum and stupid with it, not paying attention and weak as piss in mortal flesh. Though I admit I had help from Merrihew to lure him onto my patch. But he found a loophole, didn't he? He could give up the power I took to his heir when she came of age, bypassing my strictures!"

Holly pounded a massive fist into his palm, the sound almost like another gunshot.

"So it's all leaking away to you, and the oaths I've had witnessed by Coniston are coming undone, which is fucking inconvenient! We got to get them done again. So here's the deal. You freely give up your dad's power to me, and you get to live. Oh, and your mum gets to stay alive, too."

There was nothing in his face or words to give away that the men he'd sent to take care of Jassmine had fallen foul of guardians from the brook, the sky, and the earth. But Susan knew he lied. Here, even only in the beginning of her power, she could see the shape of his words and when they came straight or twisted from his mouth.

"What about my father?" she asked. She put her hands behind her back and emptied the packet into her fingers, hoping they would catch enough salt to smear upon the knife.

"He's made his choice," said Holly. "He's given up everything to you. He's fading, soon to be gone. Forget about him."

Something about that was not true, but some of it was.

"What happens to his power if it doesn't come to me?" asked Susan. "If you kill me first."

Holly grunted angrily.

"Gone. Wasted. Which will make me very, very unhappy. It's your choice. Your dad's had it, but you can live."

"You used Dad's power to make oaths binding," said Susan.

She felt the rightness of that. This was a great part of her . . . her father's . . . power. To witness oaths and make them concrete, not to be broken. He was an Oath-Maker, binding together those who asked him to witness their oaths and make them concrete. Her father was one of the benign Ancient Sovereigns.

And Holly was exactly the opposite. One of the malign Old Ones.

The big man grunted again, then flinched, and his unfocused eye filled with tears, a single drop escaping to run down his ruddy cheek.

"That's finished Merrihew," he said. "Costly, but worth it."

"What about the rest of the booksellers?" asked Susan. She edged forward a step. "Even if I give up Dad's power, let you have it, they'll kill us both, won't they?"

Holly snorted.

"Why do you think I've gone to all this effort to extend my rule over the Old World and the New, to gather under my hand such creatures as Shucks and goblins, Nikker and Boggart, Yetuns and Yallery, and all the rest, not to mention stooping to master the dreary hired killers and gangland thugs of mortal England? I was always going to deal with the booksellers. That's the whole *point*. Merrihew will only be the first to die. As befits a dupe."

CHAPTER TWENTY-TWO

>-!-‹›-O-‹›!-‹

A blood tide they called it
For even the sea could not wash clean
So many killed in so narrow a span
As between the low water and the high

>-!-‹›-O-‹›!-‹

MERRIHEW BROUGHT A GREAT STONE DOWN UPON THE SECOND Cauldron-Born, but it was too swift. It caught her and dragged her back even as the boulder rolled across. Her legs were crushed to the knee and blood already pooled about her thighs. So much blood . . .

The other Cauldron-Born scrabbled and growled six or seven feet away, pinned through the elbows by the two seventh-century seaxes Merrihew always wore hidden across her back under her fishing vest. But even the ancient, many times bespelled iron would not prevent the Cauldron-Born from eventually tearing its own flesh and bone to pieces in order to get free.

Merlin came through the fog, the old sword in his hand, with Vivien close behind.

"Good," rasped Merrihew. She pointed, weakly. "Cut that one to pieces before it breaks out."

Merlin stepped past, and the ancient sword rose and fell, rose and fell. Vivien knelt by Merrihew's side, and looked at her smashed legs, at the blood swirling its way downhill. She took a vial of Sipper blood from her inside jacket pocket, then slowly put it back.

"Yes, yes, I know," snapped Merrihew. "Too late, too late. Never mind. I go to join the Grandmother."

"No," said a soft, calm voice, but there was steel in that single word. All three booksellers looked up, and there sitting on the stone Merrihew had rolled in desperation to kill a Cauldron-Born and, inadvertently, herself, was the oldest Grandmother. The strawberry blonde in the toga-like garment. The chestnut-brown wolfhound sat on his haunches next to her, growled, and showed his teeth.

Both of them looked entirely corporeal, not like ghosts or Shades at all.

"You will not join us," continued the Grandmother. "You have betrayed the clan. You will die unlamented, your name struck from the rolls."

"I did what I did for the good of the St. Jacques!" said Merrihew. "I didn't know about the cauldron, or the . . . other matters."

"You mean Mother?" asked Merlin.

He had left the Cauldron-Born in pieces under slabs of shale and came to stand over Merrihew. He held the heavy sword negligently, point down, six inches above the older bookseller's right eye. It looked like he might let it fall at any moment.

"It was simply bad luck!" protested Merrihew. "She'd met Coniston and his woman in London, early on, and then she saw the woman again, with a child, and was going to make inquiries. She would have found out what happened to Coniston. We couldn't have that, but I didn't want her *dead*, I didn't know about it. Not until afterwards—"

The sword point dropped an inch, cold fury on Merlin's face.

"Southaw arranged it! He was concerned Antigone would release Coniston—"

"Southaw?" asked Vivien. "The London Southaw?"

"Yes, the London Southaw!" retorted Merrihew. "Is there any other one?"

Southaw was a most inimical and troublesome Ancient Sovereign, which had three entire pages to itself in the *Index*. One of the principal Old Ones of London, always in a struggle to extend his domain with his rivals, That Beneath the Tower, the Beast of Camden, the Primrose Lady, London Stone, and Oriel.

"Southaw promised peace and he delivered," said Merrihew emphatically. "We've never had such a quiet time."

"So you could go fishing," said Vivien, her voice heavy with scorn and disappointment.

"No, not that . . . you young ones don't understand, the *constant* pressure," whispered Merrihew. She had lost so much blood her face had sunken in, her skin almost translucent. "Besides, I could have fixed things. You should have told me who Susan was . . . if that last shot had killed her . . . but now Southaw's got her—"

"Southaw's here?"

Merrihew pointed with one shaking finger up the hill.

"But it can't be; we would feel the presence of an Old—" said Vivien.

"He wears a charm," said Merrihew. Her eyes lost their focus on the outer world. For the first time in many years she looked within herself. "Maybe, maybe I did make a mistake. . . ."

Vivien half expected to see Merlin drop the sword to pierce Merrihew's eye and brain. But he didn't. He lifted the blade and was gone in a swirl of fog, leaping up the mountainside. Vivien hesitated for a second, bowed to the Grandmother, and sprinted away after him.

"What about Billie?" whispered Merrihew, looking up to the Grandmother, though she could not see anything now but fog, nothing but white. Billie was her spaniel, waiting patiently at Wooten for his mistress to return.

"We'll take Billie, when her time comes," said the Grandmother. "But for her own sake, not yours. It is never the dogs who break faith."

She whistled, and the wolfhound at her side jumped down from the stone. It stalked over to Merrihew, who turned her head away as the dog's jaws closed about her throat and ripped the last spark of life away.

"So what's it to be?" asked Holly. He stood close now, a menacing presence, not simply from his bulk and height.

"I don't . . . I don't . . ." stammered Susan, and she lunged forward, drawing the knife and wiping it flat across the palm of her left hand to pick up the salt in one swift motion before tilting it to slash the sharpened edge across Holly's chest.

The knife barely cut the anorak he wore, and did not penetrate the pullover beneath. He laughed and Susan cut again, at his hand, this time slicing flesh. But no blood flowed.

"Oh, Susan, Susan, you've got guts, I'll give you that," said Holly, gripping her wrist and twisting it savagely, so she had to drop the knife. He kept hold of her and continued to speak, in a calm but bullying tone. "You've been badly taught. You forgot to say the words, for one thing, but you can't bind *me* this way. I'm not some limp lesser legend, some pathetic myth born of a piss-trickling spring or some sheep-fucked standing stone. I'm an Old One, you understand? *Old* and *mean* and *very bloody unforgiving.*"

He threw her down, shale slicing her hands when she put them out to break the fall.

"I'd hoped you would be sensible," he said. "But I see I have to do what I did to your dad and *take* your power. Which means digging him up first, I suppose. Lucky your mum had such long hair. I can use the same rope."

He turned aside and raised his hand at the cairn, as if to summon a waiter in one of the more obnoxious restaurants of the old style, where the patrons paid a premium for subservience. Susan felt power flow from the mountain through him. Her power, her father's power, usurped by Holly. She didn't know how to stop it, but she tried, willing the magic to dry up, to flow back, to return to the mountain and come to her instead.

Holly took a step aside and kicked her in the ribs.

"Stop that!"

Susan rolled away, but she'd lost concentration. Whatever Holly wanted the power for, he had enough now.

He flicked his fingers dismissively.

The cairn shifted, rocks rolling off into the fog. The platform beneath split open, the stones pushed away as if by some internal eruption.

"Come see your dad," said Holly. He walked over, supremely confident that Susan would follow.

She got up slowly, hunched over and holding her ribs, pretending to be hurt much more than she was. Slowly, she picked her way through the tumbled stones to where the cairn and platform had been.

"Leave the knife," said Holly as she bent down to pick it up. "Let's get this over with. They do a good pint and a bacon sandwich down in the village. Which you could still have if you decide to be sensible."

Susan shook her head, and concentrated on drawing more of the magic from the mountain into herself. She could feel Holly trying to take it back, but his grip was weakening. She had the right, and he didn't.

"Here he is," said Holly. "That's your dad."

Susan looked down into what was basically a rough-carved grave in the stony mountaintop, and saw her father, three feet below.

The Old Man of Coniston looked no more than forty, not old at all. His gray-streaked copper hair had grown to his waist, almost a garment in itself, and he had a beard to do the Edward Lear character proud, bushy enough to hold a dozen owls and larks and wrens. His fingernails had grown so long they curled back on themselves. His purple flared trousers were rotting at the hems, his Nehru jacket was moldy at the cuffs, and the side zips on his boots were rusted.

His eyes were partly open, enough to see a slice of slate-gray pupils. His mouth was hidden behind the whiskers. He was tied at the wrists and ankles by narrow ropes fastened to iron eye-bolts screwed into the rock.

Ropes woven from many strands of . . . raven-black hair.

Her mother's hair. Ropes of love to bind an Old One and take his power, far more stringent than any mere binding with blood and iron and salt to make a servant.

Ropes that would serve as well to bind the Old One's half-mortal heir, who loved her mother.

"Touching, isn't it," said Holly. "Like that old story. She sold her hair to buy him a present, not knowing what I wanted it for, and he risked visiting London to be with her, and they both lost out."

"That is a completely stupid misreading of 'The Gift of the Magi,'" said Vivien, coming out of the fog to stand next to Susan.

Holly started towards them, raising his fist. Susan felt him draw in power from the mountain, despite her efforts to resist. And she felt other powers, too, Holly calling on magic from far away. It was lessened here, but there was so much of it. . . .

"You bloody booksellers don't know when—"

Merlin came up behind him and swung the ancient sword in a decapitating blow, two-handed. There was a deafening, horrendous ring of metal upon metal as Holly's head flew off and bounced away down the mountainside, to be lost in the fog.

There was no blood. The body stood there for a moment, before slowly sinking to its knees. But it did not fall any farther.

Booming laughter came out of the fog, followed by Holly's voice, loud and horrible.

"Now you've really pissed me off!"

Vivien took a deep breath and held up her right hand, the luminescence growing brighter, reflecting off the swirling whiteness of the fog. Merlin stepped up next to her.

"Send him away," snapped Merlin to Susan. "Forbid him your demesne. His real name is Southaw. Use it!"

"He's still got most of Father's power!"

Vivien made a choking sound, still holding her breath. Merlin pushed Susan down and slapped the sword blade flat on the neck of the headless body as something flew in from the fog. It hit the sword, rebounded from it with another metallic clang, loud as a church bell at two paces, and would have smacked into Merlin if he hadn't dodged, so fast Susan saw him as a blur. As the thing flew past, Vivien slapped it and exhaled, her breath coming out as silver as her hand. The breath caught the object and hurled it through the air, reaming out a corridor in the fog, which closed behind its passage.

It took Susan a moment to realize the flying object was Holly's head.

"It'll be back in a few minutes," gasped Vivien, taking in a deep breath. "We won't be able to keep holding it off."

"Susan . . ."

Susan shut her eyes. She could feel the power of the mountain flowing into her, she could sense every small detail within the bounds of her father's domain, feel every living thing, the men and women and children and wildlife, the birds in the air and in the trees and on the ground, the hares and the foxes and the sheep, squirrels and red deer, natterjack toads and adders, and there were other mythic beings, too, water-fay in the lake and tarns, knocker goblins in the old copper and shale workings, the Fenris over on the western shore of Windermere . . . and halfway down the mountain on the southwestern side near Goat's Water, the awful wrongness that was Southaw, centered in the cut-off head of its mortal form.

She knelt down on the shale and spread her hands flat, calling the power into herself. She felt Southaw resisting her, but she had the right, and she reached deep inside herself for the will to use it. She was her father's daughter, and he had bequeathed his power to her. Southaw had stolen it. Now she would get it back.

Susan felt the head returning. She could sense it now as the mere tip of an iceberg of terrible power. The dismembered head was the visible presence for an unseen entity that drew upon the strength of its many, many vassals, lesser entities spread throughout the land. And it also drew strength from the Bronze

Cauldron, as great a power again as all those vassals combined.

Southaw no longer engaged in a contest of will over her father's magic; he was simply coming to kill her. The head was rising higher and higher, climbing through fog and cloud. It would fall like a falcon upon its prey, swift and terrible, too fast even for Merlin or Vivien to avoid.

"The head's going up high—it'll come straight down!" she warned, but did not open her eyes or stand up. Instead she lowered herself flat, reaching out with her arms, trying to become one with the great mass of stone beneath her. Magic rose up from the depths below, like water welling up from a deep spring. It came surely, but too slowly, and as it filled her, Susan became aware of two vital things.

The first was that the meager vessel of her body could not take in the power any faster, and the second was that she could not contain all of an Ancient Sovereign's majesty anyway. To fully take on the magic, she would have to give up her mortal form. Her body would sink into the shale; she would become a thing of myth and legend. She might take another mortal body one day, but it would be the end of Susan Arkshaw.

She would be the Old Man of Coniston. If she survived the next thirty seconds.

The head rose still higher. She felt it in the sky above, for that was also her domain, two leagues north and south and west and east, and all the air above and stone below. The magic filled her; she could feel it working through blood and bone, almost at the point of unraveling her, making her undone. . . .

She felt the head, still climbing, above the cloud now, under bright blue sky. But the magic inside her was still not enough to resist all that Southaw could bring to bear. She could not contain it. *She* was not enough and couldn't be, not in the time allowed.

Susan also saw something else, and with it came the realization that a part of what Southaw had said about her father was untrue. It was not all over for him.

She lunged for the fallen butter knife with its one sharpened edge and scuttled to the grave, almost falling in headfirst. She sawed at the rope on her father's right wrist, and it gave way as if the knife did slice butter. His eyelids quivered. She cut away the second rope and his mouth opened to draw in a rasping breath.

There was a terrible scream overhead and the head began its downward plunge.

"Guard me!" shrieked Susan to Merlin, as she swung about to cut the rope on her father's ankle. As the hair strands there parted, he sat up. Susan lurched across him, bringing the knife down on the last binding—

Merlin's sword flashed overhead; there was a flare of brilliant light and a deafening boom. Susan felt something hit her back, smashing her down. She rolled onto her side to look up, and there was Holly's head only a few inches from her face, teeth bared in hatred.

It was pierced through jaw and temple by the ancient sword. Both Merlin and Vivien strained to hold it up and away from Susan as it bit at the air, their silver hands bright as sunshine.

Gray, greasy smoke billowed from nostrils and empty eye sockets, tendrils questing towards Susan. This was the essence of Southaw, leaving the last remnant of its temporary mortal convenience, the raw mythic entity still far greater than anything Susan had become. She still lacked the power to fight it, and the smoke reached out towards her eyes, looking for a way in—

A hand gripped Susan's and she screamed in total panic, but she knew it in that same instant.

Her father's hand, which she had never felt before.

The scream became a sigh as Susan let all the power she had gathered go, opening the floodgates of her inner self, releasing the magic she had gathered, the magic stolen by Southaw, the magic still within the mountain, all rushing into one, as a long-dammed mighty river rediscovers its proper bed.

Coniston Rex took it all in, and used it.

"Go, Southaw," said a voice, hoarse from long disuse. "Get thee gone."

CHAPTER TWENTY-THREE

The day withdraws at fall of night
The night presses on, seeks a kiss of light
The two can never meet but fleetingly
At dusk and dawn, so prettily

THE INTENSELY THICK GRAY SMOKE, SO CLOSE TO SUSAN'S EYES, recoiled from Coniston's words. It coalesced into a massive, fuzzy-edged, pale raven that loomed above Merlin and Vivien, where they stood on the edge of the grave. It opened its beak to caw once in brief defiance, before rising up and winging south.

Susan looked at her father, close to her in the stony grave. He returned her gaze, before looking down at himself and his hands. He gestured. His nails fell away, and the beard and hair receded to medium sixties hippie rather than feral ancient, and his Nehru jacket, purple flares, and boots were mended.

"Thank you, daughter," he croaked. But he made no movement to hug her, or show affection, and Susan felt no inclination to do so herself. She could see some of him in how she looked herself, physically, but it was an academic observation. He might be her father, but he was still a stranger. Something about the way he looked at her suggested he felt much the same. Finding a father was one thing. Establishing any kind of relationship with him would clearly be more difficult. Made even more so by the nature of what he was.

Coniston looked up at Merlin and Vivien.

"Young St. Jacques," he said, in a not-too-friendly tone. "I trust you are not with that Merrihew who lured me to Southaw's trap. Who now lies dead upon my upper slope. What is your business here?"

"Helping Susan," said Merlin. "And you, sir."

Coniston nodded slowly, accepting that. He climbed out of the grave, paused, and held his hand out to Susan. She took it, moving stiffly and wincing as she stepped up. She'd momentarily forgotten about the glancing wound to her leg, but now the pain was coming back with a vengeance, and the cuts on her hands stung.

Coniston frowned and she suddenly felt pins and needles in her hand, and the familiar magic came back, flowing from mountain to man to her. It was like being given pethidine the time she'd broken her wrist falling off Christie, her neighbor's usually placid mare. She felt relief flowing through her veins, and the pain went away from bullet wound and cuts. But it was not only that. Her father was giving her some small part of the magic he'd taken back. A very minor part. She could sense how vast a pool of power lay within the mountain and the lake and the lands of Coniston's domain, all focused on the man in front of her, like all the sky's sunlight gathered to a lens to make one piercing ray.

"My daughter will go with you to bring the cauldron back to me," said Coniston to Merlin and Vivien. He handed Susan to them as if changing partners in a dance, and they drew her in to stand close between them.

"I will?" asked Susan.

"I am the Keeper of the Copper Cauldron," said Coniston. "After he entrapped me and took my magic, Southaw carried away the cauldron to his own demesne. It must be brought back and once more kept safe in the deep places. That seems to me fitting business for you booksellers."

"Yes," said Vivien. "It is."

"Do you know exactly where the cauldron is?" asked Merlin. "Southaw seems to have extended his realm while Merrihew . . . we . . . were not doing our job."

"Susan will find it," said Coniston. "I have given her something of my strength. So you must not kill her, as you did one of my children long ago, in the years of ice, when the lake froze from end to end."

"We did? I mean . . . no . . . we've stopped doing that. Anyway, Susan is . . ." Merlin was uncharacteristically tongue-tied. "Susan is special."

"I tire of this mortal form," said Coniston suddenly. "And I have spent too much of my strength. I must rest in the heart of the mountain, until the year's end comes round again. I thank you, daughter, for freeing me."

He leaned forward, kissed Susan very formally on top of the head, and stepped back into the grave. His feet sank into the gray shale as if it were quicksand.

"I have taken in the fragments of the Cauldron-Born. The knockers shall burn them in the lower fires, with the corpse of the Merrihew, the ashes to be strewn in the deepest chasms that extend beyond even my ken," said Coniston. "And I have stopped the hearts of the mortal evildoers below, who were waiting for Southaw's return."

He began to sink more swiftly, raised his hands above his head, and the stones that had blown away began to shuffle back across the crest and rearrange themselves, rebuilding the platform and then the cairn.

Susan, Merlin, and Vivien backed away to make room, knocking over the headless body of Holly, which rolled a short distance before crumbling into nothing, leaving only the anorak, the clothes beneath, the boots, and the silver watchband. Vivien picked that up, held it close to her eye for a few seconds, and put it in her pocket.

"Very old and *not* made by Harshton and Hoole," she said. "Which is something of a relief. One traitor is enough."

"Merrihew probably was working on her own," agreed Merlin. "Aided by Thurston being so damn lazy, of course. And others, unwittingly. Who would question Merrihew's orders, after all? Is your leg okay, Susan? We need to get moving."

"We do?" asked Susan plaintively.

"Yes," said Merlin.

"Isn't it all over now?" asked Susan.

"No," said Merlin and Vivien together.

Susan sighed, sat down on a rock, and extended her leg. The knife was back in the ruler pocket, though she couldn't remember putting it there. "I did need the knife, Vivien. But not the salt, I guess."

"Oh, maybe for this," said Merlin, taking a wax-paper packet out of his coat. "Someone left this behind at a campsite below—"

Susan grabbed the package and opened it in a single motion. A homemade roast beef and lettuce sandwich on perfect sourdough bread. She took a bite and chewed vigorously, swallowed, and looked at Vivien as she felt for the second packet of salt in her pocket.

"It does need salt! You're amazing, Vivien."

"I think I could have seen more clearly and saved us all a lot of bother," replied Vivien sardonically, watching Susan open the sandwich and sprinkle on the salt. Her hands shook a little, but steadied.

"Let me look at your leg," said Merlin, kneeling down in front of Susan.

"I think it's okay," mumbled Susan through a mouthful of bread and roast beef.

There was lots of blood on her boiler suit, and a huge tear where the bullet had ripped through, but it didn't hurt anymore. She shivered as Merlin's fingers probed the rip and then lightly touched the skin beneath. His silver hand felt slightly warmer than his right.

Susan choked a little and Merlin looked up.

"Did that hurt?" he asked anxiously. "I can't see or feel a wound at all."

"No, no, it's fine," coughed Susan. "Um, my father, when he gave me that bit of magic, I think he fixed it up."

"Oh, right," said Merlin, standing up. "We really need to get going, then. I thought I might have to carry you."

"So what happens now?" asked Susan wistfully. "I had that minute of hoping we could be . . . normal. Normal-ish, in your case. Isn't Holly . . . or Southaw, or whatever he actually is . . . finished?"

"No. He was only banished from *here*," said Merlin. "He's lost the physical form of Chief Superintendent Holly, and the charm that disguised him from those who might see him as he really is. But Southaw is a very powerful Old One, he commands many lesser entities, and he has the Copper Cauldron. He might still be able to command his gangsters as well, I don't know. He might even be able to remake his mortal shape. There's no telling what he can do, or what he wants to do, for that matter."

"He said the whole point of seizing Father's power was so he could get together criminals *and* creatures of the Old World to kill you booksellers."

"What! We have to warn them!" exclaimed Merlin. He started down the path, and for the first time Susan fully took in that he and Vivien were not only in evening dress but had no shoes, their feet already bloodied from many small cuts and undoubtedly very cold. Susan's feet even felt cold through her

Docs, particularly as she wasn't wearing winter socks.

"You haven't got shoes!"

"We're well aware of this," said Vivien. "Come on."

She started after Merlin, flapping her hands to clear a particularly thick waft of fog. Susan followed her.

"And why are you all dressed up?"

"Silvermere!" called out Merlin.

"Are we going back there, through the tarn?"

"Definitely not! We might get stuck or lose a week, or lose you again."

"So you missed me?"

"Yes!" cried Merlin, and there was such honesty in his voice that Susan didn't know how to reply and instead focused on her feet and the effort of not slipping on the loose rocks herself, and not thinking at all about how she might have misjudged him and perhaps she should give him a chance, and maybe it would work out, and it would be fun anyway and life was too short—

"Where exactly are we going, Merlin?" asked Vivien, interrupting Susan's runaway thoughts.

"The village below," said Merlin. "Phone first. The Grandmother might have warned Thurston or one of the even-handed but we can't count on that. How long do you reckon until Southaw gets back to London, Viv . . . he is a London entity, isn't he?"

"Oh yes, one of the major malevolences," said Vivien, pausing to catch Susan, who had tripped and was about to fall past her. "Careful, Susan. Uh, I don't know how swiftly he can get back . . . a discorporate entity, out of its own bounds . . . it's not something I've studied. I mean, if he keeps that smoky raven thing going and flies at the speed we saw, maybe five or six hours? If nothing stops him; I mean, he must be trespassing on many other Old Ones' domains."

"Southaw's had eighteen years of forcing oaths of loyalty without bookseller interference," said Merlin. "Who knows how far his suzerainty extends now? In both the Old World and the New? Besides, he's got the Copper Cauldron's powers."

"Yes," said Vivien. "Susan . . . where *is* the cauldron?"

"I don't know—" Susan started to say, but then she realized she did know, though in an abstract way. It would take a bit of figuring out. "Southeast, quite a distance. I guess towards London. Underground, in some sort of chamber . . . kind of earthy, with tree roots . . . I need to be closer. . . ."

The fog came with them down the mountain, heavy and far wetter than it had been up above. It was her father's work, Susan knew, so she wasn't surprised they met no one climbing up. When they got to the Walna Scar car park it was empty, save for two late-model Range Rovers. A blue one containing two dead men and two dead women, and a green one with three dead men. All of them were dressed for outdoor pursuits in brand-new clothes, some with the tags still on. Susan might have thought they were asleep, if her father hadn't mentioned stopping the hearts of evildoers below who were waiting for their boss.

Merlin opened the passenger door of the closest car and lifted the flap of the dead man's anorak pocket, revealing the butt of a Colt .45, and there was the hilt of a knife sticking out of his boot top. There was a sawn-off shotgun in a bag in the footwell, and a quick glance at the others showed they were also all well-armed, their weapons barely concealed.

"Best not to cross your dad," said Merlin. "I wonder if I should have checked with him if it was okay to ask you out, Susan."

"I make my own decisions on that," said Susan. "And I do the asking out."

"And what have you decided?" asked Merlin. He looked back for a moment, a very Brontë figure with the wisps of fog, all smiles and charm and romance. If you ignored the dead bodies in the car behind him.

"I always preferred *Jane Eyre* to *Wuthering Heights*," said Susan thoughtfully.

"Um, what does that—"

"I'd choose Mr. Rochester over Heathcliff, if I was going on a date. He always struck me as being of more practical use."

"So you will!"

"I've decided that when the opportunity presents *I* will ask *you* out for a drink," said Susan. "We'll see about anything else."

She looked at Vivien. "No warnings this time?"

"No," said Vivien seriously. "You are definitely not like the people Merlin normally . . . well, Merlin's relationships start more *quickly* I suppose and end not very long after with him sidling off. In fact I have to say I'm quite curious to see what happens. Of course, we have to survive long enough for anything *to* happen."

"We've made it so far," said Susan, finding herself unexpectedly full of something she thought must be mostly a rush of survival joy and not to do with Merlin. At least not entirely.

"Because we were here, in your father's domain, and we were lucky," said Vivien. "You could have been killed by Merrihew, let alone Southaw sticking you in a hole in the rock with your dad! And now we have to go up against him on his own turf, at the center of his power. Like tracking a wounded bear to its den. Only much, much worse."

"But not by ourselves," said Merlin grimly. He started to drag the passengers out and there was no disguising they were dead and not merely asleep. "Next time, it'll be with lots and lots and lots of well-armed, knowledgeable, and powerful booksellers."

"We hope," muttered Vivien.

"Don't be so negative and give me a hand," said Merlin, dragging the first passenger a few steps and laying her down. "Or do you want to take the blue car?"

"You don't seem bothered by dead people now," said Susan. "I thought—"

"Only the innocent ones, killed by my hand, haunt me," said Merlin somberly. "Besides, these aren't even ordinary gangsters. See those three tattoos, the rings around the forefinger? It's a Death Cultist thing. These people signed up to serve Southaw voluntarily, knowing what he is. There's always a few wannabe Satanists or Druids into human sacrifice around and malevolent entities who thirst for such blood. A tattooed ring here means a man killed; on the thumb, a woman killed; and on the little finger, a child. But I was talking to Viv about helping. You don't need to."

"No, it's okay," said Susan. She went around to the other side to remove the rear passenger. "Well, not okay. But I can cope. Particularly when they're so neat, they do look like they're asleep. He could have done that, couldn't he? Put them to sleep—"

She had to stop talking and take a breath as everything hit her. She was dragging a dead person out of a car, and there were seven more here. Her father had casually killed them, like swatting flies. From the tattoos they were murderers themselves, but did that mean they deserved to die? And she could have been killed herself, as Vivien said; a few inches across and Merrihew's bullet would have severed her femoral artery and she would have bled out. . . .

Merlin came around and hugged her. She leaned into him for a moment, feeling a sense of vast relief and comfort. For a few seconds, before she pushed him away.

"No, I'll be fine, we have to get on . . . move on, don't we?"

"We do," said Merlin. "Do you want my book?"

"You found one?"

"In Silvermere. There's a library. I think . . . anyway . . . you can read it in the back of the car."

"I can't read in moving cars," said Susan. "But thanks. Are we . . . are you going to steal a car so we can drive back to London?"

Merlin shook his head.

"We'll call from the closest phone. We have to warn them,

and there's almost certainly still a police alert out for Vivien and me. Normally, Merrihew would be the one to sort out any problem with the Home Office. She wouldn't have had time to do anything this time, of course. Or perhaps the inclination. Come on."

They laid the bodies out in a neat row. Merlin hesitated for a moment, then stripped off three anoraks, taking one for himself and handing the others to Vivien and Susan. He looked at the cultists' boots for another few long seconds, before shaking his head regretfully.

"An anorak is one thing, but socks and boots from a dead person . . . we'll have to try and get something in the village. I will take one of these handy shotgun bags, though, for the sword. Don't want to frighten the locals any more than is absolutely necessary."

They also collected the cultists' weapons and put them in the back of the Range Rover, and Merlin locked it and went over and locked the second car, where its occupants still sat, unseeing.

"No need to tempt any passersby with guns, particularly kids," he said as he climbed into the driver's seat of the green Range Rover. Vivien got in the back, nudging Susan to the front passenger seat with a kindly shove. "We'll get some local police up here as soon as possible. Though it seems your dad is keeping everyone away for now; I don't know how long that will last."

"Until the fog lifts," replied Susan automatically. She simply knew things now, within the borders of her father's realm, at least. "About two and a half hours."

Merlin looked at her and started the car.

"Anything else we need to know?"

"The Black Bull does a good bacon sandwich," replied Susan. "And there's a phone box outside."

The Grandmother *had* warned Thurston, who had taken the news of Merrihew's private dealings on behalf of the St. Jacques with a malevolent Ancient Sovereign very badly, far worse than the news of her actual death.

"Apparently, he handed the phone to Cousin Sam and went and made a kind of pyramid out of Dickens and Trollope second or later editions—he didn't disturb the firsts—climbed in, and has refused to talk or come out," said Vivien. "Anyway, Great-Aunt Evangeline is coming in from Wooten to take over the right-handed and . . . Cousin Una has taken charge of the left-handed and she's briefed Inspector Greene. The police have dropped the alert for us and Greene has organized a helicopter from RAF Catterick to pick us up and take us back to London."

"What about Holly . . . I mean Southaw?" asked Susan, through a mouthful of bacon sandwich. The roast beef sandwich she'd eaten atop the mountain had been delicious, particularly once salted, but it had barely touched the sides of her hunger.

"No sightings as yet, and nothing bad has happened.

Everyone's on full alert. Helen and Zoë are cross-indexing everything we have on Southaw. Una has sent out teams to ask the usual suspects what they know and she's going to ask Grandmother as well. Greene has got an alert out for Holly, in case he can come back in that shape, and she's organizing police watches at all our locations, under the guise of an IRA threat, in case Southaw has his gangs attack."

"An IRA threat against bookshops?"

"Important customers of the bookshops," said Vivien. "It even makes sense. Half the House of Lords buy books at the New Bookshop to begin with. I'm not sure how Greene is explaining Wooten and Thorn Hall and the Birmingham workshop and so on, but they must be secondary targets. Southaw has definitely extended his demesne, but his historical locus is somewhere in Barnet—Helen and Zoë are looking into that—and most of his vassals and servants will most likely be concentrated in or around North London."

"You need anything else, love?" asked the cheerful woman who'd greeted them at the Black Bull as if they were royalty visiting not very incognito. It only took a moment for Merlin and Vivien to realize this was all directed at Susan, another aspect of her inheritance. It took Susan herself a little longer to work out what was going on.

"No, thank you, Mrs. Staple," replied Susan. She'd known the woman's name immediately, as she did everyone else's who lived in the village, which she found rather unnerving. Not that there were very many people about; the fog was still sitting all the way to the lake, and it seemed every tourist already in Coniston or the environs had decided to stay indoors, and even the locals were inclined not to be out and about.

This was all definitely due to Susan's dad. It had even been difficult to get a pair of constables from the Ambleside police station to come out to guard the bodies in the car park until Greene could organize a proper cleanup crew. They were both locals and clearly felt a strong desire to stay away from the Old Man of Coniston, a side effect of him banishing Southaw. The Old One's "Go!" and "Get thee gone" had a lingering effect on more than the mountain's rival.

"I just realized I must have lost my job," said Susan, looking at the almost empty pint in front of her and thinking about collecting glasses. "Damn. And I don't even know what day it is. Is it Tuesday?"

"Wednesday," said Vivien. "We lost two days in Silvermere."

"I was only there for about an hour at the most," said Susan. Merlin muttered something inaudible but disparaging.

"I liked the Twice-Crowned Swan," said Susan. She sighed. "I suppose now is not the time to be worrying about having a job or not."

"You might be able to get it back. You know, once you can tell us where the Copper Cauldron is, you can probably stay out of . . . well . . . what Greene would call the weird shit."

"What? Go back to Milner Square and pick up where I left off, as if nothing's happened? Sit down for a cuppa with Mrs. L and chat about the weather?"

Merlin and Vivien exchanged an awkward glance.

"What?"

"We realized you don't know," said Merlin. "Mrs. London was killed by that Cauldron-Born."

"Oh," said Susan. "Oh . . . poor Mrs. L. I wonder who's going to look after Mister Nimbus."

They sat quietly for several minutes. Susan was remembering Mrs. London's cups of tea and small kindnesses, and the others were thinking of her, too.

Merlin was the first to break the silence, tapping his feet together in the slippers Mrs. Staple had provided for him and Vivien. Susan had been surprised to see neither bookseller's feet were badly cut, only scratched, but Merlin had shrugged it off with an offhand comment that it took things like Raud Alfar arrows to really do them harm.

"Stop that," said Vivien. "It's annoying."

"It helps me think," said Merlin. He stopped tapping his feet and began to click his teeth instead.

"You're doing that on purpose to annoy me," said Vivien.

"What? I'm thinking!" replied Merlin. But he stopped the clicking.

"How *do* you booksellers deal with an Ancient Sovereign, by the way?" asked Susan, after another minute of silence. "Since cutting their mortal heads off clearly doesn't work."

Merlin looked at Vivien.

"There are various ways," said Vivien cautiously. "I'm not sure this is the best place to discuss that sort of thing."

"I don't think Dad's listening," said Susan. It felt very strange to say that. "He's . . . here, but distant. Not exactly asleep, but . . . quiescent."

"That's pretty much what we'll try to make happen to Southaw," said Vivien. "Force him into a dormant state, only for a lot longer than the rest of the year. I've never actually been involved, or seen it done, because we haven't had to do it to any Old One in my lifetime. I guess that's part of what Southaw managed for Merrihew, the 'peace' we've had for so long. But there's a procedure I suppose you'd call it, or a ritual, which requires at least nine of the right-handed, and three even-handed, and as many of the left-handed as are needed to keep off the minions and so on while we do it. And it has to be done at the Ancient Sovereign's locus of power. Which is usually but not always something tangible, like a rock, or a mountain, a spring, or a standing stone."

"But you don't know where Southaw's locus is yet."

"We probably do know," said Merlin. "He's in the *Index*, so the right-handed will have a historical record of the bounds of his demesne and maybe the actual locus as well. It's only a matter of finding where it's been recorded."

"I doubt it will be as straightforward as that," said Vivien, somewhat gloomily. "Southaw is no ordinary entity, even for an Ancient Sovereign. He has the Copper Cauldron. I don't think any of us know what powers that gives him. . . ."

"At least it isn't our problem anymore," said Merlin. "The aunts and uncles and senior cousins can deal with Southaw and recover the cauldron. We get a helicopter ride home and hopefully everything will go back to being moderately quiet again. And Susan and I can go out for that drink."

"I'll drink to everything going back to being quiet," said Susan, draining the last swallow of her Theakston's Old Peculier.

CHAPTER TWENTY-FOUR

In my dreams I fly so, so high
Effortless, my body still
In repose, a pillow beneath my head
Yet rushing heavenwards
Falling up, instead of down

THE HELICOPTER, AN RAF PUMA HC MK 1, LANDED IN THE FIELD BEHIND the Black Bull shortly after the fog had dissipated. But even though the fog had lifted, the day was still gray, with only a little sunshine breaking through here and there. Most noticeably on the peak of the Old Man, though whether this was by her father's choice, even Susan couldn't tell.

The crew chief ran to meet Merlin, Vivien, and Susan, checked their descriptions against her notes, and carefully read Merlin's and Vivien's warrant cards.

"You're not carrying any explosives, hand grenades, flash-bangs, or anything like that, are you?" she shouted over the rotor and engine noise. She hadn't lifted the polarized visor on her helmet, so it was hard to see her expression, but her tone of voice made it clear such items would not be popular.

"No," Merlin shouted back. He indicated his yak-hair bag and pointed at his ankle, where a small lump indicated the presence of his backup pistol. "Personal weapons only. And I'm the only one armed. Oh, and the sword in the bag."

Susan held up the bag.

"A sword? What . . . never mind . . . as long as there's nothing that goes bang," yelled the woman. "I had an incident with your lot once. Could have killed all of us."

No one answered that, since the "your lot" she mentioned almost certainly were not the booksellers, but some other much more normal part of the secret world, like MI5 or SIS.

"Bend your head a bit, don't need to crouch," shouted the crew chief. "Follow me."

She led them to the open body of the helicopter, where two benches ran lengthways back-to-back down the middle of the main compartment, with net webbing to lean against between the benches. There were comms headsets on some of the seats, their cords plugged in above.

"Two this side, one the other!" shouted the crew chief, pointing to the benches. "Headsets on, seat belts on!"

Vivien went first, going around to the other side. Merlin and Susan sat down together. When they were in, the crew chief slid the door shut, lessening the noise from deafening to merely annoying, before she went back to a higher, forward-facing seat next to the left door. She would have a good view out, but the others wouldn't.

It was a bit quieter once they got the headsets on. Susan

noted the crew chief had a proper harness while the passenger seats down the middle only had lap belts, and fairly basic ones at that. As she was tightening her belt, her headset crackled, followed by the voice of another woman, but one who had the laconic drawl of pilots everywhere.

"Good afternoon. As we have been instructed that this is a no names, no questions flight to London, I will not be introducing myself or the crew, other than to say you are in good hands with Mel back there. Please study the card she will show you on safety procedures and ensure you follow her instructions at all times. Flying time today will be approximately one hundred and ten minutes; we will be landing at RAF Northolt shortly after thirteen hundred hours. It is drizzling and gray in the capital, but apart from making everyone depressed, we should have no problems with the weather. Tea and biscuits will not be served, unless you brought some with you. Sit back and enjoy the flight."

There was a click as they were cut out of the comms circuit, the turbines whined higher, and the rotor blades began to spin faster. The crew chief handed Susan a safety card that was mostly pictures.

"Read the card and pass it on. Stay seated and belted unless I tell you otherwise."

Susan had only flown once before, a short flight with her Mum to Dublin for a brief holiday when she was eleven. The passenger safety card for the helicopter was much the same as the one she'd studied so carefully then, on the VC-10. She looked at the pictures, checked her belt, looked at the door to see how it opened, then passed the card to Merlin.

The helicopter lifted off, climbed quickly, and circled to the south as Merlin studied the card. With the helicopter banking, Susan could only see sky out her window, but looking over her shoulder past Vivien, who was directly behind her, back-to-back, she saw Coniston Water gleaming below. Something inside her felt the comfortable, secure glow of knowing "that's mine," but it was at odds with her higher mental processes, which were in something of a state of anxiety as she processed what *had* happened, and worried about what was *going* to happen.

As a child, she had daydreamed about finding her father, making him a composite of all the nicest fathers of her friends at school. She'd imagined her dad returning as a long-lost sailor finally rescued, or as a recovered amnesiac like in the film *Random Harvest*, coming to his senses and returning to his lover, to be delighted to discover he had a wonderful daughter as well.

Her wildest imaginings had never gotten close to what her father actually was, and his reception of her did not match any of those childhood dreams. Susan felt this as a kind of dull ache, a weight of disappointment. He hadn't seemed to care very much that he had a daughter, and he hadn't asked about Jassmine at all. In fact, he seemed to consider Susan as a kind of offshoot of himself.

"My daughter will go with you to bring the cauldron back," she whispered, forgetting she had a microphone off the corner of her mouth.

"What was that?" asked the crew chief. "We're all one comms

circuit back here, and I don't want to know anything I'm not supposed to, okay?"

"Sorry," said Susan.

Merlin looked at her, smiled, and made a zipping motion across his mouth. Susan nodded. She didn't want to talk anyway. She leaned her head on Merlin's shoulder and back against Vivien. Merlin reached into his yak-hair bag and pulled out a book.

Susan started to read over his shoulder, recognizing the character of Harriet Vane, though she hadn't read this particular one of Dorothy Sayers's books. Merlin kindly tilted the book to make it easier for her, though she thought it irked him a little—she didn't like people reading over her shoulder herself—but she found her eyes very heavy and her head started to roll forward and before Merlin had even turned the first page she had fallen sound asleep.

She woke rather groggily sometime later—Susan wasn't sure how long—to hear the pilot's voice again, crackling in her ears.

"Hi, back there. We're coming up to RAF Northolt, but we've been instructed to land you a little over to the east at Totteridge Green in Barnet, we've received ATC clearance for that, I'm told the LZ will be secured by police and LIBER MERCATOR elements, whatever they are. I also have a message to relay, which is as follows: Southaw locus is Totteridge Yew, Barnet. I say again: Southaw locus is Totteridge Yew, Barnet."

"Copy that," said Merlin. "Uh, did they give you a particular approach, pilot? We'll want to avoid flying over or near the . . . uh . . . locus."

"Uh, no information on that. We've got the LZ. We're about five minutes out."

"If you see any weather or other unusual phenomena, I *strongly* advise . . . er . . . turning away from it, or whatever the technical term is."

"We've got a strict corridor from ATC, have to conform to that. I'll recheck."

Susan leaned forward to look out the window, which was flecked with streaks of rain. She couldn't see much more than gray sky without undoing her belt and getting up to improve the angle, which she thought would be frowned upon by the crew chief and a bad idea anyway.

"Uh, we *are* seeing something unusual ahead, a localized drift of fog between us and the LZ, but we'll clear it by a few hundred feet. We're landing on the other side."

"Go around, pilot!" snapped Merlin. "Viv! You sense anything?"

"Old One," said Viv. She pointed down. "Southaw."

The helicopter wasn't changing course.

"Pilot, *go around*!"

"We're well above it now, no prob—"

White blanketed the windows, thick as if cotton wool had been plastered on in an instant. A few seconds later everyone jumped at the sound of a heavy impact, like a thrown brick hitting the side of a car, and then there was another, and another, sharp and loud even over the helicopter's own noise.

There was confused and muffled talking through Susan's

headphones, then the pilot came on again clearly, her speech more clipped now, but without panic.

"Bird strike! We're going down! Prepare to—"

The fog split apart as a bird smacked straight into the window opposite Susan, smearing it with blood and feathers. There were thuds and bashing noises all over the helicopter now. The engine noise changed, whining higher, and the rhythm of the rotors became uneven.

Merlin ripped off his headphones and tightened his seat belt, Susan copying his actions. She could feel Vivien doing the same thing behind her.

"Lean forward and clasp your knees!" shouted the crew chief, who was pulling her straps tight and crossing her arms to grip the upper straps, her thumbs along the belt.

There were more and more bird impacts, smacking into the helicopter like heavy hail. The windows were almost completely obscured in blood and feathers, and fog blurred whatever might have been seen through the gaps.

"Can you do anything, Viv?" shouted Merlin. It was almost impossible to hear him.

The engines suddenly emitted an awful asphyxiating cough and stopped entirely. The rotors changed rhythm yet again, sounding slower and somehow less confident. The helicopter started to spin around on its axis, the tail sweeping around like a clock's second hand.

"No! It's too heavy!" shouted Vivien.

"We're autorotating!" shouted the crew chief. "Brace! Br—"

The helicopter hit the ground and slid forward with a terrifying screech of tortured metal before it smashed into something, stopped with a deafening bang, and rolled over on its right side. Susan was thrown into Merlin, who was holding on to one of the bench struts with his left hand and was steady as a rock.

Everything stopped. There were no more bird impacts, no engine noise, no *whup-whup-whup* of the rotors. Only the low, sad groan of stressed metal and composites and the sound of a piercing, high-pitched alarm.

Merlin was the first to move. He looked swiftly around, saw Vivien was hanging down but had braced her feet against the buried door, and was already moving to undo her seat belt. Susan was lying back but also wrestling with her belt. The crew chief, hanging sideways in her harness, was shouting into her helmet mike, trying to raise the pilots.

The bookseller undid his restraint and pulled himself upright to stand on the back of his seat. He slid open the left-side door, which was now above their heads. The right-side door beneath Vivien was buckled in and broken, with clumps of grass and earth visible through a long gash in the hull.

The crew chief half fell out of her harness as she tried to get a footing to reach up as well, managed to get her boots on the back of the bench, and helped Merlin with the door. She began to cup her hands to give him a boost up and out, but he simply jumped, pulling himself over the edge. He crouched there and leaned back in, offering a hand to Susan. But she passed up the bag with the sword first, which he took and hurled safely away, before Susan climbed out and up.

Tendrils of smoke were beginning to drift into the passenger compartment. Even more smoke was eddying around the hull and rising up to join the fog. Part of a rotor stuck straight up in the air, like a drowning person's arm raised for help.

Visibility was no more than a dozen feet, but as far as Susan could tell the helicopter had crash-landed in a grassy field, one littered with small rocks.

"Jump down and move away!" shouted Merlin, leaning down again to help Vivien out, and then the crew chief.

Susan jumped down, but didn't move away. Instead she circled around to the front of the helicopter, flinching as she saw the craft had slid front-first into a huge outcrop of stone. The nose and cockpit were smashed beyond recognition, pushed back to the bulkhead that separated it from the passenger compartment. There were pieces of metal and composite hull and Plexiglas strewn everywhere, all smothered in blood and feathers.

Some of the blood was not from the birds, Susan realized, and she had to look away. There was no chance the pilots had survived.

The crew chief came panting up next to her, and stared. She stood there, staring for several seconds, until Susan touched her arm.

"Mel . . . isn't it? There's nothing we can do."

Mel nodded slowly, shook herself, and stared at the thin coils of smoke starting to find their way out of the many rents and holes in the helicopter's tail and the rear of the cabin. Beyond that, the fog closed in. It was as if there was the burning helicopter and the few survivors, and nothing else, the rest of the world cut off by thick, wet mist.

"No," she said. Her voice caught for a moment, then she spoke more strongly. "We . . . uh . . . we should move to a safe distance."

Susan followed her, away from the helicopter. Merlin and Vivien were already moving, but slowly, both looking around, like scouts in enemy territory. Merlin had the sword bag, holding it in his right hand, and his left hand was in his yak-hair bag, no doubt holding the revolver as he peered through the fog. Vivien was walking slowly, her right hand held in front of her, as if she was feeling her way.

Suddenly, both looked at each other. Though they didn't speak, Susan felt that something had happened. There was a subtle change in the world around them. Nothing she could see or hear, but it felt different. . . .

Acrid smoke billowed across her face and she coughed. It not only had a chemical, metallic odor, there was also the unpleasant stink of cooking birds, all too like a rarely cleaned fried chicken shop not far from Milner Square that Susan always crossed the road to avoid smelling.

"I've never seen a fog come up like that," said Mel. "Or a flock of birds in a fog . . . and . . . where the hell are we anyway?"

Susan looked around. The fog was still too thick to see very far, but the burning helicopter had created an eddy effect that was thinning it out around the crash site. There was a very dense, overgrown forest immediately behind the helicopter, with many very tall and broad oaks, and the field they had landed in was all rough clumps of grass and was littered with stones, not at all the sort of manicured paddock to be expected in a rich outer London semirural village like Totteridge. Not to mention the massive outcrop of stone the helicopter had plowed into; that would have been broken up long ago.

"Where are we?" repeated Mel. She stopped to look back. "We were following an A road, there were big houses either side . . . nothing like this . . ."

She gestured around them, fog wafting about her waving hands, pointing at the glimpses of the tall forest and the rough field with all its stones. There was not a house or a road in sight, or any sign of human civilization at all.

Everyone flinched as something exploded aboard the helicopter. It was not the massive explosion of a Hollywood blockbuster, though it did mark the fire spreading into the main cabin. It began to burn whiter and hotter, and the many independent wisps of smoke began to weave together into a gray-black column that rose up with a crackling roar to mix with the fog.

Save for the crack and pop of the burning helicopter, it was unnaturally quiet. There were no other sounds at all, no human or traffic noise.

Something moved at the visible edge of the fog. A large dog, seen for an instant, then gone again.

"Wolf," said Merlin. "The fire should keep them off."

"A wolf? What are you talking about?" asked Mel. She

gulped, then started talking again, clearly to reassure herself. "Someone will probably have already dialed 999. Ted might have got a Mayday out . . . there'll be a rescue bird . . . we can't be more than five hundred yards from the planned LZ, the police waiting there will have heard the impact, the smoke will break through the fog layer—"

"I think there are some . . . er . . . unusual local problems that will delay rescue for a little while," said Merlin apologetically. "You should stay here, Sergeant."

"What the hell is going on?" asked Mel.

"You've signed the Official Secrets Act, no doubt," said Merlin. "Let's say it's something covered by that. Lie low, we'll send help as soon as possible."

"I should go find a phone, call in—"

A long, baying call stopped her mid-sentence. Not that far off in the fog. The call was answered by several others.

"Wolves," said Mel slowly.

"Yes," said Merlin. He spoke hurriedly, as if keen to move on. "Are you armed?"

"No! We're in England, not a war zone."

Merlin bent down and drew his Beretta from the ankle holster. He kept it pointing down.

"I think the fire will keep off the wolves," he said. "But you can keep this. Thumb safety, here. Cock the hammer to fire. Watch your grip or the slide will take your skin off."

He handed the weapon to the crew chief, along with a spare magazine from his yak-hair bag.

"But I would advise you to fire as a last resort," he said. "Keep low and quiet."

"What are you going to do?" asked Mel slowly.

"We have to go and sort someone out," said Merlin. He opened the bag and took out the sword. Surprisingly, this seemed to snap Mel out of a bewilderment that was bordering on panic.

"Is that a spatha? A Roman cavalry sword?"

"Of that general pattern, yes, though it's seventh century," admitted Merlin. "I'm surprised you recognized it."

"I'm a reenactor," said Mel. "First century AD legionary. Gladius, of course."

"As it happens I have a gladius as well, back home," said Merlin. "But it's not in the same class as *this*—"

He stopped as Vivien plucked urgently at his sleeve.

"Yeah. We can talk swords another time," he said. "Like I said, stay low and quiet. Come on."

He addressed the last two words to Vivien and Susan, as if they'd been the ones holding everything up. Vivien snorted and Susan raised an eyebrow.

"What?" asked Merlin. "Follow me."

They followed him, into the fog.

CHAPTER TWENTY-FIVE

In the dusk, she loosed without a care
The thrice-barbed arrow flew 'cross the air
Lodging not in a deer, but her lover's heart
And so they were doomed, forever to part

THEY DIDN'T GO VERY FAR BEFORE MERLIN STOPPED AND HUNKERED down, gesturing them to do likewise. Susan crouched by his side, every sense alert. She couldn't see anything through the fog, or hear anything. All she knew was that the Copper Cauldron was somewhere ahead of them, perhaps two or three hundred yards away, but she couldn't describe how she knew.

"Okay, we're far enough away from Mel to work out a plan without her flipping out," he said. He spoke quickly, obviously worried.

"Maybe I'll flip out instead," said Susan. "Where are we? What's the situation?"

"We're in Southaw's primary demesne," said Vivien bluntly. "And he's taken it—and us—out of time. Somewhat like what happened to you and Merlin in the May Fair."

"But he made a *big* mistake bringing the helicopter down when he did," said Merlin. "Spite, no doubt, because you were aboard."

"Why was it a mistake?" protested Susan. "We were almost *killed*—"

"But we weren't! And we've come down inside his demesne right at the moment he took it out of time," explained Merlin. "Great-Aunt Evangeline and Cousin Una and the troops have started to bring it back; we both felt it. So we're like an enemy inside the gates during a siege. A fifth column! A Trojan horse! A—"

"He'll know we're here, though," interrupted Susan anxiously. She pointed at the ground. "I mean, exactly here. Back at Coniston I knew where everybody was, every living thing within the bounds!"

"He can't do much about it right now," said Vivien. "The right-handed are forcing the demesne back to the New World. He'll have to use all his strength to stop them. But the contest won't take long, one way or another. We'll win, I'm sure, but to be on the safe side we should help, and we've got about fifteen minutes—"

"Fifteen minutes!" interjected Merlin. "Is that all?"

"Yes," said Vivien. She held up her right hand as if weighing some invisible object. "Maybe even less."

"What happens if they can't bring the demesne back?" asked Susan. "Bring *us* back?"

"We'll be stuck here," said Vivien. She looked around at the fog, which had not lessened. "To be honest, I'd have thought we'd already see signs of the New World coming back. . . . Southaw is more powerful than I expected. It must be because he has the cauldron."

"What does being stuck here actually mean?"

"Your usual fairyland thing," said Vivien. She was still looking around. "Time dilation. A few hours or days here, months or years in the normal world. Maybe centuries."

"Southaw will kill us straight away," said Merlin. "So we don't have to worry about that."

"So what do we do?" asked Susan.

"Find Southaw's locus," said Vivien. "Distract him. If he has to turn his power against us, he'll have less to use against the right-handed team—"

Something leaped out of the fog.

Merlin spun to meet it with his sword. Vivien dived aside, stripping off her glove and holding her breath. Susan fell over half backwards and scrambled aside to grab a big stone. When she looked back, the fog had swirled across. She couldn't see anything and could only hear an animalistic grunting, the *thunk* of Merlin's sword striking something, and Merlin's shout, "Blind it, Viv! Blind it!"

Susan raised the stone she held and ran forward, parting the fog. Suddenly, Merlin was in front of her, overtopped by a massive bear. A dead Cauldron-Born bear, its head half-skeletal, part of its skull and jaw showing through rotten fur. One eye was a bloody ruin, doubtless Vivien's quick work, but the other was bright with a coppery fire.

Merlin swung at the bear, the sword blurring in swift motion. A huge slice of decayed flesh flew from its barrel-like chest, but did not slow it or have any other noticeable effect. It was fast, faster than it ever had been while alive. Merlin leaped back from its counterstrike, his slippered foot turned on a stone, and though he recovered almost instantly, in that lost moment the bear grabbed Merlin by the ankles and twisted his legs.

Susan heard bones break and screamed, her scream drowning Merlin's own cry of pain. She threw the rock at the bear's head, striking its remaining eye. The beast threw Merlin away and rushed towards her, she scuttled back frantically, and—

Vivien stepped in front of the Cauldron-Born, her right hand raised, shining with blinding silver light, light reflecting off the shifting planes of the eddying fog.

The bear halted in place, every sinew frozen.

Beads of sweat ran down Vivien's forehead. Her cheeks were pinched, the muscles in her neck corded with the effort of holding her breath. She fought Southaw's controlling intelligence inside the Cauldron-Born bear, but she could only hold it as long as she had breath.

"Susan! Bind the beast!" gasped Merlin. He tried to stand but it was impossible, his legs were like snapped twigs. He began to crawl towards the bear, his legs dragging uselessly behind him.

Susan drew the butter knife. The blood had dried on it, and she wasn't sure that would work. Swiftly, she slashed the sharp edge across her palm, ignoring the sudden pain to wipe the blade. Then she held it tight in her bloodied hand and frantically searched her pockets for the third salt sachet.

Vivien sank to her knees, her left hand down and clenched on the ground, her shining right hand wavering in front of the Cauldron-Born bear.

Susan felt coins, a tissue, and her door key. For a terrible moment she doubted her memory of Vivien giving her *three* salt packets. Maybe it had only been two. . . .

She found it, smushed up in the corner of her pocket. She pulled it out and ripped it open with her teeth, eased her grip on the knife, and poured the salt in the gap between thumb and forefinger, like a magician stuffing down a handkerchief for a trick.

Vivien made a choking sound, but still her right hand stayed up.

Susan took the blood-and-salt-smeared knife in her own right hand and stepped forward, sliding the knife into the wound Merlin had scored across the Cauldron-Born bear's massive chest.

"I am your master!" she shouted. "You will obey!"

At almost exactly the same moment Vivien gasped for air and fell down on the spot, completely unconscious.

Unlike when she'd tried to enslave Southaw, Susan instantly felt the effect of this binding. An intense pain blossomed between her eyes, like a severe sinus pain, but through it she also felt a connection to the creature in front of her. She could see the strange golden-red fire that burned within it, the motivating power of the Copper Cauldron that had replaced the living will, and there was a line, a string of that same fire coming out of its head, rising up as if it were a puppet controlled by some presence in the sky above, beyond the fog.

She also saw the misshapen shadow that pooled behind the beast's feet, the polluted detritus of the bear's spirit, forced from it by the power of the cauldron, but still connected to the remnant flesh.

Susan bent her will upon the bear, trying to wrest control away, to become the puppet master herself. She felt a sudden flash of nausea as she lost her own vision and senses and took over the bear's, but a moment later she was thrown out, back in her own head again.

She heard Holly's bullying, confident voice right next to her, shouting in her ear, and felt his presence, Southaw's immense power.

"Mine! This is mine!"

He was too strong. She could not prevail against him—and Susan also knew she didn't *want* to; that brief, foul taste of controlling the poor bear was more than enough. She would never direct a Cauldron-Born, never.

But Susan instinctively knew there was something else she could do. She lifted her salt-stained, bloodied knife again and slashed through the fiery string emanating from the bear's head, as Southaw lifted its huge, taloned paws to strike at her.

The bright copper-red cord parted without resistance, curling back up like a burnt hair. The fire inside the bear went with it, blown out like a candle. The misshapen shadow re-formed into the true shape of a sad, bewildered bear, sank into the grass, and was gone.

Susan leaped back as the physical remains of the monster tumbled down in front of her, a gut-wrenchingly awful pile of decomposed bear meat, rank blood, and broken bones. Some of it spilled over Vivien's feet, but she still didn't move.

She looked like she was dead. Fearing the worst, Susan knelt at her side and felt for the pulse in her neck, gasping in relief as she found it. Faint, but regular, and she could see the slow lift of Vivien's chest under her eggshell-blue waistcoat. Blood trickled from her lip where she had bitten it in the effort to hold the Cauldron-Bear. And her bare silver hand still shone.

Merlin dragged himself up and Susan turned to him.

"Overtaxed her strength," muttered Merlin. "She'll be okay. . . ."

"What about you?" asked Susan anxiously. She started to pull Merlin's trousers up to see how bad the breaks were, but he stopped her, holding her wrists.

"Both legs broken," he said, grimacing. "Spiral fractures. Very bad."

"The Sipper spit . . ."

"Can't mend broken bones . . . not quickly," said Merlin. He was breathing in short pants, obviously in extreme pain. He pulled the Smython out of his bag and held it out butt first. "Take my revolver. I see your salt-bloodied knife is better than a sword against the Cauldron-Born. *You* have to distract Southaw—"

"But—"

"You can . . . do . . . what you did to that . . . one."

"But how will I even know what Southaw—"

"The Totteridge Yew," gasped Merlin. "His locus is a tree! It will be clear to you, and he'll be with the cauldron. Head for that."

"But what do I do?" asked Susan.

"I don't know! Shoot the tree, chop branches off with the knife, anything to take his attention away from the contest of wills," croaked Merlin. "I'll follow, but crawling . . . there isn't time! You're our only chance."

Susan hesitated for an instant before leaning in to kiss Merlin full on the mouth. He lifted his shaking right hand and ran his fingers across the stubble on her head. They held the kiss for an electric second, before both slowly broke away.

"Stay alive," whispered Merlin.

"You too," said Susan. If they lived, she knew there would be much more than a single date in their shared future.

If they lived.

She grabbed the revolver, hefted her knife, turned, and walked swiftly into the fog. She knew exactly where the Copper Cauldron was, and she headed straight to it.

Merlin looked at Vivien again, took a knife out of his sleeve, and sat up, grunting with the pain. He bent forward and slit his trousers from the knees, inspecting his fractured legs. With his steady left hand he drew out a vial of Sipper blood, swished it in his mouth, and spat it on his left leg where a piece of twisted bone protruded through the skin. He let it pool there, then settled his left hand on the bone and with one quick motion pushed it back in place—and fainted.

Susan did not look behind her. She walked as straight as she could towards the cauldron. She could sense its location. It wasn't far away, but the fog was still so thick she couldn't see anything but the field a few yards in front of her. The grass was higher here, strewn with stones, a natural clearing rather than the work even of primitive agriculture. Southaw had indeed removed his demesne to some ancient part of England, far back in time.

Susan readied her knife, every nerve on edge, ready for a sudden attack by a Cauldron-Born, be it human, bear, or whatever. But before she'd taken a few steps, she realized this would not work. She couldn't creep around the fog, fearing attack.

Merlin had said to distract Southaw. To do that, she had to get his attention, not skulk herself.

Susan walked faster and filled her lungs to shout as loudly as she could.

"Hey, Southaw or Holly or whatever you want to call yourself! Shithead! I'm coming for my cauldron! Yes, that's right! My cauldron! MY CAULDRON!"

Her words had an immediate effect. The fog swirled and thinned, visibility increasing enormously. Modern noises suddenly filtered in, though distant. The sound of sirens, far away, and a helicopter. Both faded away again almost at once, but the fog did not return.

Faint sunshine lit up the stony field, its light soaked up by the darkness of the ancient forest that clustered around the open space. A hundred yards in front of her, Susan saw a single, lonely tree. A yew already ancient even in this place, a cracked and gnarly thing with a massive yellowish bole that rose only three or four feet before splitting into five subsidiary trunks that rose up thirty feet. Its branches spread wide, thick with poisonous leaves and berries.

Somewhere below this yew, in a hollow between the roots, lay the Copper Cauldron. A vast bowl of hammered metal, six inches thick, big enough to hold and cook an ox, each of its three squat legs the size of Susan's torso. The metal shone with internal light, but the interior of the cauldron was darker than any night, defying all mortal sight.

Susan broke into a run, screaming words she didn't even know, some ancient war cry of her father's that had come into her head. At fifty yards she stopped to fire at the tree, but the revolver almost bucked out of her hand and the shot went wild.

But the boom of the gun did distract Southaw from his unseen struggle with the booksellers who were trying to reel him back into the flow of time. The sounds of the New World broke in again, louder and closer. Susan saw it now, like a mirage superimposed on what was already there, a blurry, double-vision view of a modern road cutting across the stony field ahead of her, a church rising up behind the yew, big expensive houses with well-clipped hedges shimmering into existence to her left and right.

There were people, too, ghostly, blurred figures. She knew they were booksellers from the blobs of bright silver that marked their hands. There were lots of them gathered in a ring around the ancient yew, like the goblins who'd danced her to the May Fair. There were even more booksellers behind them, left-handed ones with shadowy weapons, abstract lines in place of swords and axes. Susan heard Una's commanding voice, but far off, as if carried by the wind from some distant place. But there was no wind here; the air was still and wet, even though the fog had gone.

Roads, buildings, and booksellers were not yet real in this place, and might never be, if Southaw won the contest of wills. Susan stopped and held the revolver tighter, firing at the tree again, four more times, until the gun was empty. She thought she hit it, but Southaw was not distracted again.

The New World faded out again. Susan screamed in anger and ran forward, lifting her little knife high. She wanted to hurt Southaw, punish him for everything he had done. He had enslaved her father, ruined Jassmine's life, *killed* Merlin's and Vivien's mother—

No Cauldron-Born rose to stop her, no sudden flight of starlings. For a few moments a sense of exaltation filled Susan; she would reach the tree and hack at the branches with her knife . . . the sharpened butter knife. . . .

But what would that do? Shooting at it hadn't achieved anything. She already knew she couldn't bind Southaw, not with salt and steel and blood.

She didn't need to hurt Southaw. She needed to distract him. Make him fight a battle of wills with her as well as the booksellers.

Susan stopped, and raised her hands, once again taking in a deep breath.

"The Copper Cauldron is mine own! I call upon its powers and deny them to all others!"

A flash of bright copper-red light from beneath the tree answered her words. She felt a sudden giddy influx of power, only for second, before the harsh will of Southaw shut her off from it. It was not enough for her to simply claim the cauldron. It would take more than that.

The Ancient Sovereign responded in another way as well. The tree moved, a great root tearing out of the earth, or so it seemed. Susan slowed and blinked. It was not the physical tree that moved, the thing of branch and leaf and bark. It was as if the *shadow* of the tree was leaving it. But this was no shadow, it was a thing of that same intensely dense, gray, and greasy smoke she'd seen become a raven atop the Old Man of Coniston.

It was the spirit of the tree, the essence of Southaw.

Another shadowy root came free of the earth, and another, and a smoky duplicate left the actual tree, branches stretching out like grasping arms. The whorls and fissures of the physical tree were in this thing huge pupil-less yellow eyes, and the rotting crack in the bole became a gulping maw that opened and shut and ground splintered teeth together in exasperation at its challenger.

Southaw stalked towards Susan, growing taller as he came, now a fifty-foot-tall creature of dense malevolence. The real tree behind it seemed tiny now, ordinary and merely old, no longer imbued with power.

But Southaw's grip on his demesne did not waver. There was no hint of the New World, no faint vision of road or church or people.

"What does it *take*," groaned Susan, watching the apparition stalk towards her, her mind momentarily blank with fear. If she couldn't distract Southaw . . .

Bright light flashed again from the Copper Cauldron, like a beacon calling to her. She could see in her mind's eye, nestled in an earthy chamber beneath the physical yew, half-buried in the humus from the tree's dropped bark and needles decomposing over time.

Susan turned and ran, not directly away from Southaw, but at a right angle. The huge shadow tree turned to follow, moving fast, many great roots propelling it like a centipede, sending it scuttling over the ground faster than Susan could run. Its leading branches reached out fifty or sixty feet ahead, all too like a spider's forelegs, the ends curling and snatching at the air, as they would snatch at her in a very few seconds.

Susan turned again and raced for the copper-red glint. Southaw turned, too, not so swift as in a straight line, but he was already too close behind. She could hear his branches whipping the air, the roots ripping earth and stone, that smoky shadow-stuff not insubstantial at all, not here.

She would only have seconds with the cauldron, even if she got there first.

Merlin, dragging himself in agony across the field, saw Susan running, saw the monstrous spirit tree looming close behind her.

He felt a faint spark of hope leap inside as he saw Southaw was finally distracted. The New World was swimming into view, coming into focus, distant sound and wavering ghost shapes more concrete by the moment. But it was not fast enough, not fast enough by far; and Merlin cried out and tried to crawl faster as he caught the flash of light from the cauldron and saw Southaw so close, and Susan so near, and he realized what she would have to do, that he had told her himself.

If a living person is entirely immersed in the cauldron, it will shatter, its power gone forever. Oh, and the person dies.

CHAPTER TWENTY-SIX

To stand on a pivot; balanced, true
Awaiting the drop of the other shoe
A shining moment, before you fall
All things must end, but is this all?

SUSAN REACHED THE YEW WITH SOUTHAW'S QUESTING BRANCHES so close, so close behind. There was no time to consider, no time for second thoughts, no time to slow down. She felt the slash of a sharp-edged branch across her back and threw herself forward, slamming into the raw earth, sliding across and down into the cavern beneath the roots of the yew, falling in a cascade of dirt straight down—

Into the waiting mouth of the Copper Cauldron.

It was like diving into light, wondrous golden light, which enveloped Susan and took her in, Southaw too slow to catch her at the last.

A hundred yards away, Merlin saw Susan's dive. He saw the Old One lunge forward, massive branches of smoke and shadow thrashing at the earth, only to rear back with a shriek like a locomotive's locked wheels sliding into disaster, a scream of total rage.

The New World in the shape of the charming village of Totteridge rushed in to replace the Old, an unstoppable tide of color and sound and movement. Sunshine burst through the clouds, swaths of light sweeping down. The A5109 solidified in place, with flashing blue lights to north and south indicating the police roadblocks that had cut off all traffic.

On the west side of the road, huge, expensive houses rose, bordered with tall hedges to shield themselves from the passing poor. To the east a church appeared, a seventeenth- or eighteenth-century construction of dull yellow-brown brick topped by an incongruous white tower. A surprisingly low paling fence rose up around the churchyard, entered at a 1930s lych-gate, with its low peaked roof. Gravestones peppered the churchyard, amidst lesser trees.

In the middle of the churchyard, there was the Totteridge Yew.

A circle of thirty right-handed and six even-handed booksellers closed in on the physical yew tree and the raging tree monster that was Southaw, who loomed high above it. The booksellers all wore blue boiler suits, and the ugly bulbous-toed steel-capped boots that in other times would have made Merlin wince. Their silver hands were ungloved and bright, and like the goblins of May Fair, they formed a handfast ring.

Without any audible command, the booksellers suddenly stepped forward, boots crashing down as one, like the guards at Buckingham Palace. The ring drew tighter, closer to the tree.

Southaw lashed at them, long branches whipping down. But his threshing blows had no force; his smoky essence lost solidity wherever it struck, dissipating into puffs of gray dust like seeds blown from polluted dandelions.

With every blow the monstrous spirit tree became smaller and weaker, shrinking back down towards the physical yew. Again, without a word, the booksellers stepped forward, the ring tightening once more. The essence of Southaw retreated fully inside the actual tree, but it could still be seen, tree and spirit like a badly registered printing, the lines of trunk and tree and leaves smudged with gray fuzziness.

Some of the booksellers in the ring began to sing. Their voices were soft and musical, but barely more than a whisper. The words of banishment, which Merlin had learned at school but never heard in earnest. More booksellers joined in, two lines behind. Then the last group joined, also two lines behind, the song sung as a round by the three groups, each composed of a dozen booksellers, ten right-handed and two even-handed.

Dream not, thou shade
O'er an eternal night
Wake not, but sleep
In slow time's creep

Fight not, lie down
Abjure all and thy crown
Rise not, save at our behest
Sleep deep, go to thy rest

Sleep sound, Old One
Thy reign is done
Rest now, sleep fast
Thy time is past

As the booksellers in the ring sang Southaw away, forty left-handed booksellers, also wearing boiler suits and boots, worked in quartets to chop up remnant Cauldron-Born with various bladed weapons. One even had something that resembled the classic grim reaper's scythe. They were collecting the pieces in draw-stringed cotton library bags that shared a common "Wooten Library" embroidered patch along with many individual designs exhibiting the wildly variant levels of sewing expertise from several generations of St. Jacques children.

Southaw had deployed more than a dozen of the Cauldron-Born to defend the perimeter of his village lair, but had lost control when he took the demesne out of time. They had turned on whoever was closest, including each other, and some were still locked together, gnawing and tearing at decayed flesh, until the booksellers' blades chopped them into little bits.

"Where's Susan?"

Merlin was lying facedown on the grass. He rolled over and looked up, grimacing as the movement sent stabs of pain shooting through his broken legs. The sun was behind Vivien, and he squinted at her. Her chin was covered in blood from her lip, but she was smiling.

"She went in the cauldron," said Merlin dully. "That's what finished Southaw."

"That was clever!" said Vivien admiringly.

Merlin gulped back a sob.

"She went in the cauldron," he repeated, choking on the words. "She broke it to save you and me and fix Southaw and all you can say is 'That was clever'?"

Vivien frowned and pointed to where the left-handed were chopping up Cauldron-Born.

"If she broke the cauldron, why are there still Cauldron-Born flopping around?"

Merlin stared at her, then over at the tree. The booksellers stood shoulder to shoulder now, close against the bole of the Totteridge Yew. The first group of singers fell silent, and then the second, and finally the third. The round was sung, the banishing done, and with the final word the last wisp of Southaw vanished from the tree. Now, perhaps forever, it was only a yew.

Merlin and Vivien felt Southaw go, sent somewhere akin to that place of nothingness they had traversed to reach Silvermere.

The ring of booksellers broke apart, excited chatter spreading, with handshakes and embraces far more of relief than triumph. But at one spot, near the tree, several booksellers peered down into a hole lit by a faint copper-red glow. One of them called out to Una, who turned away from the Cauldron-Born she had been chopping up and marched over, her sword held ready in her silver hand.

"Pick me up!" ordered Merlin. "Fireman's carry! Get me over there now!"

"Una's not going to kill Susan," chided Vivien. But she bent down and picked Merlin up, settling him across her shoulders. "But since this will get you to an ambulance quicker, I might as well."

"Do you really think she's still alive?" asked Merlin. "Unchanged?"

Vivien didn't answer for a moment. Alive, she thought likely, given the cauldron had not shattered. Unchanged might be too much to ask.

"I don't know," she said as gently as possible.

Sirens got louder and closer, and a veritable parade of police vehicles roared in from north and south. At the same time Inspector Greene came running through the churchyard towards the yew, followed by half a dozen armed police officers in full tactical gear. Three of them carried old steel poleaxes, doubtless from the Tower of London, the others H & K MP5s.

A vicar stepped out of the front door of the church as they ran by, and looked around in extreme puzzlement at all the blue-suited, silver-handed people with medieval weapons, and the armed police.

"Go back inside, sir!" shouted Greene.

"We charge for filming here!" retorted the indignant vicar. "And no one has asked for permission! This is sacrilege and a disgrace! I will call the *actual* police!"

Greene pointed to one of her officers, who peeled off and took the vicar's arm, taking him still protesting back into the church.

Merlin and Vivien reached the yew a few seconds behind Una. But she sheathed her sword, and reached down to lift Susan up.

Her face was smeared with dirt and she was holding her right wrist up high near her neck, but otherwise she appeared to be unharmed, and unchanged.

"Put me down," said Merlin, too much aware of how he looked like a flopping fish draped over Vivien's shoulders. His sister lowered him more carefully than he deserved and helped him sit up against a tilted gravestone. Susan walked slowly towards him and sat down by his side.

They sat in silence for several seconds, looking at the Totteridge Yew and the booksellers and police bustling about it, with Una shouting orders, and Greene trying to talk to her, and a completely white-haired right-handed bookseller joined them, and there were more ambulances and police cars coming in from everywhere with sirens on, and an RAF helicopter began to circle the column of smoke from the crash site over to the west, and all was bedlam.

"I thought . . . I thought you'd broken the cauldron," said Merlin. "And . . ."

He choked back a sob and took a breath, holding it for a second before he continued, his voice regaining some of his normal, insouciant tone. "I thought it was a rather extreme way to avoid having a drink with me."

"I'd simply stand you up," agreed Susan cheerfully. "Much easier. Particularly since I seem to have broken my collarbone."

"How did you not . . . die?" said Merlin. "I saw you dive for the cauldron—"

"I couldn't think of anything else sufficiently distracting," said Susan. "But I thought there was a chance it wouldn't break, and it wouldn't kill me. Two chances, actually. One, because it is rightfully my father's and he gave me some of his power. He made the cauldron, you know; he isn't just the Keeper."

"What?"

"I don't know how I know that," said Susan thoughtfully. "But it's true. Southaw could never have bound Dad if he hadn't been so far from his own demesne, taking human form so he could be with Mum. I wonder how they met in the first place? She's never even been to the Lake District as far as I know."

"What was the second reason?" asked Merlin very slowly. He was finding it hard to concentrate. The pain in his legs was sharper and demanded more attention. It was so nice having Susan next to him. . . .

He started as Susan shook him very gently.

"Sorry, what was that . . . I . . ."

"Passed out," said Vivien, leaning in. "Stay still, Great-Aunt Evangeline is going to fix up your legs."

"As much as I can, for now," said the white-haired right-handed bookseller, clearly Great-Aunt Evangeline. "I'll see to your collarbone, too, young lady. And I'll offer you my preliminary thanks as well, for saving us all from continuing down the road to disaster paved by the unlamented Merrihew, more official thanks to be forthcoming in due course."

"They never liked each other," whispered Vivien to Susan.

"That is entirely untrue, Vivien," said Evangeline. She laid her glowing hand on Merlin's left leg, took a sudden intake of breath, and slowly let it out. Merlin grimaced, then sighed in relief as the magic took effect. "Merrihew and I were quite amicable as children, indeed might even be described as friends until she stole my young man, shortly before Waterloo. Is that better, Merlin?"

"Much, thank you, Great-Aunt," gasped Merlin. "Susan, what did you say, what was the second reason?"

Evangeline moved her hand to his right leg, muttering, "You still won't be able to walk for a week or so, but I think this will spare you a plaster cast. Two casts."

"It was what you said," said Susan, smiling at him. "You said *total immersion* in the cauldron would break it and kill whoever went in. So I grabbed the rim as I fell and kept my hand out. That's how I broke my collarbone."

"What was it like?" asked Vivien. "I can't really remember when I put my hands in our grail."

Susan shrugged, forgetting her broken collarbone, and yowled with the sudden pain.

"Ow! Ow! I can't really remember, either. I was only in it for a second or two, I pulled myself out as quickly as I could. It was full of light. Glorious light. It felt like . . . it felt like being at home. You know, when you get in after a bad day, and it's warm and well-lit and safe. . . ."

"Stay still," instructed Evangeline, moving on to Susan. "I can knit the bone, and take some of the pain away, but you will need a sling for a few days and it will hurt. You'll need to take some aspirin."

"Thank you," said Susan as Evangeline rested her right hand very lightly on her clavicle. "Could you . . . can you also tell if . . . if the cauldron has . . . has done anything to me?"

Evangeline took a breath and held it for several long seconds, the glow from her hand painting Susan's anxious face silver. When she exhaled, the old bookseller smiled gently.

"You are what you have always been, child of Ancient Sovereign and mortal," she said. "The cauldron has made you no more, and no less. But you have a rare heritage. I do not think anyone can tell you all the ins and outs of it. Our Grail-Keeper, perhaps, or your father. Though as I think you already know, though they may take human shape, they do not necessarily think or act as we do, and communication with them is rarely easy."

"I will have to take the cauldron back to Dad," said Susan. She moved her arm a little. It hurt far less, but it still hurt. "I hope you'll allow me to do that?"

"We will *help* you," said Evangeline. "Your father kept it hidden for close to two thousand years, after all, and short of breaking it—which we would not do save in direst need, for fear of unintended consequences—it is far better in his hands than any others. But for the time being, if you do not object, we shall store it with our other treasures in the New Bookshop. I suspect Grandmother will like to see it again, for one thing. And as your father has retired, I believe, until the end of the year, there is no point returning it any sooner to Coniston. But right now, both of you young people need to be taken to hospital—"

"Actually, Great-Aunt," interrupted Merlin, talking swiftly

and exerting all his charm. "I was wondering if we could put Susan up at the Northumberland because she can't go back to Greene's safe house anyway. You know those adjoining suites on the top floor, perhaps I could have one as well, temporarily of course, while I recuperate—"

"Merlin," interrupted Susan. She looked at him fondly, then over to Inspector Greene and Una, who had come over to scowl down at them both, as if they expected to see them mortally wounded, and together would have to do the paperwork to explain this fact to sundry secular powers. Though there had already been a discussion along the lines of the vicar's serendipitous comment, that maybe it could all be explained as a big budget film shoot that had gotten out of control.

"Merlin," repeated Susan. "I'm going to take the advice I was given when I first got here, and go home to my mum."

Merlin's face fell, his expression equally disbelieving that his charms had been so comprehensively rebuffed, and shattered because he truly did care for her.

Susan enjoyed this for a very brief moment before she added, "Only for a week or two, until I've recovered. And I'd like you to come with me."

"She got you good, brother," said Vivien admiringly, as Susan and Merlin kissed.

EPILOGUE

THE BROOK BURBLED LOUDER AS THE TAXI DROVE UP AND SWUNG around in the graveled parking area in front of the farmhouse. It was a black cab, a London one at that, which was highly unusual here, close to Bath. The crows on the chimney of the barn Jassmine used as a studio eyed the vehicle askance, and several small stones rolled down the hill where the earth shivered, as if it was about to move more weightily.

But the entities of water, air, and earth settled back with a collective sigh of relief as Susan got out of the back of the cab, away from the mass of shielding iron. It was not a sigh that could be heard or seen by ordinary mortals, but Susan felt it, and looked to the brook and the ravens and up the hill, and waved to each in turn, before leaning back in to get Merlin's crutches out of the car. He edged out gingerly after them, and took the crutches from her, got himself up and balanced, and slowly moved from the graveled car park to the flagstoned path leading to the front door.

Susan was wearing a new blue boiler suit, another one exactly her size being found easily, much to Merlin's surprise. He had adopted a dashing ensemble he was sure would impress Susan's mother, a pale blue long-sleeved shirt with ruffled cuffs, a Black Watch kilt, and despite Susan's frowns he'd cross-gartered dark green ribbons over the bandages that ran from ankle to knee, above carpet slippers, also in tartan. The ubiquitous tie-dyed yak-hair bag was over his shoulder, where it annoyingly swung against his crutches every now and then.

Audrey got out and removed Susan's backpack and Merlin's suitcase that had perhaps once been Noël Coward's out, and four cardboard book boxes. These had handwritten labels in bold marker pen over the publishing house logos: "Sayers-Allingham-Marsh-Christie," "Vivien's Recs—None too difficult for Merlin," "Rare Edns, We Want These Back," and "Best Novels in English and Translation 1920–1950." As soon as she had stacked the boxes up, Mister Nimbus jumped up on top and surveyed what might be his new territory, though he did incline his head to the ravens, suggesting he had the wisdom to share.

"Meter says two hundred and sixty pounds," said Audrey cheerfully. "But I'll settle for a cuppa char before I go back."

"You can have several," promised Susan. "And probably some cake, or at least biscuits. It rather depends on what Mum's been—"

"Susan!"

Jassmine came flying out the farmhouse door, struggling to take off her painting smock to show the vintage violet silk dress beneath but succeeding only in breaking the necklace she wore, sending beads spraying everywhere. She laughed and let the smock fall, enfolding Susan in a careful embrace that avoided her slung-up arm and shoulder.

"My shoulder's a lot better," said Susan, forestalling Jassmine's question. "Mum, this is Merlin. Merlin, this is Jassmine."

"Oh, poor Lenny," said Jassmine, staring at Merlin appreciatively. "Though I did hear he's already taken up with Kerry O'Neill. She plays clarinet, you know."

"Does she?" asked Merlin blandly. "I understand clarinet goes very well with the French horn."

"It does, doesn't it," said Jassmine.

"And this is Merlin's aunt Audrey," said Susan. "Who was kind enough to drive us here."

"Delighted to meet you, Jassmine," said Audrey, without a trace of Cockney at all. She offered her hand, but it was not the bare right that Jassmine looked at, but the gloved left. She hadn't noticed Merlin's, because he was gripping his crutches and leaning forward.

"Oh," she said faintly, stepping back. "You're one of *those* booksellers. Like the one . . . the one . . ."

"No, not like Merrihew," said Susan quickly, taking her mother's arm. "Merrihew was a . . . a . . ."

"Traitor," said Merlin bleakly. "And we will do everything

we can to try to make amends for what she did."

"I didn't remember," said Jassmine slowly. She had a faraway look in her eyes, but also seemed to Susan to have come more into herself, to be fully present, always a rare occurrence in the past. "I couldn't remember . . . but a few days ago it started coming back. . . ."

"I found Dad," said Susan quietly. "He was made to leave you, Mum. It wasn't his fault."

Jassmine nodded slowly. She wiped a tear away, and smiled, a smile of fond remembrance.

"I know," she said. "It would never have lasted anyway."

"What?" asked Susan.

"Rex and me," said Jassmine. "We had fun, but we were from different worlds. Him and his mountain and the lake, and me all for the city and the music scene and everything. Back then. To be honest, he was often rather selfish. We never would have stayed together."

Susan stared at her. This was not how she had imagined her mother taking the news of her father's discovery and potential reappearance.

"But I got you from it, darling!" said Jassmine brightly. "That was the best thing!"

"I agree," said Merlin. He pointed to the fallen beads with the ferrule of his right crutch. "Should we pick those up? I say we, but I mean Audrey."

"Oh no," said Jassmine. "Leave them for the ravens, they like that sort of thing. Come and have some tea! I'm dying to hear about everything that's happened. I've made the blue room up for you and Merlin, Susan—not yours; I thought you'd prefer the *big* bed—"

"Good idea," said Susan gravely, while Merlin pretended to be scandalized.

ACKNOWLEDGMENTS

I first visited the United Kingdom (from Australia) in 1983, when I was nineteen. I was very fortunate that my aunt Judy married Gerry Heavey, an Englishman who returned home for a visit at the same time I was there, and he and his parents extended their kind hospitality in London, providing me with a base of operations for my travels over the next six months. I owe many thanks to Gerry, and his parents, Mr. and Mrs. Heavey (as I called them; it was a more formal era). It was during this time that I decided I wanted to try to become a writer. In fact I wrote the first short story I ever sold during that trip, on a Silver-Reed typewriter that I had to sell in order to buy a bus ticket to Heathrow, having a return air ticket to Sydney but otherwise having spent every penny.

I walked up the Old Man of Coniston in 1983, and again

when I returned the next time, in 1993. I have to thank Arthur Ransome for that, for the Swallows and Amazons books I loved as a child (and still do), which provided an impetus to visit the Lake District that first time, and numerous times since, including my honeymoon in 2000, when my wife, Anna, and I stayed in a hotel on the shores of Lake Windermere and a sudden fog came up and rolled over the lawns, across our balcony, and into our second-floor room. . . .

I have returned to the United Kingdom and to London in particular numerous times since that first visit, these visits often made easier and more pleasant due to the hospitality of my sister-in-law, Belinda McFarlane. Not to mention extremely cultural, since she is a violinist with the London Symphony Orchestra and always gets us tickets for wonderful concerts and performances.

Many of my visitations to the United Kingdom have been working ones, to promote my books, and I have been fortunate to have been so well looked after by publicists, editors, and other staff from my various publishers over the years: Harper-Collins, Egmont, Bonnier (Hot Key and Piccadilly Press), and now also Gollancz.

The initial idea for this book actually came when I was on tour for my book *Goldenhand*. I was signing stock at the Ocean Terminal Waterstones in Leith, and I noticed the bookseller was left-handed, and commented on it. He said *all* the booksellers in the shop that day were left-handed. Please forgive me that I didn't note your surname, Stephen the bookseller of Leith, and thank you for the spark that led to this book.

I also am grateful to my friends Inspector Roger Nield MBE (Surrey Police, rtd) and WPC Lucy Nield (Surrey Police, rtd) for answering my questions about British policing. If I've gotten something right, it's thanks to Roger and Lucy; if wrong, it's all my fault. Or it's different in this somewhat alternate 1983. . . .

I must thank my agents for their expertise, encouragement, and unfailing business acumen: Jill Grinberg and her team at Jill Grinberg Literary Management in New York; Fiona Inglis and the gang at Curtis Brown Australia; and Matthew Snyder and his associates, who look after film/TV for me at CAA in Los Angeles.

My publishers help me in many different ways to do my job and make beautiful books; they also market and sell them superbly, and I am honored to be on their lists: Katherine Tegen and the HarperCollins crew in the USA; Eva Mills and everyone at Allen & Unwin in Australia; and Gillian Redfearn and the team at Gollancz in the United Kingdom. I have also been very lucky to work with fantastic audiobook publishers, at Listening Library/Random House, Bolinda, and Brilliance. I am also very grateful to the translators and publishers who make my books work in other languages and countries.

Booksellers have been absolutely essential in helping my books reach readers. I am grateful to all booksellers, not only for supporting my own books but for everything you do to connect people and reading. I would particularly like to thank Margaret and Teki Dalton and the Dalton family, and everyone

I worked with at Dalton's Bookshop in Canberra, way back in 1987 when the height of bookshop technology was calling the Penguin warehouse every evening to recite a list of ISBNs for restocking.

I should also mention that the modern-era Foyles bookshops have all the good aspects of the fabled older store at 121 Charing Cross Road, but not what might perhaps be called the negative eccentricities. The St. Jacques booksellers are also biased, of course.

Similarly, the actual ancient yew, village, and church of Totteridge, and whoever was vicar in 1983, are not the same as in this book, which depicts an alternate, imagined 1983 and not the real places or persons.

I am eternally grateful to my wife, Anna McFarlane, who not only manages a very busy career as a publisher, but also our family; and to our sons, Thomas and Edward, who are very understanding of their father's foibles and limitations, so often related to at least half my mind being absent in a book.

Flip the page to return to the Old Kingdom with
the long-awaited prequel to SABRIEL,

TERCIEL &
ELINOR

Prologue

THE FIG TREE was ancient and huge, its lower trunk buttressed by enormous roots that rose out of the lawn around it like the fins of some vast subterranean creature, while its upper branches topped out at two hundred feet, a full hundred feet higher than even the red-roofed tower of the Abhorsen's House nearby.

A boy, perhaps eight years old, brown-skinned, dark-haired, thin in the face and everywhere else from lack of food, was climbing swiftly up through the branches of the fig with fierce determination. He was wearing ragged, many-times-repaired breeches and a new linen shirt, far too large for him, that had been cinched in the middle with a silk scarf, also new, to make a kind of tunic, and his bare feet were extremely dirty.

It was very quiet in and around the tree, but the boy climbed in a frenzy, as if he were pursued. Several times he almost lost his grip or footing, but he didn't slow or falter. Finally, as he neared the top and the branches became slimmer and began to bend and creak, he slowed down. Soon after, reaching a point some twenty or thirty paces short of the crown, he stopped and straddled a horizontal branch, setting his thin shoulders against the gnarled trunk of the mighty tree.

He couldn't see much from his vantage point. The leaves were too thick around him. But there were a few spots where the foliage thinned. Through these gaps he could catch a glimpse of the red-roofed tower house below and the white limestone walls that surrounded the island it was built on, an island in the middle of a broad, fast-rushing river that only a few hundred yards to the south plunged over a massive waterfall.

The boy stared at the mist rising along the line of the cliffs, marveling again at the quiet, the roar of the falls held back from the island by magic, or so he supposed. It had been noisy enough on the riverbank, and almost deafening when the old woman had jumped across the stepping-stones with him on her back, gripping her so hard around the neck she'd told him crossly to stop choking her or they would both die.

The old woman. She'd said she was his great-aunt, but he didn't think that could be true. She'd repeated this claim to the beadle at the workhouse in Grynhold, and the mayor, so they would let him go, but they wouldn't have stopped her anyway. They were all bowing and begging her pardon and asking if she wanted wine or oysters or cake or anything at all the town might give her.

But all she had wanted was him, and they had been happy to hand him over. No one had asked what he wanted.

There was a rustle higher above, and a crunching, snapping sound. For a moment the boy thought it was a branch breaking, but the sound went on too long. A continuous crunching noise. He stood up and parted the branches immediately above him. All the boy saw was glaring green, elongated eyes and a broad open mouth full of very sharp white teeth.

He flinched, lost his footing, and almost fell, but sacrificing skin, he managed to keep his grip on the higher branches. He swung there for a heart-stopping second before he scrabbled his feet back onto a thicker, lower branch.

Branches creaked above, as if suddenly bearing more weight, and the foliage moved so Terciel got a proper look at what was above him. He was surprised to see it was a man, or sort of a man, because his first, half-seen impression was of something smaller. That said, this man was no taller than Terciel, albeit much broader across the shoulders. He had an odd pinkish nose and there was that hideous, many-toothed mouth and the huge emerald eyes. Adding to his strangeness, his skin was entirely covered in fine, very white fur or down, which grew longer on his head and chin to give the appearance of hair and a beard. He had been eating fig-bird chicks out of a nest, crunching their tiny bones. There was a feather in the corner of his mouth and a single drop of blood on his broad white chest.

A red leather collar was fastened tight around his neck, a collar that swarmed with Charter marks to make some sort of spell, and a tiny silver bell hung from the collar. The boy could see the clapper swing inside, but it made no sound, at least not one that he could hear.

"So," said whatever this thing was, spitting out the feather. His voice was that of a grown man, and sardonic. "You're her new one."

The boy crouched lower on the branch, ready to drop down to the next branch below, to climb down as fast or even faster than he had climbed up.

"Don't fret," said the creature. "You're safe enough from me."

"What are you?" asked the boy nervously. He had one foot on the branch below, but he stayed where he was. For the moment. "I mean who? Sir."

"Many things once," said the stranger, yawning. His teeth were even longer and sharper than they had seemed at first, and there were more of them. "I am a servant of the Abhorsens. Or to be more accurate, a slave. I have had many names. Your mistress calls me Moregrim."

"The Abhorsen. Her, down there," said the boy, frowning. He gestured at the house. She'd taken him inside as soon as they arrived and handed him over to two strange magical servants she called Sendings. They were like daytime ghosts, their skin and eyes and hair and everything all Charter marks, uncountable tiny marks in different colors, swarming and crawling about to create the illusion of living people. The Sendings had tried to give him a bath but he'd managed to escape and climb the tree.

"Yes indeed," replied the dwarf, his green eyes sparkling with mischief. "Her down there is the current Abhorsen, and you, I presume, are her latest Abhorsen-in-Waiting. Terciel, that's your name, isn't it?"

"How do you know that?"

"I listen at doors," said Moregrim blithely. "And windows. Both the real and the metaphorical."

Terciel frowned again, not understanding what the strange creature was talking about.

"Tell me," said the dwarf idly, not even looking at the boy. "Have you wielded the bells yet? Touched the handles? Worn the bandolier at least?"

"What?" asked Terciel. He still wasn't sure whether to flee down the tree or not. He had climbed it with the idea of hiding there until nightfall, and then trying to escape this island, but with this magical slave of the Abhorsen's here, that plan had already failed. He looked around, wondering if there was somewhere else he could hide. Apart from the main house and its immediate gardens, there was an orchard, and lawns, and a strange little house or shed to the south, but nowhere that would offer safety from a search.

He tried not to think even farther ahead, to how he might cross the river, so swift, with the vast falls so close. The stepping-stones were too far apart for him to jump. Maybe there was a boat. He was good with boats, a true child of the fishing port of Grynhold. Launched from the northern end of the island, where the current would be weaker, maybe—

"Have you wielded the bells?"

The bells.

The sudden change in Terciel's admittedly already difficult life had started with the appearance of seven bells in a bandolier. One moment they had not been there, and then there they were, in Terciel's most secret eyrie in between the chimney stacks on the roof of the Grynhold Fish Hall. He'd been steeping a stolen piece of salt fish in a rain bucket, heard something strange, and looked away for less than a second. When he looked back, there was the bandolier, with the mahogany bell handles sticking out of the pouches that kept the bells silent, the handles and the leather crawling all over with glowing Charter marks, which slowly faded from too-bright brilliance as he watched, though they remained visible.

Terciel had left the bells and his fish, departing across the rooftop in a great rush that set the roosting gulls flying. Despite having the forehead Charter mark himself, he had never been taught magic, since he was an orphan of no account, merely a line in the register of the Grynhold Workhouse, an annoyance to the beadle who oversaw the children there, and nothing more than that to anyone else. His parents, who might have taught him Charter Magic, had drowned when he was two, and his much older sister, Rahi, who had looked after him for a while afterward, had disappeared before he was four. Or thereabouts. He had no memory of his parents at all, and only a vague recollection of his sister.

Everything he knew about them came from rare answered questions or from overhearing people talk about him, which happened even less frequently. Mostly he was ignored, apart from a cuff to speed him out of the workhouse to the oakum-picking shed, or a cuff to get him back in again at the end of the day, with an occasional caning thrown in if his absence from the daily work was noticed.

All Terciel knew about magic was that the old healer Maralide made Charter marks appear from nowhere, sketching them in the air and on broken skin and bone, and sometimes they healed a hurt or cured a sickness, and sometimes they didn't. And what Terciel knew about magical bells came only from stories whispered at night in the workhouse dormitory, whispers backstopped by the constant gurgle of the north aqueduct close by, whose swift running water kept the town safe from the marauding Dead, terrible creatures who were brought back into the living world by awful necromancers *who used magical bells.*

Seven bells, carried in a bandolier, worn across the chest.

Three days after the bells had appeared in Terciel's eyrie, the old woman had arrived in Grynhold, and shortly after that Terciel had been called to the beadle's office and then when he had fled instead, since he had numerous petty crimes of fish theft and other misdemeanors that might have come to light, he had been apprehended by an unprecedented collegiate effort on the part of the beadle and her associates, the Grynhold Town Watch, and a large number of fisher-folk who were ashore waiting for the tide to turn before they went out again. It was the last group that had soured Terciel's attempted escape. The fisher-folk had never bothered the boy before, and he had been hiding among the drying nets.

They had dragged him before the old woman, and he had met her piercing black eyes, seen her horrendously white face, so much paler than anyone's ever should be, and then he had looked down to the seven bells she wore in a bandolier across her chest, over an armored coat of unusual design, made of many small interlocking plates, several scored with the mark of weapons that had failed to penetrate.

Terciel had screamed when he saw the bells, and it had taken the combined effort of the mayor, the beadle, and the woman herself to convince him that she was not a necromancer come to steal his life and use his dead body for some terrible unspecified purpose. They'd explained that bells with Charter marks were special, not the usual necromancer's tools, and they also were *not* the same seven bells that had appeared in his eyrie.

Those bells had come to him specially, the woman said, and it meant he had to go and get them and then he would have to come away with her. That was when she had said she was his great-aunt and her name was Tizanael, and he could call her "Aunt Tizzy."

Terciel had noticed everyone else called her "Abhorsen" and bowed low, something the free fishers of Grynhold didn't do for anyone else.

With the fisher-folk turned against him, there was nowhere Terciel could hide. He'd climbed the fish hall and carefully picked up the bandolier by the very end of one strap, carried the bells down, and handed them over to the Abhorsen. She said she would keep them until his training began, when they got to the "House," wherever that was. They'd left soon after, walking out under the aqueduct in the late afternoon, something that filled Terciel with terror. To go beyond the safety of running water, with the night coming on?

But nothing had happened, then or in the next three days and nights. After a while it occurred to Terciel that this was because he was traveling with someone the creatures of the night were afraid of themselves. He wanted to run away but dared not try anything, not when she was so close.

Now he was trapped here, on this island on the edge of a waterfall, and he didn't know what to do.

Moregrim asked the question again, but Terciel didn't answer.

"Could you take my collar off? It itches."

Terciel shook his head slowly. He hadn't touched the bells and he wasn't going to touch a collar with all those marks glowing and floating upon it, not least when he didn't know what this creature was.

The strange man slid along the branch above on all fours, a curiously nimble movement. Terciel noted his fingers were very stubby and ended in claws and were covered in the same short white hair that was all over his body. He also appeared to have a vestigial tail.

"Take off my collar!"

Terciel lowered himself to the branch below, and then the next, climbing down as rapidly as he ever had to escape the workhouse, with the beadle shouting at him from the window above.

There was shouting here too, but it came from below.

"Come down at once!"

"I am coming down!" he shouted back. He could see her now, on the lawn below the tree, one hand raised in a beckoning motion. For a second he thought there was a bright star on her finger, before he saw it was the afternoon sun catching the ring she wore at the right angle to make it flash.

"Not you!" called Tizanael, the fifty-first Abhorsen in a line that stretched back over centuries to the very first, whose name had become synonymous with the office. "Him! Come down at once!"

A white form leapt past Terciel, too close for comfort, gripped a branch with those taloned hands and swung down farther, switchbacking down the branches in swinging falls and crouching leaps, the blocky body moving with incongruous mobility. The boy followed more slowly, losing sight of both the creature and Tizzy as he entered the denser foliage of the lower branches.

When he finally reached the ground, the dwarf was kneeling in front of Tizanael, his head tilted at a very inhuman angle that obviously was no discomfort. The Abhorsen no longer wore the armor, bell bandolier, and sword, but a robe of dark blue embroidered with a multitude of tiny silver keys, a golden rope in place of a belt, with a small dagger in a metal sheath at her hip. She held her left hand high, the silver ring on her finger still catching the afternoon sun.

"You were forbidden to leave the house, Moregrim."

"This whole island is often termed the 'House,'" said the dwarf with a yawn. "I thought that was what you meant."

"I meant the structure to my left," said Tizanael shortly. "I will now be more specific. You are to remain within the walls of the building I am indicating until I give you leave otherwise."

She pointed at the whitewashed, red-roofed house with its sky-blue door and the door knocker in the shape of a lion's head, a ring held in its jaws.

"I also did not give you leave to change your shape," added Tizanael. "Whether for the purpose of climbing trees or anything else."

Moregrim emitted a high-pitched hissing noise and stood up. For a moment Terciel thought the strange, short man was going to attack Tizanael, but instead he bowed low. As he straightened up, he changed, suddenly more humanlike. Now his skin was as pale as the Abhorsen's, his hair and beard were no longer fur-like, though still luminously white, and he was clothed in a shapeless white smock. The collar that had been around his neck had become a broader red leather belt hitched around his waist, and the small bell swung inside a large bronze buckle. The vestigial tail had entirely disappeared.

Moregrim bowed, turned away, and headed not toward the front door of the house but to an open gate in the wall on the right-hand side, which led to the kitchen garden. When he was about ten paces away, he turned and snarled, green eyes directed piercingly at Terciel.

"She killed Rahiniel!"

Tizanael raised her hand. She did not do anything Terciel could see, but Moregrim writhed and fell over his own feet, rolled twice, and yowled exactly like the cats that frequented the Grynhold Fish Hall, before he got up again and stumbled away through the garden gate.

Tizanael turned to look at Terciel. Her face, as ever, was set. Not angry or antagonistic, like the beadle's so often was. This was simply an absence of emotion. Terciel had no idea what she was feeling or thinking.

"Who's Rahiniel?" he asked.

"Your sister," said Tizanael, watching him carefully. "I believe she was generally known as Rahi."

"Rahi?"

Terciel took in a slow breath. He could almost remember Rahi. At least, he had the faint recollection of someone wrapping him up in a blanket and kissing his forehead as hail clattered on the roof. It had been cozy and warm, so not the workhouse. That was more likely to have been Rahi than his mother. He had been too little when his parents died to remember anything of them.

But that was his only memory. She had left, and he had always presumed she was dead anyway. What did it matter how she died?

"I did not kill her," said Tizanael. "She was my Abhorsen-in-Waiting. It is a dangerous office we hold, and she did not survive one of the many tests we face."

"That man, or whatever he is, Moregrim. He wanted me to take off his collar."

"You would not have been able to," said Tizanael. "Not yet. But Moregrim lays his plans long ahead. For now, simply remember that if you take off his collar, he will kill you."

Terciel shrugged, attempting to show he wasn't scared. But he was, and they both knew it.

"You are to be my new Abhorsen-in-Waiting," said Tizanael. "That is why the bells came to you."

"Why me?" asked Terciel.

Tizanael did not immediately answer. Terciel shifted, lifting his heels nervously, as she continued to look at him, gaze unblinking.

"It is a very difficult thing to be the Abhorsen," she said finally. "Many different strengths are needed. These tend to occur more frequently in those descended from the first Abhorsen, who was given many gifts by her . . . mother . . . you might say. So the bells often choose one of that line, however distant. Like your sister, Rahiniel, and now you."

"You're not my aunt," said Terciel defiantly. He didn't really understand what she was going on about.

"No," replied Tizanael. "I am your great-great-aunt. You have something of the look of my brother, Herranael, your great-grandfather."

"Where's he, then?"

"He is dead," replied the Abhorsen. "They are all dead now, of that line, save you."

Her expression didn't change, nor her tone of voice. She might have been speaking of the weather, or the time of day.

Terciel scowled, and scuffed the dirt with his heel.

"Did they drown?" he asked. His parents had drowned. Most of the orphans in the workhouse had lost their family to the sea.

"No," replied Tizanael.

"Everyone dies," said Terciel.

"Yes," said Tizanael. "In the right time. And it is my task . . . our task . . . to make sure they stay dead."

"How?" asked Terciel. He felt suddenly tired, and hungry, and overwhelmed by all things he didn't understand. His entire world had changed, and it seemed unlikely to be for the better, even though his old life had been bad enough.

"I will teach you," said Tizanael. "But first, you must bathe, and put on clean clothes, and then we will eat a proper dinner. No more travel bread and water."

"Salt fish?" asked Terciel.

Tizanael shuddered, the first time he had seen any kind of human expression pass over her statue-like mask of a face.

"Definitely not salt fish," she said.

Terciel nodded, and walked ahead of her back to the blue door with the lion knocker. It was that simple reaction that convinced him there was hope in this new life after all.

He was so tired of eating salt fish.

From bestselling author Garth Nix comes the story of an ageless young woman with terrifying angelic powers, bent on reuniting with her lover—no matter the cost to anyone else.

An epic feminist fantasy set in a dazzling new world

READ THE LONG-AWAITED PREQUEL TO A CLASSIC FANTASY SERIES!

Return to the Old Kingdom by global phenomenon Garth Nix

JOIN THE
Epic Reads
COMMUNITY